ROGUE Romeo

PAMELA O'ROURKE

Cover Design: Lori Jackson

Cover Photographer: Michelle Lancaster

Cover Model: Eric Guilmette

Editing & Proofreading: Mackenzie Letson

Formatting: CPR Editing

Content Warning

This book contains the following:

- Attempted Sexual Assault (not by MMC)
- Mention of Emotional Child Abuse
- Terminal Illness
- Physical Assault
- Consensual Solicitation
- Loss of a Loved One
- Sexually Explicit Content
- Profanity

WHAT MATTERS MOST
IS HOW WELL YOU WALK
THROUGH THE FIRE.

-Charles Bukowski

For anyone who's struggling.

MAY YOUR DAYS BRIGHTEN. MAY YOUR BURDENS LESSEN.

PLEASE REMEMBER THAT WITHOUT THE DARK, WE'D NEVER SEE THE STARS.

- “Innocence and Sadness” – Dermot Kennedy
- “Before You” – Benson Boone
- “Let It All Go” – Rhodes & Birdy
- “Everything Has Changed” – Taylor Swift & Ed Sheeran
- “Forever and Ever and Always” – Ryan Mack
- “Perfect For Me” – Bradley Marshall
- “Still Falling For You” – Ellie Goulding
- “Shape of You” – Ed Sheeran
- “Already Gone” – Dermot Kennedy
- “Thinking Out Loud” – Ed Sheeran
- “Despacito (Remix)” – Luis Fonsi, Yankee & Justin Bieber
- “Say You Love Me” – Jessie Ware
- “South of the Border (Cheat Codes Remix)” – Camila Cabello & Ed Sheeran feat. Cardi B.
- “You’ve Lost That Loving Feelin’” – Righteous Brothers

Prologue

ALEX

SIX YEARS AGO
LONDON

"The longer you keep this up, Alex, the longer you'll need to see me."

Dr. Schneider leans closer, her short blonde bob curling in against the sides of her pale cheeks. "Your brother is adamant that you need to talk to somebody—"

"I. *Don't*. He's. Wrong." My waning patience makes my words more clipped than I would like. "I'm fine. He's fine. We're all *fine*. There's nothing else to say on the matter."

She watches me closely as my face remains as impassive as always. Images of entering the foyer of my childhood home moments after my mother was killed are playing through my mind, and still, I feel nothing.

I feel *less* than nothing.

And I continue to keep my mouth shut, knowing I can't tell anyone *anything* without breaking my silence about life with Lauren DeMarco as my primary caregiver.

No one loves you, Alexander. No one cares.

Her often-spoken, never forgotten words linger in my mind, reminding me of times best left alone.

"What about your life growing up, Alex? Might you tell me what kind of mother she was to you?"

"She was my mother. Nothing more, nothing less."

My lips twitch when I see Dr. Schneider surreptitiously glance at her wristwatch, clearly hoping the session is almost at an end.

Dropping her notepad onto the desk and interlocking her fingers, she fixes me with a more determined stare than I've seen from her thus far.

"Alex, if I may be so frank..."

My interest is sufficiently piqued, and so I give her the smallest nod of assent.

"Your brother will find another therapist, and another, and another, until you eventually give him what he wants. Which is the peace of mind that he helped you grieve the loss of the only parent you had left."

I heave a deep sigh, knowing full well that she's right. He's relentless, and he won't stop until he gets what he wants. I drop my head back onto the chaise and allow my eyes to drift closed.

What does she want me to say?

That I want to forgive my mother for sexually assaulting my older half-brother, Henry? An act that ultimately saw me left alone with her at age ten?

That I understand her reasoning for kidnapping my best friend, Liv, and my younger half-sister, Mila? That it's all water under the bridge?

That I deeply miss the woman who would beat my knuckles raw if I missed a note during my piano lessons or slapped me across the face if I conjugated my French verbs incorrectly.

Or perhaps she wants me to say that I grieve the loss of the woman who paid a prostitute to take my virginity on the day of my sixteenth birthday. Her twisted *welcome to manhood* gift that ruined my ability to view sex as anything other than an exchange of pleasure.

But it would all be a lie. Because when I saw her lying there lifeless on the marble foyer floor, all I felt was an overwhelming relief that she was gone and I was finally free.

So what kind of monster does that make *me*?

"She wasn't overly maternal, Dr. Schneider." I open my eyes, fixing my stare on an obviously pleased therapist, as I repeat the lies that I've told for years with far more conviction than the truth would ever sound. "She spent a vast amount of time away from the house, and I had so many extra classes for languages and arts that we didn't spend much quality time together."

"And how does that make you feel?"

I *almost* snort at the ridiculously generic question.

I hope Henry's not paying through the nose for this one.

"It makes me a little bit sad, actually."

She leans even closer, her eyes flashing in delightful conviction, fully sure she's made a breakthrough.

"And why is that, Alex?"

I frown, as though in deep thought, before nodding slowly. "Because I would give just about anything to see her again. One last time."

So I could be the one to end your miserable life, Mother.

One

REYNA

PRESENT DAY
MANHATTAN

"See you tomorrow, Reyna."

I wave at Simon from Legal, the last straggler heading for the elevator at Freemont Insurance, before I return to the mountain of paperwork in front of me.

Blowing out a breath through the side of my mouth, my overly long dark brown bangs fly skyward before I grab the top file from the stack on my desk.

I'm three files in and wholly absorbed, when a voice pulls my attention from the task at hand.

"Reyna?"

My boss's boss stops at my desk, a frown marring his handsome features. "What are you still doing here?"

"Oh my gosh, Mr. Freemont!" I clasp my hand to my breastbone as I sit up with a jolt. Having been so involved in my files, I'd not heard his approach. "You scared me half to death. I thought everyone else had finished for the day."

He smirks, flashing his perfect white teeth, teasing a singular dimple that drives the girls in the office insane.

Chad Freemont, the only son of the owner of Freemont Insurance, Dwight, is under thirty and single, with the face of a god and the body of an Olympian.

And the man absolutely knows it too.

Grace from Underwriting swears his penis is magical, although Hadley in Claims is thoroughly convinced it was his tongue that made her see stars.

The thought of lunchtime gossip makes my cheeks flame bright pink as the man in question surveys me with a knowing glint in his light blue eyes.

"I'd love to take you for dinner, Reyna…if you're free."

My brows almost hit my hairline as my jaw falls open. "Umm… I—I'm flattered, Mr. Freemont—"

"Please." He leans down right over my desk and into my personal space. "Call me Chad."

His smile widens, showcasing the matching dimple, and my mouth goes dry as an absurd thought flies through my mind.

Is he flirting with me?

I didn't think he even knew I existed, truth be told, lowly paper pusher that I am.

I clear my throat, not knowing how to process this newfound attention. "I'm so flattered, Mr…I mean…*Chad*. But I really need to get this paperwork finished. I'm so behind this week."

He nods with a furrowed brow as understanding softens his chiseled features. "Ah yes, I heard. Your grandmother hasn't been too well this past month, has she?"

That would be an understatement.

My Nana, or Lita, as she prefers, had been diagnosed with dementia shortly before I left our home in Connecticut to attend the world-renowned Pearson School of the Arts here in Manhattan six years ago.

While still in complete control of her actions, she'd organized to be placed in Sunrise Harbor, an assisted living facility in Staten Island, the only one close enough to Manhattan that our insurance would cover.

The plan had been that her life savings would continue to cover the rest, alongside affording a small stipend for me to help with what my scholarship didn't.

But neither of us could have known the road ahead and how that decision would irrevocably change my future.

"She's okay, Mr. Fr—"

My boss clears his throat in a gentle reminder, and I smile up at him from underneath my bangs. "Sorry, I mean, *Chad*."

I glance back at the desk, suddenly embarrassed under his intense scrutiny.

"So, what do you say we grab that dinner, hmm?"

A part of me is utterly exhilarated at my handsome boss's blatant attention. I mean, it's been a long time since I've allowed myself to feel attraction. My life simply doesn't allow for the emotion or the time in which to express it.

But there's a bigger part of me—the intuitive side my abuelita always insisted I listen to—screaming to run away. As fast as I can.

I raise my eyes one final time, allowing a soft smile to play across my lips, and then I see it.

A predatory grin plays across Chad Freemont's beautiful face, turning him into an obscene parody of himself, and Lita's much-repeated words echo through my mind.

Your intuition is your gift, mija. Listen to it!

"I'm so flattered, Chad, but I really *do* need to finish this paperwork. Perhaps another time!"

My smile is exaggeratedly bright as I tilt my head back down to my work. He waits for a beat, then a moment longer, before he starts to walk away, calling over his shoulder.

"I'm a persistent man, Miss Marquez. Patient too! I can wait as long as it takes."

His loud laugh booms through the stillness, and it sends a ripple of fear down my spine.

Once I hear the *ding* of the elevator, my shoulders drop, alerting me to the fact that I've been on edge this entire time.

I laugh aloud to dispel the heaviness surrounding me, and then, taking several deep breaths, I dive back into my mountain of catching up.

The following hour passes quickly and quietly, and before I know it, I've reached the end of my filing.

With a thankful heart, I grab my bag and my light jacket from the back of my chair and all but skip to the elevator.

I press the call button, blowing out a breath and longing for the comfort of my bed.

My eyes fall closed momentarily, remembering that glorious year at Pearson before everything went to crap. That year when I'd danced to my heart's content, even being scouted as a background dancer for several contemporary and modern productions.

Ballet had been my true passion, though, and the Master at Pearson had frequently said that I was undoubtedly headed directly for Prima status.

And I'd believed her, because I could feel it in my *bones* that I had been born to dance.

Until my piece of shit father lost Lita's house in a game of No Limit Texas Hold 'Em and disappeared, having cleaned her bank account for good measure.

The main problem was affording to barely survive while

attending school *and* earning enough money to cover half of my grandmother's care now that her life savings had been depleted.

I suppose I could have opted to move her to a different facility; however, her dementia had progressed, and truthfully, I didn't have the heart to uproot her already tumultuous life. And so, I'd taken a year off, which had turned into two, which had eventually led to dropping out entirely.

I'd tried my hand at barista work and discovered it was *way* more complicated than it looked.

I had been an usher at a theater, a pizza delivery girl, and a cocktail maker at an upscale bar off Broadway – I learned how to be a Jack of all trades pretty damn quickly because life *doesn't* come cheap. Especially in the city that never sleeps.

Add to that the half of Lita's care that wasn't covered by our insurance—especially now with her current health status—and it's safe to say that I needed to work in order to barely survive.

Finally, I found a cleaning job with an agency and took as many shifts as they'd allow, and eventually, dancing, alongside the joy it brought to me, faded into a distant memory.

I happened to meet Carter Reese, head of Human Resources here at Freemont, while cleaning these very offices one evening. He'd been working late and had spilled coffee on his shirt front when he was due to meet his wife for dinner across town.

I'd given him a little of the vinegar-cleaning solution I'd had on hand, and with a bit of help, the stain was removed in no time.

We'd gotten to talking, and he told me about the entry-level admin position he wanted to fill if I felt I was up for the task.

I'd confessed that I needed some flexibility to visit Lita, but he'd assured me that we could deal with that on an as-and-when basis.

So, I started work less than a week later, continuing with my agency cleaning job when I needed to pick up a shift, though the regular over-time at Freemont meant I didn't need to very often.

I was busy. Content. With a roof over my head and food in my stomach. Lita was well cared for, and I couldn't ask for anything more.

The elevator doors slide open, and I step on with a pep in my step at the thought that I was fated for this job. Meeting Carter that evening had changed the trajectory of my life, and I'd been able to keep Lita in her Staten Island assisted living debt free.

Jamming the button for the ground floor, the door begins to close but stops suddenly when a hand grabs one side of the silver panel, forcing it to glide open fully once more.

Chad's face comes into view, and I frown deeply despite the giant grin on his face.

"Told you I was patient, Reyna." He tosses an exaggerated wink as he steps in beside me, nudging me with his shoulder. His grin is nothing short of self-congratulatory as alarm bells ring in my head. "Now, where did you want to eat?"

The elevator door closes as I continue to hold his stare, repeatedly blinking in silent disbelief.

"Sushi sound good to you? There's a little place not too far—"

"Excuse me?" I cut him off, putting another foot of distance between us when I step backward. "I *believe* my answer was no, Mr. Freemont—"

"Chad." He quirks a brow.

I cross my arms, standing firm. *"Mr. Freemont."*

His gaze holds mine, and the light blue of his eyes darkens turbulently to send a shiver of panic straight to my marrow. But even so, I'm immovable.

I've always been bull-headed when I'm firm in my decisions, and now is no exception.

"This conversation is *highly* inappropriate, sir, and I would very much like to pretend that it never occurred."

I twist my body to face the elevator doors; arms still crossed defiantly as I watch the floor indicator slowly edge its way between floors.

Four. Three. Two. One.

I can feel the elevator settle on the ground floor even before the indicator changes to tell us that we've arrived at our destination.

But just as I'm about to expel a silent sigh of relief, Chad leans across me to harshly tug the emergency stop lever.

I raise wide eyes to find his expression is nothing short of vicious. The mild-mannered flirt from before is long gone, and in his place stands a frenzied version that scares the living shit out of me.

"Now, now, beauty." He leans down to get right in my face. "This can go one of two ways, okay?"

My mouth is like cardboard, nausea rising in the depths of my stomach, and words escape me.

"I said *okay*?" Chad's bark makes me physically jump, and I nod frantically, my heart pounding against my breast painfully.

He reaches out, grasping the side of my long bangs to twirl it around his index finger before drawing the digit from my temple, along my cheekbone, and down to rest on my trembling bottom lip.

"This can go the *easy* way, beauty…" He watches his finger twist the strand of hair around and around as though hypnotized. "You come back to my place and *give* me what I want…"

His finger drops from my lip, down my chin, and along the seam of my blouse, covering my heaving chest, flickering at the top button. His eyes follow his actions with intensity.

"Or…I can just *take* it."

He pops open the first button, followed by the second, baring my old off-white cotton bra to his avid gaze.

"P-p-please, Mr. Freemont—"

"I said it's *Chad*!" His nostrils flare as he cuts me off to grip the cheap material of my blouse, ripping it halfway off my body. My cry of pain puts a smirk on his face that widens enormously when I feel tears crest my lower lashes of their own volition to streak down both of my flushed cheeks.

"Oh *yes*, beauty. I like it when they scream."

Planting his hands on either side of my head, he effectively cages me in as his features take on a predatorial look.

My heart hammers against my rib cage as sweat beads on my brow.

He leans closer until his chin rests on my shoulder, and his words ghost across the shell of my ear. "The next time your superiors honor you with their attention, you'll know to be grateful for the privilege."

I cry out in pain when he roughly nips my earlobe as my knees threaten to go out from under me. He presses a firm close-mouthed kiss to my arched neck, and my eyes flick around the small space, frantically trying to find a way out.

He grips my hips, pressing me back against the wall of the elevator, and chuckles darkly. "I'm going to take my time with you, beauty."

NO!

My fight or flight kicks in at that, and before he can take anything else from me, I bring my knee upwards to drive it full force into his unsuspecting groin.

He falls to the elevator floor with a howl, and I waste no time hitting the emergency stop button. The floor indicator immediately changes to zero, with the doors opening an instant later.

"You'll fucking pay for this, *bitch*!" Chad's words are a pained hiss at my fleeing back, sending a jolt of fear clear through me.

I run from the elevator without looking back, tossing my light jacket over my shoulders and pulling it closed over my ruined blouse as my feet fly across the lobby, out into the cool spring night.

My heart is still pounding in my ears when I make it to the parking garage around the corner on William Street.

"Everything okay, Reyna?"

Leonard, the parking attendant, steps outside of his office with a worried look on his face when he catches sight of me trying to go unnoticed.

I keep my eyes on the ground beneath my feet as I murmur, "I—I'm fine. Truly."

Thankfully, he keeps his distance, allowing me to slip into Lita's beat-up, much loved, dark blue Toyota Corolla without any further questioning.

The thirty minutes back to my shared rental house in Staten Island feels like it takes forever. I've just gotten the trembling in my hands to stop when I pull into the driveway, only for my world to tilt on its axis for the second time today.

I get out of the car, instantly recognizing the luggage outside the front door as the set I'd bought for moving to the city when I joined Pearson.

My clothes and a handful of other belongings are strewn along the porch of the house I've been renting with three other girls from somewhere in Europe who have barely a word of English between them.

As I get closer, I spot a notice hanging on the front door, and my stomach drops along with my spirits when I read the heading.

Notice of Eviction

Without warning, my stomach revolts, emptying its little contents on the threadbare brown mat outside my old house. I retch again and again as defeat takes over my body.

When I feel like I have nothing left inside of me, I straighten and run my hands down the sides of my hair, attempting to fix my dishevelment.

I inhale deeply, the cool air filling my lungs and bringing a modicum of peace to my fraught mind. Scrubbing my palms down my face, I wipe away the evidence of my distress and face the small pile of belongings that amounts to everything I own in the world.

"It could always be worse."

I voice my thoughts out loud, and almost in answer, the sky rumbles overhead. Shaking my head, I set to work, packing my things into the Corolla, trying not to let the events of the day overwhelm me.

And failing miserably when I realize my tears have intermingled with the rain I didn't even notice was falling.

It could always be worse. It could always be worse. It could always be worse.

Two

ALEX

"And you're absolutely *positive* that this is the real deal, Burton?"

My palms bead with sweat as I pray for my friend, Vaughn, to tell me this is all one cosmic joke. Or even a fucking prank.

I'll take a good, old-fashioned punking over this shit any time!

"When it comes to this, you know I don't dick about, DeMarco. My guy is good. Trustworthy. You can believe me when I say there's a shitstorm headed straight for you!"

I huff a dark laugh. "Christ, sugarcoat it for me, why don't you!"

My friend snorts but doesn't elaborate because there's little he can say to make this any better.

"How the fuck did one of them even get a device into the goddamn hotel suite? It's never happened before."

"Doesn't matter *how*, Alex. What matters is how you handle it. You know that better than most." I find myself nodding along with his voice over the receiver. "Get ahead of it. *Call him.*"

My stomach churns at the thought of calling who I need to call. Of facing his wrath, but even worse, his disappointment.

Of showcasing my failures to the head of our company, my older brother, Henry, and his wife—my best friend—Olivia. I don't want them to look at me like I'm less than the man they see me to be.

Like I'm less than the man I present to the world every fucking day.

It's tiring, and sometimes I need to blow off some steam. If that happens to be with a beautiful woman or two, no harm, no foul.

We're all consenting adults, after all. I'm not doing anything he didn't do when he was single, for Christ's sake.

Quit making excuses, you damn coward.

"I'll call him now. Pour me a drink. I'm going to need it after I face the firing squad."

Vaughn murmurs his assent before the line goes dead, and I wait a moment to gather myself—and my waning courage—before dialing Henry's UK cell number.

I realize on the third ring that, in my idiocy, I've forgotten the five-hour time difference, with him being in London. I'm on the cusp of hanging up, when his voice calls down the line.

"It better be a matter of life or death, Al, 'cause I'm kind of in the middle of something."

Liv's inimitable giggle comes down the line, putting a wistful smile on my face as I long for simpler times when it was the two of us against the world.

"Henry!" Her chastising tone elicits a huff of annoyance from my easily irritated older brother.

"Cut to the chase, Alex. What's got your panties in a bunch that it couldn't wait until business hours?"

My mouth opens, but the words stick in my throat. I clear it harshly and swallow before slowly and succinctly spilling the proverbial tea.

"I've just been made aware that someone made a sex tape last year." Silence follows, and I rush to fill it without registering my words.

"Of me—without my knowledge, *obviously*—and the maker is in talks to sell it to a media outlet. A friend is working on making a deal before it gets out. I *swear* I didn't mean for this to happen. I've always been exceptionally discreet."

I'm met with another silence that extends for so long that I feel the need to speak again. "Henry? You there?"

"I'm going to murder you. When I get my hands on you, little brother, you are minced-fucking-meat, you hear me? I'll—"

There's a scuffle on the other end of the cell, and suddenly, Liv's centering voice comes down the line, calm and soothing as ever. I can instantly feel my shoulders relax, knowing she's going to fix everything.

"Alex?"

"Oh, sweet girl, I—"

She cuts me off, her tone brooking no argument. "*Don't* 'sweet girl' me, Alexander Sebastian DeMarco."

My eyes blow wide open, and I push my overly long hair back out of my face as I exhale heavily.

"This is why you left early, isn't it?"

I murmur an affirmative, knowing she's referring to my nephew Nathan's christening earlier today in London. I'd gotten both the call from Vaughn alerting me to my impending doom and another from the guys in IT regarding a possible hack into our systems.

I'd practically run from my sister Mila's penthouse without so much as a farewell, flying straight back to New York within an hour of leaving.

"Sit tight." Liv's firm voice comes down the line. "Henry's on his way to you."

"More."

Vaughn tilts his head questioningly, quirking a dark brow. "Shouldn't you be keeping a clear head in a crisis?"

"Shouldn't you be pouring me more fucking whisky?"

I blow out a breath as he fills the tumbler, then I return my face to my hands to ponder how I could have fucked up so monumentally.

"A sex tape!" The words are muted behind my palms, so I drop my hands to repeat myself louder this time. "A damn *sex* tape, Burton. It *can't* see the light of day."

A tumbler of whisky finds its way into my hand, and I raise it to my mouth, grimacing as the gulp I inhale burns all the way down. I feel it warm the recesses of my stomach, welcoming the pain. Deserving the pain.

No one loves you, Alexander. No one cares.

My mother's sharp words from that day long ago ring in my mind, and I forcibly push them away with a deep gulp from my tumbler.

Shifting back around behind his desk, Vaughn barks a laugh. "You afraid the world's going to see your pencil dick?"

"Don't be jealous 'cause I got the most perfect of Goldi-cocks, Burton!"

He snorts as he takes a sip from his own tumbler, settling into the chair opposite mine. "Great title, actually. 'Goldi-cocks and the Three Beavers' has a nice ring to it."

I squint my eyes, shooting daggers at this asshole who somehow has grown to attain the title of friend since my move to Manhattan to run the US Headquarters for DeMarco Holdings six years ago.

Vaughn is the only bastard son of his prolific late father, Valentine Burton, owner of two elite member-only sex clubs.

Valentines in London is currently being run by Vaughn's legitimate half-sister, Vivienne. Valentines in Manhattan *was* being run by Verity, Vaughn's other half-sister, until their father died. He'd never acknowledged Vaughn—another topic we bonded over—and so Vaughn had made Verity an offer she couldn't refuse, though he'd kept the details to himself.

She'd up and left Manhattan, paving the way for Vaughn to dismantle Valentines in order to build his own legacy while pissing all over his sperm donors. He'd renamed the club Rogue, implementing all new requirements for entry and membership, making it the hottest spot in the country right now.

"You're a proper asshat, you know that, right?"

Vaughn shrugs wryly, then chuckles into his whisky as a sharp knock sounds on his office door, but before he can acknowledge it, the door swings wide open to admit my Chief Financial Officer, Grayson Hunter.

He's wearing a skeptical look on his face as he surreptitiously closes the door behind him.

"If Talia knew I was here, she'd have a damn fit."

He's not wrong. His childhood sweetheart turned wife, and mother of their four-year-old twins, would *not* be happy if she knew her husband was visiting Rogue.

Sliding into the chair beside mine, he gratefully accepts the tumbler of whisky Vaughn offers. "What in the name of God is wrong that it couldn't wait until tomorrow at work?"

I slide a glance at Vaughn, who all but buries his smirk in his glass, sheer devilment dancing in his onyx eyes.

Rolling my eyes at him, I pivot in my seat to take in a clearly peeved Grayson.

Might as well rip off that Band-Aid, buddy!

And so, I deadpan, "I got a call that there's a sex tape featuring yours truly about to break, and I need you to have my back when Henry inevitably tears me a new one tomorrow."

With each word that falls out of my mouth, Grayson's eyes get disturbingly wider until I'm altogether sure they're on the cusp of falling clear out of their sockets.

Silence rebounds through the small office as Grayson empties his tumbler in one fell swoop, then holds it out for a refill.

"I'm gonna need more, Burton. The secondhand fear is *real*."

REYNA

My ringing cell wakes me from a dead sleep, and I jolt upright, only for my head to harshly connect with the ceiling of my Corolla.

"Ouch!"

I rub my forehead, blinking repeatedly as I scan the floor of the car for the chiming cell that I'd thankfully been able to charge at the nearest Denny's following my unceremonious eviction.

My forehead breaks out in a cold sweat, remembering the true extent of how bad yesterday *could* have been had I not gotten free of that wolf in sheep's clothing, Chad Freemont.

Spotting the device half hidden by the layer of clothes I slept underneath last night, I push those thoughts firmly aside as I yank it out, only for my heart to drop into my stomach when I spot the caller.

Sunrise Harbor, Lita's assisted living center, flashes on the screen, and without further thought, I swipe to answer.

"Hello?"

The caller clears their throat, and I shoot up a silent prayer that this isn't the call.

Please let her be okay!

"I'm sorry to bother you so early, Reyna..."

My shoulders descend from my earlobes when I hear Penelope, one of Lita's Memory Care specialists, on the other end.

"Not at all, Pen. Is Lita okay?"

"She's...she's asking for you, Reyna."

My mouth drops open, and tears fill my eyes.

Her doctors spoke to me recently, advising that there had been some symptoms of possible terminal lucidity in recent weeks. She'd requested her favorite gelato a couple of times now and even given her tamales recipe to Penelope the other day.

They'd said there might be a possibility of her asking for me. I just never dreamed I could get her back for any period of time.

I glance at my watch to see it's 6:14 am.

"I'll be there in five."

And true to my word, less than five minutes later, I'm jogging through the parking lot at Sunrise Harbor. The name is very apt this morning, with the sun shining low across the bay as it makes its ascent for the day ahead.

It's comforting, almost hypnotic, and I feel a wave of serenity wash over me despite the wretched evening I'd experienced. It's almost like the world is trying to tell me that everything is going to be okay.

Ringing the bell at the front door, I'm buzzed in immediately. I toss a quick nod at whoever is at reception, not stopping to identify who I'm acknowledging as my feet fly across the linoleum flooring that lines the hallway.

As I skid to a halt outside my abuela's door, I take a moment to collect myself. Blowing out a breath, I inhale through my nose deeply to calm myself. A smile threatens my lips at the thought of what I might encounter when I open the door before me, and with that, I step forward, pushing the door wide.

"Lita?"

I poke my head hesitantly around the corner of the door, finding the woman in question immediately, alongside a grinning Penelope. She's sat next to my grandmother, playing a card game—rummy, no doubt, knowing my abuela—and she smiles broadly as her eyes find mine.

"Mariana! Look who's here."

She stands, setting her hands on the tray table between them.

My abuela's concentrated gaze lifts from her own hand of cards to meet my hopeful gaze. Her big brown eyes light up, and tears fill my matching doe eyes as she drops her cards to open her arms wide.

"Ah, *mija*! Come to me, *mi conchita linda*."

My pretty little seashell!

Tears fall unheeded down my cheeks when I hear the much-loved nickname, and I close the distance between us, falling ungracefully into her warm embrace. "Lita! I missed you so much."

She rubs the top of my head soothingly as I inhale her homely scent. "I saw you yesterday, *mi amor*. Surely you couldn't have missed me that much!"

Her chest rumbles with a chuckle as my heart breaks at her words. She's not had any lucidity in well over a year.

Terminal lucidity. A blessing and a curse.

Even so, I embrace this special gift, this dear time with her, before the end. Because once she's gone, I'll truly be all alone.

Plastering a smile on my face, I sit back and cup her cheeks. She mirrors my actions, using her thumbs to wipe the tears from beneath my eyes.

"I know, Lita. I just missed you, that's all."

"Oh, *mi conchita linda.*" She brushes her knuckles across my cheekbone as her eyes hold mine intently. "You don't ever need to miss me. I'm right here." Raising her hand, she gently taps my temple before dropping her other hand from my cheek to rest over my heart.

"And here."

My bottom lip trembles under the force of my emotions, her words meaning more to me than she could possibly comprehend right now. I tug the offending lip between my teeth, biting harshly in an attempt to keep myself together.

Lita turns to Penelope. "Did you know my Reyna was the lead in the Pearson School of the Arts Christmas Gala last year?"

My heart stutters as her chest puffs out with pride, and she smiles brightly. That concert was five years ago.

"She played the Sugar Plum Fairy, and it was the most beautiful sight these old eyes have ever seen." I'm unable to keep the smile from my lips at the sheer joy shining on her face.

"I've seen the footage, Mariana." Penelope nods in my direction with a sad smile. "She was beautiful."

My abuela shifts her gaze back to me, clasping her hands together in excitement. "Would you dance for us, mija? Please!"

"Of course, Lita." I smile into her deep brown eyes. "I will *always* dance for you."

Three

REYNA

Crap, crap, crap!

I fly around the corner of William Street, spilling out onto the hustle and bustle of Wall Street and narrowly missing a group of Japanese tourists slowly ambling by.

"Excuse me!"

Shouting my apology over my shoulder, I continue to run barefoot at full tilt until the doors of Freemont Insurance come into view. When I'm within reach of my offices, I drop my half-size-too-big, thrift store black pumps onto the pavement and slide my feet into them once I've dusted the streets from my soles.

"Morning, Miss Marquez," Fred, the building's security guard, calls across the foyer as I march directly toward the elevators.

"Morning, Fred." My smile is genuine, and I slow my footsteps to toss him a wink.

"Suzie said to make sure to thank you again for the cake for Harris's birthday. They didn't stop talking about it all day."

"Tell Suzie she's more than welcome. My abuela has the best

recipes!"

Fred's answering smile is wide as I step onto the waiting elevator, shooting him a small wave of farewell before the doors close.

After I hit the button for the seventeenth floor, I take a moment to check myself in the mirror.

I shake my head at my reflection, smoothing the strays into place as best I can. My cheeks are flushed, and the mascara I applied whilst sitting in midtown traffic for longer than anticipated is not as sleek as I'd thought in the car.

Using my pinkie finger, I fix my lashes and nod to myself.

You'll have to do.

Having danced for Lita and Penelope, breakfast was delivered to the three of us. We'd sat chatting about nothing and everything until Lita noticed the time and insisted I go to class.

My stomach had churned with nausea the whole trip into the city at the thought of being in the same vicinity as my would-be attacker—the same man who dogged my uncomfortable rough sleeping last night—but to make matters worse, thanks to a delay on 278, I was now late.

I'd called ahead, but my gut was telling me that Chad Freemont will be out for blood following the events of last night. A man like him would *not* take kindly to a rebuff, let alone one as harsh as mine.

A shudder glides up along my spine at the revelation as I reach my floor, and the elevator doors glide open soundlessly.

Wide eyes belonging to Mary, the motherly receptionist sitting behind the desk facing me, land on my slightly disheveled state before jerking her head to the right.

"The head honchos are asking for you, sweetie. Boardroom five." Her thick Jersey accent softens. "We all make mistakes. It'll be okay."

My heart drops as my stomach swirls, knowing instantly that Chad Freemont is at the center of whatever is happening here. "Did you pass on my message?"

She nods sadly, her sincere eyes holding mine as I fill my lungs and exhale a grateful, "Thanks, Mary."

I square my shoulders, ready as I'll ever be for what's to come, as I stride across the lobby and into the office beyond.

The layout of Freemont Insurance is open plan, with rows of neat little desks running the length of the entire floor, separated by sheets of frosted glass to give the illusion of privacy.

Dozens of eyes swing around to land on me, and my feet almost falter under the scrutiny but I catch myself, absolutely refusing to show weakness now.

Clearly, they're in on something that I have no idea about, and it doesn't bode well. But hell will freeze over before I'll let him try to take my pride today following his attempt to invalidate my choice last night.

Yes, I need this job, but I've been down before. I can rise again.

I know I can.

With steel in my spine and determination running through my veins, I cement a smile on my face.

Head held high, I walk briskly past every turned head, ignoring each one, with my eyes trained on the three men awaiting me behind the glass walls of Boardroom five, dead ahead.

The savior who hired me, Carter, is the first to notice my approach, and I can clearly see him mutter something to his colleagues that makes each head swivel in my direction in an almost practiced move.

I allow my eyes to linger on Carter first, who's looking guilty, and more than a little shamefaced. I narrow my eyes minutely as

I hold his gaze, smirking internally when he visibly squirms.

Spineless prick!

I flick my stare onto Finnegan Bradley, my point manager and ultimate brown noser, who glances at his wristwatch before pinning me with a slitted stare. I quirk a brow, my confidence rising with each step closer I take to my inevitable doom.

If you're going down, go down swinging, Marquez.

The thought bolsters me further as my eyes land on the third man, Chad Freemont.

His face is practically gleeful, and I know without a doubt that my tardiness of this morning will be used as his way of getting rid of me before I can cause any fuss about last night.

I'm not stupid enough to think any of the building's security footage will remain untampered. Clearly, from his own words, it wasn't his first time assaulting a woman who had blatantly rejected him.

I push open the glass door, tilting my chin ever-so slightly as I enter the boardroom.

Bradley and Freemont each take a seat at the opposite side of the table as Carter closes the door before slipping into his own beside them.

Chivalry is well and truly dead with these guys!

I slide into the seat, resting my hands on my lap while keeping my face clear of all the mutinous thoughts running riot inside my brain.

Finnegan speaks first, his tone holding even more impatience than his posture.

"Late again, Marquez. Third time this month."

I incline my head. "Yes, sir. I believe I made up for the lost time. Also, when I was hired, Carter knew of my situation, and there was no issue with it."

"It's Mr. Reese, Miss Marquez."

My eyes glide over to land on a smirking Chad Freemont, and I grit through my clenched jaw. "Apologies. I didn't realize we were being so formal."

It's his turn to incline his head, his smirk widening enough to make my stomach churn. When he speaks again, I very nearly empty my morning coffee onto the table between us.

"Now, Miss Marquez. I believe you are not so uneducated as to misinterpret our presence here today, hmm?"

Carter fidgets in his seat. His eyes are cast downward, and he is thoroughly unable to even look at me.

I focus all my attention on the smiling prick to my right. "I couldn't possibly misinterpret your presence today. Uneducated, I am not. After all, I was valedictorian of my graduating class, *Chad*."

"It's Mr. Freemont—" my useless point manager tries to interject, but I cut him off.

"That's not what you were insistent upon last night, is it, *beauty*?" The last word is spat with as much venom as I can muster while rage circulates in my veins.

My gaze rests on each man opposite me as silence stretches between us until Chad speaks again. "Tread lightly, Miss Marquez."

"Or what? You'll fire me? That's clearly what's about to happen here, so do me a favor and cut to the goddamn chase."

Freemont's eyes narrow into slits. "Carter, enlighten Miss Marquez as to why we're all here today."

Carter slowly lifts his stare from his lap until he meets my eyes. He swallows roughly before clearing his throat. "I'm afraid you're being let go…" He trails off when I quirk a brow.

"I've been advised that illegal substances were found in your desk following an anonymous tip earlier—"

Mary's comments from before and my colleague's stares make complete sense now.

I begin to slow clap with my eyes trained on Freemont's smug grin, and it halts the bullshit spewing from my "savior's" mouth.

"Bravo. Nicely played!"

I push myself to stand before planting my palms on the desk between us and staring down at the three bullies before me.

"I'm no stranger to adversity. I've had to fight tooth and nail almost my whole entire life, and I'll be damned if I let entitled assholes like the three of you get the better of me."

Standing tall, I look down my nose at them, disgust featuring heavily on my face. Carter is staring at his lap, and even Finnegan's eyes are cast downward, unable to meet my uncompromising stare.

Freemont, on the other hand, steeples his finger and taps the index ones against his smirking mouth as he leans back in his seat like he doesn't have a care in the world.

"This won't be the first time you've pulled shit like this, but you can bet your ass it *will* be the last. You won't get away with this, Chad."

I spin on my heel, pull open the door, and flick a final glance back over my shoulder. "I promise you that. Karma's a motherfucking bitch!"

ALEX

"Alexander DeMarco, are you even listening to me, for Christ's sake?"

I scrub my palms along my weary face before running my

hands through my unkempt hair. My eyes land on my irate older brother, Henry, as he glowers at me from *my* seat behind *my* desk.

His face is flushed, and his own usually immaculately styled hair is falling over his forehead, causing him to raise a hand to brush it away impatiently as he holds my gaze.

I open my mouth to speak, but the words won't come.

"*Speak,* damn you!" Henry's roar of frustration reverberates through the office, making Grayson flinch openly. "How could you be so fucking stupid, Al? A motherfucking *sex tape*! If this gets out, our reputation may never recover."

He throws his hands up in exasperation, giving me his back as he plants his hands against the glass walls overlooking Wall Street below us.

Henry's mumbled words land on my ears. "An orgy, by the sounds of it, for fuck's sake."

I'd learned from an early age to keep a cool head in a crisis, to think before I act, to always uphold the DeMarco family name—despite the fact my father never wanted a damn thing to do with me—and I'd always played my part.

Until now.

Henry's surprisingly soft voice carries easily through the silent space.

"I told Liv I was going to scale back at the company, Alex. Last night, minutes before your call. I told her I was giving your sorry ass more responsibility. And that I was going to be there for her and the kids."

My heart clenches in my chest, and my lungs constrict at the thought of disappointing my best friend in the world.

"She's carrying twins, Al."

A lump the size of a boulder makes words an impossibility as Henry slowly continues. "She's given me a life I could never have imagined. Not in my wildest dreams, Alex. And what do I give her?"

He pivots about, his face is thunderous, as he answers his own question in a yell that carries beyond this office. "A workaholic husband with a complete *fuck-up* for a brother, that's what!"

I hold his glower as I lean forward, resting my elbows on my desk, Liv's undoubted disappointment spurring me to action. "My source has the best of the best on this, Ri. Give me time—"

He cuts me off, his eyes flashing green flames. "This isn't the first time, Al. There's been stories that have needed to be squashed, almost scandals that we've narrowly avoided. This is the first time that you just might get caught red-fucking-handed."

His exhalation weighs heavily as he regards me with exasperation.

"When are you going to quit fucking around? I know all about your time at Rogue with that reprobate, Burton. That's a given; I was young and stupid once, too. But even I knew to maintain *discretion*. For you, this is a million times worse than if it had ever been me."

I shake my head, my hair landing in my eyes. "No, that's not fair—"

"He's right, Alex."

Grayson cuts me off this time, and I quickly level him with a stare of betrayal.

I don't even attempt to keep the disdain out of my tone. "And how, *pray tell*, is he right, *friend*?"

My CFO swallows roughly. "You're the face of the company now, Alex. You have been since you took over the New York branch six years ago. You made time for things Henry would never have. You attend galas, fashion shows, and red-carpet events. You're photographed with the crème de la crème of high society. You're a celebrity in your own right, whether you want to be or not. If this footage makes the tabloids, it will do irreparable damage to your name—which is the brand that this company stands on."

My stomach churns nauseatingly, and my vision grows spotty as his words sink in.

He's right.

Fuck!

"You're one of the most eligible bachelors in the Northern United States. You could have any woman you wanted." Henry scrubs his hands down his face, clearly frustrated.

"When are you going to grow the fuck up, brother?"

His forehead is deeply furrowed, and for the first time in my life, I see a weariness on my brother's face. Guilt cuts me like a knife at the knowledge that it's *me* who's put that there.

"Take the rest of the day, Alex—"

"No! I want to help. I can't—"

Henry holds up his palms, and I immediately stop speaking, not wanting to make things worse between us.

"Take the day, Alex. That's not a request. I need to run interference before the Board catches wind of this, and I can't do that when I'm liable to say something to you that I know I'll regret."

Four

REYNA

I shoot a watery smile at Fred, not trusting my voice to bid him goodbye as I exit the building that houses Freemont Insurance, walking out onto a bustling Wall Street.

The rush of adrenaline I'd felt while facing those assholes dissipated almost immediately, and I came crashing back to reality with a bang.

My hands are trembling, and my knees feel more than a little unsteady. I lean against the side of the building, digging deep to find the will to keep moving forward, when my cell vibrates in my crossbody bag.

I slip it out, almost dropping it from my shaking grip, and my stomach knots when I see it's Sunrise Harbor for the second time today.

"Hello?"

"I'm sorry for interrupting you, Reyna." Penelope's voice seems loud, almost booming, in my ears. "I wanted to let you know that Mariana's episode has passed, unfortunately." My shoulders drop as she continues. "I just didn't want you rushing back from work..."

Her words become white noise as a buzzing sound clouds my mind. I stare numbly into the distance for a long beat, my heart shattering beneath my breast.

"Thank you, Penelope. I'll be by again tomorrow."

Without waiting for her response, I hang up. My feet begin to move without conscious thought, and suddenly, I'm back at my car with no idea how I got here.

I glance around the parking garage, noting that Leonard is looking at me from his small glass office with a look of concern on his kind, round face. I glance down along my body to find that, somewhere along the way, I lost my half-size-too-big shoes.

My feet are filthy with grime from the street. I blink heavily, feeling as though I'm on the cusp of a breakdown, and I mentally scramble to stop my unwanted spiral.

"Reyna?"

My head shoots up, finding Leonard standing not ten feet away. He gestures to my bare, dirty feet, his hands encompassing my whole self in general, as he smiles softly.

"You look like you've had a rough twenty-four hours."

I work my throat, but the words don't come. Instead, my bottom lip trembles dangerously, so I suck it into my mouth to stop the rush of emotion.

"I'm not going to ask you to tell me any of it...but my ma always said that it costs nothing to be kind."

He looks uncertain all of a sudden, his Irish accent becoming stronger with each word spoken.

"I'd like to help you if—if you'll let me."

I allow my eyes to fall closed as my lip pops free, and I nod slowly in silent reply. When my eyes open, Leonard has moved closer and is holding a hand out to me.

"My sister has a place nearby. You can clean up there if you like."

"I—I—"

My words are broken, my mouth absolutely refusing to cooperate, and I can feel my face scrunch up in frustration.

I point through the window of the old Corolla. "Clothes."

He nods gently, and I drop my keys into his waiting hands.

Once he's opened the door, I lean into the back seat, ignoring the pitying look on Leonard's face when he sees the evidence of my recent eviction. I quickly grab some clean clothes and spot an almost empty CVS bag on the floor to carry them in.

The pill packet and wet wipes from inside go directly into my handbag, and I quickly shove the necessary items into it.

Almost as an afterthought, I pluck an old pair of flip-flops from underneath the passenger seat. Then I straighten to look at Leonard, dropping the flip-flops onto the ground to slide my feet into them.

I'm thankful to feel a little more centered, having done something as normal as putting on footwear.

"Come on, Reyna." Leonard moves off toward the pedestrian exit, and I follow gratefully.

Less than five minutes later, he pushes open the door to an Irish bar on the corner of Broad Street called Molly Malones.

"We're closed!"

A voice rings out from behind the bar, and a flame-haired, exceptionally short plus-sized woman turns to us with a scowl that transforms into a worried expression upon spotting Leonard.

"What's going on, Leo?"

She rounds the end of the bar, coming closer as Leonard gently grips me underneath my elbow. "Darcy, meet my friend, Reyna."

Darcy smiles brightly, dusting her palms off on her black work pants before extending her right hand. "Nice to meet you, Reyna."

I slide my hand into hers, wincing slightly when her grip belies her stature. "Sorry, lovely." She smiles self-deprecatingly. "I'm stronger than I look."

The Irish lilt in her voice is much more apparent than in Leonard's, I note, as though from a distance.

"Reyna's the baker of all of the desserts I've been bringing home."

Darcy chuckles. "Ah! You're the reason I'm not bikini ready, is it?"

She taps her rounded hips as she pops a brow playfully. The gesture tugs a small smile from my weary lips, and with that, I feel instantly at ease despite never having met her before.

Leonard gently urges me closer, a deep chuckle rumbling in his chest before he sobers. "Reyna's down on her luck at the minute, Darce. Umm…"

He trails off, and I can feel his eyes on me, asking for my assent. I nod once, and he carries on.

"She's had some trouble with work—though I'm not privy as to what exactly—and judging by her car, I'm fairly sure she's living out of it."

My stomach dips, hearing the sorry state of my life spoken aloud for the first time, and before I can help it, my breath hitches on a sob.

Leonard stiffens beside me as his sister springs into action.

"It's okay, lovely. It'll all be just grand." She hooks my other elbow. "You're safe here."

"I need to get back—"

Darcy cuts her brother off by raising her free hand. "Go on, Leo." She squeezes my elbow lightly. "We're all good here."

"I'll be by once my shift is finished to check on you." Leonard slowly lets go of my elbow, and I look up at him to send him a small smile of reassurance.

He returns it softly before giving us his back while Darcy leads me behind the bar, toward a door labeled *Staff Only*.

"There's a small apartment in the back, lovely. Let's get you all cleaned up, yeah?"

ALEX

"What the fuck was that, Hunter?"

Grayson jogs to keep up with my brisk strides, despite having a good inch on my 6'3" frame. "What was what?"

I stop suddenly, rounding on him as he almost plows into my back.

"You're a fucking turncoat, Gray. You were meant to have my back, and instead, you pissed all over me!"

My CFO has the decency to look slightly ashamed before opening his mouth to speak, but I cut him off.

"Give me your cell."

I extend my hand, nodding with raised brows when he looks at me in question.

"Give me your damn cell."

He shifts his gait to one foot, glancing to the side, and I know I'm right.

"He texted you to keep an eye on me, didn't he?"

"Alex, he didn't—"

"Don't fucking *lie to me*!"

My shout has every head on the floor turning toward our spat, including my assistant, Bailey, who frowns as he presses his finger to his lips in a shushing motion. But I'm too far gone, so I firmly ignore his attempted warning.

"I don't need a damn babysitter, Gray. I *needed* you to have my back today."

Pointing in the direction of what *used* to be my office, I snarl in a tone that's utterly unlike me. "Go shadow *him*, the almighty savior, who can do no wrong, and leave the fuck-up to do what he does best, hmm?"

My friend lifts sorrowful eyes to mine as conflict makes him fidget under my cool stare.

The elevator chooses that moment to arrive, its doors gliding open with ease. I step back onto it, my eyes never leaving Grayson's as I hit the button for the ground floor.

Grayson, clearly making a decision, moves to step forward, but I hold up a quelling palm.

"You made your bed."

The doors start to close, and I narrow my eyes to slits as I hiss, "Now, lie in it."

My friend's pained expression is all I see as the doors align and the elevator begins its descent.

"FUCK!"

The single expletive is a roar that echoes through the elevator, and I feel a pang of guilt at my treatment of Hunter.

He was right, after all. My face *is* the brand upon which DeMarco Holdings has elevated to new heights here in the United States.

I pivot to observe my image in the elevator mirror.

Tailored suit. Designer scruff. A body that I work damn fucking hard for.

Simple brown hair that's immaculately styled, as always.

Tanned complexion, courtesy of my absentee father.

Amber eyes, courtesy of my deranged mother.

There's nothing notable about me, at least that I can see. I can hold a decent conversation. I have a sharp wit and a semi-photographic mind, which means I'm never short of an anecdote or two.

Charismatic.

That's the word the rags have used to describe me when I've been to an event or other.

Truth is, I'm a fucking fraud. I plaster a smile on and do what's expected of me, just as I always have. And all the while, I'm screaming inside, hating the face I show the world, and wanting nothing more than to wipe the slate clean and start all over.

But when you're a DeMarco, that's not possible.

No one loves you, Alexander. No one cares.

Those ever-present words rattle around inside my brain. They're always in there, behind every interaction I've ever had.

My eyes bore into my reflection, noting the rising flush in my cheeks, and suddenly, I feel too hot. I shuck my jacket, dropping it to the floor of the elevator without thought.

Having arrived on the ground floor, the doors open into the pristine lobby. Wall Street is bustling just outside, and I cross the space, marching onto the Manhattan sidewalk.

As always, my driver, Damien, is curbside, awaiting my instructions. He opens the back door of the uniform black town car, waiting on me to slide inside as I normally do, except my feet don't move.

I glance to my left, then to my right, and then left again. Holding my hand up, I indicate to Damien that I'm going to walk, and turn left, vaguely noting his surprised expression.

My cell vibrates in my pants pocket, so I slip it out, and seeing Grayson's name on the screen, I quickly power it off.

Take the day, Alex.

I nod succinctly to myself. "Yeah. I think I *will* take the damn day."

Having made a firm decision, I quicken my pace, unfastening the buttons on my shirt sleeves to roll them up to my elbows. I unknot my skinny blue tie, dropping it into my pocket before I open the top three buttons of my dress shirt.

I run my hand through my hair, mussing it up as I smile to myself in silent rebellion.

I feel freer already. Like I've discarded the shackles of my heritage in one fell swoop, and the thought is liberating.

My feet take me left and across a pedestrian crossing before I take a sharp right, coming to a standstill outside of a bar called Molly Malones. The words *Traditional Irish Pub* stand proudly beneath the name.

I've been here with Grayson a time or ten, and at this time of the day, it's practically guaranteed to be empty.

Which is precisely what I need. No outside noise.

I step forward, pushing the heavy oak door inward to find an ornate, old-world quintessential Irish bar.

There's a long, wooden, immaculately clean counter that runs the length of one wall, with matching wooden stools along the outside. I move closer, my shoes clacking noisily on the marble flooring beneath my feet.

I grab a stool and slide onto the wooden seat, glancing around in search of the owner, a flame-haired Irish ex-pat named Darcy.

There's an array of signage plastered to the walls with advertisements such as 'Guinness is good for you,' and the entire wall behind the bar is packed with every kind of Irish whiskey known to man.

But the place itself is exactly the ghost town I predicted until a girl emerges from the door marked *Staff Only* and rounds the bar to slip onto a seat at the end of it.

She side-eyes me, shooting a forced half-smile in my direction before focusing her stare on her hands, which are clasped and resting on her lap.

My brows draw together as I observe her, and I can't help but think that she's having a day as bad as mine.

"Have you ever seen *Harry Potter and the Prisoner of Azkaban*?"

The question is out of my mouth before I know what I'm doing. She twists in her seat, her head raising as her eyes find mine.

I can't help noting that this woman is a fucking knockout, even with her freshly washed long brown hair surrounding her like a halo. She's wearing an oversized grey sweater over black leggings while looking at me with big brown eyes that have clearly been crying and cheeks flushed with emotion.

Even so, I force the thought from my mind, all too aware that thinking with the appendage in my pants is what put me in the direct line of this shitstorm in the first place.

"Y-yeah. Why?" Her reply is hesitant, but I can hear a sprinkling of genuine curiosity in her tone.

My mouth lifts in a lopsided grin. "Remember Hermione had a time-turner?"

She nods, her eyes tracing the lines of my face with clear interest, and I continue. "I'm having a day where I could really use one. You ever feel like that?"

And at that, her face lights up with a smile that almost knocks the breath from my body.

"I can absolutely relate." She laughs softly. "A time-turner is *exactly* what I need right now."

Just then, Darcy emerges from the back, her eyes landing directly on me as a smile tugs at the corners of her mouth.

"Long time no see, Alex!" She glances at the clock behind her. "Bit early for the likes of you."

I shrug, shooting her an answering smile. "It's Happy Hour somewhere, eh?"

She rolls her eyes as she shakes her head. "Alright, pretty boy. What'll it be?"

"Macallan 64. Neat." I slide a glance down the bar. "And please add whatever the lady would like to my tab, Darcy."

For some reason that truly escapes me, I have the overwhelming urge to just sit and talk. To make her smile. To lift her spirits.

And I push that thought out of my head as quickly as it entered.

I don't *do* friendships. Outside of Liv. Possibly Vaughn and Gray, too – when he's not being a dick.

The knockout shakes her head, opening her mouth to undoubtedly decline the offer, but I pre-empt her despite my internal reservations. "No pressure. Though my best friend would tell you that misery loves company."

Five

REYNA

"That Alex sure is a pretty one."

Darcy's smile is mischievous as she nods at the retreating back of the man in question while he strides toward the restroom, and I can feel my cheeks heat under her knowing gaze.

"I hadn't noticed." I pretend not to hear her snort, and shrug with a nonchalance I don't feel. "I don't have time for guys anyway."

It's true, too. I haven't so much as kissed anyone in years.

At first, I'd been too focused on succeeding at Pearson, a relationship was the last thing on my mind. I'd had one hook-up that could have become more had I wanted it to, but I was determined to succeed.

Eventually, that determination had morphed into being too busy when I entered the workforce.

Even if I did have the time, I doubt I'd have the inclination at this point. If nothing else, my morning proves that men are misogynistic assholes.

"Appreciating a man as gorgeous as that one doesn't need to be anything more than what it is." She winks easily before moving off down the bar. "At least let him buy you a few drinks. From the sound of things, you deserve it, lovely."

I swallow the sudden lump in my throat while she goes about her business.

Darcy has been a Godsend.

Having unburdened my circumstances onto the willing ears of a complete stranger, she'd floored me by offering me room and board in the small apartment attached to the back of the pub while I find my feet again.

She was sad to say that she had no extra shifts to offer me. However, she said she would be only too glad to help train me up as a bartender, citing that tips in some upscale places in Manhattan would help cover the exorbitant cost of Lita's care.

At least until the end…

I'd been so overwhelmed by the support of someone I'd literally just met that I'd all but run to the restroom to sob uncontrollably.

When I'd finally gathered myself together enough to re-emerge, I'd been mortified to find a handsome stranger had taken up residence at the far end of the bar. But once he'd begun talking, I'd strangely felt at ease.

"Liv—that best friend I mentioned—would say 'penny for your thoughts' if she were here."

His entirely delicious British accent sends a shiver along my spine, and I glance over my shoulder as he sits on the stool beside mine. My stomach dips precariously when his scent engulfs my senses, setting them alight.

When my eyes land on his face, my pulse kicks up a hundred notches, and butterflies *literally* take flight in the recesses of my stomach.

He is, without a doubt, the most attractive man I've ever seen up close.

Brown hair falls across his face, almost covering the most expressive and unusual whiskey-colored eyes I've ever seen. His olive skin makes those distinctive orbs even more devastating.

His face is a masterpiece of unparalleled beauty when his mouth lifts in a devastating smile that assuredly has had more than its fair share of women bending over backward just to catch a glimpse.

It's like the sun appearing in the sky after a thunderstorm.

Blindingly beautiful while warming me to my very marrow.

I don't have time for guys...

I repeat my mantra from before while I ignore the tingles his woodsy scent is sending to my long-unused female parts as I rapidly scan the recesses of my suddenly incompetent brain for a reasonable reply. "I was just thinking that I don't know you, and my abuela told me all about stranger danger, so…"

A deep laugh rumbles in his broad chest as I trail off, taking a sip of the rum and Coke in front of me.

"I'm Alex." He extends his hand. "I'm twenty-nine. A Leo through and through." He flashes an entirely too contagious shit-eating grin that makes my lips tug upward despite myself. "I work at DeMarco Holdings on Wall Street, though I'm originally from the UK, and, random fact, my favorite food is arancini."

I smile, sliding my palm along his and squeezing lightly as my pulse quickens from the simple act of shaking this man's rugged hand. "I'm Reyna. I'm twenty-four. A Capricorn, if you must know, and I'm currently unemployed as of this morning." Understanding lights his face as I continue. "I grew up in Connecticut, but moved to Manhattan for school when I was eighteen. And *my* favorite food is my abuelita's tamales."

Slowly shaking my hand, his smile reaches those warm amber eyes. "It's a pleasure to make your acquaintance, Reyna."

His hand lingers in mine for a beat longer, making my heart hiccup in response. His eyes languidly drift across the contours of my face before he severs the connection to pluck his tumbler of whisky from the bar.

"I'm sorry to hear of your recent unemployment. I can talk to HR to see if there's a suitable position at DeMarco—"

I cut him off before he can finish that sentence. "Thank you. Truly, but I think I'm done with Wall Street and the hordes of assholes it seems to breed. No offense."

He chuckles into his whisky. "None taken. In fact, I concur wholeheartedly. They're a load of wankers."

My smile is bright, and the weight on my shoulders feels lighter as I take another sip of my drink. I settle deeper into my stool, feeling a variation of relief for the first time in what feels like forever.

"What did you study?"

I turn toward him, setting my drink back on the bar. "Dance. I was at the Pearson School of the Arts…for a time."

His brows almost hit his hairline. "Wow, that's amazing!" He shakes his head in disbelief. "They're notoriously picky. You must be really good."

"Once upon a time, maybe." I can't help the self-deprecatory laugh that spills from my lips. "I don't remember the last time I danced for anyone besides *mi abuela,* to be honest."

My gaze drops to my lap when a frown overtakes my face as I remember how purposeful my life had felt back then.

"Lita got sick, and her care was…I mean, her care *is* expensive. Reality took over, so now I guess dancing for anyone else reminds me of a dream that died."

Silence hangs heavily between us for a weighty beat until Alex lays his hands atop my clasped ones. The simple contact sends a wave of unmistakable calm through every inch of my body, and for some reason that I can't fathom, this man's touch centers me enough to stop my rising emotions in their tracks.

"The sunshine after the storm has passed will be all the sweeter if you can learn to dance in the rain."

I raise my head at those words—words that speak to my soul—to find those beautiful eyes of his trained solely and intently on my face. Our gazes hold for endless minutes, time seeming to stand still.

My breath quickens as his eyes darken to a deep brown to match my own until Darcy's voice calls out from the back room, and I sever the connection, quickly averting my gaze.

"There's an old jukebox over by the restrooms if you fancy taking her for a spin around the floor, pretty boy." She chuckles loudly enough to be heard despite the distance. "I'd pay good money to see you attempt it."

I begin to shake my head, but Alex springs from his stool with an enthusiasm reminiscent of Fifi, the Golden Retriever I'd had as a kid.

His strides eat up the distance in mere seconds. He reaches his destination before my body catches up with my brain, and I slip from the stool to speed walk after him.

"What was your favorite dance?" He glances at me, then continues to scan the song choices before him.

"I'm *not* dancing today."

He turns to face me as I reach him, his expression more than a little sheepish, and I can already feel my resolve waver.

"Okay, so hear me out." He tilts his head to the side, sending me the biggest puppy dog eyes so that all I can do is nod as I press my lips together to stifle my rising smile.

"I was born with two left feet. Without an ounce of rhythm in this most perfect of bodies." He shrugs as he brushes non-existent dust from his chest, his lopsided smirk growing by the second. "I mean, I'm not perfect, but I'm damn near close."

My smile splits my face, lighting me up from within as he gently grasps my upper arms. "Teach me some simple steps, and I'll be *forever* in your debt, Reyna."

I exhale heavily through my nose, narrowing my eyes at him. "Fine. You win. Some *simple* steps, purely because I could use some comedic relief, Leftie."

He leans closer with a self-congratulatory smile. "I'm a fast learner, I'll have you know."

I shake my head before moving around to stand beside him.

"I'll be the judge of that statement."

He looks down at me, all signs of mirth gone from his face, now fully prepared to learn, and I feel a small hum of excitement building in the depths of my stomach at the thought of dancing again.

"We'll start with the box step, and once you have that, we'll take that spin around the tiles."

He nods succinctly, and we both turn our focus toward the floor.

"Okay, so your feet will step like this. Forward on your left, to the side with your right, and bring them together."

I show him what I mean, and he copies me after a beat.

"Now, you'll repeat the movement, but like this. Back with your right foot, to the side with your left, and then bring them together."

I shoot him an encouraging nod with a smile, and this time, he executes the steps instantly.

"Very good. Now let's repeat."

A handful of full turns later and Alex sends me a smug grin before he turns back to the jukebox, looking through the music in his apparent readiness.

The day has taken a sharp turn, and the constant smile that's plastered to my face is all down to the man with the time-turner.

My misery most definitely loves this guy's company.

He turns to me with a confused expression, holding a black Amex in his right hand. "Where's the contactless tap thingy?"

My brows knit as I replay his question, and I laugh out loud when realization dawns.

"Oh, Alex! You can't tap your card here." I nudge him to the side with my hip as my laugh dims to low chuckles while I scan the list of songs. "This thing is probably older than the building."

I catch him face-palming in my peripheral vision, and fresh laughter bubbles from my lips when my eyes land on the *perfect* waltz song choice. Slipping some change into the machine, I hit my selection and turn to face my newly acquired protégé, holding my right hand out for him to take.

The opening of "Thinking Out Loud" by my absolute favorite, Ed Sheeran, hits our ears at the exact same time, and his mouth twitches with a grin he can't restrain.

"I'm friends with Ed, you know."

"You are *not*!" My voice is high-pitched in my incredulity.

With my mouth dropped open, he clasps my outstretched hand with his left, leaning closer. "You're right. I'm not, but it would make for a great story, right?"

"Careful, pretty boy, or the deal's off."

Alex smirks as he lifts a brow. "Ah, so you think I'm pretty."

"Darcy called you that earlier. I was just—"

He interrupts my huff with a snort of laughter, and I narrow my eyes as best I can.

"You are *incorrigible*. Do you know that?"

"So I've been told a time or two."

He slides his right hand around my waist, completely distracting me when the simple movement sends a shiver of awareness through me. His masculine and thoroughly intoxicating scent invades my senses, and my head feels lighter at our proximity.

"Okay, time to get down to business."

I glance up at his words, my forehead creasing in confusion. "Huh?"

He tightens his hold on my waist. "We do it like this, right?"

I can feel my cheeks heat as I nod. "Mm-hmm. Yup. That's right." Gently laying my palm on his shoulder, I push the insinuating thoughts in my head aside and let the beat take the lead.

"Wait for the beat...and forward, side, together, repeat. Forward, side, together, *good*."

He smiles proudly at my praise, and I answer him with one of my own.

Once he's gotten the hang of it, I widen our steps to cover more of the floor space.

When Ed hits the bridge of the song, Alex surprises the crap out of me by urging me into an underarm turn. Laughter bubbles up my throat, spilling from my mouth.

"What are you doing?"

He spins me out and back in against his body as our box step is thrown clean out the window before he sobers slightly, and our eyes hold. "Dancing in the rain with you."

Tears prick my eyes at the kindness of this complete stranger who feels like *so* much more, and we continue to sway slightly for long minutes, eventually realizing the music has stopped.

My chest feels tight, my throat is clogged with emotion, and I'm filled with such an overwhelming feeling of gratitude that I could burst.

Alex's hand on my waist tightens as his jaw ticks almost imperceptibly. His eyes are stormy, raging in the silence hanging between us.

My mouth moves to ask him what's happening here, and his eyes are drawn to the movement, the pupils dilating when I tug my bottom lip between my teeth.

"I thought you might need some clothes…"

Leonard's voice calls over my shoulder, breaking the moment, and Alex steps back, digging his hands deeply into his pants pockets as he rocks back on his heels.

"Come on, Leo," Darcy calls out from her place behind the bar, where she's sat on a bar stool, clearly having been watching us the whole time. "Mammy always said if you were twice as smart, you'd still be stupid."

Six

REYNA

"There is no *way* the new Top Gun is better than the original. I call bullshit!"

Alex's chest rumbles with laughter as he nods. "I'm telling you, you're missing out."

I shake my head, grinning at his insistence. "I'll take your word."

Music sounds through the speakers dotting the expansive pub just as the front door opens, and suddenly there's an onslaught of customers flooding inside, scrambling over one another to get closer to the bar.

What begins as a dim hum of voices blares to life in a cacophony inside the space of two minutes, all while we watch in amazement. Shortly, the entire place is heaving full of business types, utterly at odds with the décor of the bar.

Darcy and two of her employees spur into action as my eyes find Alex's. He tips his head toward a free booth in the back of the pub in silent question, and I nod my agreement enthusiastically.

He grabs my hand, interlinking our fingers as though it's the most natural thing in the world. His eyes catch mine, and he brushes his thumb across the back of my hand in reassurance. My stomach dips when the simple touch sends a jolt of electricity up along my arm while he leads me through the mass of customers.

Once we reach the booth, he gestures for me to sit on one side.

I fully expect him to sit opposite; however, he surprises me by sliding in alongside me. As though in answer to my unspoken question, he grins lopsidedly. "If I sit opposite, I might not hear you properly."

Makes sense.

"Is it always this hectic?"

Alex glances about, taking in the jam-packed space, before turning back to face me and slowly lifting a shoulder. "Upon occasion. Though I can't say I've been here often enough to make me an expert on anything Molly Malones related. I'd have to ask my assistant to know for sure."

His eyes sparkle playfully, and my face splits in a smile. He glances at his watch, looking back up at me with incredulous eyes. "Christ, Rey. I walked in here five hours ago!"

My own eyes blow wide at the thought, vaguely registering his abbreviation of my name.

"Wow, that was the quickest afternoon of my life!" I shake my head, laughing softly in disbelief.

Alex chuckles at my reaction, turning just in time to catch the eye of a passing barman. He holds up two fingers, and the barman nods before turning back toward the bar.

"Talking with you has made a really unpleasant day so much more bearable." I glance down almost shyly, unable to meet his eyes, when he turns back to face me. "Thank you for lifting my spirits, Alex. Despite your own day being less than stellar—"

He cuts me off. "What gave me away?"

I press my lips together before raising my eyes to find his. "Well, you did lure me in with your phrase 'misery loves company.' It's not your average chat-up line, and you've been utterly respectable to boot. You've spent the day cheering me up and avoiding mention of your own reason for wanting a time-turner, which leads me to deduce your day drinking is connected to a work-related mishap that occurred sometime before noon."

He sniggers easily. "You're quite the sleuth, Rey."

"Just call me Reyna Holmes!" I waggle my eyebrows playfully.

Alex throws his head back, laughing long and loud, uncaring that his unfiltered bellow draws the attention of several bystanders who continue to stare, talking quickly among themselves.

I don't give them much thought, as his mirth is infectious, and soon I'm laughing alongside him.

Darcy appears almost out of nowhere, depositing two steaming bowls before us. "Irish stew. My mother's recipe, just so you know." She puffs out her chest with pride at that, and I smile my appreciation in return, knowing just how special old family recipes are.

"I'll add it to the ever-mounting tab, pretty boy." Then she winks before disappearing through the throng.

I peer hesitantly into my bowl, the scent of the dish hitting me square in the nostrils.

"Oh my God, it smells *so* good."

I pick up my spoon and dive straight in. A moan of delight escapes my lips, and my eyes fall closed as I savor the divine flavor in my mouth.

When I open my eyes, I find Alex watching me with a grin. "It's good, right?"

I nod enthusiastically and tuck back in as he picks up his own utensils.

The noise of the customers is the only sound between us until our bowls are empty. I drop my spoon into the bowl and sit back to rub my stomach.

"I think I'm having a food baby."

Alex mirrors my actions, rubbing his own clearly taut stomach as he deadpans. "I think I'm having Irish twins."

I catch his laughing gaze as a smile takes over my features. His eyes move along the contours of my face, sending butterflies swarming in the full depths of my stomach until his smile dims as his brows furrow.

I'm about to ask what's wrong, when a voice behind Alex sends a chill racing along my spine.

ALEX

Christ, she's beautiful. Inside and out.

If someone told me six hours ago that today would end up being one of the best days I've had in *years*, I'd have called bullshit.

I walked into Molly Malones, expecting to have a few drinks before heading over to Vaughn to get an update on the brewing scandal, only to get swept up in Reyna.

When she'd slipped to the restrooms, I'd asked Darcy to close the bar off to other customers for a bit and add it to my tab, which she'd done with a smirk.

Except now it feels like those five hours weren't enough.

I really do *need a time-turner!*

I feel as though my thoughts are showing plainly on my face until Reyna opens her mouth to speak, only to clamp her lips closed as plain horror mars the perfection of her features.

"Look what the cat dragged in."

I spin in my seat to find an acquaintance of mine, insurance mogul, Chad Freemont, standing over our table.

"Not your usual scene, is it, Freemont?"

He arches a brow, his eyes flitting to Reyna at my back, and I feel her body stiffen under his steely perusal.

"Christ no, DeMarco."

I let my eyes fall closed in resignation at Chad's divulging of my surname. I'd purposefully left it out of our conversation, unwilling to be one of those Wall Street wankers in Rey's eyes.

I twist my neck around, seeing no recognition in her wide eyes, and a bolt of relief shoots through me.

"Felt like slumming it this evening." His predatory gaze slides to Reyna, and the sight sees protectiveness well up inside of me before he follows it with, "Seems you did too, friend."

I fly to my feet, grabbing him by the collar of his shirt to hiss into his face. "Say that again, asshole, and I'll make sure that you live to regret it. You hear me?"

Chad smirks smugly, shrugging his shoulders as though he doesn't have a care in the world, and my attention is suddenly drawn to the wall of faces staring at us.

People in the midst of dancing, some in the middle of taking a sip of their drink, every single body in Molly Malones has stopped in their tracks to level their attention upon Freemont and me.

I drop his shirt, stepping back with my hands up, knowing that if I make a scene here and word gets out—which it inevitably will—Henry will undoubtedly cut off my balls and wear them as earrings.

"Fuck off, Freemont."

The prick tosses a wink in Rey's direction, and I grit my teeth as he leans close, whispering for my ears alone, "Enjoy my sloppy seconds, DeMarco. She's a real screamer. Tell her I liked it a *whole* lot."

He leans back, a smug-as-fuck smile on his face. And I've reached my limit.

Fuck it!

I ball my right hand into a fist and lean back before propelling myself forward to slam my knuckles into his egotistical face.

Satisfaction fills me from head to toe as he flies backward, landing flat on his back with a heavy thump. I step closer to loom over him, fully aware of the look of unconcealed rage on my face.

There's the sound of cameras clicking and lights flashing as bystanders take photos, but I'm entirely too focused on the piece of shit beneath me to give a rat's ass.

A surge of protectiveness flows through me, the likes of which I've only ever felt toward Liv and my nephews, and at that moment—as bizarre as it makes me feel to acknowledge it—I know she's gotten under my skin.

I want to take care of her. The way she deserves to be cared for. The way she hasn't been cared for in a very long time, by the sounds of it.

I want to be the shelter in the raging storm for this tiny girl with the big chocolaty brown eyes that see me—the real me—and I know I'll never allow anyone to disrespect her. *Ever.*

"If you so much as even glance in Reyna's direction *ever again…*" I trail off, narrowing my eyes into slits. "I'll *not* be held responsible for my actions."

I straighten, glancing to my left to find Rey standing stock still at my side. When I extend my hand, she grabs hold of it like it's a lifeline, and I tug her behind me as the wall of bodies parts like the Red Sea.

I don't stop until I've reached the bar, ducking around the side of it and slipping behind the Staff Only door at the back.

Once we are safely away from prying eyes, I round on a wide-eyed Reyna.

"I need to go and run some damage control. It's going to be a long night at the office for me." She deflates right where she stands, and I rush to follow to soften the blow. "I'll come back tomorrow to check in. You'll be here, right?"

She worries her lip between her teeth before slowly nodding. "I want to visit Lita early tomorrow morning, but I'll be here otherwise, I'm sure." Her brows knit with obvious worry. "I have nowhere else to go, seemingly."

"Give me your cell." My words are sharper than I'd intend, but even so, her eyes remain on mine without an ounce of judgment.

She tugs a clunky cell from a pocket on her sweater, thrusting it into my hands with eyes that are more pupil than iris in their intensity.

Ripping my gaze from hers, I key in my cell number and smirk when I save it under Pretty Boy. "Text me when you are back here, and I'll come to you. We can talk about finding a more permanent residence and employment—"

She cuts me off. "Why do you want to help me? You only just met me today." She shakes her head, her forehead knitting as she clearly searches for an answer to her own question.

Before I can think of an answer, my mouth is moving as I spill my truth in a way I haven't ever before. Not even to Liv.

"When I was a kid, my brother was the only person who ever gave a shit about me. He was my brother, my mother, my father, and my best friend, all rolled into one. It was us against the world. But...something happened that made him leave home."

I inhale deeply through my nostrils and blow out a steadying breath as she watches me with rapt attention. "I was so thoroughly and completely *alone*. My mother used me as a bargaining chip to get everything she wanted. The surname that my absentee father bestowed upon me opened plenty of doors that would have been otherwise closed firmly in her face."

I pour every ounce of emotion into my next words as I hold her gaze.

"So I know what it's like to be alone. I know what it's like to think that people could give less of a shit about your issues because they're neck deep just trying to make it through their own. But I also know what it's like to have a person who believes in you. Who makes you believe in yourself and your dreams just by being there when you need them. Liv was that friend for me… so *maybe* this is my chance to pay it forward."

Our eyes continue to hold when I finish speaking, and hers fill with unshed tears before she closes the distance between us to slip her arms around my waist, tucking herself in against my chest.

Her sweet floral scent dances along my senses as my arms wrap around her small body.

She fits so perfectly.

My eyes fall shut as she rubs her cheek against my chest and exhales heavily, a little of the tension leaving her body in the safety of my hold.

"I've got you, Rey. I'll weather the storm with you."

Seven

ALEX

"Morning, princess."

I sit up with a jerk, my eyes bleary with lack of sleep as they land on a fresh-faced, smiling Grayson Hunter.

"What time is it?" My words sound slurred as I rub my eyes. "And where's the fucking coffee?"

Grayson drops a travel mug down in front of me. "Macchiato from Pearse's." He looks at me pointedly. "You're welcome."

I close my hand around the handle and bring it to my lips with a grumble. "If you're looking for a thanks, you won't find one here. Today was *your* turn."

"Actually, *yesterday* was my turn, but that meeting with Henry fucked with our routine, so..."

He trails off with an expectant look on his face. And considering the mess ahead of me, I know I'll get through it faster with his help. *"Thank you."*

Tipping his head, my CFO slides into the seat opposite mine, and without waiting—which is one of the things that makes him so damn good at his job—he gets ahead of the game, even surprising me this time.

"Your debacle at Molly Malones is being handled. Why you thought you needed to do it yourself is beyond me."

My forehead creases as visions of my scuffle with Chad Freemont—and of a tiny dancer with chocolate eyes and smooth, tan skin—flit through my sleep-addled brain.

"How did you know?"

He barks a laugh while shaking his head. "Ah, DeMarco, DeMarco, DeMarco. Use your brain for once."

I narrow my eyes as I take a big gulp of the steaming brew in my hand, but he disregards me entirely. "It was a simple matter of following hashtags, my friend. Vaughn's tech guy used some hashtag tracking software, setting it up from the second you left here yesterday, and when the hashtags that were most apt—like your name, for instance—started to be used, we were able to get them removed or restricted within moments of each upload."

I take another sip of my coffee, nodding my head. "So... sleeping on my desk was—"

"Classic Alex." He shrugs before leaning back in the chair, steepling his fingers and resting them on his stomach.

I open my mouth to disagree wholeheartedly with that statement, when there's a knock on the office door.

"Come in."

Bailey's head pops around the door. "Henry's just arrived. He's asking for you both in Boardroom Three."

He presses his lips together, almost in an apologetic move, and I know that what I'm about to face is the worst of the worst. "Thank you, Bailey."

Grayson stands first, giving me a pitying look as Bailey closes my office door behind him. "Let's just get this over with."

I stand to face him, giving him a sharp nod. "It can't possibly be worse than yesterday's meeting."

But less than two minutes later, I'm proved completely wrong.

"A fake relationship, Alex. It's more common than you'd think. Don't be so fucking obtuse." Henry rolls his eyes as he tosses an armload of black folders across the table. "I expect you to come to your decision quickly and efficiently."

"You expect *what*?"

Henry levels me with a look that brooks no argument before leaning back in his seat and folding his arms across his chest.

Despite being seated, while Gray and I stand, my brother is the one with all the power here.

"Don't play dumb, Al. You heard me. You need a girlfriend to clean up your image. A relationship will take you off the market, there'll be less of a target on your back, and it will look good to the Board members, some of whom are hoping to see you out on your ass due to rumors swirling that I can't control. Something needs to change, and fast."

His eyes pierce me with their severity. "A girlfriend or you're out, little brother. The choice is all yours."

A cold sweat emerges on my brow as panic wells in the pit of my stomach. I glance sideways at Gray, finding his eyes bulging from his head with a matching perspiration-soaked forehead of his own.

"I really don't think choosing an actress as a fake girlfriend is the answer to—"

Henry rises to his feet in one fluid movement, his eyes spitting angry green flames that see both Grayson and I openly flinch.

"I've been able to make this unholy mess of yours go away, Alex. Through great personal sacrifice—not to mention a pretty penny and favors I'll be paying back on my death bed—I've done my best by you." He carefully places his clenched fists on the table between us, leaning closer to growl dangerously, "*Now* it's your turn. You play your part—and you play it damn-fucking-well—or you're *out* of the company. Permanently."

I hold his gaze as rage bubbles up in the pits of my churning stomach. "It was *one* mistake, Ri. One—"

"Of many, little brother."

I try again. "Come on. You *can't* be serious—"

My brother's fist comes down on the desk, halting my plea. His eyes pin me in place as he enunciates each word. "Don't. Test. Me."

We stare one another down for a long beat, even as Gray begins to fidget beside me.

Henry gestures at the piles of folders strewn across the boardroom table. "Pick one you won't fuck. That way, you can keep it purely business."

"I am focused on *this* business, not the business of maintaining a sham relationship to placate you and the board. The company is where I'm best—"

My brother cuts me off as though I haven't even spoken. "As of today, you're on extended leave, little brother. Liv is bringing the kids, and we'll be Stateside for the foreseeable."

Guilt gnaws at my insides at that. At the stress being put on the people I care for the most.

"Pick one of these girls and come back to me when you're ready to organize the contracts. It will involve a lot of public appearances to sell this charade, so pick one that has semi-decent conversational skills for your own sake."

My brain whirrs to keep up with just how fast everything has turned to shit, and before my brain catches up, my mouth blurts out words I can't take back.

"I already *have* a girlfriend."

Shit! Did I just say that?

"What the actual hell?"

Gray rounds on me with eyes that threaten to fall clean out of their sockets while Henry just tilts his head to one side in complete skepticism, but instead of crumbling under their joint looks of disbelief, I double down.

I feel myself standing taller as I clear my throat, and my brain finally catches up with my mouth. "It's been ongoing for…" I trail off as the lie sticks in my throat, but I grit my jaw and force out the words. "For six months now. And it's…serious. *Very* serious."

My earnest eyes hold Henry's, fully invested in my lie now. I'm not about to let my own brother force me from my birthright. Damn him.

"It's the reason I wanted to quash the sex tape, Ri. I—I don't want her to find out about past indiscretions."

My brother's face is impenetrable as he assesses me, and while he picks apart my words, I wait with bated breath for his ruling.

"Do I know her?"

I shake my head, praying he won't ask me anything further, but my prayers land on deaf ears.

His face looks skeptical as he stares me down. "Who is she?"

Shit!

I force my face to remain impassive as my mind races, searching for an answer I don't fucking have until my cell chimes in my pocket. I slide it out to check the sender.

UNKNOWN

I'm back from Staten, Pretty Boy.

Deep brown eyes float at the front of my vision.

Oversized sweats and a dancing smile that lights up the room.

My lips twitch at the memory, despite the severity of this moment.

Maybe this *is why we met. Maybe* this *is how I can take care of her like she needs.*

"Her name is Reyna, and she's…" My forehead creases in thought, and I trail off, momentarily unsure of what to say, until the words just come to me.

"She *matters* to me, Henry."

The emphasis placed on that statement is eerily accurate despite our short acquaintance, but I can see the moment Henry realizes I'm one hundred percent serious.

And then, in typical Alex fashion, I drive my point home in style. "I want to marry this woman."

In for a penny and all that!

Unrestrained delight lifts his heavy brow as his eyes soften openly. His mouth lifts in a broad smile that shines from his cheeks. "Christ's sake, Al. Couldn't you have led with that?"

His laugh is brimming with relief as he rounds the table to clasp my shoulders, tugging me against his chest and into a bear hug. "I only want your happiness, little brother. And if she is important to you, then I'll welcome her with open arms."

Gray claps his hand atop my shoulder from his place at my back, and I close my eyes for a moment to allow my guilt to settle.

I don't like lying to the few people I care about, and the ease with which I've just told this lie makes me sick to my stomach. Despite my best efforts, I'm just like my fucked-up parents.

Showing the desired image to the world, all while being twisted and broken on the inside.

Henry pulls out of our embrace, gripping my upper arms, and I swallow that thought along with my guilt, pushing everything as deep down as I can, just like I've done for as long as I can remember.

"When do we get to meet my future sister-in-law, Reyna?"

"Well, you've just gone and shit the motherfucking bed, DeMarco, haven't you!"

I narrow my eyes at my pseudo-friend as he begins to slow clap. "Well done. This is next-level screwing up, even for such a seasoned—"

"Christ almighty, Burton." I cut him off before he manages to piss me off even further, but all he does is smirk. "I came here for some damn advice, so do your part, and get me out of this mess…"

I trail off, my face turning sheepish as I murmur, "Again."

The bastard laughs in my face before suddenly rising to stand.

"Come on. I have a club to run, and you're eating into my valuable time."

He reaches the door of his office above Rogue, where he can be found at almost any hour of the day or night, swinging it wide open before beckoning me to follow.

"The least you can do is keep me company while we talk it out."

I follow after him, lengthening my strides to catch up with his as we cross the staff quarters, that are, even at this time of the afternoon, bustling with a flurry of activity.

Catching my eye, Vaughn merely shrugs. "You *know*, debauchery never sleeps, my friend."

He's not wrong. If the walls of this place could talk, the stories they'd tell would undoubtedly destroy lives.

He marches through a seemingly hidden door on the far side of the vast staff area, leading us into *Risqué*.

There are three tiers to Rogue.

The first, *Rapture,* is the main club area decorated in hues of blue and green to almost give the impression of being underwater. Nightly shows, parades, and a multitude of A-listers make it a top-class night out.

Masquerade masks are not uncommon and are actually a requirement for *all* staff on the floor. It adds to the mystery, according to Vaughn.

The second, *Risque,* where we are now, is a maze of dimly lit hallways and curtained alcoves, purpose-built for secret interludes and rendezvous away from the prying eyes of the masses.

Private rooms dot the hallways, hired out at a rate of five thousand dollars per half-hour with staff called performers within to fulfill any kind of fantasy your body may desire. Many of these doors are closed, meaning they're in use despite the tender hour.

Debauchery never sleeps, indeed.

Coming to the end of the long, winding corridor, I spy the hot pink neon sign for the third and final tier, *Ravish,* come into view.

My feet automatically grind to a halt, disapproval filling my mouth with a bitterness I can almost taste. "You never said you were coming over *here.*"

Vaughn stops with a heavy sigh. "Calm your tits. It's empty at this time of day, idiot."

He rolls his eyes before continuing closer to the biometric hand scanner that grants only a select few access to possibly the seediest aspect of the club.

The door swings open with a loud beep, admitting us into a lowly lit large space that I typically avoid.

I swallow my disgust and voice the question. "Is there one tonight?"

Vaughn grunts in confirmation, moving off to check on

something behind a low bar to our left.

Neither of us is comfortable being here, but Vaughn hides it exceptionally well, standing tall and unafraid in the only part of his father's legacy that he couldn't dismantle, much to his revulsion.

Having established his London club first, Valentine Burton had expanded the menu for his North American clientele, going so far as to offer sex auctions, among other unsavory events.

These had made him a fortune, putting his name well and truly on the map, and so, Valentines of Manhattan had quickly become home to a great many powerful men and women.

It was when Vaughn had rebranded as Rogue that the shit hit the proverbial fan. People were threatened, lives were lost, and Vaughn was backed into a corner.

Keep the auctions and everything that goes with them, *or else.*

"Okay, so you have two options, DeMarco."

Vaughn's voice echoes through the space, pulling me from my musings. I shift my eyes to my left, where he's stood before a computer, tapping away with his eyes glued to the screen before him.

"By all means, feel free to spit it out sometime this year."

He finishes up, lifting his head with a heavy eye roll. "Wanker."

He comes closer, hitting a light switch on the wall as he passes that illuminates the bars running on either side of the space and the elevated runway in the center of the room with the same hot pink neon as the sign outside the door.

"Choice number one. Tell Henry you're a liar. Go back to the office, and tell him you'll do what he wants. You'll do the bought-and-paid fake girlfriend just like he's demanding. Toe the line, and keep the Board happy."

I nod as he pauses, signaling for him to continue.

"Choice two. Ask this mysterious Reyna to be a willing accomplice—"

I cut him off. "No one would agree to marry me, no questions asked, purely because I need a fake fucking wife. Especially not a girl like this, Burton. She's…she's…"

I trail off, unsure of how to conclude that thought, but Vaughn jumps right in to fill in the blanks when he deadpans. "She's practically homeless, jobless, and has a grandmother with huge healthcare bills. It's safe to say that she needs you as much as you need her."

My brows crease as I weigh up his words.

Maybe she really does *need me.*

I sigh heavily as he regards me with his hands clasped in front of his waist.

"You don't trust people easily, DeMarco. I get it. We're alike in that sense. *But*, from what you've told me, she's somehow made it past the walls you use to keep the world at bay. Perhaps meeting her yesterday was meant to be."

Vaughn's words knock around inside my head as he checks things over for tonight's auction, eventually realizing that choice two is the better option here.

In hindsight, I'd known it before I'd come to him, but an objective opinion never hurt anyone.

He ushers me back the way we came, having shut off the underlighting, and I stop when he comes to the biometric scanner to allow us to leave *Ravish*.

"Thank you for this, Burton."

He nods as the door beeps loudly, swinging toward us to showcase the darkened hallways of *Risque*, and as I step past him, he cranes his neck with a frown.

"Sorry, what was that, DeMarco? I'm afraid I couldn't hear it over the sound of how awesome I am."

He grins as I roll my eyes.

Prick!

Eight

ALEX

Shit. Fuck. Wanker. Bollocks.

I've run out of expletives by the time my feet have easily found their way back to Molly Malones.

When I push open the heavy oak door, my eyes unerringly land on the vision behind the bar.

Reyna is holding a clipboard while she checks the inventory behind the bar on the opposite wall.

I stop dead in my tracks as the light from outside floods the dimly lit interior. It travels across the marble floor, streaking along the bar to illuminate her and draw her attention toward me.

Her face is brighter than the sunlight I've just left behind, and I feel a warmth in my chest as I bask in her attention.

"Alex."

My name is a whisper on an exhalation, and my stomach dips when my cock stands to attention.

Down, boy. Rey is off-fucking-limits. We're her shelter.

Much to my relief, the thought immediately deflates my

swelling dick, and I stride closer as her smile grows ever brighter.

"You came back."

I'm helpless to stop my mouth from drawing up like a bow as I reach the bar and take a stool. "I told you I would, didn't I?"

Reyna blinks slowly before tipping her head to one side as her face scrunches up playfully. "I'd be in for a world of disappointment if I believed everything I was told. A promise is easily made and twice as easily broken."

"I'm a man of my word, Rey. You don't ever need to doubt that I mean what I say, and I say what I mean."

She smiles, dropping her clipboard onto the bar as Darcy pokes her head out from the back.

"Oh, it's just you, pretty boy." Her eyes dart from me to Reyna with a smile. "I'll be back here, lovely, if any *real* patrons wander in."

Reyna grins as she nods, turning back to face me when Darcy closes the door again. "Can I get you anything?"

"I'm here for you, Rey."

Her eyes blow wide at that statement, and I rush to follow it up. "I need your help, to be precise. I have a…" I trail off, unsure of how to describe it, and suddenly wondering what the actual fuck got into me at the office to make this sound like a reasonable idea.

"You have a…?" Rey prompts, nodding her head encouragingly.

Fuck it.

"Okay, so hear me out. I need to ask you something. It's a little bit out there, even for me, but I'm going to do it anyway. So here it goes."

I inhale deeply before launching into it, realizing as I go that it's the most insane idea I've ever heard of, let alone had.

"A year ago, I was filmed while being intimate with a woman… or two." Her brows raise slightly, but I keep going. "Okay, full disclosure, there were three."

I wait for her reaction, expecting judgment, but just receiving another nod to go on.

"Anyway, my position at DeMarco Holdings is held by the grace of my brother, Henry, and our Board of Directors. But recently, my friend, Vaughn, discovered an underground sale of the footage to a newspaper here in Manhattan."

Rey's gasp of shock cuts me off.

"Yeah, I know, right? Bad enough that it was done without my consent, but to make money from it too."

I shrug, blowing out a heavy breath. "Anyway, I needed to let Henry know, and between him and Vaughn, they were able to bury it."

"Oh, thank goodness for that, Alex. You poor thing." Reyna's face is the very picture of concern, despite the sordid story that's just been dumped on her lap.

"I'm grateful for their help, but Henry blindsided me this morning at the office. He decided that he was going to employ an actress as my fake girlfriend to clean up my image. To dispel rumors and to keep the Board happy." I roll my eyes exaggeratedly. "Henry is married to Liv, my best friend. The woman is a walking angel. My brother knows *exactly* how lucky he is to have found her. And so, he's convinced that I can only be happy if I find the same happiness, clearly."

"That's sweet of him, though I suspect the fake girlfriend was a step too far, right?"

I throw my hands up. "*Bingo*! I'm all for cleaning up my image and keeping the damn Board happy, but employing someone to be my fake girlfriend is just asking for trouble. I mean, people break NDAs all the damn time. They're not worth shit!"

Reyna's infectious laughter rings throughout the pub, and I chuckle along with her before sobering to hold her gaze.

"But asking a new friend to pretend to be my girlfriend in exchange for taking over her lita's expenses isn't out of the realm of possibility, hmm?"

REYNA

Alex's whiskey eyes hold mine with a plea that speaks to my whole self. I know before he's even finished his sentence that, despite the insanity of his suggestion, I'll say yes.

Something about this man calls to me, and if I can help him out while making sure Lita is cared for in her final days, then I have no qualms about doing what he asks.

My intuition is never wrong, and it's screaming to trust my gut here and now.

"I'll do it."

His brows fly up in blatant disbelief, and his jaw slackens, making it impossible for me to keep a straight face. He looks so incredulous; it's endearing.

"Am I insane?" I shrug as I chuckle and answer my own question. "Clearly, *yes*! However, you're the one who cooked up this idea, so apparently, we're two peas in the same pod."

His bark of laughter echoes through the bar, and he strides closer. "You'll really do it? I mean, I don't have a plan, really—"

"I'll do it." I tuck my hair behind my left ear, looking up at him from underneath my lashes with serious eyes. "You made yesterday *bearable*—no, actually, you made it amazing despite the crap I was dealing with."

A smile makes the corners of my mouth twitch, and I shrug playfully. "Plus, I mean, it's not like you're a horrible person to be around, you know!"

The fact that he simply makes me feel safe, secure, and protected in his mere presence doesn't hurt either. His defense of me last night had compounded what my gut had already surmised – this man is *special*.

He's one of a kind.

A smile grows on his face with every word I speak until his feet begin to move, taking him down and around by the end of the bar. His long strides cover the distance between us, and when he finally reaches me, he tugs me into his warm embrace.

My cheek is pressed to his chest, and I can hear his heart beating solidly beneath my ear. Long moments pass, and he lays his own cheek atop my head, his breathing even and slow.

"Well, you sure move fast, pretty boy." Darcy's voice sees us jump apart as though caught with our hands in the proverbial cookie jar.

Alex's grin is lopsided and thoroughly contagious. "My brother always says, when you know, you know." He tosses me a wink before turning to face a smiling Darcy.

"Now, can you show me to Rey's room? We need to get moving quickly."

"Moving where?" Mine and Darcy's voices ring out in unison, concern etched on her face as it most assuredly is on my own.

"To my penthouse, obviously." Alex turns to face me, and whatever he finds there makes him rush on as though afraid I'll change my mind about the whole thing. "Or I'll buy you your own. Would that work?"

"No, no, Alex." I shake my head rapidly. "That's entirely unnecessary. However, we *do* need to discuss this before jumping headfirst. I know you said you don't have a timeline, but—"

Darcy cuts me off by popping her head up behind Alex's shoulder. "Christ's sake, lovely. Don't look a gift horse in the mouth."

She quirks a brow, and her lips twitch suspiciously. "Especially one as pretty as this!"

Having gathered everything of value from my Corolla earlier this morning, it takes us less than ten minutes to pack, and once we bid Darcy farewell—ensuring her with a hug that we'll be back soon—we exit Molly Malones to find a black town car awaiting us at the sidewalk.

"I could have driven us, pretty boy."

I arch a brow pointedly, and Alex smirks as he gestures for me to go first.

"Ah, but that would do Damien here out of a job, Sunshine."

As I slip into the car, sending a smile of gratitude toward a stoic Damien, I pin my new fake boyfriend with a questioning stare. "Sunshine?"

He slides in beside me while Damien softly closes the car door behind him.

Alex grins lopsidedly, and my foolish heart thumps traitorously beneath my breast.

Give it up, idiot!

"Yeah, I mean, if we're in this, I feel a nickname is required, no?"

He rolls his eyes, shaking his head. "Henry is big on nicknames."

I shrug indifferently. "Why Sunshine?"

He chuckles, gripping my hand in his much larger one as he

wriggles his eyebrows. "Because you're a Rey of Sunshine."

My face splits in a wide smile, and Alex reaches across with his free hand to dust his knuckles along my cheek. "See? A smile like sunshine."

My pulse kicks up at the sentiment, and my cheeks blush furiously.

Stop it. STOP IT, *Reyna.*

His eyes soften for a moment, then he pulls back and pats my hand before tugging his palm from my hold.

"Some ground rules then, okay?"

I nod succinctly. "Okay. Shoot, pretty boy."

He slides me a narrow-eyed look that makes me belly laugh.

"Well, if you get to call me something ridiculous, then it's only fair that I get the same courtesy."

"Fine." He grins, transforming his whole face. "Henry will eat that shit up."

My chuckle tugs an answering one from Alex before he dives right in.

"So first, for as long as we're in this, neither of us can see anyone else. Okay?"

I nod my agreement, finding zero fault in that rule. Dating is not my gig.

"That includes casual sex, Alex." I quirk a brow.

His lip twitches. "Only sex with my fake girlfriend. Okay, got it!"

I reach across the seat between us to shove his shoulder. His laugh is thoroughly infectious. "You are—"

"Incorrigible, Sunshine. I know!"

He wriggles his eyebrows, the very picture of hilarity, and I can't even keep a straight face. "The only sex in your future is with your hand. That's the first rule right there, pretty boy."

Despite the laughter in his eyes, he nods solemnly and crosses his heart before moving on to the next rule. "Second, you will need to live in the same building as me. Preferably on the same floor – *ideally* in my penthouse. I don't want to make you uncomfortable, but we *may* need to cohabitate for a period of time…"

He trails off hesitantly, and I rush to speak, wanting to ease his concerns. "You are clearly a public figure, going on what you've told me, so I'm going to go out on a limb here and say you're not a serial killer."

He flashes his teeth. "Only a serial screw-up, if that's not a deal breaker."

My lips twitch. "I'm good with that, roomie. What else?"

"Well, there will be a number of high-profile events we'll need to attend as a couple. You'd need to be okay with the attention. On *both* of us. We'll need to play the role perfectly in these instances, in particular."

My face freezes, and Alex rushes on. "There will be security in place for you, of course. And an Amex in your name *should* be waiting at the penthouse, so money won't be an issue."

He takes my hands in his, holding them as lightly as his gaze is firm. "For my third request, all I ask is that you have my back because I'll always have yours."

The car glides to a halt, and Damien exits the vehicle quietly.

I bite down on my bottom lip, simultaneously overwhelmed by everything he's just laid on me, and dumbstruck, unsure of what to say in response.

The door opens beside Alex, flooding the car with daylight. He gives me one final look before slipping from his place beside me, then he reaches his hand back inside to assist me.

When I exit the vehicle, I instantly note that we're on the Upper East Side, and everything surrounding us screams money.

"Thank you, Damien."

Alex reaches for my hand instinctively, pulling me along beside him as I nod to our driver in silent thanks. "What about my bags?"

"Damien will see they are sent up, Rey."

I can't stop the giggle that pops out of my mouth as we cross the threshold of a clearly uber-swanky residence. This feels so surreal, and I'm entirely sure that reality hasn't sunk in just yet.

The elevator pings open before we reach it, and a tall, blonde woman steps out, her eyes instantly landing on Alex.

"Alex!" His name is practically purred from her pouty, glossed lips, and his grip on my hand tightens noticeably.

"Krista, you're back in Manhattan. How was Ralph's seventieth birthday trip? Is he back too?"

I chance a look at him, finding his face pained. His eyes are darting around, clearly looking for an escape route.

"Pffft, he's somewhere nearby." She winks broadly. "I'm sure he wouldn't mind if you took me for a drink tonight. He loves knowing I'm being taken care of, you know. Swing by my place around seven."

My mouth almost hits the floor at her audacity. Alex goes to speak, but I beat him to it.

"Alex is busy tonight, and every other night, *Krista*." It's my turn to wink exaggeratedly when I hold up our clasped hands. "We'll be spending the foreseeable future christening every surface of *our* penthouse."

I raise our joined hands to my lips, pressing a kiss to the back of Alex's before stepping around a clearly affronted Krista.

But something takes hold of me, forcing me to stop at her side and whisper in a honeyed tone filled with as much condescension as I can muster, "Have fun with Ralph's saggy old man balls."

We step onto the elevator, and Alex hits the button for forty-six. Krista's stunned face is the last thing I see before the doors close silently.

Alex's howl of laughter fills the car, and he throws his head back in abandon. "Oh shit, that was priceless, Rey. Absolutely fucking priceless."

I shrug as I chuckle. "Well, one of the rules is not seeing anyone else. Obviously, I was *helping* you stick to the rule you set."

He sobers, leveling me with a look before he steps closer and palms my cheeks. His hands are warm, singeing my skin as his eyes pierce my soul before his words permeate my heart.

"That is one rule I would never, *ever* break, Reyna. I can't promise to make all your problems disappear, but I *can* promise that I'll be here to share the burden with you."

His eyes travel along the contours of my face, and in this moment, I feel precious, safe, and cared for.

Things I have not felt for a long, *long* time, and I can't help the flash of fear that shoots through me at the thought of all of this falling apart.

Because despite only finding the beauty and strength of this man *yesterday*, I'm getting altogether too reliant on how he makes me feel.

Your intuition is your gift, mija. Listen to it!

My abuela's words of comfort soothe my anxiety, and all I can do is hope that he doesn't leave me more broken than he found me.

Having reached our destination, the elevator doors ping open to reveal a cavernous apartment with a double vaulted ceiling and huge Monolithic windows looking out onto the city beyond.

My gasp of delight is muted by Alex's laughter. "It's quite something, isn't it? It's owned by the company. My own taste would be far less ostentatious."

I step from the elevator, spinning a full turn to take in the entire space. "Wow! It's *huge*."

"That's what they all say."

I shoot Alex a playful glare, to which he just grins. "Incorrigible, pretty boy."

"So you've told me, Rey."

He strides forward into the open-plan kitchen to pluck an envelope from the counter, quietly murmuring, "That was fast."

Ripping it open, he slides a black credit card from within. He presents it to me with a flourish and my eyes bulge as I note it's in my name. "It's limitless. Buy whatever you'd like."

He glances upward in thought, lips scrunched into a pondering pout. "Well, it's limitless within reason – Henry would blow a fuse if he needed to explain away the purchase of a small country in the company's income tax returns."

My gaze flicks from Alex to the card and back again as I blink owlishly.

"I—I—" I swallow harshly and try again. "You don't need to do this. I—"

"I *want* to. That's the difference." He comes closer, smiling down at me before locking me in his embrace. "You haven't had the ability to put yourself first since you moved to New York. Let me put you first. Let me take care of you the way you deserve, Reyna. Let me be your person."

He presses a kiss atop my head, and the simple gesture has my stomach turning somersaults as I inhale his woodsy scent in deep lungfuls.

"Tomorrow, we'll go shopping and get everything set up for Friday."

My words are muffled against his shirt. "What's Friday?"

I can feel him tense up slightly before he answers. "Liv and the boys arrive tomorrow, and we're having lunch here with them on Friday."

Nerves rush through me, and he blows out a breath. "Time to get this party started, Sunshine."

Nine

REYNA

I wake to an empty penthouse.

A note on the table by the elevator explains everything.

> Morning Sunshine,
>
> The jet with Liv and my nephews on board landed while you were sleeping. I needed to go to meet her and the boys, but I'll be back soon.
>
> Get ready for a big ass day!
>
> Thinking of you,
>
> Pretty Boy

I glance around the empty penthouse as my stomach grumbles. Loudly.

Breakfast it is.

I drop the note onto the table and march straight for the

kitchen as my pajama shorts tickle my upper thighs. I spot an Apple smart speaker on the countertop, and excitement zings through my entire body.

Glancing upwards, I can't help but zone in on the ignored acoustic ability of this place.

I bite my lip, bouncing back and forth on the balls of my feet. Blowing out a breath, I squeeze my eyes shut and utter the glorious words, "Siri, play Ed Sheeran."

As though fated, "Thinking Out Loud" booms out through speakers clearly dotted throughout the space, and I smile brightly as I open the refrigerator, ready to cook up a storm.

My eyes land on the carton of eggs, so I grab them along with some milk and butter and set about making French Toast, having noted some vanilla flavoring in the well stocked pantry as we'd eaten Thai takeout before I'd gone to bed last night.

The music shifts to "Shape of You," one of my Ed favorites, and my hips understand the assignment.

I crack the eggs into the bowl, then add the milk and vanilla before I grab a whisk from the well-stocked drawer and set to whipping.

The beat takes over, and soon I'm gyrating all over the kitchen without a care in the world. My voice decides that now—thanks to the vaulted ceilings—would be a great time to try to debate my tone-deafness, and before I know it, I'm screeching the lyrics at the top of my lungs.

I spin around and around, egg mixture flying left and right as my body is utterly consumed by the music, until I spot a flash in my peripheral vision.

I stop dead in my tracks, eyes landing unerringly on a laughing pretty boy whose cell is pointing right at me.

"Siri, pause."

At my words, his lips lift in that lopsided smile that makes my stomach dip so that I can only shoot him a nasty look that sees him grab his chest in feigned pain.

"Don't stop on my account, Sunshine."

I push my mussed hair back out of my flushed face, belatedly realizing there's egg mixture all over my hands—and now, in my hair.

"Ugh!" My huff of annoyance echoes through the space as I place the bowl on the countertop and glance around in search of cleaning products.

Alex edges closer. "How about you grab a shower, and I'll sort breakfast. I have *quite* the day planned for us."

"It's my mess—"

"And I'm plenty capable of cleaning it while you get ready." He comes closer, swatting me lightly on my hip. "Now go shower, and wear something that slips off easily."

My eyes blow wide as my jaw damn well almost hits the floor.

Alex snorts a laugh. "You'll see what I mean."

Shaking my head, I pad in the direction of the room he'd assigned to me last night and make short work of showering.

Once I've dried my hair, I tuck my bangs behind my ears and quickly look through my clothes, landing on a simple white jersey dress that I found in a thrift store last year, but haven't had a casual occasion to wear it to before now.

I slip it on, tie a slim brown belt around my waist, and loop a small brown cross-body bag over my head before slipping into a pair of white sneakers.

Taking a look in the mirror, I nod to myself, then make my way back out to the living area.

The smell of French Toast hits my nose, making my mouth water. "Holy hell, that smells divine."

Alex smiles over his shoulder from his place at the hob. "Take a seat at the breakfast nook." He jerks his chin, indicating a small table by one of the many windows that I'd not noticed before now.

I smile brightly when I see he's set the table with a host of side items, including what looks like freshly squeezed orange juice and a barrage of fruits, including strawberries that are almost as big as my fist.

Before I can decide what I want first, Alex drops a plated stack of powdered French Toast down in front of me. I look up into his smiling eyes, nodding my thanks as my stomach rumbles loudly.

He laughs easily. "There's more where that came from."

My eyes feast on the food before me while Alex slides into his seat opposite. I grab the knife and fork, cut into the fluffy bread, and shovel it directly into my waiting mouth.

A moan of sheer joy echoes between us, and I speak around my mouthful of heaven. "Sweet baby Jesus, this is *amazing*."

"I'm glad you like it." Alex pours himself a coffee from the carafe on the table, gesturing to my cup, and I nod as I happily gorge on more of the deliciousness.

Once I've demolished my food, I add two sweeteners to the steaming coffee he poured me, along with a little creamer, before I settle back and focus all my attention on him.

"Where did you learn to cook like that?"

He swallows his mouthful before answering. "The family cook, Iris. When my brother left home, she took me under her wing and kept me out of my mother's path as much as possible."

His eyes remain on mine when he shrugs as he takes a sip of his black coffee. "Her domain was the kitchen, so it was only natural that she taught me some recipes. As it turned out, I'm not half bad."

"Not half bad?" I pop a brow. "You can feel free to perfect your skills on me anytime, pretty boy."

His lips twitch as I realize the loaded innuendo in that statement, but I push the thought from my mind as I take a strawberry from the spread between us.

I bite into it, juices dripping down my fingers and staining my plate. "Mmm, these are *so* good. You *need* to try one."

His hand darts across, plucking my half-eaten berry from my fingers before sliding it between his own lips. He cleans his thumb and index finger, releasing them with a pop as I watch his mouth raptly.

My eyes rise to his, and I swallow hastily, my eyes widening at the swirling intensity in his gaze.

Beautiful amber eyes sparkle as they travel the length and breadth of my face before they shutter closed. His jaw locks, and he rises to stand. "I'll be in the foyer when you're ready."

ALEX

Having reached the foyer, I've had a hot minute to cool off.

I hadn't planned on taking the berry from her hand. I'd been utterly impelled to do so. By a force stronger than myself.

I bet she tastes sweeter than this strawberry.

The second the thought had crossed my mind, I'd known I'd stepped over a line in my head and needed to get the fuck out of my—no, *our*—penthouse before I did something far worse.

Like slamming my mouth to hers to check if I was right.

What is going on with you, idiot? She's off-limits.

When I'd come back from meeting Liv and the boys to find her gyrating around the penthouse, I'd been too intent on watching her to give it any thought. But when I was cooking breakfast, alone with only my thoughts for company, I came to the realization that—to my detriment—I am very much attracted to my new housemate on a physical level. I mean, I *knew* she was attractive, but when I put forward my proposition, I didn't quite think through what that could translate to between us further down the line.

And this is one relationship I can't fuck up because she *needs* me. Probably more than I need her, if I'm honest with myself.

I could have easily gone back to Henry, tail between my legs, and come clean. He'd have been spitting mad, but nothing I haven't seen before.

I'd been fully ready for Reyna to tell me to get lost when I propositioned her in Molly Malones. The fact that she'd answered yes instantly, her face lighting up with pure, uncomplicated happiness, had made my heart swell with longing.

I'd felt the most overwhelming need to take care of her. To protect her. To be her person.

Damn you, Grey's Anatomy.

The elevator pings open, and out walks the Sun, beaming a smile that lights up my entire vision.

I'm fucking screwed.

"This is absolutely unnecessary, Alex. I don't need a shopping spree."

I slide from the back of my town car, holding my hand out to assist her, which she takes with a grateful smile.

"You deserve it, Rey. Indulge me. Please?"

Her inner struggle plays out clearly on her stunning features, hesitance warring with desire until I clasp her right hand in my left and tug her toward our first stop.

I can see the moment desire wins, and her face blooms with a dazzling smile that makes my chest feel tight.

"Bergdorf Goodman!"

I smile indulgently as I dust my thumb across the back of her smooth hand. She squeezes lightly, her strides lengthening as her smile grows impossibly wider.

Once we're inside, my eyes land on the four stylists I had my assistant, Bailey, organize for the occasion. All four are upon us immediately.

"Welcome to Bergdorf Goodman, Mr. DeMarco. I'm Jessica, your primary stylist, and we are just *thrilled* to have you with us today."

"Thank you, Jessica." I flash her a smile before twisting my head around to Reyna, who is taking the store in with wide brown eyes. "My girlfriend, Miss Marquez, is your client today. I'm purely here to give my opinion if required."

Holy shit! That word fell from your mouth way *too smoothly, DeMarco.*

All four sets of eyes swing around to Rey, who regards the stylists hesitantly.

"Excellent." Jessica recovers quickly, turning her full professional attention to Rey. "I have some wonderful pieces that I think will look simply divine on your figure."

The stylists crowd around Reyna, moving her in the direction of a private fitting room, and I follow, stuffing my hands in my pants pockets with a self-congratulatory, shit-eating grin.

Once we are settled, flutes of champagne in hand, each stylist brings forth outfit after outfit, but for some reason, Reyna stays seated, only nodding now and then.

"Ladies, if you'll excuse us for a moment." My sentence is

spoken softly but firmly.

The four stylists, the epitome of professionals, drop what they're doing and file from the fitting area in the blink of an eye, leaving me to turn to Reyna.

"Is there nothing that you liked?"

She lifts her disbelieving eyes to mine. "Everything is *so* beautiful, Alex. It's like a dream."

"Do you want me to get them to just ring everything up without trying them on?"

She bites her bottom lip before shaking her head vehemently. "No, please don't do that."

I scratch my forehead. "Would you like to visit Saks? We can try as many places as you—"

She cuts me off when she blurts out, "But everything is so expensive! I saw a tag on one blouse, and it cost more than I'd make in a month at Freemont."

My eyebrows draw together in a deep frown.

"*Expensive*?" A deep chuckle leaves my chest. "Sunshine, make no mistake, we are here to spend a damn fortune. That's non-negotiable."

"Alex, I—"

I exhale in frustration, mumbling under my breath, "I thought every female liked shopping!"

"I *do* like shopping, Alex, but I feel like I'm taking advantage."

At that, I push to my feet, cross the space, and kneel on the plush carpet at her feet.

My eyes lock on hers, holding her in place while I grip her hands in mine. "Reyna, when I said I want to take care of you, I meant it. In every way. Now, for the love of all that's holy, get your ass up out of this seat and into these clothes before I lose the will to live. There's only so much Bergdorf this body can take."

Ten

REYNA

"Turn to me now, Miss Marquez. Oh, yes. That mulberry is stunning against your skin tone." Jessica leans closer conspiratorially. "Mr. DeMarco will absolutely adore it, mark my words."

I can feel my cheeks flush, and my pulse kicks up no less than ten notches. I inhale deeply to try to calm my breathing as Jessica continues. "The way his eyes follow you is nothing short of true love. Hold on to that one." She catches my eye and winks with a sweet smile. "He's a keeper."

I blow out my held breath as she strides from the changing area back out into the fitting room, where Alex is being entertained by a short blonde named Tiff. She's fawning all over him, much to the disgust of the other three stylists—and myself, if I'm honest.

He's not yours. This is just pretend.

Yeah, tell that to my foolish heart.

Alex lifts his head, his eyes lighting on me as they take in every inch of my body.

I'm wearing a mulberry purple ballgown that sits slightly off my shoulders, is cinched tightly around my small dancer's waist that I've somehow hung onto, and flows into intricate ruffles that trail all the way to the floor.

His eyes finally come to a stop on my face, and he smiles then, so brightly, he looks lit up from within. My face answers unknown to myself until I eventually lower my gaze as a blush covers my face and decolletage.

"I did say you could mark my words, Miss Marquez."

My blush deepens, and Alex prowls closer with a darkened gaze that does crazy things to my insides. "Excuse us, ladies."

His words are once again obeyed immediately and without question.

Once we're alone, he closes the distance between us. "You look amazing, Rey."

His eyes flicker back and forth between mine. "Every single thing you tried on today was spectacular. It will all be delivered to the penthouse later."

I open my mouth to protest, but his index finger lands on my lips, halting my dissent.

"And that's the last I'll hear on the matter."

His eyes tell me that he means what he says, so I nod slightly.

"Now, I'm going to leave for this next part, but you're in safe—"

"I don't want you to leave." I step back, away from his quelling index finger, tilting my chin in opposition, but he only chuckles as he looks at the carpet and shakes his head.

"Oh, Sunshine…" He lifts his eyes to mine. "I am just a man, and sticking around to witness your undoubtedly perfect body as you embark on lingerie shopping might just kill me."

He grins lopsidedly, making me smile, before he reaches

between us to pinch a ruffle between his thumb and index finger. "This dress is perfect for an upcoming event that we'll be attending."

Dropping the ruffle, he presses a kiss to my forehead before taking a step back. "I have the perfect accessory in mind. I'll make a call while I wait."

ALEX

"Thank you for waiting."

I turn at the sound of Reyna's voice as she exits the fitting rooms. She's flushed, and her hair is all over the place – and I've never seen anything as beautiful in my life.

Even as I tell myself to stop it, I step closer, running my hands through her silky locks, taming them once more as she chortles in self-deprecation. "Sorry, guess I should've taken a second to fix myself."

I tuck her hair behind her ears with a smile. "You look perfect."

I slide my hand down to grasp hers, the move coming to me as easily as breathing, and I tug her toward the front door. "Come on, let's grab a bite before going back to the penthouse."

We step out onto the sidewalk, eyes fixed on one another and totally unaware of the ambush awaiting us.

One flash after another after another until we're almost blinded. Paparazzi hit us from all angles, and a small cry of fear bursts from Reyna as she steps closer to me.

I loop my arms around her, cursing myself for not already having security in place. Clearly, I wasn't thinking with my brain.

I try my best to shield her from the onslaught as media hounds bark question after question at both of us.

"Who's the mystery woman, Alex?"

"How long have you been dating?"

"Are the sex tape rumors true?"

"Are you with him for his money?"

Rey turns wide, frightened eyes up toward me, and I'm filled with the need to protect her. To make her safe once more as I attempt to edge us out of the fray.

"Get out of the way, you damn vultures."

Relief fills my chest cavity when I catch sight of a man cutting through the crowd, wearing a familiar black Stetson that makes an already tall man even more imposing.

Vaughn's head of security, Ford Holloway, strides through the crowd easily when most of the paps catch sight of his trademark scowl. "Get on with y'all. Shoo!"

Despite his recent years of living in New York, his Texan drawl is still thick upon occasion.

He reaches us in no time, his face splitting in a grin when he catches sight of Rey snug against my chest. His snort is barely audible, but I can see the knowing look in his eyes.

"Come on, you two lovebirds. Vaughn's around the corner." He glances around us at the somewhat dispersed, still snapping paps. "He got a tip that news of your…*status* had gotten out."

His gaze shifts to Reyna, and he shoots her a reassuring wink before grimacing at a pap who's gotten too close, barking menacingly, "I said get gone!"

Ford leads the way through the gathered media right to the edge of the sidewalk, where there's a waiting black SUV with blacked-out windows.

He opens the rear passenger door, and I help Rey inside as Ford rounds the car to hop into the driver's seat. Once I've slid in, I've barely closed the door before he zips out into traffic.

"Well, well, well." Vaughn twists his head around the passenger seat, smirking openly. "If it isn't Goldi-co—"

"I *swear*, if you finish that sentence, Burton, I will maim you alive and dance on your motherfucking grave!"

He grins, turning his attention to a wide-eyed Reyna as he extends his right hand. "Pleased to make your acquaintance, Miss Marquez—"

"How do you know her name? How did you know we were going to be ambushed?"

I drop my head into my hands. "I need a damn whisky."

"Calm your tits, DeMarco. I've been tracking everything related to you online since Grayson asked me to the other day. An as-yet unknown source disclosed your whereabouts to several media outlets about forty minutes ago."

I sit up in the seat, reaching for Reyna's trembling hands to rub them soothingly. "It's okay, Sunshine." I bring her hands to my lips, pressing a soft kiss to her fingertips, and she scoots closer along the seat, seeking the comfort of my embrace, which I give without hesitation.

"I need some security in place, Burton."

Vaughn snorts a laugh. "Not like you to be as unprepared as today."

The words hang in the silence of the SUV as it travels across Midtown.

"I know. I *know*." I exhale heavily, scared to think of how aggressive things might have become had Ford not stepped in. "Have you got any connections or not?"

Ford speaks up. "I'm branching out into private security. I'll do it."

The tension in my shoulders and chest eases slightly at his words. "Thank you, Ford. I'll let you know what our upcoming schedule is."

"Food's ready."

My announcement rings through the penthouse before Rey shouts from upstairs, "Coming!"

I set to plating up the traditional Italian dishes I've made, courtesy of my sister Mila's massively successful cookbook, Nonna's Kitchen.

I've opted for an easy Penne alla vodka with two sides: simple garlic bread and, of course, my personal favorite, arancini. The smell of the food fills the entire open space and having not eaten since breakfast, my stomach is now screaming for sustenance.

I've just tossed a ball of arancini into my mouth, moaning in bliss as the cheesy goodness bursts on my taste buds, when my eyes catch a movement on the stairs.

Reyna is wearing a silky white robe over pajama shorts with a matching camisole. Her long brown hair has been braided over one shoulder, and the smile spreading across her face warms me to my core.

Her eyes alight when they land on me, and she lets her gaze drift down along my body in open appreciation. I inhale sharply when she tugs her bottom lip between her teeth, hiding a coy smile – only to suck the half-chewed ball of cheesy risotto into the back of my throat.

My eyes blow wide open as my hand flies to my throat, and I reach to my left to grab the countertop as though that can help me.

I inhale a frantic breath as Reyna rushes down the remaining steps. She runs her hand down along my bicep in an attempt to soothe me.

"I need you to bend forward and cough as *hard* as you can." Her serene voice dims my blind panic somewhat.

I do as instructed, and as I cough, she harshly pounds on my back several times until I feel the arancini give way. It flies from my mouth, landing innocently on the tiled floor.

My breathing is ragged, and my heart rate is through the roof as I slide to the floor. I scrub my hands down my face before raising wide, grateful eyes to Reyna, who has dropped to a crouch beside me.

Concern mars her exquisite features when she raises a hand to palm my cheek. "You scared me half to death."

Her chest is rising and falling rapidly, and her eyes are shining with tears that she's managing to hold on to by a thread.

And despite my own fear, despite my own desire to be comforted and told everything will be alright, I'm quite simply overwhelmed with the visceral *need* to bring her peace.

I palm both her cheeks, bringing her head closer to rest our brows against one another. Our breaths mingle as we struggle to regain composure.

"Lucky it was only half to death, Sunshine. The death of my new live-in fake girlfriend *might* be a scandal that gives Henry the stroke he's narrowly avoiding."

She pulls back on a snort, her eyes finding and holding mine as their willing captive before she shakes her head. "That was *dark*, pretty boy."

I shrug, closing the distance to press a chaste but slightly overly long kiss to her cheek, then I drop my chin to her shoulder, whispering against her earlobe. "That's not even the half of it."

Pulling back, my gaze locks with hers. "Tonight is about getting to know one another on another level." I heave a sigh, my throat mildly burning, and I shoot a hateful glance at the arancini on the tiles beside me.

Go fuck yourself, cheesy goodness!

When I bring my eyes back to Rey, she's pink-cheeked, wide-eyed, and slightly open-mouthed. "Another level, Alex? Umm… the rules…umm…say that…"

I cut her off with a chuckle. "Oh, Sunshine. I know the rules. Sex with my hand for my foreseeable. I would never fuck with this…this…"

I trail off, uncertain of the word that I'm searching for, but she hits the nail on the head. "Bond?"

"*Yes*!" I grin. "I would never, *ever* mess up this bond we have formed so effortlessly, Reyna. I don't *do* relationships. Or even friendships, to be fully honest. I rely solely, and happily, on myself. It's been like that since—"

I abruptly cut myself off, pushing my back against the wall behind me and using it to help me to rise. I hold my hand out to Reyna as I stand over her, which she takes with a furrowed brow.

"Let's eat some pasta before we dive off the deep end, okay?"

I grab the plated arancini from the countertop and, with a deep scowl, toss them right into the garbage disposal. "These wankers can fuck right off!"

Eleven

REYNA

I relax into in my chair, expelling a sigh of contentment. "That was entirely *too* delicious!"

Alex swirls his glass of Sauvignon Blanc, tipping his head in thanks before he takes a sip.

Pushing to stand, I reach for our plates, only for Alex to place a firm but gentle hand on mine. "I got this. Sit back, enjoy your Sauv, and I'll be back in two."

I open my mouth to protest, but he arches a mischievous brow. "Drink the damn wine, and let me look after you, Sunshine."

My lips twitch when I hold my hands up in surrender. "Fine, but on *one* condition."

He narrows his mirth-filled eyes. "Depends on the condition."

"Let me make lunch for everyone tomorrow. I really want to keep my hands busy…" I tilt my head to the side, trying to find the right words. "I guess I'm feeling a little anxious about playing a role in front of your loved ones."

Our gazes hold for a beat before he shrugs. "Sounds like a win-

win. You've got yourself a deal."

I sit back again, mentally running through what groceries I need to order for delivery so that I can make some of Lita's traditional Costa Rican recipes. By the time Alex has everything cleared away, I have a solid menu already formed inside my head, and I'm rearing to get down and dirty in the state-of-the-art kitchen I've been surreptitiously admiring since arriving yesterday.

Alex tops up both of our wineglasses before depositing them on the coffee table in the center of the open living area. "Come on, Rey. Let's get comfortable."

By the time I make my way over, he has settled into the oversized deep purple L-shaped sofa with his left hand draped along the back.

I pluck our wineglasses from the table, passing one into his right hand before I sink down on his left side.

He reaches out with the index finger of his left hand to tuck my hair behind my ear, and I tamp down on the urge to look at him when a slew of goosebumps arises in the wake of that barest of touches.

Stop. It. Now!

The foolish heart of a foolish girl beats rapidly in my chest, and I take a large gulp of my wine in an attempt to distract myself from my newly discovered weakness: Alex DeMarco.

It's an arrangement between…friends? Get that into your head, Marquez!

"I was hoping we could play a game, Rey."

I twist my head toward Alex, shoving all thoughts of this foolhardy attraction into a box in the deep recesses of my mind.

"What kind of game, pretty boy?"

He presses his lips together, clearly subduing a smile. "I think that with Henry and Liv being here tomorrow, it would be beneficial to know more about one another. I propose we do our own version of twenty questions, but not limited to just twenty. You ask one, I answer honestly, no matter what, and then vice versa."

I shrug, then take another sip of my wine. "I'm game. Do you want to go first, or—"

"I'm the epitome of a gentleman, I'll have you know." His eyes twinkle with sheer mischief as one side of his mouth tugs up in a devilish smirk. "Ladies *always* come first, Sunshine."

My snort of laughter only sees his smirk grow even broader. "*Incorrigible*!"

He tugs the shorter hairs at the nape of my neck playfully. "You know you love it."

Then he allows the threatening smile to bloom on his face, making his eyes shine with unconstrained pleasure. I feel my chest expand in delight, wholly sure that this is a side of Alex that not many people get to see.

And I bask in the sheer privilege.

"So, shoot. Hit me with your questions." He holds his hands up. "I'm an open book."

I chew my lip in thought for a hot minute, realizing I should probably start with the basics. "When's your birthday?"

"July twenty-fourth. When's yours?"

"December twenty-fifth."

He winces, and I laugh easily, savoring this organic connection between us. "Siblings?"

Alex's face transforms, his smile genuine as his eyes glow with sincerity.

"My younger half-sister, Mila, is the one you can thank for that Penne alla vodka recipe. She lives back in the UK, for the most part, with her husband and my nephew, Nathan. She's a pain in my ass."

He shoots me a wry grin. "I think you'll like her."

I playfully slap his knee as he chuckles low in his chest.

"Then there's Henry. He's my older half-brother. He's the dour one who's married to my best friend, Liv. Stick up his ass a mile long, but he's…"

He trails off, suddenly growing serious, his forehead crinkling. "He's the one who keeps us in line. Who deals with the shit so that we don't have to."

His eyes return to mine, breath-taking in their intensity. "He's the best man I know."

Silence echoes between us until the corners of his mouth curl upward. "And the reason we're both here right now."

I crack a grin at that.

"What about you? Any siblings? Family?"

"Just Lita." I shoot up a quick prayer, hoping he won't ask me to elaborate, but it falls on deaf ears.

"She raised you, right?"

I nod, chewing on my lip in silence.

"Your parents?"

I close my eyes tight, and his hand brushes off my shoulder. The simple touch is enough to bolster my confidence, and I inhale deeply before opening my eyes once more, finding his concerned gaze fixed upon my face.

"My mother disappeared when I was a week old. She left me at the local church with a dirty blanket and a short note. It said she wasn't fit to be a parent."

I drop my gaze to my lap, fidgeting with the stem of my wineglass as I continue. "The priest knew Lita and brought me home to her. My father—if you want to refer to him as such—spent years flitting in and out of our lives. Out, more often than not, *thankfully*."

Blowing out a breath, I close my eyes and remember the times he *was* around. The tension that flowed through the house, the strangers who came and went at all hours.

The time he broke my pinkie finger for not fetching his cigarettes quickly enough…

A shudder runs through my body, and Alex places his hand on my shoulder encouragingly, silently bolstering me to continue.

"He spent a lot of time behind bars for various offenses. Theft, breaking and entering, assault and battery. He always said, 'tough times don't last, but tough people do, *niñita*.'"

I shake my head with a frown. "Maybe he thought he was teaching me a life lesson. Who knows."

My lips downward as I shrug. "Eventually, when Lita had settled in Sunrise Harbor, and I was happy at Pearson, he lost the deeds to our house in a game of poker, along with draining every dime from Lita's savings before he disappeared too, skipping out on bail in the process."

Silence fills the room, and I exhale heavily, feeling unburdened, having shared my deepest, darkest secret with this man who makes me safe enough to be my true self.

Warts and all.

"We can't choose our family."

I lift my head at his words, finding his whiskey orbs intently focused on my face.

"But we *can* choose one another, Sunshine."

His mouth lifts in a crooked grin that makes my heart sing, and in this moment, I feel *seen*.

I grin back, deciding to shift the conversation to lighter topics. "Favorite…color?"

He doesn't miss a beat. "Gray."

I snort a laugh. "Gray is *no one's* favorite color."

"It's mine." Alex shrugs, quickly moving on as I raise my glass to my lips. "Favorite vacation spot?"

It's my turn to shrug as I swallow my mouthful of wine. "Never been on vacation. What's—"

"Change of question. Favorite place you've ever been?"

I narrow my eyes, but answer anyway. "The Koch Theater. Lita took me to see the New York City Ballet perform The Nutcracker when I was eight, and I *knew* it was where I was meant to be."

Alex regards me with unreadable eyes for a moment as the fading memory of that perfect day runs through my mind until I snap back to reality. "Favorite food?"

My question catches him utterly off guard, and he barks a sudden laugh. "Well, it isn't arancini anymore, that's for damn sure!"

He grimaces as he massages his throat with his free hand before pouting in thought. His eyes flare, and his mouth tugs upward as he asks, "What's your best trait? What's your favorite thing about yourself?"

"Eh...that's two questions!"

He rolls his eyes with a wide grin. "Then you can have two once you've answered mine."

I incline my head in acceptance. "My best trait...well, that would be my determination. Whatever I put my mind to, I *will* give it my absolute all."

"Okay, I can see that. One hundred percent. So, what's your favorite thing about yourself?"

I nibble on my lower lip, realization dawning as Lita's words come to mind.

"My intuition. It's *never* wrong. When I have a gut feeling, I trust it. *Implicitly*."

I glance down at my wineglass, suddenly shy. "It's the reason why I'm here. It's the reason why I…why I trust *you*."

Silence follows until Alex drops his arm around my shoulder, tugging me against his side before pressing a fleeting kiss to my temple. "I trust you, too, Sunshine."

I look up to catch his eyes and smile brightly. "Your turn, pretty boy! Best trait?"

When he places his arm on the back of the couch, I feel his loss immediately, despite telling my wayward heart to get a grip.

"My best trait has to be my charm. The gossip rags say that it's the most memorable thing about me."

He huffs a self-deprecatory laugh as my brow furrows. "I thought we needed to be honest."

Alex instantly stops laughing while a confused look overtakes his handsome face. "I *am* being honest, Rey."

"*No*. You're telling me what other people think is your most memorable trait." I hold his gaze firmly. "I asked what is your best trait? *Your* best. Not what anyone else thinks."

His face creases in thought, and he chuckles low before emptying his glass. "I'm decisive. Does that suit?"

I nod, placated for now. "And your favorite thing about yourself?"

He doesn't miss a beat.

"My monster cock, obviously."

I throw my head back, laughing uproariously as he continues. "As my girlfriend, Henry will expect you to know all about my perfect penis. He's an authority on the appendage, considering he was the one who used to change my nappies."

I sober enough to ask, "What on earth are nappies?"

"Shit, sometimes I forget I'm Stateside. I meant *diapers*."

I nod even as I continue to chuckle at what seems to be his

cheekiness. "I'm *sure* your brother won't ask me about our bedroom activities, no?"

Alex laughs even harder. "Oh, sweet baby Jesus. Henry has precisely zero fucks to give." Dawning horror makes my eyes widen. "There are *no* lines he's not willing to cross. In *any* aspect of his life. We need to sell it *hard* tomorrow, Sunshine."

"Just when I was feeling okay about meeting him!"

He chuckles. "You'll do just fine, Rey. He'll love you."

I smile back before he takes his turn. "Do you want a big family?"

My eyes blow wide as I nod excessively. "*Yes*! Being an only child was lonely. I want a house full of kids.

He chuckles even as he shakes his head indulgently. The idea of a mini-Alex running around does strange things to my insides, and I can't help wanting to know his own thoughts on the matter.

"And what about you?"

He snorts a laugh. "Not a damn hope."

My chest tightens as he continues. "There's not a hope I'd inflict my messed-up genes on another generation." He holds my eyes with a small smile. "But your kids would be pretty damn perfect."

Alex brushes the back of his knuckles across my cheek, and I can feel them blush at the contact, so I pull back enough to take another sip of my wine.

"How many sexual partners have you had?"

The wine goes down the wrong way, and I begin to choke.

Alex pats my back gently while my mind flounders on what to say. Once I've gotten myself under control, my gaze finds his. "You okay?"

I nod, pressing my lips upwards in a semblance of a smile.

He looks even more interested now, and I just want the ground to open up and swallow me whole as I utter. "Less than yours, apparently."

His face adjusts visibly, his forehead contorting into a massive frown. "Why do you say that?"

I chuckle, almost uncomfortably, but fully confident in my honesty. "Well, you slept with three women last year—on the low end, I'm assuming."

His face falls as he realizes where I'm headed. "I've slept with *two* guys in my entire life, so…there's that."

"*Shit*, Rey. I didn't—"

I hold up a quelling hand. "I know, Alex." I shrug as my mouth turns down. "I'm not the norm, and I'm good with that."

I place that same hand on his creased forehead, smoothing the indentations of frustration. "Just as I'm good with you being a normal man with normal desires and a wholly healthy sex life. You *never* need to feel like I would judge you. For *anything*."

He relaxes visibly, the previous tension ebbing away under my absolute lack of condemnation.

"Damon was my boyfriend in high school, and I was in a sort of friends-with-benefits situation with Todd, a guy at Pearson." I shrug, easily disclosing these intimacies despite the tender age of our relationship.

I quirk a devilish brow while my mouth lifts on one side. "What's *your* number, pretty boy?"

His face pales slightly, and his eyes widen. The sight is all too hilarious, and I struggle to contain my threatening laughter.

"Umm…well, I think…umm…it's not as many as all that… umm…"

His floundering is too much. "Oh, Alex. I'm kidding."

He narrows his eyes at me before playfully mopping his brow. I giggle at his easy recovery, emptying my glass.

"Favorite movie?"

I snort. "Can I plead the fifth?"

He sits forward, depositing his glass of wine on the coffee table as his vibrant eyes sparkle with intrigue. "Not a fucking hope, Sunshine."

I expel an almost pained sigh before deadpanning. "Top Gun. *The original*!"

His mouth twitches, mine mirrors it, and suddenly our joint laughter rings out across the penthouse's vaulted ceilings.

"Christ, Rey. I think we need to have a designated movie night going forward."

My laughter turns to hiccups before I abruptly stop. The events outside Bergdorf Goodman, along with the casual mention of a timeline that hasn't been ironed out, encourage the next words to tumble from my mouth.

"And how long do you reckon those movie nights would run on for? A month? Two, perhaps?"

Alex's smile dies on his face before his eyebrows pucker together. He scoots closer on the seat, gently plucking my glass from my fingertips to deposit it on the coffee table before enfolding my hands in his much larger ones.

His eyes are brimming with a deep resolution that I can't put my finger on, but it affects me down to my marrow.

"Reyna, when I said I don't have a timeline, I wasn't referring to me being a part of your life. You can rest assured that, in one capacity or another, I will have your back. Rule three will *always* stand."

He draws me in against his chest, allowing me to breathe a heavy sigh of relief. I pinch my eyes closed tight, my next words spilling heedlessly from my lips.

"I-I feel something for you, Alex. Something I can't quite

place. And I'm terrified of letting myself get too close." I swallow roughly, huffing a mocking laugh. "I don't let people in, and I've been alone for so long."

His arms tighten around me almost painfully, and I revel in the clear fact that my words have resonated with him.

Silence envelops us, allowing me to focus on the lulling cadence of his deep, even breathing and the low, steady thump of his heartbeat beneath my ear. A feeling of complete and utter peace and safety surrounds me, and I slam my eyes closed while committing this feeling to memory, needing to file it away for nights to come.

"My mother used to hurt me. Physically. Mentally. Emotionally. She was a twisted individual who pretty much *ruined* my faith in humanity."

ALEX

I stop at Reyna's sharp gasp, allowing my eyes to fall closed as I place my whole trust in someone for the first time in my life.

"I've never told another living soul—not even the therapist my brother made me see for an entire year following her murder. Not even Liv, and she knows just about everything there is to know about me. And *especially* not Henry, because I can't have him blaming himself for circumstances that were not his doing."

I inhale her sweet fragrance, and it buoys me to continue. "My mother forced Henry from my life when I was ten. I know *now* that he didn't want to leave, but for the longest time, I *hated* him for leaving me with her. To Lauren DeMarco, I was nothing more than a commodity. The child she tricked my father into conceiving when he was grieving the loss of his wife. Unwanted and unloved by the people who created me. Abandoned by my brother…"

I trail off when the long-buried feelings threaten to choke me.

Her arms tighten around my waist, and her quiet strength encourages me to continue.

"It wasn't until I met Liv when I was fifteen that I could believe I deserved to be happy. That I wasn't at fault for the circumstances of my birth. It took a long time, but *eventually*, I was able to begin to trust in the friendship she painstakingly built."

I palm Rey's cheeks, angling her head up toward mine to hold her eyes with a burning intensity.

"Once I let her in, I knew I would do *anything* and *everything* to protect her and our deep bond. And for a time, I did."

My lips twitch slightly, remembering how much of a pest I must have been for Henry when he was attempting to win Liv over.

Reyna's eyes dart to my mouth at the movement, and I close the distance between us to press a kiss atop her forehead before murmuring softly against her smooth brow.

"And that's exactly how I felt when I met you in Molly Malones, Rey. I knew immediately that I wanted to keep you safe—that I would do whatever was in my power to protect you. I recognized the feeling because of how close Liv and I are, and I can tell you with one hundred percent certainty—"

I pull back, holding her swirling chocolaty gaze intently. "I will always be here to weather your storms. To dance in the rain and to celebrate your rainbows, Sunshine. Don't *ever* doubt that."

Twelve

ALEX

"On your knees, Sunshine."

Rey's big brown eyes hold mine as she sinks to her knees with a smirk. Her small hands reach for the buckle of my belt while she licks her lips in anticipation, and my dick jumps under her touch.

She makes quick work of pushing my pants down my legs, placing a kiss over my underwear-covered cock as he leaks a steady stream of precum.

"Fuck my mouth, pretty boy."

"Come on, it's late, Alex!"

I wake to the smell of pungent spices tickling my nose and the sound of Reyna calling me from downstairs.

My cheeks heat at the memory of my dream, and I adjust my morning wood with a grimace.

Throwing back the covers, I quickly use the toilet, wash up, and leave my bedroom without bothering to cover up.

It's a warm spring day in Manhattan, and I'm cursing myself for not having left the air conditioner on the right setting overnight.

When I reach the top of the stairs, I spot Rey in the middle of the kitchen, pirouetting from one pot to another, clearly in the midst of cooking lunch as promised.

The smells are familiar but different, and despite being drawn toward the delicious scent, I take a long moment just to appreciate her doing something as normal as cooking in my mostly unused penthouse.

Her hair is pulled up in a knot on the top of her head, exposing the slender line of her neck, and a sharp vision of drawing my tongue from the cleft of her breasts all the way to the tip of her chin assails me.

The thought is so vivid that my dick is instantly rock hard, and I swing about to head back to the bedroom to cover my chub before she sees, only to be pulled up short.

"Morning, pretty boy. You certainly got your beauty sleep. It's so late!"

I twist back to face her, making sure to angle my body so that my horn is hidden, praying that the fear of being found out is enough to make that fucker deflate.

She smiles up at me, and my heart rate kicks up twenty beats. "Come on down, your breakfast is getting cold!"

"You didn't need to cook for me, Sunshine." I descend the steps, making my way into the kitchen and easing onto a high stool at the counter to watch her work, at ease now having successfully hidden the evidence of how much this girl turns me on.

Pick one you won't fuck. That way, you can keep it purely business.

Henry's words flit through my mind, and I can feel my brows draw together.

I won't fuck Rey, I *know* I won't, because I've never slept with anyone I've given a shit about before. And I won't make the exception for her either, because she deserves better than what I can give her.

"Penny for your thoughts?"

Rey drops a plate of eggs and bacon down on the counter with a grin before spinning back around to the stove, where there's a big ass pot that I didn't even know I owned.

I dig into the eggs, moaning in delight when I taste them. "Christ, what did you put in these? They're hands-down *the* best eggs I've ever tasted."

Chuckling, she keeps her back to me. "It's amazing what some seasoning does for your taste buds." She turns slightly, resting her chin on her right shoulder. "It's a tease for what's coming."

I smile before turning my attention back to my plate, scarfing it down in record time.

When I'm finished, I rub my toned stomach while Rey grabs the plate to drop it into the sink, but not before she takes a veiled look at my exposed torso.

The covert glance makes my cock pulse once more in my underwear, and I curse my piss-poor decision to leave the sanctity of my bedroom in only my fucking Calvins.

"How do you feel about Costa Rican for lunch?" She doesn't turn from her task, the muscles in her shoulder working beneath the skin in a way I simply can't tear my eyes away from.

That fucking dream!

"I'm making Lita's tamales, and I've been up since the crack of dawn getting everything ready."

She spins about, my eyes instantly landing on her breasts, rising and falling with each breath as a result of her exertions.

I need a cold shower.

"Could you grab me a water from the refrigerator, please?"

She tilts her head to the side, clearly confused, but does as I've asked, and as soon as she has her back turned, that's my cue.

I'm halfway up the stairs, almost to my room, when I hear her call from behind. "Hey, didn't you want your water?"

I pick up my pace, practically running now. "Got to make a call. I'll be back."

Once I reach my door, I throw it open and dive inside, marching straight to the shower, ripping off my underwear as I go.

I step under the cool water that *should* be making my boner fuck off, but it's not working, and I *know* it's a result of my damn dream.

Pinching my eyes closed tight, my hand strays to my throbbing cock, pumping it up and down once, twice. The vision of Rey's shoulder stirring that pot vigorously makes me moan, and I know I won't make it through the day without rubbing one out.

"On your knees, Sunshine."

I focus on big brown eyes, a warm mouth taking my dick deep inside, sucking and bobbing. I fuck my hand slowly, savoring the vision of Rey's mouth around my cock until I'm right on the cusp.

"Fuck my mouth, pretty boy."

I explode, throwing my head back against the wall with a dull thud as I come in thick streams against the side of the shower. I'm completely unable to stop the guttural groan that spills from my lips.

"*Rey*! Fuck, yes, Sunshine."

My chest heaves while my mind spins for a hot moment, having come ridiculously hard until the icy cold water begins to bite into my rapidly cooling skin, and the guilt of what I've just done starts to gnaw at my insides.

REYNA

"They're here!" My breathless exclamation is a whisper through the kitchen where Alex and I have been finishing up the Costa Rican spread I've put such effort into.

Alex spins to face me as the elevator chimes, announcing the arrival of our anticipated guests.

"I've got you, Sunshine." He tugs me in against his side, his scent enveloping my senses as he presses a fleeting kiss to my temple.

"*Thank you* for doing this." He pulls back, his whiskey eyes filled with something I've never seen before, and the sight makes my stomach dip even as goosebumps scatter along my entire body. "It means more than I could possibly—"

"Ah, there you are, Al!"

A tall, exceptionally handsome man with striking green eyes enters the kitchen with a small boy who's his miniature in his arms.

He holds out his hand, his eyes almost blinding in their intensity, and I instantly spot the similarity. "I'm Henry, Alex's older brother." He flashes a smile that softens his features immeasurably. "It's a pleasure to meet you, Miss Marquez."

Alex lifts the child out of his brother's hold with a grin for his nephew as I accept Henry's hand. "The pleasure is all mine. And *please,* call me Reyna."

He inclines his head, his smile dimming to a smirk as a stunning blonde comes into view behind him, holding the hand of another one of Henry's doppelgangers.

"Uncle Al!"

The dark-haired boy's face breaks into a wide smile, displaying the most gorgeous pair of dimples, that I soon realize he's inherited from his mother when her face copies her son's.

"Bash, my man!" Alex drops to his knees, catching the other

boy with his free arm to hold both brothers close against his chest. "Oh, I missed you guys!"

His eyes fall closed as he drops his head atop the older boy, inhaling his hair with a smile that makes my heart flip-flop beneath my breastbone.

"I'm Liv, Alex's sister-in-law—"

"Excuse *me*, sweet girl." Alex cuts her off as I take her extended hand in mine, and we both swing our heads around at the sound of his voice while Henry tuts behind me. "I think you'll find that you were my best friend before you were my anything-in-law!"

Liv shakes her head as she rolls her eyes good-naturedly before Henry cups my elbow to draw me away from the kitchen and toward the living room. "I'm going to need a stiff drink if he's starting on this shit already."

Liv's laughter chimes behind us. "You know he likes to get a rise out of you, Henry."

Having reached the sideboard containing a barrage of all sorts of alcohol, Henry turns to me. "What would you like?"

I shake my head. "I'm okay for now, thank you." He then makes short work of pouring a whisky for both himself and Alex while Liv and I get settled on one of the sofas.

"Lunch will be ready shortly. We've made my grandmother's traditional Costa Rican recipes."

Alex strides into the living room, a boy in each arm, pinning me with a pointed stare. "*We* didn't make anything. *You* did all the hard work, Sunshine."

I catch Liv and Henry exchanging a look in my peripheral vision before my attention is claimed entirely by Alex's nephews.

"I'm Sebastian, and I'm four years old." The older of the two thrusts his hand out confidently, and for the first time, I notice golden flecks in the depths of his big green eyes. "Mumma said you're Uncle Al's girlfriend and that I simply *must* be good today."

I take his small hand, smiling my brightest smile. "I'm so glad to meet you, Sebastian. And who's this?"

I shift my gaze to his blatantly shy younger brother, but Sebastian answers for him with an eye roll far beyond his years. "This is Theo. He's a *baby*."

Alex chuckles at that, though his oldest nephew is quick to silence him with a look that is entirely his father.

I shoot him a playful wink, taking the heat off of a rebuked Alex. "How would you like to help me assemble everything for lunch? I'm in need of a big, strong helper."

Sebastian puffs his chest out almost comically in that way that only four years olds can as he nods.

Alex sets him on the ground as Theo cuddles closer, content as a church mouse snug against his uncle's solid chest.

Taking my extended hand, Sebastian turns to his mother and whispers way too loud, "See, Mumma. Told you I could be good."

"Reyna, that was absolutely divine." Liv drops her napkin beside her plate, rubbing her slightly rounded stomach. "My compliments to your grandmother."

My cheeks heat even while I nod. I've cooked and baked for a lot of people, but for some reason, Henry and Liv's approval means a great deal to me. I *need* them to like me for Alex.

But even more than that, I *want* them to like me. For me.

I move to clear the table, but Alex stops me with a gentle hand on my wrist.

"You did all the hard work, Rey. Allow me."

He shoots me those damn puppy dog eyes that he's so fond of, and I'm utterly helpless to do anything other than nod dumbly. He gathers an armful of dishes before heading in the direction of the kitchen, leaving me alone with Liv.

Henry has escaped to Alex's room, putting Seb and Theo down for a much-needed nap due to jetlag, though both boys were nothing short of angelic throughout the meal.

Seb had taken great enjoyment in telling everyone all about the tamales and the simple rice and beans I'd served alongside. He'd listened in rapture when I'd explained the process of wrapping the tamales in cooked banana leaves, and I was relatively confident that I'd made a good first impression on the little sweetheart.

"I've never met a girlfriend of Alex's before – despite knowing him for half of my life."

Liv's words are soft, her hands clasped over her small baby bump and her eyes fixed on mine. "I'm going to be frank, Reyna, if I may?"

I nod, swallowing roughly as I prepare for her next words.

"I've never seen Alex look at a single person the way he looks at you, outside of his nephews—who I know for a fact he loves dearly. He looks at you like you are the center of his world."

A kaleidoscope of butterflies swarms to life in the depths of my stomach, and I fight to keep my face neutral, losing spectacularly when my lips edge upwards in a tremulous smile.

She stops, leaning closer and extending her hand palm up. I rest my trembling hand atop hers, and she squeezes gently. "I am *so* happy that he's finally found you. I've been waiting a long time for him to pull his head out of his ass long enough to realize that he's beyond worthy of love."

Tears fill her eyes and a lump forms in my throat that makes speech an impossibility.

"Don't let his demons ruin what I'm sure is the start of

something life-altering for you both."

I smile hesitantly, tears welling in my own eyes before Henry jogs down the stairs, and both Liv and I lean back in our seats. She sends me a small, meaningful smile.

"They've finally given up." He rolls his eyes. "Have kids, they said…"

He shoots me a wink and a grin before pressing a kiss to the top of his wife's head and then sliding into the empty chair beside her. He gently palms Liv's stomach, his eyes glowing in reverence. "But I wouldn't change a thing."

Closing the gap, he brushes his lips across his wife's before glancing around the penthouse.

"Where's Al gone off—"

The unmistakable opening bars of *"You've Lost That Loving Feeling"* by The Righteous Brothers echo through the penthouse on the innumerable speakers dotted throughout.

Before anyone can utter a word or go in search of the clear culprit, Alex walks in from the kitchen, literally knocking the breath from my body when he does.

He's dressed in a full-body Naval jumpsuit identical to Maverick's from *Top Gun,* a shit-eating grin plastered to his face as he sings along completely out of key, "You're trying hard not to show it, *baby*."

My own lips are helpless from joining him in his blatant delight, and my belly laugh rings loudly throughout the space.

I hear a mumbled, "What the *actual* fuck?" from Henry's direction, but I pay no heed, fixated as I am on the man before me.

Until that man shocks the hell out of me when he drops to one knee and opens his fist to display a small, square navy box in his hand.

My breath comes in short bursts while my smile threatens to

slip from my face, though I manage to hold it in place through sheer force.

He grasps my quivering hands in his free left one, rubbing his thumb soothingly along my skin.

"I know this is new between us, Rey. I know that you could do *so* much better than me, with your smiles that light up a room and eyes that truly see the *real* me."

His pupils have widened enough that the unique irises of his eyes are almost entirely covered, and butterflies burst to life in the depths of my stomach at the intensity held within them. "But I'm asking you to *please* consider this."

He looks down as he cracks open the box to display a large square-cut diamond ring, that takes my breath away, before turning those big, wide eyes back to mine. "I can't promise things will always be easy, but I *can* promise to have your back forever and a day. Please, Reyna Marquez, be my wife, and let me take care of you for all of our days."

As he swallows roughly, so do I. Time seems to stop as my mind races to catch up with his words, with his true intentions.

My eyes fall closed, holding back the tears that threaten to blind me, and it's at that moment, my stomach drops as I realize it's a ruse. It's part of *the* ruse, the one I'm here to play, and I curse myself for forgetting—if only for this afternoon—that none of this is real.

You stupid girl.

But I gave him my word to help sell this relationship to his brother. To always have his back. And so, it's with that singular thought that I open my eyes with a bright smile and launch myself into his waiting arms.

"Yes, Alex. Of course, I'll be your wife."

Thirteen

ALEX

Once Liv and Henry left with two cranky little boys, I'd turned to find Rey had disappeared upstairs, and didn't re-emerge for the rest of the evening.

I'd tidied up the mess downstairs and decided to call it a night, lingering for long moments outside her bedroom door with my hand poised to knock, *needing* to clear the air between us.

But I'd given her the space she clearly desired, slinking off to my own room to aimlessly flick through endless TV stations and streaming services, settling on rewatching *Grey's Anatomy* from season one.

Liv and I had a long-standing weekly *Grey's Anatomy* night until I'd been shipped off to the States. I'd continued to watch every week, clearly too far gone in my *Grey's* era to quit, so leaving it on in the background whilst debating my feelings and actions is like the presence of a long-used comfort blanket.

Despite my churning stomach, I can't help but close my eyes to remember the vibrancy of Rey's smile when I walked into the dining room as Maverick. The pure, unfettered joy that had filled her face, the mirth that had rolled off of her entire body…I'm pretty sure I could live off of the memory for years to come.

It had been *everything*.

Seeing her smile start to drop as realization took hold made me wish I'd opted for another place and time to ask her to marry me.

When I'd come up with the idea to sell this relationship to Henry, I hadn't known how real it would feel in the run up to it. How connected I would be to Reyna. How right things felt between us.

Be my wife.

The damn words had fallen from my mouth as easily as breathing, much to my inherent disgust.

I'd wanted nothing more than to rid our home of my brother, my best friend, and my beloved nephews so that I could iron things out. So that I could make things right because, in the immediate aftermath, I knew without a doubt that I'd fucked up.

I'm neck-deep in self-loathing as episode two of season one starts, when there's a loud bang on my door that makes me sit forward in shameless anticipation.

"Come in."

The knob twists open quickly, the door slamming open to admit a blatantly irate Rey, and I welcome it.

"Okay, pretty boy. First thing's first." She strides closer, clad in that far too sexy silky pajama set that does things to my damn brain, not to mention my cock. I blink heavily to dispel the visions of bending her over my bed and ripping those tantalizing shorts to bits with my motherfucking teeth.

Get a grip, DeMarco!

"The ground rules need to be expanded. *Now*."

Her eyes skim across my exposed chest and my grey lounge pants so quickly I'd have missed it if I wasn't fully intent on watching her every little move.

I move over, making room on my left side for her. "I agree."

She holds out her hand, palm facing me. "I need to stand for this, Alex. I *need* you to hear me, okay?"

I nod slowly, and she continues. "Firstly, never, *ever* blindside me like that, Alexander DeMarco. I agreed to enter into this arrangement because I. *Trust.* You." I flinch at that, and she steps closer, pinning me with an uncompromising stare. "Shit like this will chip away at that trust, and I'll be out of here faster than you can blink. You got me?"

"Yes, absolutely. I'm so sorry—"

I get the palm again and fuck me if this rage of hers isn't a total turn-on.

"A simple nod will suffice." Her words are clipped as her eyes flash like obsidian. "Now, secondly, being your fake girlfriend is one thing. Your fiancée is a whole other ball game, pretty boy. I'm going to need a more concrete timeline when it comes to this."

She inhales through her nose, exhaling slowly through her lips. "Now, you may speak."

I swallow roughly before I begin. "Okay, so first…I truly *am* sorry for how today went down. Full disclosure, when I told Henry that I had a girlfriend, I knew he would need something *more,* so I told him that I wanted to propose to her."

She sighs heavily, shifting closer as I continue. "Initially, I had the idea to pop the question today while he was here, and I wanted to get your fully surprised reaction for *his* benefit."

I rise onto my knees, crawling to the edge of the bed to extend my hand in a silent plea. "It wasn't until we were in that moment that I realized how thoughtless I'd been toward your feelings, and for that, I feel like the biggest piece of shit. All I can say is, if you chose to stick around, I *swear* to never blindside you ever, *ever* again. I will forever put your thoughts and feelings above all others. This is my promise to you."

I let my head drop as I finish. "I understand if I've broken your trust, Rey. And for that, I'm sorrier than you know."

After a beat, her small hand lands in mine, and I raise shocked eyes to hers as relief fills my chest.

She moves closer, climbing up to kneel on the bed opposite me. "I believe you, Alex. I *know* I can trust you. My gut doesn't lie."

Our gazes hold, and I can see her soften, but even so, I need to show her how truly sorry I am. "Okay, hear me out."

She nods, shifting closer until our knees are touching.

"Marry me in six months, divorce me six months later."

Her eyes blow wide, and she moves to speak, but I gently press my finger over her soft lips. "Be my fiancée, and my wife, and one year from now, I'll give you anything you want. You want me to buy the Pearson School for you, Sunshine? Consider it done. A house, and staff in any country of your choosing? Piece of cake. I'll give you the world, just please…say you'll stay."

I allow my hand to drop away from her mouth, and she regards me for long moments with serious eyes. "My own studio. For under-privileged children. All costs covered."

My heart clenches at her selflessness, even when she could have *anything* for herself, but I nod softly, willing to give her the world if she asked for it. "It's yours."

Rey smiles brightly as I open my arms, and she slides hers around my neck, allowing me to enclose her in my embrace. I hold her for a long moment, her soft breath tickling my neck as the tension ebbs away. "I'm truly sorry."

"I know." She pulls back enough to look into my eyes. *"Don't* do it again, okay?"

I nod. "I will always be honest with you, Rey." I pinch her chin gently between my thumb and index finger, my eyes holding hers firmly. "Whatever you're feeling, share it with me. Talk to me; never shut me out, okay?"

She tugs her bottom lip between her teeth, my eyes following the movement. "It's a deal, pretty boy."

I hold out my arms playfully. "Fancy sealing it with a kiss?"

She throws back her head, exposing the delicate column of her throat as she laughs loudly and freely, and I can't help joining in.

"In-fucking-corrigible!"

She slides her cell from her pocket and deposits it on my nightstand with a wry smile. Then, flopping back onto my bed, she lies back against the headboard to side-eye me.

"So, what are we watching?"

REYNA

"You feel so good, Sunshine."

Alex's hard body grinds against my ass as his tongue caresses the delicate skin on my neck, sending goosebumps scattering along every inch of my body.

"Touch me, Alex. I need you to feel your hands on my skin."

His hand snakes down my stomach and inside my silky shorts. His gasp of delight turns to a groan when he finds me bare beneath them. Dipping lower, his middle finger slides between my slick folds, circling my clit with a promise of more to come.

A promise of something I've never experienced.

"So fucking *wet."*

My deep groan fills the air, the noise pulling me from the most dangerous sort of dream.

I expel a heavy breath, even as my entire body cries out for Alex's touch.

I snuggle deeper against my pillow, desperately trying to go back to my dream, and at that, Alex's woodsy scent fills my nostrils.

My eyes fly open when I remember precisely *where* I am. I fell asleep in Alex's bed last night, having binged the first season of *Grey's Anatomy*.

Shit!

Gingerly, I look over my shoulder, finding Alex on his back. His left arm is thrown over his face, blocking me from his view entirely.

I move to slide from the bed, barely holding in my gasp of surprise when my eyes travel to the huge hard-on in his indecent grey lounge pants.

He wasn't lying when he said he had a monster cock.

I press my thighs together shamelessly at the sight, a flush building along my breastbone that swiftly rises to engulf my entire face.

Move your ass, Reyna!

I edge off of the bed and gently swing my legs over the side, careful not to wake him, but a deep groan stops me in my tracks.

My eyes are magnetically drawn back to Alex, who's on the cusp of wakefulness and has slid his hand into his pants, fisting his morning wood with relish beneath the thin material of those damn pants.

"Mmmmm."

His low moan tears through me, and I can't move, can't breathe, can't think. I can only watch his hand pump up and down while his chest tightens and flushes a deep red.

I know I need to move, but I watch on in utter thrall until the shrill ringing of my cell on the bedside locker breaks the spell I've been under.

Alex jerks his left arm from across his face while tugging his hand free of his pants, an expression that's a mixture of intrigued horror when his eyes find mine.

I grab the cell, and upon seeing Sunrise Harbor calling, my heart drops as I answer immediately, forgetting everything that just happened in an instant.

"Penelope? Is everything okay?"

"Firstly, Reyna, calm down. Everything is good. It's *better* than good!"

My chest expands with hope, and my voice is shaky when I attempt to speak. "Is she…is she…?"

I can hear the smile in Penelope's voice when she replies, "Get your ass over here pronto!"

Alex had insisted upon coming with me to Staten Island once I'd relayed what Penelope had said. Neither of us had mentioned what had gone on prior to the call, and I didn't dwell on thinking about where things might have escalated to had we not been interrupted.

Once Alex had given our route to Ford, he'd proceeded to leave the penthouse via the underground parking lot in the most luxurious car I have ever seen.

He'd run his palms reverently across the silver bonnet of his Bugatti before climbing into the driver's side.

The ride had been silent, each of us clearly lost in our own thoughts, though I felt his questioning eyes upon me more than a handful of times. When he pulls into the parking lot at Sunrise Harbor almost two hours after my voyeurism, the air between us is heavy.

My cheeks heat at the thought, and I reach for the door handle, only for Alex to stop me with a hand on my knee.

"Wait, Rey. I just wanted to say—"

But I cut him off before he can get any further.

"I'm sorry, Alex. I didn't mean to let things go as far as they did this morning. I should have made my presence known." I raise my eyes to his. "I'm *sorry*."

He squeezes my knee before patting it softly. "I just wanted to say, if you ever find yourself in a situation like that again…" He winks with a cheeky as fuck grin. "Feel free to give me a hand."

And just like that, the tension dissipates. I shake my head with a smile. "I'd call you incorrigible, but it doesn't seem to make any difference at this point."

I slip from my door, and he does the same, finding my eyes over the roof of the car. "I did warn you that I was a serial screw-up…"

Rounding the car, his hand finds mine as he presses a kiss to my forehead. I can feel him lending me his strength in this moment, and my heart is filled with silent thanks for the soulmate I discovered entirely by accident.

Or perhaps it was fate.

We cross the relatively empty parking lot, and I press the familiar buzzer as a mixture of apprehension and excitement dances in the pit of my stomach.

We're buzzed in by Joaquin, one of the orderlies, who smiles broadly at both Alex and me.

As I move down the corridor toward Lita's room, Alex halts

abruptly, fixing me with an intense stare. "I'll wait out here. You should get this special time alone with—"

I tug his hand, forcing him to step closer. "I would really like for her to meet the *other* most special person in my life."

His jaw tics and he swallows roughly before nodding, his feet falling into step with mine once more.

I slowly push the door of her room open, poking my head around the corner to find Lita sitting up in a high-backed chair at her small table. Penelope and Vanessa, one of the higher-ups, are sitting with her, all three chatting animatedly.

"Lita?"

The woman in question turns toward me, her big brown eyes—the ones identical to my own—lighting up with unadulterated love and affection. "Ah, *mi conchita linda*! There you are. Come, come."

She gestures for me to come closer, patting the arm of her chair. "Sit by me, and tell me all about your day."

I move farther into the room, Alex's hand still clasped in mine, and when her eyes land on the sight, her entire face beams as she exclaims with a high-pitched voice that utterly doesn't sound like her own, "Pen! Nessa!! Look, *mija* brought a friend to visit today."

She turns to her carers, openly winking at them with a wry grin on her face. "And what a sight he is for these sore eyes, hmm, ladies?"

Alex chuckles behind me, and his lips graze the shell of my ear, sending shivers running the length and breadth of my spine. "If only they knew the sights you've seen this morning."

Incorrigible!

Fourteen

ALEX

"Did you know my Reyna was the lead in the Pearson School of the Arts Christmas Gala last year?"

Rey's smile is a little tight, and I have a feeling this is a memory her abuela has spoken of before.

"She played the Sugar Plum Fairy, and she was spectacular. You've always been so special. Do you remember when you were ten, *mija*? That recital where you let little Ariana Cramer take the solo because…because—"

Reyna cuts her grandmother off gently when she appears to lose her train of thought. "Because she needed the distraction. I remember, Lita."

As Rey turns to me, she holds out her hand, palm up. I walk closer, taking her proffered hand and squeezing it lightly. "Lita thought I was insane, passing it up, but my gut told me that Ariana needed it more than I did."

"And she did! Her parents were going through a divorce—

something she hadn't told anyone." Rey's grandmother's chest puffs out with pride. "It was the first time we witnessed your gift. The first of many."

"Your gift?"

Rey twists her head up toward mine. "My intuition, Alex. Lita has always said that it's my gift."

They smile softly at one another as the two caretakers exchange a glance. The taller of the two, Vanessa, steps forward and places a hand on Reyna's shoulder. "I have a little paperwork for the insurance that requires your autograph, sweetie. Could you come to the office with me for a minute?"

Rey looks hesitantly from me to her abuela and back again. She rises to stand, and I immediately enfold her in my arms with a reassuring hug. "Go, Sunshine. I'll keep Lita company."

"It's Mari to you, handsome."

Reyna's groan against my chest makes everyone laugh before she withdraws from my hold and gives both me and her abuela a serious look. "I'll be back in five. *No* exchanging horror stories, you two."

She follows Vanessa from the room with a worried backward glance that I try to ease with an encouraging smile before settling into the seat opposite Mari.

I pick up the deck of cards from the table, shuffling them rapidly. "What would you like to play?"

Mari surprises me with a speed I wouldn't have expected of her when her hand darts out to halt my motions. "Pen, give us a minute, please."

Penelope looks up from her knitting in the far corner of the bedroom before nodding with a small smile. "Course, Mariana. I'll be back in two."

Once she's closed the door, Mari turns to me with a serious

face. "What are your intentions with *mija*? My Reyna is an exceptionally special person, and I refuse to allow her to settle for anything less than an extraordinary life, *comprendes*?"

I take a moment, soaking in the sheer love that this small, frail, ferocious old lady has for the woman who's upended my life, and it fills my chest cavity to almost bursting.

I reach across the table, grasping Mari's hands in mine and holding her gaze with a vehemence I feel in my bones. "I can *promise* you that my intentions toward Rey are absolutely in her best interest. I…I…"

My sentence trails off as my forehead creases in thought, unable to find the words to express what she means to me.

"These eyes may be old, Alex, but they can clearly see that the bond you share is very real. The love between you both is palpable, and it soothes my soul to see she's found it while I'm still here to witness." Her brown eyes, so like Reyna's, glisten with unshed tears. "So like the love I shared with my Thiago, Reyna's abuelo, may he rest in peace."

Silence hangs between us before something flickers across Mari's kind old face. She leans closer across the table. "A girl like my Reyna deserves the world. And I believe you might just be the one who can give her that. She's been burdened by our family for far too long. It's time she got to live those big dreams of hers."

"I will do everything in my power to see that happen, Mari. I swear to you now."

She smiles, squeezing my hand lightly. "She's always wanted to go home." Her eyes take on a dreamy look. "Not back to Connecticut, I mean, *my* home. Where my Thia and I immigrated from. To walk the streets of my girlhood, to swim the waters of my youth."

She gestures toward her bedside locker. "In the top drawer,

there's a green book. Take it. Please, Alex. Read it yourself, if you like, but *please*...give it to her." Her eyes darken to almost black in their intensity. Goosebumps scatter along my skin, and I know she's more aware right now than she has been in quite a very long time. "When the time is right."

"How will I know, Mari?"

She smiles softly in a way that both fills my heart and breaks it at the same time. "You'll know, *mijo*."

Our gazes hold for a long moment until I stand to cross the space to the drawer and hold up the well-used green book within. "This one?"

She nods with a bright smile. "Now, that's done. Come tell me all about how you plan on spoiling my little dancer."

I find myself nodding, a smile blooming on my face. I'm completely unable to stop myself from uttering my next words when I slip back into my seat opposite her. "We're getting married, Mari."

Her eyes widen in a shock that rapidly transforms into sheer delight as I rush on. "And I promise to always take care of your girl."

It's at that very moment Rey steps back into the room. She's clearly been crying, but I don't get a second to question it because Mari's eyes drop to Rey's left hand, landing on the huge diamond ring that I put on her finger less than twenty-four hours ago.

"*Ay Dios mio, mija*! Come closer. Let me get a look at that rock."

Reyna's eyes dart to mine in question even as she closes the distance, perching her ass on the arm of my chair. I wrap my arm around her waist, tugging her closer as she holds her left hand out, much to Mari's blatant delight.

"Oh, *mi amor*! You *must* wed on *Dia de Juan Santamaria*, just as we did." Reyna stiffens minutely, and Mari looks up with tears on her cheeks. "Yours is a true love match, *si*? Just like your abuelo and me, *mi conchita linda*."

She twists about, checking what appears to be an old calendar on the wall by her bed.

"Yes, yes. Six months is *plenty* of time to prepare."

Her smiling eyes catch mine, and she reaches for my hand, which I take with a genuine smile and a light heart. I can easily see why Reyna is the beautiful human she is today, having been reared by such a woman as Mariana Marquez.

"Come, mijo. The gardens are this way."

I help her stand, gently hooking her arm through mine as Rey splutters, "The gardens? Why on earth are we going outside, Lita? You haven't been mobile for…"

She trails off, clearly not wanting to upset Mari before she rephrases.

"Please, Lita. You might fall. You might get hurt. You might—"

She's cut off by a grinning Mari. "And pigs *might* fly, *mija*. Now, grab that door and tell Pen we're on the move."

The courtyard at Sunrise Harbor is enclosed in a square shape and filled with all manner of shrubbery and flowers.

Rey is standing to one side with Penelope while Mari and I take a seat on one of the many benches dotted throughout the place.

"I hope she dances to my favorite."

I slide my gaze to Mari with a slow smile. "What's that?"

She grasps my nearest hand in hers as she smiles, but doesn't answer my question. Instead, she focuses on settling it on her own lap as though she's known me my whole life, and the simple gesture is nearly my undoing.

I inhale through my nose to gather myself, entirely blown away by this tiny Costa Rican lady with a heart of gold. A heart that she has so blatantly passed along to her magnificent granddaughter.

"Alex, mijo." She squeezes my hand without looking at me. "My Reyna is exceptionally talented—in *many* aspects of her life—but she is also utterly selfless when she *loves* someone."

Mari slowly shifts her gaze to mine. "She is a free spirit who cannot be tamed, though she sometimes requires a strong hand. She is a caring individual who will place the needs of everyone above her own. She is the embodiment of my love for Thia, my dearly departed husband, and the antithesis of her toxic father, Victor."

I desperately want to ask what she means, but as I open my mouth, she holds up a palm. "Love is the ability to see someone for who they truly are. Beneath the façade, behind the mask. And true love is the ability to love one another regardless, flaws and all."

Before we can delve deeper, a guitar strums over the speakers, and my eyes are instantly drawn to Reyna. She's slipped into a worn pair of ballet slippers, and she strides forward with pure elegance with a smile on her face that is all for Mari.

A piece of classical music sounds over a speaker, and it takes me a second to recognize it. Mari spots the confusion on my face and quietly murmurs for my ears only, "It's her piece from The Nutcracker. The—"

I cut her off softly when awareness strikes. "The Dance of the Sugar Plum Fairy."

Mari nods with a smile, then deadpans, "Though I am partial to the Bieber remix of Despacito."

I barely contain a snort of laughter, and Mari chuckles softly as

I turn my intrigued eyes toward Reyna.

Her body is moving in fluidity along with the music. She's poised and graceful. Her face is so serene that I'm altogether sure that inside her head, she's a million miles away, performing on stage under spotlights.

Because she certainly looks the part, even without the leotard and tutu.

I'm positively glued to her performance from beginning to end, and when she breaks into a series of spins, my mouth drops wide open.

Each intricate spin glides smoothly into another, and another, until she finishes with a flourish, arms raised elegantly, with a bright smile on her joy-filled face.

The courtyard erupts in catcalls and applause, and I realize with a start that we're surrounded by, possibly, the entire population of Sunrise Harbor.

Rey steps closer to us, grasping mine and Mari's hands in hers before dropping to her knees and placing her head atop our clasped palms as the commotion around us eases.

She raises those stunning chocolate eyes first to Mari's, who is smiling in nothing short of motherly pride, to mine, and it takes me a hot minute to focus on anything other than how fucking proud I am right now before the wind is taken utterly out of both of our sails.

"Who…who are you?"

Mariana jerks her hand from both mine and Rey's, the confusion on her dear face making my heart clench in pain.

"Where am I? Where is Thiago?" She rises from her seat as Penelope and two other staff arrive out of nowhere.

Rey stands, holding my hand like a lifeline as the caretakers for her abuela rally to care for her.

"Don't you want to—"

She cuts me off with a soft voice. "Let's just go, Alex." Her eyes find mine. "Today was more than I could have ever dreamed of. To know that you met her, and even though this engagement is a lie, she was fully behind it…" She trails off, exhaling a heavy sigh. "It meant the world to me."

Mari has been taken back inside, seemingly less distraught already in her familiar inner surroundings, and Rey shoots a pained smile at Penelope when she gives her the thumbs-up from inside Mari's room.

"Come on, let's go."

Once she's slipped into her shoes, we start for the exit, but I draw up before we have even exited the courtyard. "Rey, I want to honor Mari's wish. I want to get married on…on…what was it called?"

"*Dia de Juan Santamaria*? Umm, pretty boy, that's—"

I spin around, uncaring of where we are, and drop to my knees, a plea and a prayer on my face. "Rey, I want to make your abuela happy, your abuelo proud—and…"

I shrug as a grin splits my face. "And sticking it to Henry is an added bonus, I won't lie."

She giggles softly, glancing about at the bystanders as I edge closer on my knees, wrapping my arms around her slim waist.

"Let's do it. Let's do it for her." I raise my biggest puppy dog eyes to Rey, resting my chin on her belly button.

"Let's get married on *Dia de Juan Santamaria*. Let's give Mari the day she wants for you, Sunshine."

Rey cups my cheeks in her soft palms, tears threatening to spill from her dark lashes.

"You realize *Dia de Juan Santamaria* is in *six days*, right? That calendar in her room is years out of date!"

"Six days? Six months? Rey—" I stand smoothly, grasping her cheeks in my palms and dropping my forehead to hers.

"The timing doesn't matter because you're stuck with me forever. I know I'll be in your life in whatever capacity you need me. When I said always, I meant it."

Tears crest her lashes, and my thumbs brush them away as they glide down her cheeks.

"I've said it before, I'll continue to say it until I'm blue in the face. *I've got you,* Sunshine."

Fifteen

REYNA

"You look simply stunning, Miss Marquez."

Simona, the stylist Alex had insisted upon, beams a bright smile as she slowly steps back.

Her entourage of hair stylists, make-up artists, lash and nail technicians, and heaven knows what else, are all wearing matching wide smiles as they watch Simona walk over to the long, full-length mirror that, up until now, has been covered.

She whips the white sheet from it with a flourish, and for a moment, I don't recognize myself.

Stepping closer, I tilt my head in wonderment. I run my hands along the mulberry ruffles and gently slide my fingertips along the band that's cinching my waist.

My eyes follow the movements, trailing higher along the gentle curve of my breasts, up to my bare collar bone that's on full display thanks to the mass of curls piled artfully atop my head.

Simple diamond earrings sparkle in my ears, and other than my engagement ring, they are the only jewelry I'm wearing.

My make-up has been kept to an understated elegance, with slightly smoky eyes and a deep red matte lipstick.

Simona steps forward, passing me my silver, rhinestone-encrusted clutch bag, and it's only then that I notice the rest of her team has filed out of my bedroom.

"Thank you so much. You've worked wonders."

She shakes her head with a smile. "My job is always easier when the client is a natural beauty."

I can feel my cheeks pinken under her compliment right as there's a gentle knock on the door, followed by Alex's husky baritone that makes my skin tingle. "Are you ready, Rey?"

My stomach dips even as I call out. "Almost. Just a sec."

"Okay, I'll be in the living room." I can hear his footsteps as he walks back down the hall and eventually downstairs.

"He's going to fall head over heels for you all over again tonight." Simona begins to back out of my room, throwing me a wink before she slips out the door. "Mark my words."

I blow out a breath, smooth my hands down along my ruffles once more, and leave my room on wobbly legs.

When Alex had mentioned a future event that we'd be attending whilst on our shopping trip to Bergdorf Goodman, I hadn't realized that he meant the Spring Gala at the Koch Theater.

It's a full red-carpet event, and to say that I'm nervous would be the understatement of the century.

He'd broken the news to me when we'd left Sunrise Harbor yesterday, stating that if we were to be getting married on *Dia de Juan Santamaria* five short days from now, it would be a good idea to have at least one public appearance as a couple beforehand.

When I reach the top of the stairs, I slip my heels off, afraid I might fall courtesy of my knocking knees. I pick them up and carry them in my left hand, with my clutch tucked underneath my arm, while clinging to the wrought-iron banister with my right hand.

I am so focused on making it down without a mishap that I don't notice a waiting Alex until I'm almost upon him.

Oh my God!

My breath catches on a gasp at the sight before me, and I stop dead in my tracks on the second to last step, taking a moment to appreciate his utter magnificence.

He's wearing a black tux that was assuredly made to fit his too-perfect body. His hair is immaculately styled back from his face, and my palms itch with the sudden desire to mess it up. To run my fingers through those soft locks and trail my nails along his scalp.

Desire pools within me despite myself, and I know in this instant what it is to want to lose all control and surrender to my most baser desires.

His gaze is fixed on me. Stormy eyes rove across every inch of me, and I feel completely exposed, my nipples pebbling into awareness beneath my dress. His eyes caress my body as intentionally as the touch of a skilled lover, and I feel myself stand taller, more confident under his obvious approval.

Until I stumble as I hit the last step. A squeal erupts from my mouth as I fall forward, ramming my eyes shut as the ground rises up to meet me.

Except, instead of the hard marble surface of the penthouse, I feel strong arms wrap around my body, holding me in place before raising me back up to stand.

"I've got you, Sunshine."

I bite down harshly on my bottom lip to stop the multitude of completely inappropriate words that flash through my brain from pouring out of my mouth.

Instead, I inhale through my nose before slowly blowing the breath out through my mouth. "Thank you."

Having set me to rights, he lets go of my upper arms and steps back to ram his hands into his tux pants pockets. A lock of hair has fallen loose from his carefully styled hair, and before I know it, my hand has crossed the distance between us to oh-so gently set it back into place.

As my arm falls away, Alex's hand reaches out to encircle my wrist. He smooths his thumb across the soft skin over my racing pulse, the simple move setting fire to my sex.

"I've never seen anything as beautiful as you. Right now. At this moment." He takes a breath as I blink furiously, my cheeks heating under his stare. "You're like the sun appearing from behind the clouds in the aftermath of a storm."

He raises my hand to his mouth, pressing a soft, lingering kiss to the back of mine. *"Voglio assorbire la tua luce e conservarla per sempre."*

My breath hitches at his gravelly tone. "What does that mean?"

He doesn't volunteer a translation; instead, eyes still holding mine in complete rapture, he digs his free hand into his pants pocket, pulling out a sparkling diamond bracelet.

He twists my wrist around, letting his eyes drop to his actions as he fastens the bracelet, fixing it just right before he lets go, severing the connection between us.

In a move that shocks me, he drops to the floor at my feet, fishing my discarded heels from their place on the floor beside us. He raises the hem of my gown, and gently lifts my bare feet to slip first one, then the other, into my shoes.

Once I'm all set, he settles the dress back into place, smoothing his hands along the ruffles and, by proxy, my body, making me swallow harshly as I hum to life beneath that barest of touches.

He stands without a word, taking in my surely flushed cheeks and the rapid rise and fall of my chest before offering me his arm. "Shall we, Sunshine?"

ALEX

Rey is fidgeting in her bag, checking her lipstick and her hair in the small compact mirror, and generally doing anything and everything to distract herself from both the obvious sexual tension back at the penthouse and the rapidly encroaching red-carpet appearance.

And there's something underneath, underlying all of that, that's an utter mystery to me, though for the life of me, I can't put my finger on it.

But Christ almighty, when she appeared at the top of the stairs, I'd been a hair's breadth from breaking the rule that's keeping her safe from me and selfishly taking what I know we both want.

"Voglio assorbire la tua luce e conservarla per sempre."

I scratch my temple, hoping she didn't understand my sudden burst of Italian but also knowing that the words are entirely true.

I *do* want to absorb her light. I *do* want to keep it. *Forever.*

But I can't allow my selfishness to ruin her.

Yes, I know pretty much all there is to know about sex. How to make it good for one another. I have no doubt I could make her come harder than she's ever come in her life—and I do want that. *Badly.*

But I don't know *anything* about love. And if there's one thing I know about Reyna Marquez, it's that she deserves to be loved completely and endlessly.

No one loves you, Alexander. No one cares.

The never-ending repetition of those damn words runs through my head again, driving my point home all too well.

Fuck you very much, Mother.

Rey's trembling hands see her drop the compact mirror onto the floor at her feet. She reaches down to pick it up at the same time I do, our fingertips colliding, and I swear I can almost feel the charge of electricity run through my veins from that accidental brushing of skin.

She pulls away, turning wide, scared eyes to mine as I rescue the mirror from the floor of our town car.

Once I've dropped it back inside her bag, I slide along the leather seat, draping my arm across the back to pull her in against my side whilst ignoring the shot of longing that almost rips my entire body apart.

Instead, I focus solely on being her comfort.

"There's nothing to be scared of, Sunshine. I'll be with you the entire time."

She turns her face up to mine, her hands still fidgeting in her lap. "I—I'm afraid I'll do something wrong. Say something stupid. I—I don't fit in with these people. They're—"

"They're *so* far beneath you, Reyna Marquez."

I softly cover her twitching fingers. "Try to see yourself the way *I* see you, and you'll soon realize that I'm right. You're kind. Funny. Thoughtful. You're a beautiful person, both inside and out."

I lift my hand to pinch her chin, tempted beyond all good reason to kiss her right now. Whatever she sees in my eyes makes her tilt her chin even higher, angling her mouth just right to be utterly consumed by mine.

I brush the pad of my thumb across her bottom lip, grazing it back and forth slowly. My eyes follow the movement as though hypnotized, and I can feel my nostrils flare as my dick presses painfully against the strict confines of my tuxedo pants.

She inhales sharply, and my eyes travel from her ensnaring mouth to her mesmerizing eyes. She's watching me from beneath her long black lashes, desire plain as day in the depths of her beautiful orbs.

I pull down on her bottom lip with my thumb, and, ever-so slowly, she runs the tip of her pink tongue along her top lip, never once breaking eye contact with me.

"It's a dangerous game we're playing, Rey."

The car rolls to a slow halt then, breaking the spell in the nick of time.

I suck in a deep breath before sliding back across the seat, taking a second to adjust my rock-hard cock as I go. Rey's eyes follow the move, widening in surprise.

"Don't look so shocked, Sunshine." I grin, shoving all thoughts of kissing her to the very back of my mind. "To pretend the mere sight of you doesn't get me harder than granite would be pointless, especially if you're about to be my wife."

My grin widens at her sudden gasp. "Don't worry. I'll look my fill so I'll have plenty for the wank bank when I inevitably need to fuck my fist every night for the next year." I wink just as Ford, who's driven us, opens the door behind me, and cameras begin to flash. "I won't touch you, though. You're far too good for the likes of me."

Her brows draw together as I slip from the car, nodding to our new security guard before plastering my media face on so that I can smile brightly for the surrounding cameras and watching celebrities.

News of my newly found relationship status has traveled far and fast. Vaughn—the only one in the know outside of the

Malones, whose silence Bailey was obviously able to ensure—was able to "leak" information on how long I've known Reyna and how we met, among the other lies he was more than willing to help me concoct.

I do so appreciate my exceedingly morally grey friend.

However, tonight will be the first time anyone has heard of our impending nuptials, so things will surely be interesting.

I twist about to assist Reyna, and she takes my outstretched hand with a gentle smile that does nothing to help the semi that refuses to deflate beneath my dress pants.

She steps from the car, and I'm utterly helpless to stop myself from bending down to press a soft, lingering kiss to the silky skin of her cheek.

Pulling back, I catch and hold her eyes as I mouth the words she needs from me. "I've got you, Sunshine."

I straighten with a smile, tuck her arm into the crook of mine, and together we step forward into the blinding flash of camera lights, leaving Ford at our rear.

The red carpet is a long, tedious affair. Media outlets shout for our attention, desperate to be the first to speak with the only woman I've ever brought as a plus-one, outside of Liv or Mila, of course.

I murmur words of encouragement in Rey's ear as we pose for endless photos, and her small intimate smiles of gratitude see me preening shamelessly like a motherfucking peacock.

We've almost made it inside the Koch Theater when I finally spot Kennedy Sawyer, the young intern at DeMarco Holdings who's been promised a permanent position if she asks the questions I've especially mandated for mine and Reyna's first informal interview.

"Let's answer some questions before we go inside, Rey."

I drop my hand to the small of her back, ushering her toward a delighted Kennedy.

"May I ask you both a couple of questions, Mr. DeMarco?"

I flash what I know is my most charming grin. "Of course. Shoot."

The surrounding outlets watch on, practically ignoring everyone else as they wait with bated breath to see what happens next.

Kennedy takes out her list of approved questions, and a sudden gust of wind knocks them from her hands. "Oh, I'm sorry. Hold—hold on."

She scrambles after the card, leaving a gap in the surrounding news hounds. They begin to shout again. The questions are more easily heard now that we're standing closer to them.

"Is that an engagement ring, Miss Marquez?"

"Are you *really* pregnant?"

"Word on the street is he *paid* you to be his girlfriend. Can you comment, Miss Marquez?"

I grit my jaw at that last one, and with no sign of that damnable intern returning, I press a comforting kiss to Rey's temple before taking her hand in mine. As we're moving away, I halt when the crowd's shouts all seem to unify, one word echoing on repeat as the entire gathering screams for one thing.

The very thing I've been fighting for far too long now.

"Kiss! Kiss! Kiss! Kiss!"

Fuck it!

Rey has moved several steps ahead, and without analyzing it any further, I tug slightly on her arm. She spins about as I close the distance, sliding the tips of my fingers along the side of her jaw, eventually resting on the back of her neck.

Our eyes hold and the whole world around us fades into

oblivion. Her breathing kicks up a notch, and her nostrils flare as I brush the pad of my thumb over the delicate skin of her nape.

"*Kiss me*. Alex."

The words leave her mouth on a pleading breath as her fingers flex over my jacket-covered chest. Her eyes flare with unflinching desire when I nod almost imperceptibly, ready and willing to break all the rules for one taste.

I angle her head just right as she wets her lips with the tip of her tongue, her eyes watching in thrall as I close the gap between our wanting mouths.

Her moan of pleasure hits my ears at the barest brush of my lips across hers, and her arms encircle my neck, pulling me impossibly closer, opening her mouth to mine in the most glorious surrender.

Our tongues collide, twisting and coiling around one another, almost fighting for dominance until I rein things in, needing beyond measure to savor this moment because it will *not* happen again.

It can't.

And so, I slowly take her mouth, sliding my tongue along hers, nipping her bottom lip, and leisurely exploring her sweetness as every nerve ending inside of my body awakens. This kiss is like nothing I've experienced in my entire life, and in the back of my mind, I wonder what I've been doing wrong because this kiss…

This kiss is *everything*.

I inhale sharply through my nose, exhaling a groan deep inside my chest, and her answering moan suddenly makes me remember where we are.

Slowly and begrudgingly, I break our kiss and slowly watch as her eyes flutter open. As she comes back to awareness.

Her eyes hold mine as their willing captive, and she blinks rapidly before reaching up to cup my cheek. She presses a chaste kiss to my lips, then smiles brightly, her next words affecting me more than I'd like.

"I think that was enough to throw them off the scent."

Sixteen

ALEX

"I need to use the restroom."

Rey rises from her chair with the grace of a natural-born dancer, shooting me a little smile before she moves off toward the facilities, her hips swaying deliciously.

I rip my treacherous eyes from that *perfect* fucking ass, forcing myself to do anything but watch her walk away.

"Lovely seeing you again, Alex."

Dwight and Norah Freemont, who had sat at our table all evening, nod in my direction as they make their way out of the Koch Theater. Luckily, their asshat of a son isn't in attendance, or I'd have had a job for Ford.

"Evening, Norah. Dwight." I tip my chin with the smile they've come to expect of me at these damn events.

The meal and dancing portion of the evening is over, and things are beginning to wind down. I check my wristwatch, noting that it's not yet midnight, and I brighten at the thought of potentially a third night in a row of binging *Grey's Anatomy.*

I'm getting altogether too fond of waking up surrounded by a certain woman's radiance.

Pulling out my cell, I shoot Ford a quick text.

ME

Pull the car around in fifteen.

I'm met with a Ford classic that makes me laugh far too loudly.

FORD

K.

He's a man of few words. I won't complain, as his lack of conversational skills suits my needs.

I glance around in search of Rey, but she's still AWOL.

Instead of waiting here for her return, I grab her bag from the table and go in search of her. I don't have to travel far before I hear her inimitable laughter ringing out like a siren call.

I round a corner to find her in conversation with one of the male dancers from the performance.

"Well, I'm glad you thought so, Reyna, because Veronica is going to—"

I close the gap, instantly noting how this guy is looking at *my* fiancée.

Woah, tiger!

Yet even as I tell myself to keep my calm, it's like a car crash, and there's no hope of slamming on the brakes.

"Hey, Sunshine." I wrap my arms around her waist to rest my chin on her bare shoulder before I press a kiss to her soft cheek, never once taking my eyes off the insipid blue ones of the blonde kid in front of me. "Ready to go home?"

"Alex! I'm so glad you're here." Her happiness at my presence is evident in her voice, but the dipshit loitering before us clearly doesn't give a rat's ass, because he narrows his eyes when he observes my hands resting possessively on her slender waist.

"This is Todd, an old friend from college."

The name sounds far too familiar…though I realize why almost instantly.

The friend-with-benefits guy!

"Todd is part of the company now. Isn't that wonderful?"

She angles her face toward mine, utterly oblivious to the silent undercurrent running between me and Todd.

"That's amazing, Rey. Ford is bringing the car—"

Todd, clearly not picking up what I'm putting down—or maybe just too fucking dumb to know when to quit—cuts me off when he steps closer to playfully swat at one of the ruffles on Reyna's hip.

"There's an after-party across town. I could get you in as my plus-one." He arches a questioning brow. "For old time's sake, hmm?"

Rey raises wide eyes to mine, but my complete attention is on the dick bag that is Todd. She turns back to him with a hesitant smile. "Thank you for asking me, Todd. I—"

"Oh, now I know who he is." I clap my right hand across my forehead, as though realization is suddenly dawning. "*You're* the Todd with the teeny-weeny cock!"

I lean down to whisper loudly in Rey's ear, keeping my eyes on Todd's reddening face. "Is it *really* the size of a *pickle*?"

Rey gasps, and Todd stares at me as though I've mortally wounded him before turning to Rey with accusing eyes. "Real nice, Reyna. At least my dick works. You're broken—"

I take a menacing step toward the little shit, fully aware that this conversation has taken a swan dive, and we need to get out of here. "Leave *now*, and I won't tell Veronica you were fraternizing with the patrons."

He wavers, clearly needing to say more, but the threat of his job is enough to see him shuffle off begrudgingly.

"Rey, I—"

She holds up her palm. "I don't want to talk about this right now, Alex. I had it under control, but you insulted him—"

"Not my fault that it was clearly *true*!"

"That's not the point and you know—"

"He could see we were together, and *still,* he wanted you to go with him to some shit hole across town. For very obvious reasons, I might add!"

"And I was about to turn him down if you hadn't steam-rolled in." She exhales in plain annoyance. "I *really* don't want to argue with you about this, Alex. I'm going to the restroom. When I return, we will leave, and we will *not* talk about this conversation again."

She sidesteps around me and marches directly toward the restrooms. It takes my feet a second to catch up with my brain, but when it does, my brow knits, and I jog after her.

"What did he mean about being broken, Rey? Did somebody hurt you? Did *he* hurt you?"

I can see her spine stiffen, but her stride continues to eat the ground.

Before she can reach the sanctity of the women's restroom, I grab her arm and spin her around the corner, taking her through the first door I find.

Once we're inside, I close the door behind us, realizing that we are in a small ballet studio.

She rounds on me; the fire in her eyes appears to have dimmed in the darkened space but is no less intense.

"What on earth are you doing, Alex? I need to use the restroom—"

"No." I cut her off with a single word before prowling closer. She backs away until her ass hits the barre that runs the entire length of the floor-to-ceiling mirrors of the studio. "You don't need to use the restroom, Rey. You wanted to avoid talking to me."

Despite the darkened room, I can see the flush that climbs from her chest all the way to her cheeks. "No, that's not true at all."

She tilts her chin, and her defiance is honestly the sexiest thing I've ever witnessed in my whole fucking life.

"Tell me what he meant then."

Chewing her bottom lip, indecision plays across her features. "I don't want to, Alex. I can fight my own battles."

I move closer and closer still until she's within arm's reach. My words are low and filled with barely constrained anger at whoever it is that forced her to fight *any* battles. "If anyone hurt you, Rey…if someone tried to break you somehow—"

She leans forward, stopping me when she plants her palms on my cheeks. "You have it all wrong. Todd didn't mean that I was broken *by* someone. He—he meant that…"

She trails off, allowing her hands to fall away as her chin drops to her chest with a heavy sigh. When she speaks again, her words are so softly spoken I need to strain my ears to hear them.

"He meant that *I'm* broken…when it comes to sex."

"I don't understand—"

"He wasn't able to make me…you know…"

I gulp in an attempt to quell my rising heart rate.

There's no way *she's saying what I think she's saying…*

"He wasn't able to *what* exactly, Rey?"

She lifts her head, clearly annoyed at having to spell it out. "I've never had an orgasm, okay? Happy now?"

"As in *ever*?" I strive to keep the incredulity from my tone, and fail miserably.

She huffs as she moves to step around me, but I palm her upper arms gently, halting her to bring her in against my chest. I wrap my arms around her, holding her tight against my body until I feel the tension begin to ebb from her shoulders.

"You're not broken, Sunshine." I press a kiss to the top of her head. "Learning how to play a woman's body is like blind reading sheet music for a complicated piece by Chopin."

I smooth my hand over the back of her head, drawing it slowly down across her exposed spine, allowing myself a small smirk when I feel a shiver run through her body.

It feels as though I'm having an out-of-body experience when I run full throttle right into the fire.

"It takes *time*."

I press a lingering kiss to one flushed cheek, utterly ignoring the alarm bells that are going off inside my head.

"Patience."

Then I kiss the other before pulling back to spear her with an intense stare.

"Attention to detail."

I fist her slightly disheveled hair to tilt her head to one side. The move exposes the delicate line of her shoulder and neck, allowing me to bend lower to graze my teeth across the smooth skin.

As another quiver rocks her body, I ghost my mouth across the shell of her ear. "It takes the *desire* to please." I nip the lobe between my teeth, and her sharp inhalation is like a call to motherfucking action.

"I'll show you how wrong he is, Sunshine. Say the word."

I pull back enough to pierce her with a look that says I'll do anything she wants of me right now. Because it's true.

However it happened, Reyna Marquez is the center of my

universe, and I will do *anything* to make her happy.

Her eyes are unsure, even as her tits press closer against my chest, seeking something she's dubious of. "Alex, I don't want things to change between—"

I press the index finger of my left hand over her plump lips, entirely sure that we can have this moment. This one time to show her what she's missing, and everything will stay exactly as it is between us.

"Nothing will change, Rey. I only want you to understand that you're *not* broken." My right hand slides reverently along her mouthwatering curves before dipping around to cup the ass I've been doing my best not to notice and pulling her firmly against my blatant hardness.

"*Please*. Let me show you."

I rock against her, drawing a low moan from her barely parted lips.

"I've got you, Sunshine."

Her eyes are like pools of molten lava when she expels a breath that's more like a moan before giving me the barest nod.

I walk her backward until she's flush with the mirror, our eyes never once leaving the other's.

It's like the floodgates have opened, and there's no stopping the oncoming tide even if I wanted to.

"Turn around."

Her brows pull down in a confused frown. "What? I—"

"Turn. Around."

She swallows roughly as her nostrils flare at the deeper-than-usual baritone of my voice, but she does what I say.

I lift her hands to plant her palms on the mirror on either side of her face as she watches me in our reflection.

Pressing a kiss to her exposed shoulder blade, I fist the ruffles of her skirt, slowly drawing it higher and higher until it's bunched around her waist.

My heart almost stops, and my mouth goes dry when I slide my palm over her smooth ass to find that she's not wearing any panties. My eyes find hers in the mirror as I groan, "Dirty fucking girl, Sunshine."

She arches a brow in rebuke, a move that goes directly to my straining cock. "The store said a thong would work best for this gown, but I couldn't deal with that string riding my ass all night, so…"

I press a kiss to her shoulder, arching an approving brow. "Good call."

Holding the bunched dress with my left hand, I run the fingertips of my right down the silky skin of her stomach, stopping to dance lightly across her bare pubic bone. Rey cries out at the barest touch of my fingers, and I move my mouth close to her ear once again.

"Watch yourself fall apart on my fingers." My voice is a growl from deep in my chest that sees goosebumps scattering across her exposed shoulder. "Keep your eyes on us."

Without warning, I nudge her legs apart with my foot, and my hand drops between her shaking thighs.

Her low moan of pleasure mixes with my deep-seated groan of delight when my middle finger slides over her slick clit before dipping lower into her tight core.

"*Shit*." My breathing is shallow, and my rough exhalations whisper across her skin, driving us both wild with want.

"You're so fucking tight. Your pussy would choke my cock *real* fucking good."

She gasps, her eyes holding mine in the mirror. "But my fingers are all you'll get."

I slowly pump my finger in and out, pushing farther with each thrust, and her eyes fall closed as she arches her back against me, seeking more.

"*So* wet for me, Sunshine. Fuck, you're dripping down my hand."

As I add a second finger, my hips pump against her perfect ass, and she searches for my reflection in the mirror as a look of abandon consumes her beautiful face.

My thumb glides across her throbbing clit in an alternating pattern of hard grinds and soft brushes, and her core tightens perceptibly around my fingers.

"Oh my God. *Yes*! Don't stop."

I lave wet kisses along every exposed inch of her neck and upper back, nipping with my teeth, soothing with my tongue, until she throws her head back, eyes open in wonder as they land on mine.

A desperate panic enters her voice, and I know that she's about to fall before she whispers, "Kiss me, Alex. *Please*. Kiss—"

And despite my earlier promise to myself, I'm helpless to deny her. I cut her off, slamming my mouth to hers to swallow her cries of pleasure like the gift I know them to be.

Her pussy constricts around my fingers, taking everything and begging for more as she shatters for me. It's one of the most beautiful sights I've ever seen, and I know I would die a happy man right now, having witnessed such perfection.

Our lips never part, tongues undulating against one another's while aftershocks ripple through her soaked pussy, and she slowly comes back down to earth.

As I break our kiss, her eyelids flutter open, and a single tear glides down her flushed cheek. I kiss it away and gently remove my fingers from her pulsating center, unwillingly leaving the warmth of her behind.

I let go of her now-crumpled gown, allowing it to fall to the floor, covering the evidence of what just happened here.

She slowly spins in my arms, her eyes wide in disbelief as she plants her trembling hands upon my chest. "I didn't know I could feel so—"

I brush my lips across her kiss-swollen mouth, my eyes never leaving hers while my heart palpitates at the gravity of what's passed between us.

And even knowing that we've crossed that invisible line in my head, I desperately try to backtrack, opting for some signature humor in my need to keep this desire for her firmly under control.

To keep from screwing this up, as I inevitably do with everything in my fucking life.

"Todd's dick was no bigger than a triple-A battery, and you won't convince me otherwise."

She giggles behind her hand, her eyes glowing in the wake of her first orgasm, and as I look at her, my chest fills with some ridiculous caveman version of pride at being the one to deliver it.

My left hand catches her right one while I slide my orgasm-coated hand into my pocket to clean the slick digits lest I succumb to the near-overwhelming need to suck those fingers dry. My desire to know if her cunt is as sweet as her berry-flavored mouth almost brings me to my damn knees.

I swallow hard, shoving that thought clear out of my head, disgust settling in the pit of my stomach at my complete and utter lack of self-control.

"Come on, Sunshine." I squeeze her hand lightly, sending her an encouraging smile. "There's an episode of *Grey's Anatomy* at home with our name on it."

Seventeen

REYNA

"Are we doing this or what, Rey?"

Alex's voice calls up the stairs through my open bedroom door, and I quickly throw some dance shoes on my feet before heading down to get started.

In the three days that have passed since the events at the Koch Theater, we'd dove head-first into wedding preparations.

Alex had rung his sister in the UK the day we'd returned from Sunrise Harbor following Lita's lucidity, so she had arrived in New York early this morning with her family in anticipation of our big day. Henry was already here with his, and Alex had a handful of friends and business associates to invite outside of that.

Even so, our guest list is sitting somewhere around two hundred – with only Leonard and Darcy Malone on my side.

Having discussed everything with Vanessa at Sunrise Harbor and signing the paperwork for Lita to receive respite care, I knew she wouldn't be able to come. It stung, but marrying on her and my abuelo's anniversary was what she had wanted, and I could give that to her.

There had been no mention of what had happened between me and Alex at the Spring Gala. Our interlude had been brushed firmly underneath the rug as though it had never occurred, which simultaneously gave me relief because we could carry on as before, but also gave me irrational anxiety that it would never happen again.

Christ, Reyna. You're not making any sense!

When I reach the open-plan living space, I find that Alex has pushed all the seats back, giving us a wide space in which to practice our first dance. His concern to do well at something so trivial warms my heart, and I'm entirely unable to stop my mouth from smiling ridiculously wide at the thought of spending this time with him.

He holds his hands out, palms facing up, puppy dog eyes front and center. "Teach me a lift, oh most amazing of dance masters."

I giggle loudly, and the sound fills the huge space. "Nuh-uh. Not happening."

When I shift his arms around into a waltz frame, he sighs even as he holds the pose. "Spoil sport."

I smirk at his knowing grin.

Placing my right hand in his left, he slides his other one around my waist, pulling me close, and when his scent fills my senses, I drop my head as my eyelids flutter shut. Taking half a beat to relive the feelings and sensations this man—my off-limits husband-to-be—stirred to life inside of me less than seventy-two hours previously.

"Rey…"

Alex's hesitant voice whispers across the top of my head, and I raise my eyes to his, plastering a smile on my face as I do.

"Sorry, pretty boy. Just taking a second to think of a song."

His eyes tell me that he doesn't believe me, but thankfully, he just nods.

"Siri, play 'Thinking Out Loud.'"

The following two hours pass quickly, and my body gets lost in the music rather than the sight, touch, and smell of my dance partner.

"You've really gotten the hang of it." I beam a proud smile that turns into a chuckle. "You were right in Molly Malones when you said you were a fast learner."

Something unreadable crosses his face before he gives me his back as he begins to set the furniture back in its place. "It's not so much picking things up fast as opposed to learning from my mistakes. And not repeating them."

I stiffen and flinch at the double meaning in his words, my hand immediately reaching to rub at a sudden sharp pain in my chest.

"Okay, well…that's good to know." I force a sliver of enthusiasm into my voice, needing to get out of here fast. "I—I've got to wash up. There's a dress fitting at 4:45, and then dinner with your family this evening…"

I trail off, lengthening my strides until I make it to the foot of the stairs.

Alex appears behind me as though out of thin air. "Rey, I'm—"

I spin to face him, pressing my index finger over his kissably soft lips and piercing him with a stare. "Okay, so now you want to talk about the goddamn elephant in the room, is that it?"

"Rey—"

I press more firmly over his mouth, stopping him before he can start. Needing to get this out.

"I'm well aware that the proverbial love hearts in my eyes

haven't gone unnoticed these past three days, Alex. So do me a favor, okay?"

He nods mutely as a frown mars the perfection of his features.

"Cut me some slack."

His shoulders deflate, but I power through, determined to make my point.

"So I have a small crush on the first guy who's been able to get me off. *It means nothing*. It's the equivalent of your erection before the gala. Let's refer to this as my lady boner stage, okay?"

He doesn't move a muscle, and the silence is deafening, so I continue, and when I do, I inject every drop of sincerity into my words as I hold his eyes unwaveringly.

"I'll get over it. It's a stupid infatuation." I shake my head with an attempted smile before dropping my finger and gently cupping his cheek. "Besides, it's best not to complicate our marriage by making it into something it's not before it's even begun, right?"

His eyes are sorrowful, almost pained, as he nods. "I'm sorry, Rey. I never wanted to hurt you."

I turn slowly as I swallow my emotions before ambling up the stairs without a backward glance.

Too late.

"Thank you for doing such a wonderful job at this late notice, Yvette."

My seamstress waves her hand at me. "It's been no problem, Miss Marquez."

I twirl once more, checking the dress in the mirror one final time before nodding at my reflection.

It truly is the dress that little girls' dreams are made of, and I wish so much that Lita was here to see it.

Maybe I can wear it to Sunrise Harbor…

Alex had said I could have whatever I wanted, and for most grown women, that would mean a bridal gown simply dripping with jewels and gems. However, for me, I had wanted a plain white satin dress that sat off my shoulders, Hepburn-style, and that cinched at my waist, falling to the floor in beautiful waves – and Yvette had delivered precisely that.

No bells. No whistles.

Just me.

"I will make the final adjustments and have it prepared for the big day." Yvette's eyes widen playfully. "Will you be staying here with Mr. DeMarco between now and then, or will you move elsewhere?"

I stop for a moment, realizing I haven't thought that far ahead, but I'm saved from answering when the elevator chimes and Alex steps off.

He's back from his friend Vaughn's club, and his face looks troubled until his eyes land on me.

All the breath leaves my body when he stops dead in his tracks.

"Christ, Rey." He blinks heavily, his sole focus on me.

"No, no, no, Mr. DeMarco." Yvette steps in front of him, trying to shield me unsuccessfully as I make a dash toward the stairs. "You shouldn't be here."

"Rey, wait." I stop just as I reach the stairs, and turn to face him.

His whiskey eyes hold mine, roving over every contour of my face, never once descending lower than my chin, but I feel his perusal as intimately as if it were his hands caressing me.

"You may leave, Ms. Williams. I'll have the dress couriered to your workshop shortly."

His words are sharp, though he softens them with a "Thank you so very much."

I can hear her gathering her things from my spot at the base of the stairs, but my eyes don't leave Alex's. They couldn't even if they wanted to – and they don't.

Once Yvette has left us, we continue to stand enthralled in one another's eyes until I break the silence with a whisper, "It's bad luck to see the bride—"

Alex's swift strides eat the space between us, and he cuts me off when he kneels at my feet. His eyes hold an ocean of sorrow and nothing short of a million and one regrets in their unusual depths.

"Rey, I'm so fucking sorry to have blurred the lines between us. That was *not* my intention, I prom—"

"You didn't blur any lines, Alex." I cup his cheeks in my hands. "I know where we stand. I know what we are. And my dumb crush will pass soon, I promise. What we have *right now* is too precious to screw up. I know that."

I lean forward to kiss his forehead gently, and when I straighten, he stands with me.

His eyes don't leave mine as he tucks my hair behind both of my ears before palming my cheeks ever-so gently. "You are so *special,* Reyna Marquez. You don't know just how much you mean to me."

Tears fill my eyes at his declaration as I feel his every word in the farthest reaches of my soul.

"And I will do everything—*every-fucking-thing*—within my power to *not* mess this up." Regret darkens his usually light features. "I should never have touched you. It's as simple as that."

He exhales a heavy breath, the sincerity in his eyes almost my undoing.

"I'm *sorry*."

I nod mutely, afraid to answer; otherwise, I plead with him to reconsider.

And so, I do the only thing I *can* do.

"I absolutely agree. And I'll move past crushing on you, pretty boy. All you have to do is be a little less like yourself. Perhaps you could try to model yourself on the one and only Chad Freemont."

I shoot him a wink, praying that a return to our regularly scheduled humor will dispel the tension. "Do that, and I won't be able to stand the damn sight of you."

His eyes flicker with a stirring of mirth as his lips twitch.

"Sounds like a plan, Rey. I'll get to work on my assholisms. Might even swing by Freemont to get pointers."

"It would take years of practice to become as polished as that self-entitled asshole."

I shudder as I push the memory of being trapped in that elevator with him firmly out of my head. "He's rotten to the goddamn core."

Alex opens his mouth to speak but stops himself, his forehead creasing in thought.

"What's the matter?"

His eyes are fixed intently on mine. "He said you were a screamer."

I blink rapidly, my mouth going dry as I try to swallow the nausea that bubbles in my stomach. "*What*?"

But Alex's eyes shift away from me as he continues, as though speaking to himself. "But how could he know that if you'd never orgasmed before..."

He trails off, his gaze returning to mine. "Why would he—"

"Because..." I cut him off, my head dropping before I can find it in myself to continue. "He cornered me one night in the office.

I was working late, and he wanted to go for dinner. I said *no,* and he…well, he didn't like that very much."

Alex steps closer, pinching my chin between his thumb and index finger to lift my face to his. His eyes are as kind as ever as his stare penetrates me.

"Did he hurt you, Rey?"

I shake my head. "N-no. I kicked him in t-t-the nuts before…b-before…"

As I trail off, unsure of how to finish that sentence, Alex pulls me in against his chest, and all memory of that horrible event is utterly purged by the feeling of all-encompassing safety that surrounds me when I'm in this man's embrace.

"Thank you for telling me, Sunshine." He plants a lingering kiss atop my head. "No one will hurt you *ever* again. Not so long as there's breath in my body."

Long minutes pass, and neither of us speaks a word until the elevator chimes.

"Shit, they're here!"

Eighteen

ALEX

"I don't want Italian."

Liv and Mila's heads swivel about in sync, eyes blown comically wide. "*What*?"

I shrug, not wanting to expand on that statement. "I already made a res—"

"Who are you, and what have you done to my best friend?" Liv steps closer, pressing her palm to my forehead. "Are you ill? You never pass up the chance to stuff your face with arancini."

I swat her away. "I just don't fancy it tonight, okay?"

"Don't fancy what?"

Rey steps off the bottom of the stairs, wearing a simple black dress with small flowers dotted throughout. There's a split on one side that goes to her mid-thigh, and her legs look like they go on for days thanks to the strappy heels she's wearing.

When I'd come home to find her standing in this same spot wearing the wedding dress she'll wear when we tie the knot two days from now, I'd been floored by the need to clear the god-awful tension between us.

I've been utterly miserable since letting my cock do the thinking back at the Gala. Yes, she's the most stunning woman I've ever met, both inside and out, and the more time we spend together, the more I want her, but I *won't* risk losing her presence in my life just because my dick thinks we can have our cake and eat it too.

I get her in my life for the next year. My place at the company will be secured, and Henry will be off my case, hopefully for good.

She gets her ballet studio, Mari's care covered, and anything else her beautiful heart desires.

Sex is a meaningless complication that will *ruin* everything for both of us.

Remember that in the future, you stupid wanker!

"Alex doesn't want Italian." Liv's appalled voice breaks my observations before I can stare too hard.

Rey presses her lips together, devilment flashing in her wide brown eyes, but she says nothing, and it appears as though my secret shame is still a secret when Mila strides forward with her hand outstretched.

"Since my brother is clearly a pig, *I'll* introduce myself." Rey takes her hand as I tut loudly.

Siblings!

"I'm Mila, and I'm *thrilled* to meet the woman who captured our playboy bro—"

I cut her off, indignance featuring heavily in my tone. "Gee, thanks, sis!"

My younger sister shrugs while Rey giggles. "And this is my husband, Nathaniel."

Nate Hawthorne unfurls his large frame from the sofa, offering his hand to Rey with a small nod.

"Pleased to meet you both."

Rey glances between them almost shyly. Between my sister's extrovert tendencies and Nate's outward appearance, she seems slightly overwhelmed.

Only one thing for it.

I sigh exaggeratedly. "Go on then, Sunshine. You can tell them."

She slides her eyes to mine and steps closer, threading our fingers together. "Nah, I'm good. What happens between us stays between us, pretty boy."

Her mouth turns up in a radiant smile before I slip my free hand around the back of her head, pulling her closer to press a kiss to her forehead.

"Aww!" Mila and Liv's combined voices break the moment, making me and Rey turn to our guests.

Liv chats animatedly with Mila. "I told you they were perfect together."

"So stinking cute!"

I roll my eyes while Reyna blushes furiously. "Okay, enough is enough. I've already made a reservation at Koi, folks. Let's move."

"And we can absolutely help in any way you need us, Reyna."

My best friend's signature selflessness lands on my ears as I bid farewell to my brother while Ford has gone to bring around our town car.

Liv and Henry are staying out for another while, a child-free evening being exactly what they need, especially with two more on the way and Liv's preference for keeping the kids with her instead of their nanny.

"Don't forget the rehearsal dinner tomorrow night, Ri."

My brother nods, glancing around at his wife chatting to Rey animatedly before turning to me. "Christ, she fits right in."

We chuckle together, and Henry claps his hand on my shoulder. "I'm happy for you, little brother. I'm happy for *both* of you."

I nod in thanks as Rey and Liv move closer. "Mila texted to say Nathan finally settled for them."

Henry expels a heavy breath. "That kid has got to be the worst sleeper."

He spins to me, a wry smile on his lips. "Kind of reminds me of you, Al. Jesus, you were so bad! You'd only settle when I kept you in my bed."

My chest tightens uncomfortably at the reminder that my brother was the person who raised me despite only being seven years my senior.

"What age were you when Alex was born, Henry?"

Liv slides a hesitant glance in first Henry's direction, then mine at Rey's innocuous question.

"I was seven, Rey." Henry's face splits in a huge grin. "I'll never forget the day he came home from the hospital. He was so small and angry, but *my God*, it was love at first sight."

I glance around at Liv and Rey, matching broad smiles on both their faces as Henry continues. "I seem to have a habit of falling in love at first sight. Right, Peach?"

Liv nudges him playfully. "You DeMarco men are emotionally stunted, but when you guys love, it's with your whole entire selves."

She winks at Rey. "We're very lucky ladies to be on the receiving end."

My cell chimes with a text.

FORD

Outside.

I shake my head at his predictability as I pocket my cell. "Ford's waiting out back, Rey. Are you ready to go?"

My fiancée nods as I reach for her hand. "See you two tomorrow. Don't stay out too late. The rehearsal is tomorrow, with or without you!"

Henry flips me the bird before catching Liv's hand to pull her into his arms. "Dance with me, Peaches."

We slip out through the service elevator, having had Ford organize security in advance. As expected, news of our whereabouts had leaked, and paparazzi had been swarming at the front of the hotel long before our arrival.

The only issue with this is the fact that the service bay has two large trucks taking up the space where Ford had planned on picking us up, so he needed to park a little ways down a side alley.

Rey is smiling brightly as we step out into the cooler night air. "They're so sweet."

She looks up at me, those damn love hearts in her big brown eyes that make my pulse pick up speed despite myself. "He does have his moments, I guess."

I press a kiss to the tip of her nose, and she giggles softly. As I drop my arm over her shoulders, she slides her arm around my waist, pressing close against my side like it's the most natural thing in the world.

A part of me knows I should discourage this behavior because it's just feeding into her crushing on me. But a bigger part of me can't deny her.

Or myself, truth be told.

"Your family is so wonderful." She beams up at me. "Do you miss them since moving here?"

"At times."

Her body tenses slightly with her next question. "Have you

ever thought about moving back home?"

I snort. "Fuck *no*. I like it here." And the tension ebbs from her shoulders. "Would you miss me if I did, Sunshine?"

She shoves me away playfully, and I can't help ribbing her further. "It would help you move past your crush, you know."

I shoot her a wide smirk that sees her shaking her head as she rolls her eyes. "Oh, you are—"

"Go on, say it. I'm incorrigible, right?"

We reach the car, and I open the door, gesturing for her to go first. She deadpans, "Oh, you already *know* that you're incorrigible. What I was going to say is that you're an *asshole*."

A loud bark of laughter bursts from my mouth as she moves to slip past me into the back seat, only to stop and bop me on the nose with her index finger before she winks. "But a super sexy asshole with a big heart...so you're not a *total* lost cause, pretty boy."

REYNA

My body is reaching higher and higher, searching for something just *beyond my reach, when Alex increases the pressure of his thumb on my clit, and suddenly, I'm right on the precipice, terrified of falling.*

"Kiss me, Alex. Please. Kiss—"

His eyes darken, noticeable even in the dim light of the ballet studio, before he slams his mouth to mine, devouring my cries of pleasure, and I come apart all over his hand.

My core clenches his fingers while his mouth consumes me, driving an already intense moment to rapturous heights.

He groans deeply, and I feel the sound reverberate through my body, landing directly in my center, ready and willing to do whatever this man wants with me.

We kiss forever, heartbreakingly languorous kisses that are a direct line to my foolish heart, and in that moment, I know, as surely as I know my own name, that I am falling madly in love with him.

My eyes fly open as the realization flows through me.

I'm falling in love with Alex DeMarco!

We had stayed up late, binging several episodes of *Grey's Anatomy* last night after returning from dinner. His disgust at the fact that I hadn't watched it before now was only offset by his joy in experiencing it as though for the first time through my eyes.

And, as has become my bad habit at this stage, I'd fallen asleep beside him, migrating closer to his side overnight, longing to be closer to him even in my sleep. I can only be thankful that I seem to wake first almost every morning, putting enough distance between us so that I can watch him sleep.

My guilty stalker-like pleasure.

I glance toward the wall clock by the television on the opposite side of the room, noting that it's 10:24 a.m., and we have an obscenely busy day ahead of us.

But still, I can't force myself to move.

My eyes slide across the bed to land on Alex's glorious sleeping form. He's face down on the white sheets, clad only in those indecent grey lounge pants that are currently molded to his perfect ass. His broad, tanned back is rising and falling as he breathes softly in his slumber.

A lock of hair has fallen across his forehead, giving him an innocent, boyish look that makes my heart clench, and it's at that precise moment that his long black lashes twitch, parting to reveal those honeyed eyes I've come to adore.

A smile lights up every single contour of his handsome face, and butterflies take flight in the depths of my stomach. "Morning,

Sunshine."

His words are edged with sleep, and I smile back fondly before reaching across to smooth the errant lock away from his brow.

"Morning, pretty boy. Did you sleep well?"

He nods against his pillow, then rolls onto his side so that we are facing one another. "Like a damn baby, Rey."

His satisfied tone makes me chuckle. I move to sit up, but he stops me with a gentle hand on my arm. "Let's just talk for a couple of minutes before the day begins."

I lie back down beside him, tucking my hands beneath my cheek with an easy smile. "Sounds like a wonderful way to start the day."

He brushes my hair behind my ear, then smooths his thumb across my cheekbone. My whole self lights up at his touch as a smile tips his lips.

"I just wanted to check in and make sure you're okay with everything."

Concern colors his face as he holds my gaze with clear purpose, and it warms me to my marrow. "It's all happening so fast. I don't want to see you overwhelmed with all the organization that goes into this stuff."

"*Truly*, I am fine! The wedding planner is doing her thing, the dress…" I trail off with a snort. "Well, you know exactly how the dress is."

He shrugs with nothing short of a shit-eating grin.

"Everything is organized, Alex. Other than the rehearsal tonight, we are full steam ahead for tomorrow! Though I *am* nervous about this photoshoot that you said we need to do in order to keep the media off our backs."

He nods in approval, pushing himself up onto one elbow to look down at me. "It will all be fine. Trust me. And you will make the most stunning bride, Rey."

His eyes are soft, his smile is bright, and my heart accelerates beneath my breast as an almost overwhelming desire to share my newly realized true feelings for him overtakes me.

I open my mouth, the words forming on the tip of my tongue, even as I scream at myself to shut the hell up.

"Alex, I—"

My cell cuts me off with a shrill ring, and I find myself both angry at being disrupted and relieved at being saved from making an idiot of myself.

I twist about, grabbing the chiming cell from the bedside locker at my back.

My stomach bottoms out when I see Sunrise Harbor is calling, and the conversation with Vanessa from earlier this week flits through my mind.

"It's only a matter of time, Reyna. These episodes of lucidity are a gift that not many families receive."

I sign the paperwork, drop my pen heavily, and find Vanessa's kind eyes. "How long?"

She shakes her head sadly. "Outside of these two occasions when she's remembered you, Mariana is mostly quiet and unresponsive. Otherwise, she just sleeps. Alongside other factors, I'm confident that this is the right call, Reyna. There's really no telling how much longer she has left, but hospice care will ensure that she's comfortable. For however long that may be."

"Rey?"

Alex's voice brings me back to the still-ringing cell that's gripped tightly in my hand. I raise horrified eyes to his while Lita's much-loved words flit through my suddenly pounding head.

Your intuition is your gift, mija.

Unable to hear the words I *know* are about to be spoken, I thrust the cell toward Alex in a silent plea. He takes it without hesitation, answering immediately.

"Hello, Reyna's cell. Alex speaking."

As though in slow motion, his face starts to fall with each word spoken into his ear until, eventually, he speaks with his pained eyes firmly holding mine, lending me a strength I know I'm going to need.

"We're on our way."

Nineteen

REYNA

A short ninety minutes later, Ford pulls the town car into the lot at Sunrise Harbor.

He parks and immediately exits the vehicle, giving me and Alex a moment alone.

I inhale shakily through my nostrils, holding it for a beat before I slowly exhale through barely parted lips, willing myself to keep a handle on my emotions for as long as it takes.

Alex is watching me with concern etched on his handsome face. "Rey. Come here, Sunshine."

He opens his arms, and I slide across the seat to allow him to shroud me in his warm embrace, more grateful than he could ever understand for the comfort he's unquestioningly offered.

"Tell me again, please. What did they say?"

This is the third time I've asked, and he answers as patiently as he did the first time.

"They said that she's comfortable. And that she's not in *any* pain, but it's highly unlikely that she will regain consciousness before…" His heart hiccups beneath my ear as he trails off. He expels a heavy sigh, then murmurs lowly, "Before the end."

I slam my eyes closed, holding back the tears threatening to blur my vision. I've spent the years since Lita's diagnosis preparing for this day, researching how things will go and what questions to ask. Rallying my heart to do what I need to do…but *God,* it hurts so bad.

It doesn't matter how much I've readied myself. The time is here. And I'm not sure I can do this.

Right then, as though he can hear my unspoken fear, Alex pulls back enough to palm my cheeks, tilting my head up. His eyes are fierce dark pools brimming with concern, and I can *feel* him filling my heart with the strength to face the pain, to survive the grief.

"I'm here. You're not alone." He swallows harshly, then brushes his lips across my forehead before whispering, *"I've got you, Sunshine."*

My chest burns with the force of holding myself together, and I take another moment to breathe deeply of Alex's comfortingly familiar woodsy scent before I slip from his hold.

My eyes find his as I straighten my spine. "I'm ready."

His nod is heavy before he exits the car, coming around to open my door to take my hand and lead me to the front entrance.

The doors are wide open, with two orderlies standing on either side. They exchange a look when they notice a stoic Ford trailing along behind us, and it almost makes my lips twitch.

His height and black Stetson make him stand out in any crowd, let alone on the front steps of a quiet facility like Sunrise Harbor.

We walk inside to find the corridor is interspersed with medical personnel, clearly from the respite team alongside the usual staff from the nursing home. I nod at everyone whose paths I cross, not really taking note of the faces in my stupor until we eventually reach Lita's room.

I hesitate for a split second until Alex pops his head around the door first before walking inside, pulling me after him.

"Reyna!"

Penelope drops her knitting and practically leaps from her seat by Lita's bedside before enfolding both myself and Alex in her arms. "Mariana would be so happy that you're *both* here."

My eyes land on the still figure on the bed, starting at her feet and slowly traveling up to her face.

A sob catches in my throat when I see how pale she's gotten, even since I'd FaceTimed Penelope yesterday.

She's connected to the same IV fluids they'd administered earlier this week, but there are more monitors and wires than I'd have thought, and the sight is more than a little upsetting.

Penelope releases me from her hold, and I immediately move past her to sit on the edge of Lita's bed. I take her familiar hand in both of mine, suddenly remembering in rapid succession other times when I've needed to hold this same hand.

On my first day at kindergarten.

On my twelfth birthday, when my father sold my beloved Fifi to help pay for gambling debts.

The day I got my full ride to Pearson.

At the appointment where she got her diagnosis…

Two fat tears fall from my lashes, landing on the sheet covering her as I forcibly stop the onslaught of memories from overwhelming me.

Alex gently places his palm on my shoulder, bolstering me, and I inhale a wobbly breath.

"Hey, Lita. We're here."

My words sound much too loud in the room, along with only the rhythmic beep from one of the monitors, and I flinch, lowering my pitch.

"We are going to stay if that's okay." I lean over, pressing a kiss to her wrinkled forehead before whispering against her skin. "I promise you, I'll be right *here*. Until..."

I break off on a hiccup. Alex's hand squeezes my shoulder, and he steps closer behind me, buoying me with his unwavering strength. "I'll be here until the end, Lita."

ALEX

"I appreciate everything you've done today, Bailey. It was no easy feat."

Canceling all the wedding plans for tomorrow, notifying the guests, and keeping the never-ending media at bay a while longer, my stalwart assistant will most definitely require vacation days going forward.

Bailey sighs sadly down the line. "Not at all, Mr. DeMarco. I'm always here to help you, sir."

I murmur my thanks before ending the call and take a beat to check my reflection in the mirror. My hair is in complete disarray, and my cheeks are flushed bright red. I splash water on my face, then heave a deep sigh, wishing to whatever higher power there is to *please* allow me to carry Rey's pain for her.

My eyes slam closed when the image of how dull and drawn she's become in the twelve hours since we arrived at Sunrise Harbor swims before my vision. She hasn't moved from Mari's bedside, not even to use the restroom.

"I need to be with her."

Rey's pain cuts through me like a fucking blunt machete. I can feel it on a visceral level; our connection is *that* real. I only wish I could bear the full brunt of it on her behalf because right now, it's tearing her apart, and the sight is *killing* me.

I exit the restroom, my eyes searching for Rey, who's moved from her high-backed chair at Mari's bedside to climb onto the bed beside her beloved abuela.

She's lowly humming a familiar piece of classical music. It takes me a minute to realize it's the piece she'd have danced to in that year she'd spent at Pearson.

The Dance of the Sugar Plum Fairy.

Tears are streaming down her face, and matching ones fill my own eyes as I close the distance between us, needing to touch her, desperately wanting to share her pain.

To *steal* this wretched agony from her bowed shoulders.

I sit on the other side of Mari to clasp both hers and Rey's hands in mine before joining in with Rey's off-key humming. Our eyes hold while I send every ounce of courage that I can muster to my tiny dancer with the heart of a lion.

As we hum the final bars of the song, Mari's hand twitches in mine and Rey's entire body stiffens abruptly.

Our gazes shift to Mari's face, finding her eyes open and focusing intently on me.

"*Holy shit*!" The words leave my mouth of their own volition as Rey gasps in shock.

Mari's lips attempt to smile, only to fail miserably.

"Lita, oh, Lita!" Reyna gently kisses her abuela's cheek, reaching out blindly to grip my hand in hers. "I *knew* you'd come back to say goodbye. My gift told me you would."

Mari's mouth ticks once more before she angles her head toward the old calendar to her right. She tries to speak again.

"D-dia de Juan…"

She trails off, her breathing labored. I reach forward, brushing my free hand along the side of her face while she watches me with intensity.

"To-today."

The singular word comes out a hoarse croak, but we both know instantly what she means, and our gazes clash when the realization strikes us.

I slide a glance at the wall clock, noting that it is now past midnight, meaning that today is the eleventh of April—our intended wedding day—and so, without a word, I gently press a kiss to Mari's forehead, cupping her cheek with a fond look before instantly jumping into action.

The room is darkened, only lit by candlelight, and even so—dressed in simple black leggings and a cropped grey T-shirt—my bride is the most stunning thing I've ever seen in my entire life.

Rey's eyes hold mine from the opposite side of Mariana's bed, one hand cradling her abuela's while the other sits gently in my grasp.

Her vows are enunciated slowly and with purpose, and I can't help but think that perhaps if I were a better person—someone deserving of the love that I *know* she's capable of—then this could be real.

"I, Reyna Marquez, take you, Alexander DeMarco, as my lawful husband, to have and to hold from this day forward, for better, for worse, for richer, for poorer, in sickness and health, until death do us part."

Reyna blows out a heavy breath and sends me a wobbly smile while a single tear trails down her emotion-stained cheek.

Fr. Thomas, an old friend from my teen years in the UK, had

flown out earlier this week to marry us at the private event that would no longer be taking place later today.

Instead, he'd had a rude wake-up call when Ford had sped to get him from the hotel he was staying at downtown with Liv, Henry, and the boys.

He nods to me now, indicating that it's my turn. I start out haltingly, but gain confidence as I repeat the words after him.

"I, Alexander DeMarco, t-take you, Reyna Marquez, as m-my lawful wife, to have and to hold from this day forward, for better, for worse, for richer, for poorer, in sickness and health, until death do us part."

I look down into Mari's smiling eyes when Fr. Thomas asks for the rings. I shoot her a wink before pulling the two of them from my jeans pocket.

Fr. Thomas is talking, but my eyes are fixed on Rey, and I hear nothing outside of my own heartbeat as I wait for the moment when I can show her the inscription on her wedding band.

She holds up mine, sliding it onto my ring finger as she repeats the words after Fr. Thomas.

Before I do the same, I hold her wedding band up, showing her the engraving on the inside that reads:

I've got you, Sunshine.

Her eyes sparkle with tears, piercing mine, as Penelope, our witness, sobs quietly at the foot of the bed beside Fr. T. I repeat the same words as Rey did previously before easily sliding the band onto her ring finger.

My eyes meet Rey's as she lifts her gaze from the shining band on her left hand. Her face is puffy, red, and tear stained. Her emotions, her easy display of love, grief, loss, and hope—of *everything*—I'm enraptured by it.

I'm enraptured by *her*.

"You may kiss the bride."

Fr. T's words have barely left his mouth before we simultaneously close the gap, our lips meeting far too fleetingly before we both pull back. Rey's eyes flicker open, finding mine for a beat as I feed her as much strength as I can muster.

Mari lightly squeezes my hand, drawing my attention from Rey's wide brown eyes to hers.

"Mijo."

A lump in my throat makes breathing damn near impossible, and I clench my jaw so tightly I genuinely fear I'm about to shatter my damn teeth.

Rey chokes on a sob opposite me, and I grip her small hand even more tightly as I bend over Mari. I press a kiss to her cheek and take a moment to whisper in her ear.

"Abuela de mi corazón, por siempre."

When I straighten, her eyes are shining with joy as they shift from my face to Rey's.

"I love you, *mija*."

Rey releases my hand from hers, dropping onto the bed beside Mari as sobs overtake her small body. Her shoulders heave with the force of her grief while tears crest Mari's lashes, sliding down each side of her face heedlessly, and I'm helpless in the face of love like I've never before experienced.

The love between a parent and their child. Because that's what Mari is to Reyna.

Her mother.

And all I can do is continue to hold Mari's hand while rubbing a soothing palm along Rey's trembling back until she eventually succumbs to an uneasy rest.

Mari drifts off to sleep, her right hand somehow finding its way up to rest atop Rey's head.

At some point, Fr. T and Penelope leave us, and several caretakers take their place as non-invasively as possible.

Wires are unhooked, and various tests are performed – I'm entirely *not* paying attention, because my eyes never once stray from the women before me.

My cell vibrates God knows how many times. Innumerable calls and texts, and at one point, I can hear Ford lowly conversing with someone—possibly Vaughn—in the corridor beyond, yet still, I stand silent, watching over these two amazing women.

The bay outside the window is beginning to streak with the rising sun when Mari stirs.

The beeping monitors from before have been muted, disconnected, or switched off entirely, and the room is utterly silent.

Penelope is sleeping in the high-backed chair by the door, and Rey is still fitfully dozing at her abuela's side when a calmness as I've never experienced before descends upon the room.

Mari's eyes focus clearly on me, and she smiles with her whole face before her hand gently smooths across the back of Reyna's head.

Rey stirs instantly, her eyes fluttering open as she slowly sits up to look down on her serene-faced Abuela.

Mari's eyes drift from my face to Reyna's, and something tangible passes silently between the two of them. Their eyes hold for a long while as the room fills with the dawn's early light until Mari's attention shifts slightly, her eyes moving to something behind her grandchild.

She inhales suddenly, and a smile overtakes her face, her eyes shining with uncompromising delight.

"I'm on my way, Thiago."

Her eyelids slowly close with a small smile tipping the edges of her mouth. The light fades from her face, and her breath leaves her body in a low, contented sigh as her grip on my hand slackens.

The sound of Rey's quiet sobs calls me to her side, and I pull her into my embrace as grief washes through the room with the devastation of a hurricane.

And all that I can do is hope that I can be strong enough to help my sunshine to find the rainbow waiting on the other side.

Twenty

REYNA

I'd been in complete and utter denial after we'd gotten Lita's diagnosis in my final year of high school. I think we *both* had.

In accepting the scholarship to Pearson, I know *now* that I'd believed I could have it all.

Even when my father had lost the house and taken all of Lita's money, I had truly believed that everything would be okay.

Denial.

I'd lived and breathed it for over a damn year, eventually giving way to a slow-burning annoyance when I had to start working a million and one odd jobs just to make ends meet.

Never once did I associate the fact that I'd had to pause my time at Pearson with my underlying exasperation and a deep-seated sense of unfairness. I was too busy trying to get by and ensuring Lita was being cared for that I didn't notice the near-constant tension in my body.

It was only in hindsight that I saw that two-year period for what it was.

Anger.

And it only ebbed—never leaving entirely—when I eventually left Pearson altogether, telling myself that one day I'd go back if I did my job well. If I attempted to live a life outside of my passion. If I was a good, dutiful employee, neighbor, granddaughter, friend…

If, if, if.

Bargaining.

Not that I realized it all those years. It became ingrained in my everyday life. Be good, be kind, be courteous, and maybe, just *maybe,* I'd wake up back home in Connecticut to find that everything had just been a bad dream.

That my future at Pearson and on the stage was still bright and waiting for me in the city that never sleeps.

And so, I really shouldn't have been surprised when I sank into a chasm of hopelessness in the days following Lita's memorial service. Innumerable days and nights ran into one another as the gravity of loss permeated my bones, making the effort of even getting out of bed too much for my weary body.

I was present, yet wholly distant, and even as the worry in Alex's whiskey eyes grew with each passing hour, I could feel myself sink deeper.

Depression.

Then, the darkness consumed me, and I willingly gave myself over to its numbing embrace.

Time passes, or maybe it doesn't. I feel nothing. I'm in a waking sleep, hearing people come and go around me, but nothing matters beyond the veil of a soul-deep darkness that surrounds me.

It has become its own entity in the black void I've sunk into.

And still, light finds a way.

The bed dips at my back as I feel Alex lie down beside me, rousing me from my half-sleep.

I feel removed, almost as though I'm floating above my bed, staring down at the scene unfolding rather than being an actual participant.

Alex smooths my knotty hair back from my face, his hand lingering on my shoulder for a beat before encouraging me to roll over onto my back.

His concern-filled eyes rake across my face and his jaw tics. "Rey, this can't continue. It's been three weeks."

I blink heavily, expelling a breath as my chest tightens.

Three weeks without her. A lifetime to go. And I can't find the strength inside of me to rise like I know I need to.

"Something has to give, Rey. You're not eating. You're barely drinking. I've watched you grieve for three weeks, and every day you've drifted further away." Alex's brow creases, and he blows out a breath. "I'm sorry, but I can't sit here and do nothing anymore. I can't watch you disappear right before my eyes."

He raises himself to kneel on the bed before scooping me up into his arms, and there's a crack in the shroud that has been my safe haven these past weeks.

"Hey, put me *down*!"

He doesn't listen, instead standing and marching toward the ensuite, where he unceremoniously dumps me onto my ass in the freestanding shower before turning it on.

"What the fucking hell!" My shriek of outrage echoes throughout the space as cold water rains down on me.

Alex steps in with me, kneeling beside me on the tiled floor with a pained expression. "She wouldn't want you to mourn like this, Sunshine."

He clasps my face in his warm palms as I slam my eyes shut against the welling emotions that I long to suppress, even for just a while longer.

"*Please,* Rey. If not for yourself, then for *her*. Let me help you."

My eyes open as icy water drips from my lashes, mingling with the tears I can no longer restrain.

Emotion bubbles up my throat, almost choking me as a keening cry spills from my lips, and the dam bursts.

"I—I can't. I—" I gulp air frantically, trying to fill my lungs, but even so, I feel like I'm suffocating.

Alex places a palm on my heaving back as my despair takes over, and all the feelings I've withheld slam into me like a freight train. Harsh sobs wrack my frame as the water pours over both of us. Alex sits on the wet floor before gathering me in his arms, cradling me in the comfort of his strong embrace.

My cries eventually turn to hiccuping sobs, mostly drowned out by the sound of the water splashing over us, and I lift my head from Alex's shoulder to find his eyes filled with tears of his own, his face stained with the color of his emotions.

I press my palm to his flushed cheek, and he swallows harshly as he brings up a hand to softly grip my wrist.

"Please don't leave me, Rey." The desperation in his tone rests heavily on my heart as his voice drops to a whisper. "I *can't* lose you."

We sit in silence for a long while until a shiver wracks my body.

He shifts me from his lap before adjusting the water temperature.

"Are you up to taking a shower?"

I nod gratefully as the water begins to heat, warming my icy skin.

Alex grips my ring finger, sliding my forgotten-about wedding band from my hand and sliding it into the back pocket of his saturated jeans.

"Let me help you." He lifts the hem of my dirty pink T-shirt and encourages me to strip out of my wet clothes before leaving me in my underwear.

"I'll take these, and you can follow me down when you're up to it."

He lifts my chin, pinning me with an intense stare. "Take your time, Sunshine."

The water is a balm to my soul, miraculously washing away *some* of the constant aching loss and helping to make me feel slightly like myself once more.

I switch off the shower once I've finished washing and towel dry my thinner-than-usual body in the ensuite, already feeling so much better than before. The pain is still there, but somehow it doesn't feel as sharp following Alex's heartfelt plea.

I feel seen. Cared for. I feel human enough to throw on a pair of old black sweatpants with a baggy grey Tee and venture beyond my bedroom door for the first time since Lita's service.

Has it really *been three weeks since the service?*

It had been an intimate farewell with just a handful of staff from Sunrise Harbor, Penelope and Vanessa among them, along with Alex's siblings, his work colleague, Grayson, who'd looked as miserable as I felt, and his friend Vaughn.

Ford had stood sentinel, silent and stoic as always, as we'd paid our respects, and Alex had even given a beautiful eulogy when I'd been unable to form a basic sentence.

I'd held it together long enough to get home from the service and then disappeared into my grief, where time had ceased to exist for me, apparently.

Three weeks!

My bare feet slowly and silently descend the staircase, and my eyes land on a dry-clothed Alex as he flits from the dishwasher to the stove in the open-plan kitchen.

He's wearing the same clothes as I am, except his T-shirt is black, and his sweatpants are grey. The corner of my lip tics in the first sign of joy I have felt in what feels like forever just as he raises his head.

He watches my slow approach, leaving his place at the stove to meet me at the bottom of the stairs.

His arms encircle me before I've made it past the last step, and he picks me up, locking me in his strong embrace. He stands there for a long beat, burying his nose in my neck and inhaling deeply.

I can *feel* sheer relief emanating from his body.

When he gently sets me back down, he presses a kiss to my brow before interlocking our fingers and tugging me after him toward the kitchen.

My nose twitches when I smell the inimitable scents of tomato and garlic with each step closer to the kitchen. A large pot on the stove confirms my suspicion.

"Spaghetti?"

Alex answers over his shoulder with a soft nod. "I wanted to make you some comfort food, but I'm afraid tamales are not in my wheelhouse."

My chest swells at his thoughtfulness. "Spaghetti is the perfect comfort food for today."

I slide onto a stool at the kitchen island, watching as he moves fluidly from one task to the next. He shoots me an easy grin as he adds a ladleful of sauce to a pan of pasta, coating the noodles with several flicks of his wrist.

He plates it with ease before dropping a bowl down in front of me with a smile. "Eat up, Sunshine."

When I twist some onto my fork, he watches as I bring it to my mouth.

"Mmm!" A moan of delight escapes my lips when the taste of a well-seasoned sauce explodes on my taste buds.

"This is *so* good."

He moves around to the opposite side of the island and plates up his own dish before tucking in. I can feel his eyes on me while I eat, but I'm too absorbed in filling my stomach to do anything further than vaguely note it.

I'm full to bursting by the time I've even made it halfway through my food, and I sit back, rubbing my slightly-less concave stomach in complete disappointment.

"I can't eat another bite."

He chuckles around a mouthful of spaghetti as I dab the sides of my undoubtedly sauce-covered mouth with my napkin. "Don't worry. I have plenty of other meals up my sleeve. We'll round out those curves again in no time."

I ball up my napkin with a fake gasp of indignation before tossing it across the island, hitting him square in the face.

The fork of spaghetti that was poised at his mouth goes flying, sending saucy noodles splattering across his T-shirt before landing with a wet *plop* on his lap.

My eyes blow wide while my mouth forms an O as he looks down at the mess I've made. He lifts his head, quirks a brow, and smirks.

"So that's how you want to play, Sunshine?"

He grabs the pasta from his lap, and I jump to my feet, pivoting to make a dash toward the stairs when I feel the noodles hit me in the center of my back.

I spin around just in time to see him fist another handful of food from his plate to raise it up with a devilish smile.

"Don't. You. *Dare*!"

I narrow my eyes as menacingly as I can, and he shrugs before I find myself with a face full of spaghetti.

Noodles cover my line of sight, and I gingerly pluck them from my face, dropping them to the tiles beneath my feet with an arched brow and a curled lip.

His howl of laughter reverberates through the penthouse, and even covered in spaghetti sauce, I feel a pinprick of light shining in a world that has been wholly dark for the last three weeks.

"Ooh, pretty boy!" I step closer to my half-eaten plate of food, taking relish in the slippery texture of the noodles when I grab a handful, and flick my gaze to a grinning Alex. "You asked for it!"

I launch the spaghetti, and it lands on his shoulder, so I immediately reload while cursing my aim before ducking behind the island.

"Come out, come out wherever you are..."

I can hear Alex squelch his hand in some pasta, and so I drop to my knees to scurry around the island, ducking out to surprise him from behind.

"Yoo-hoo!"

He spins at my exclamation. "Have some—"

I cut him off when I fling the spaghetti, hitting him between the eyes. His shout of disgust makes me snort, and I quickly shuffle back to my almost depleted pasta dish to scoop up the last super saucy remnants.

Silence follows after I duck behind the island again, pressing my back against it as I listen closely for a telltale sign that he's about to attack.

My eyes shift left then right as my heart palpitates in my chest, waiting on the inevitable retaliation.

A sharp whistle from above makes me look up, surprise painting my face. Alex is kneeling on the island, his half-eaten dinner in hand, while his face wears *the* biggest self-congratulatory grin.

The dish tips over, sending the spaghetti careening down and onto my surprised face almost in slow motion.

My cry of indignation is met with a full-body laugh before Alex drops down beside me, holding his stomach.

"You should—" Chuckle.

"See your—" Howl.

"Face!" Snort.

He throws his head back as laughter wracks his body, and beneath the faceful of spaghetti, I pop a brow before thrusting my own sauce-filled hand forward to connect cleanly with his smug face.

His mirth freezes on his features, moving closer to pull me onto his stained lap. He clucks me under the chin with a tomatoey index finger, his smile making me genuinely *smile* like I haven't in so damn long.

"I love a girl who can hold her own, Sunshine."

His eyes are brimming with admiration, even when dripping with spaghetti sauce, and he suddenly shifts, digging his hand into his right pocket.

"But a *wife* who can hold her own…" He trails off as he flourishes my wedding band before sliding it onto my stained finger. "Now that shit is elite."

I'm helpless to stop a grin from blooming on my face, and I shove his chest playfully.

"Incorrigible asshole." I narrow my eyes exaggeratedly. "Now I have to shower again!"

He snorts, palming my cheeks before bending my head to peck my nose briefly. "In all fairness, you could do with it."

I tilt my head. "Huh?"

He scrunches his nose and shakes his head. "No showers for three weeks, Rey? One word – *smelly*!"

ALEX

The sight of Rey asleep in my bed is one that, at times, I thought I may never see again.

These past three weeks following Mariana's ceremony were some of the darkest days I've ever had – and for *me*, that's really saying something.

Today marked the four-week anniversary of Mari's passing, and I'd woken up this morning *knowing* I couldn't allow things to continue as they had been. I'd not known exactly what I was going to do, but seeing her so despondent on the bed like that, I'd just acted.

I run my fingers across her slightly damp hair, tucking it behind her ear so that I can soak up her natural beauty.

My eyes instantly note the changes these three weeks have wrought. Her complexion is dimmed, darkness mars beneath her eyes, and her cheeks hold a gauntness I long to banish.

If she knew the month I've had since Mari's passing, she'd sink even further into the abyss, so I mention nothing of the incessant media that are raking through every part of her life—of *our* life.

And I won't say a damn thing about the tragic death of Grayson's wife a few short days after Mariana's service.

I shiver at the knowledge that life can change in the space of a heartbeat, and before I know what I've done, I'm gently nudging my sleeping wife—*my wife*—awake.

Her eyes slowly open to half-mast. "Hmm?"

She buries farther into her pillow, but I'm unstoppable now, so

I gather her close in my hold despite her cries of annoyance.

"Rey, baby?"

I dimly note that, to my knowledge, I've never referred to her in such an intimate tone, and clearly, she does too, because her eyes fly open. "Yes?"

"How would you feel about a little…road trip, of sorts?"

She blinks heavily once, then twice, before her face lights up in her signature Sunshine smile.

"Where do you want to go, pretty boy?"

ALEX

"So…was your first flight everything you wanted it to be?"

My question is met with silence, followed by an agitated murmur.

"Why won't you tell me where we are?"

Rey's eyes are narrowed as she watches me from the seat opposite mine on the private jet owned by DeMarco Holdings.

The wheels have just hit the tarmac on the runway of our destination, and I've had the flight staff pull all the blinds for the entire trip, so Rey has no clue where we are right now.

My lips twitch, and her eyes narrow further when she notices.

As she folds her arms over her sweatshirt-clad chest, she settles deeply back against her seat to regard me with openly suspicious eyes.

"Time will tell, Sunshine." I grin back at her, refusing to say more.

She checks her watch. "Around five hours in the air, right?"

I tip my head in acknowledgment.

"West Coast? Vegas? Mmm…" She pouts in thought. "Vancouver? Am I getting close?"

I arch a brow, keeping silent as she leans forward, placing her elbows on her knees.

"Is it warm? Cold? I didn't pack any long johns if there's going to be snow, pretty boy."

I allow myself a self-satisfied grin, but still, I say nothing. She huffs before sitting back in her seat.

"Incorrigible asshole."

My bark of laughter fills the plane, and I spot her own lips tipping upwards in an unwanted smile.

"You love it, though."

She arches a brow. "I really don't."

My smile grows even wider. "Yes, you do, Sunshine. You like my special brand of assholism, don't even try to deny it."

She chuckles as she shakes her head. "You are the *worst*."

Tanya, our flight attendant, pokes her head around the door with a massive smile. "Everything is ready for you."

I stand, holding my hand out for Rey, which she begrudgingly takes. Then she rises alongside me, following me to the front of the plane.

Light from beyond the open door floods inside, and I usher her forward toward the top of the waiting airstairs.

She stops, clapping her free hand over her eyes, and I follow suit when we're both blinded by the sunlight outside the darkened body of the plane that we've left behind.

Once our eyes have adjusted, we move onto the top step. I'm standing at Rey's back when she stops suddenly, and a gasp tumbles from her mouth.

"*Oh my* God!"

A white SUV is parked not twenty feet from the base of the stairs, where two men—one being our driver, the other our pilot—are standing on either side of the vehicle. They are each holding one end of a sign that reads:

BIENVENIDOS A COSTA RICA

Rey pivots on her heel, launching herself into my waiting arms.

"I can't *believe*—" She breaks off on a sob, then nuzzles her head deeper in against my neck. I hold her even closer, soaking up this moment as I take a deep breath, inhaling her essence.

"Believe it, baby."

Pulling back, she pierces me with glistening doe eyes containing a look that makes my heart skip a beat. Her palms gently cup my face, utterly at odds with the fervor in her gaze.

"Thank you!"

She dusts her thumbs along my cheekbones before pulling my head down, grazing her lips off of mine as though it's the most natural thing in the world.

Dropping her hands, she moves away, giving me her back. Automatically, I step closer to align my chest with her spine as she looks out at the waiting car, my body registering the loss of her warmth instantaneously and not taking kindly to the sensation.

My mouth drops to her ear, whispering against the shell. "The sun will always set, Rey. But even when everything is dark, you can take heart in the fact that it will rise again tomorrow."

She tugs my arms around her waist, cuddling back against my body, and I feel a wave of possessive contentment wash over me, knowing that I'm bringing the sunshine back into her life.

"Have a wonderful trip, Mr. and Mrs. DeMarco."

Tanya's well wishes make my feet falter as we begin to descend the airstairs, and I dimly note, somewhere in the recesses of my subconscious, that despite Rey's joy at the moment, given her crush from last month, this trip might not have been the brightest idea.

REYNA

"This place is like something out of a movie!"

I race up the stairs with the enthusiasm of Fifi, laughing wildly when I fly across the wooden floor to the balcony beyond the living room.

The view outside of the private casa that Alex has rented for the next couple of days is awe-inducing.

A canopy of treetops stretches all the way to the turquoise ocean beyond. My eyes drink their fill as Alex's footsteps sound behind me.

"This has to be the best thing I've ever seen."

My face hurts from smiling so hard, living a dream I've had for as long as I can remember.

Touching down in Tamarindo was quite easily the biggest shock of my life.

The entire car trip from there to here had been spent alternating between pointing at the scenery as it flew by and thanking Alex profusely for his beyond-thoughtful gesture.

In my despair since Lita's passing, one of the hardest parts was knowing that I'd never again experience the easy joy and soothing calm of her presence. Until I'd stepped from the jet and felt the breeze of her homeland wash over my skin, bringing her back to me in a way I'd never have thought possible.

Alex's arms wrap around my waist, and his chin rests on

my shoulder. He presses a kiss to my cheekbone, tightening his hold, and I inhale his inimitable scent, allowing my eyelids to fall closed in pure joy.

"Thank you, Alex."

He snorts softly. "You don't need to thank me. Your happiness is thanks enough, baby."

Baby.

I try and fail to push down the familiar rush of butterflies in my stomach at his casual use of the intimate word.

There's a knock on our door, and I spin in his hold, our faces *almost* touching.

"Who could that be?"

He rubs the tip of his nose off mine with a lopsided smile that sets my foolish heart fluttering before gathering me in against his side so we can both cross the wide-open living space to answer the door.

What greets us is nothing short of a whirlwind.

A man dressed in chef whites breezes past us with three helpers scurrying after him.

Five women, each pushing a rack of various items of clothing, file in one after the other, nodding at both of us as they stride down the hall toward one of the many guest bedrooms.

Two men follow them, stopping for a moment to address Alex.

"Where shall we set up, Mr. DeMarco?"

Alex sends me a wink. "The third bedroom on the right should be large enough, Federico. *Gracias.*"

Once everyone is inside the huge casa, Alex closes the door and turns to me with a devilment-filled smirk. "Surprise!"

I'm helpless to stop the smile that undoubtedly lights up my face, and I step closer to encircle his waist, pressing my cheek against his chest. His arms go around me, and he drops a lingering kiss to the top of my head.

"Thank you."

"Anything for my Sunshine."

We stand like that for a long moment, the sounds of the other occupants of the house reaching our ears, and still, we don't move. Until a voice sounds behind us.

"We're ready for you, Mr. and Mrs. DeMarco."

I blush furiously at the easy use of my married name, the thumb of my left hand immediately grazing across the underside of my wedding band.

Alex catches my right hand, and we move down the hall to the third bedroom on the right.

Once inside, I spot two massage tables that have been set up alongside one another in the candlelit space.

I inhale sharply. "Oh my!"

Alex squeezes my hand as the two masseuses slip from the room. "A full body massage is exactly what you need after that flight, and…" He trails off as his forehead puckers. "Well, after everything, Rey."

I swallow with a gulp, blown away by the sheer thoughtfulness. "Thank you."

He nods softly in acknowledgment before dropping my hand to point out a door behind me. "There's a bathroom there if you'd like to get ready."

"Ready?"

He grins, then hands me a soft white towel.

"Take off everything, including your panties." His grin broadens as his eyes sparkle with mischief. "If you're wearing them, that is."

Swatting him away, he slinks off to the opposite side of the room with a howl of laughter.

I slip into the ensuite with a parting shot over my shoulder that makes him laugh even harder. "Incorrigible asshole."

Once I've stripped, I wrap myself in the towel Alex gave to me and step back into the bedroom.

The air is knocked from my body when my eyes land on a bare-chested pretty boy leaning back against one of the massage tables. His head is down, his legs crossed at the ankles, and the skimpy towel that's slung across his hips does precisely nothing to conceal what lies beneath.

I blow out a breath through almost pursed lips, and the sound draws his attention.

His eyes slowly climb my body, affecting me as deeply as if it were his hands gliding over each and every curve until his gaze finds mine. His jaw clenches noticeably, and his white towel begins to tent.

I inhale sharply before he moves swiftly to lie face down on the table, but not before openly adjusting himself.

He looks me up and down once more before speaking as though to himself. "Definitely *not* one of my brighter ideas."

There's a knock at the door before I can ask what he means, and Alex buries his face in the hole at the top of the table, calling out, "Enter."

I hastily settle atop the table as the two men re-enter.

"Here, Mrs. DeMarco. Allow me to help you."

The taller of the two rushes toward me, making short work of assisting me into place. "I'm Bastiano, and I shall be your masseuse. My colleague Federico will work on your husband today. Please just relax and tell me if you need me to go harder or softer at times, okay?"

I settle into the table, but instead of putting my head down as Alex has, I rest it on my forearms so that I can look at him.

His masseuse, Federico, has already begun kneading the olive skin of Alex's muscular back, and I'm utterly enchanted at the sight of the glistening oils moving across the smooth expanse.

I watch Federico's hands for a long while as Bastiano works on the tense muscles in my shoulders.

A moan escapes my lips when he works on a particularly large knot above my right shoulder blade, and my eyes close as the tension in my body begins to shift.

"Mmm, right there, Bastiano."

My lids are hooded in unconcealed bliss when I feel Alex's eyes on me, and I shift my gaze from his back toward his face.

He's taken the same position as me, his eyes burning amber flames as he glares at Bastiano's hands. He moves his eyes up to mine, holding me in his fiery stare.

My breathing accelerates, and my heart hiccups as undeniable desire flows between us in a look that neither of us is willing to break. Our gazes continue to hold, the tension building to unbearable heights, and each flare of his nostrils or tic of his jaw sends a ripple of want straight to my disgracefully wet pussy.

"That'll be enough for today, Federico." Alex rises in one fluid movement, giving me his back as he folds the towel around his waist. "Thank you."

Without another word, he leaves the room, leaving both masseuses with puzzled looks on their faces.

"I'm good, too, Bastiano. Thank you."

My masseuse instantly removes his hands from my calves where he was diligently working out the kinks, and both men leave the room without another word.

With a furrowed brow, I rise from the table and shower immediately, washing the fragrant oils from my body. I'm confused and horny, and it's *not* a nice combination.

I've just toweled myself off, when I hear a knock on the door of the ensuite.

"Yes?" I keep my reply short, knowing it can only be one person.

Alex clears his throat. "I brought you some clean clothes. I'll leave them on the table."

My stomach swirls despite myself. Having been the one taking care of Lita and disregarding myself for so long, it feels strange and so damn nice to have someone looking out for me.

"Thank you."

I peek into the room, finding it empty, and then slip into the simple white cotton dress that he'd left for me. My bare feet pad from the room and down the hallway, finding Alex waiting by the front door.

"Did you enjoy your massage?"

His words are carefree, his tone light, but there's *something* in his eyes that I can't put my finger on.

"It was glorious. Thank you."

I close the distance between us, desperate to bridge the invisible gap that has somehow formed in the space of the last hour, and tuck myself in against the firmness of his chest.

His arms wrap around me, and I feel like I can breathe again as I'm cocooned in a feeling of belonging, of safety.

Of devotion.

And salvation.

I exhale a sigh of sheer contentment, and Alex's arms tighten around me as his breathing accelerates.

"Rey, I—" He stops as a voice calls out behind him.

"Dinner is ready, Mr. and Mrs. DeMarco."

I register two things simultaneously.

Firstly, I'm *far* too fond of my new title, and secondly, the smells wafting from the kitchen make my stomach scream with hunger.

Alex steps out of my embrace and intertwines our fingers before leading me to the stairs with a small smile.

"What did you want to—"

He shakes his head. "Nothing, baby. I just wanted to say I'm glad you had a nice massage."

My smile is bright, even though I know that's not what he was about to say.

"The dining area is up here."

I follow after him, my mouth dropping open wide most unbecomingly when we step out onto an elevated platform designed entirely to take in the incredible view.

The sun is hanging low in the sky, casting a multitude of shades across the darkening sea. The treetops that stretch across the distance between us and those waves are teeming with life.

There's a low table set for two that's surrounded by throw pillows in a variety of deep hues, and the whole space is lit up with lanterns that dot the floor.

"*Wow*!"

My whispered exclamation reaches Alex's ears, and he smiles broadly while he helps me get comfortable before lowering himself to the cushions opposite me.

We've barely gotten settled when the chef's helpers begin to bring course after course up the small stairs directly to our table.

My mouth waters when platters of tamales, tortillas, and tacos ticos land on the table between us. Bowls of chifrijo—pork rinds on beans covered in chimichurri—and gallo pinto—a simple side of beans and white rice—soon follow.

"Are you planning on feeding a small army?" I pop a brow, trying to suppress my rising smile.

Alex snorts, arching a brow of his own as his eyes drop down my body before returning to mine. "I told you we'd round out those curves again, Sunshine."

The sound of my belly laughter fills the late evening sky surrounding us and clearly startles some of the wildlife beneath the sea of trees when a shrill screech erupts from somewhere to our left.

I shake my head as I reach for a tacos ticos. "I can't even be mad at that because *this* is perfection."

Taking a bite out of the crispy taco, my eyes roll back in my head. "Mmm! This is absolutely out-of-this-world good. Here." I thrust my half-eaten taco forward. "Take a bite."

He leans closer, taking a huge mouthful with his eyes fixed firmly on mine the entire time. He nods as he chews, and I watch how his jaw works, utterly caught up in the movement as I nibble on my lip.

"Delicious." His tongue darts out to lick his lips.

My eyes shoot to his guiltily, and he sends me a knowing smirk as he reaches for a bowl of chifrijo. "I see that crush is still hanging around."

He chuckles, his eyes holding mine mischievously.

I narrow my eyes and pop the remaining taco into my mouth. Once I've swallowed, I lean across the table, a pout playing on my lips.

"I did tell you to be a little less like yourself, Alexander DeMarco."

Then I throw my arms out wide, gesturing around us. "However, I don't think you understood the assignment."

He throws his head back when he laughs loudly, and several more screeches ring out from the forest beneath us, which only makes us both laugh even harder.

I compose myself faster than him, shooting him a narrow look.

"You really are striving for perfection, aren't you, pretty boy? Next, you'll tell me you can speak five languages and are some kind of math whiz!"

I playfully roll my eyes, and he shrugs as he swallows a mouthful of food. "I'm an accomplished pianist also, Sunshine."

My mouth drops open. "You're fucking with me, right?"

He chuckles as he chews a mouthful of his food before shaking his head, making his hair fall across his face.

"Nope! 'Fraid not. Good old Mother, may she rest in Hell, was meticulous in ensuring that I excelled at everything she believed would make me a better heir to the company than Henry."

Blowing out a heavy breath, he puts his half-eaten chifrijo back onto the table between us. "It wasn't about helping me be my best self, it was always about how things appeared on the outside. How my talents reflected upon *her*."

My heart breaks for the beautifully flawed man before me as he chooses to share his decades' old, but still very fresh, wounds with me. And my need to comfort him, to bring him even a small measure of peace, flows through me.

I crawl around the side of the low table, and kneel beside him, placing my palms on his chest as my eyes hold his.

"The heart that beats in here"—I gently pat his chest —"is because of who you *are,* not what you can *do,* or what you can *give* to others. You are the best man I've ever known, Alex DeMarco. Our past is not a reflection of our future. *You* are not the sum of *their* mistakes."

He gathers me in his embrace before I've even finished speaking, and we just hold each other as the sounds of the rainforest beneath us fill the evening sky.

Eventually, he spins me around, settling me in against the crook of his arm. "Look, the sun is setting."

The colors that light up the sky as the sun sets on the horizon are breathtaking, and I watch in rapture.

"It's so beautiful."

My words are murmured low, but Alex reaches down to grip my chin with his index finger and thumb. He tilts my chin up so he can watch me with an intensity that makes the whiskey of his eyes darken to black pools, and my stomach swirls.

"It's the most beautiful sight I've ever seen in my life, Sunshine."

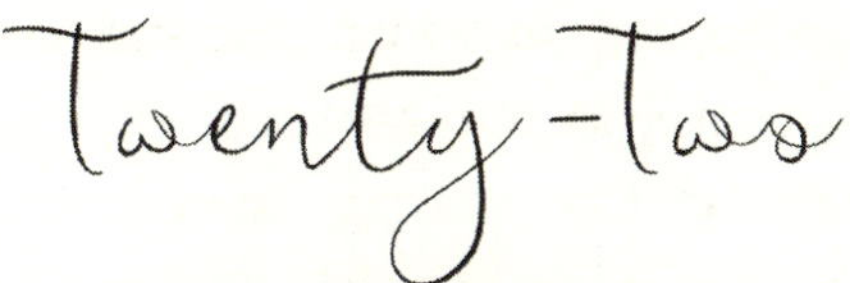

ALEX

My eyes follow the curve of Rey's bare shoulder as it rises and falls with each soft, even breath.

Her back is facing me, her long dark hair fanned out across the white pillows of our bed, and I don't even bother to try to control the urge to run my fingers through those smooth locks.

The silken strands tickle my fingertips, and I close my eyes, relishing the feeling of contentment that resonates through my whole body.

Visions from yesterday of Reyna wrapped in a small white towel assault my mind, and I inhale a deep breath when my already hard cock throbs against my Calvins.

The moan she'd made during the massage had almost destroyed me. I was instantly transported to when she'd come undone for me at the gala back in Manhattan.

"Kiss me, Alex. Please."

The memory of her erratic breathing as her undoubtedly sweet cunt drenched my fingers before I'd devoured her orgasm with a savage kiss is one that lives rent-free at the forefront of my mind.

I revisit that moment more often than I should—more often than is sane, to be truthful—and the more I remember, the less I care about crossing that invisible line I've drawn between us.

The one that keeps her safe from being inevitably ruined by me and my serial screwing up.

A woman like Rey deserves the best that this life has to offer. She deserves the life my brother has given to my best friend. A home filled with love, light, and children who are reared by parents who wanted them and who care for them beyond measure.

That is something I don't think I would be able to give her.

I wouldn't know how. Barring a damn miracle.

Rey stirs, and I slowly withdraw my hand from her hair before she turns over onto her back with a smile that outshines the early morning sunlight filtering into our room.

"Morning."

I smile in reply. "Sleep well?"

"*So* well. Thank you."

I'd had our long-standing *Grey's Anatom*y ready to go after dinner last night. We'd managed a whole episode before she'd passed out, and I'd been only too glad to follow suit.

I'd not even bothered having one of the other eleven bedrooms made up for Rey. I'm past the point of pretending I'm not thoroughly addicted to the simple act of being in her presence.

"Have you made plans for today?"

I shoot her a wide smile, mentally ready for what's to come, even if my dick has yet to get the memo.

"There's a gift for you in the top drawer of your nightstand. It will explain everything." My brow creases. "Trust me when I say everything will be okay. *I've got you*. Always."

She regards me with questioning eyes, and then nods slowly before stretching her limbs with a yawn. Her chest strains against the satiny fabric of her nightdress, and my ravenous eyes watch her slightly pebbled nipples press against the material.

Checking myself before she notices my downright lecherous stare, I take the opportunity to slide from the bed, giving her my back while I march intently toward the open door of our ensuite.

"Where are you going?"

Confusion colors her tone when she calls after me, and I stop to glance over my shoulder.

"I'm going to take a hot shower, Sunshine."

Her eyebrows hit her hairline. "In this heat?"

I smirk when she takes the bait. "Well, it's like a normal shower, except it's got me in it."

Her laughter follows me into the shower, where I step under icy cold water that does sweet fuck all for the boner that won't get a clue.

REYNA

When I've finally stopped laughing, I reach for the nightstand with a smile that turns to a frown when I find a green, well-used book.

I settle into the Lotus pose in the middle of the bed and gently open the first page.

When I note Lita's familiar handwriting, my breath hitches.

Your Roots

My teary eyes slowly rise from the book to the closed door of the ensuite before drifting back down when I hear the sound of the shower running.

Trembling hands turn the page, and a half-sob, half-laugh tumbles from my mouth.

There's a black-and-white photograph of a small baby in the arms of a smiling woman, a preening man at her shoulder with a matching broad smile. My beautiful abeula's neat script is underneath.

Born June Fourth in Santa Cruz to Julio and Inez

Once I've studied the image to my heart's content, I carefully turn to the next page, where I find a photo of a teenage girl, clearly my abuela, holding the hand of an exceptionally handsome older man. I peer closely at the image, my eyes bulging when I realize that she's with my abuelo.

He's looking at her as though she hung the moon while she smiles brightly for the camera.

Met Thiago Marquez. January First

I swallow roughly at the significance of that date for me. The day my mother disappeared, leaving me at a church with nothing and no one.

I move on with a lump in my throat that is dislodged by a low sob when my eyes see the third image. Lita is wearing a very simple bridal gown, beaming a smile at my abuelo, who's only got eyes for his new wife as they stand on church steps, confetti falling all around them.

Married in Santa Cruz. Dia de Juan Santamaria

My index finger gently traces every part of the image as my emotions bubble up, spilling down my cheeks in bittersweet agony. I slam my eyelids shut, inhaling sharply through my nose as I attempt to get a handle on my runaway feelings.

Several deep breaths later, I've composed myself enough to open my eyes and study the image once more.

They look so happy.

A tremulous smile hangs on the edges of my lips when I scan the image, finding nothing but love painted across every part of it.

I turn the page with a soft smile that turns to wonder at the next image. It's a photo of a heavily pregnant Lita, one hand resting on the curve of her belly while the other points at the camera as though she's playfully rebuking the person snapping the picture.

Delivered Victor at home. April Ninth

My chest tightens with a soul-deep sadness for my strong abuelita, knowing how the child she carried in this picture is a no-good, weak-willed degenerate, and I simply can't reconcile how he came from the pure love that my grandparents shared.

I turn the page again, finding one last picture, and the emotion I'm barely keeping a lid on comes rushing to the surface.

It's a photograph of me as the Sugar Plum Fairy backstage at the Pearson Christmas Gala on the night we'd performed with text beneath that both breaks my heart while simultaneously healing it.

My greatest achievement in this life. Manhattan

Sobs consume my frame as a deep, keening cry spills from

my lips, and I bury my face in my hands, giving myself over to feeling everything I know that I need to feel in order to keep from sinking back into that bone-weary depression.

Her greatest achievement… Oh, Lita.

And that's how Alex finds me when he opens the ensuite door moments later.

"Oh, Rey."

He crosses the space, dropping onto the bed beside me to gather me in his shower-damp arms, allowing me to fall to pieces in his embrace.

"Shush, Sunshine. It's okay." He rocks me like he would a newborn, the gentle rise and fall soothing me until I've gotten myself mostly under control.

"Did you know? Did you read…?"

He murmurs softly. "Yes."

"How did you get this?"

I turn my tear-stained face up to his, and he meets my gaze with a comforting warmth. "She gave it to me. At Sunrise Harbor, the day you danced in the courtyard."

He swallows heavily. "She asked me to give it to you…but only when the time was right."

My entire self fills to bursting with undeniable love for this man—my off-limits *husband*—and I settle myself even farther into his arms, wanting nothing more than to embed myself so deeply underneath his skin that he can't help but love me back.

"Have you read to the end, Rey?"

I shake my head against his chest. "No…I couldn't." I pluck the book from the sheets, turning my head to face him again. "Could you…would you, please—"

He gently takes the book from my hand, palming the back of my head with his other to pull me close enough to dust his lips across my forehead.

His whispered words are a balm to the ache in my heart. "I've got you, Sunshine. *Always*."

I cuddle in against the width of his chest, and he reaches around me to hold the book open so that both of us can see. He moves past the picture of me onto the next page, where there's a hand-drawn map of Costa Rica.

I squint my eyes as they dart from one marked location to the next.

Several small locations within Santa Cruz are marked with an X, and a list of each location is neatly written across the end of the page.

Realization dawns, and I sit up with an exclamation. "It's a map of her life!"

Alex closes the book, tugging me close against him before burying his face in my hair to whisper, "And today, we're going to follow her footsteps, Sunshine."

Our first stop was the house of Lita's childhood, followed by the Iglesia, where she had been a bride, but sadly both were no longer standing. However, even just being in the same place where she'd been was enough for me.

I felt her presence as clearly as I felt Alex's hand in mine. As clearly as I've felt her since stepping off the jet.

The marketplace where she'd met my abuelo was teeming with vendors and tourists. And Alex and I spent several hours testing foods from different stalls and conversing with the super-friendly locals.

It was so busy today that I couldn't imagine how my

grandparents had found one another here, but I could envision them stealing away to dance in some quiet corner just like they had when I was a child before Abuelo's accident.

Having visited the three locations marked in Santa Cruz, we moved on to a town called Brasilito, where my grandparents had settled when they got married – or so I thought.

The SUV continues driving through the streets, bypassing the town altogether.

I shoot Alex a questioning look, but he simply reaches across the seat to take my hand in his, rubbing his thumb back and forth across my knuckles.

We soon roll to a stop at a pier, and Alex side-eyes me. "I hope you don't get seasick."

"I've never been on a boat!"

He slips out his door, coming around to open mine as he likes to, and helps me from the SUV with a smile. "Well, that's about to change right now."

There's a small boat waiting for us, gently rocking on the waves of the harbor, and once we've both gotten settled on it, the motor flares to life, taking us away from land at speed.

"Where are we—"

Alex cuts off my question with a finger pressed to my lips. "You know I won't spoil a good surprise, Sunshine." He raises a brow. "I'm an excellent secret keeper."

I push his hand away with an exaggerated pout that only makes him chuckle. Then he pulls me in against the side of his body to press a kiss to my temple.

"We'll be there in a couple of minutes. But while we wait…" He trails off to present the green book with a flourish. "How about you finish reading?"

I falter for a moment before finding my voice. "Wh-what do

you mean, f-finish reading?"

He opens the book to the map, turning it over to display a final page that I hadn't seen earlier. Right there, in black ink, is Lita's tidy handwriting.

I swallow the ball of emotion that clogs my throat, and then stiffen my spine before I start to read.

My little dancer,

Today was your first day at Pearson, and I couldn't be prouder. I spent the entire day telling every single person at Sunrise Harbor all about my beautiful mija who's destined for greatness.

I say this without an ounce of bias. You got your gift from me, you know!

It's a simple fact and something that I have always known. My only regret is that I won't be there to see it— or perhaps I will in body, but not in mind.

Already I can feel myself slipping away further with each passing day. Small things that would mean nothing to someone else, but I know in my heart that it's the turning of the tide.

So, I'm making this for you—and for me, I think, for the days when I need to be reminded—so that you will know where your roots began.

And if I have done my job right, then I pray to the

Lord that you spread those wings I gave to you so that you can soar to the heights that I know you will.

When you make it back home, I hope you'll visit the places that are part of your heritage and think fondly of me. Know that I will be with you every step of the way, mi conchita linda.

Always.

And if you can, try to visit my favorite place in this world. Playa Conchal is a beach near our home in Brasilito, and it holds some of my fondest memories.

I'll be waiting there with your abuelo.

Te amo, Reyna. Te amo infinitamente.

My eyes scan the last line once, then twice, before the tears fall, and I turn into the comforting embrace of my person.

Twenty-Three

ALEX

My eyes are closed tight as I rest my cheek atop Rey's head, holding her as she succumbs to the emotions Mari's words have pulled from her, as I'd known they would.

It would be impossible for *anyone* who'd seen the love they shared to have been unmoved by that damn green book.

I open my eyes when I feel the boat tilt to the side slightly, knowing from my previous research that we should be rounding the edge of the bay now, but even so, I'm unprepared for the sight that greets me.

"Look, Rey!"

At my request, Rey lifts her tear-stained face from my chest, and when her eyes land on the bay before us, her expression shifts to sheer wonderment.

"Is that…are we…?" She turns wide, hopeful eyes to mine.

I nod easily, and those chocolaty orbs fill with fresh tears.

"*Yes*, baby. It's Playa Conchal."

The idyllic shoreline grows nearer and nearer until the boat moors on the empty shoreline.

The entire strand is devoid of all signs of life except for a small white gazebo that's set up away from the shore, the white fabric sides gently fluttering in the breeze.

This day has been a while in the making. Having read the green book in the days after Mari's passing, I'd gotten the ball rolling on securing this beach for our private use.

One special day for closure.

For Rey.

And for Mari.

I disembark, holding a hand out to assist a wide-eyed Rey as her eyes devour the scene before her.

"No wonder it was her favorite place."

Her words are softly spoken, and despite the tears glistening in her eyes, her mouth draws up like a bow with a smile so dazzling I'm mesmerized.

"I can *feel* their presence so powerfully." She looks around the empty shore, her eyelids softly closing as she raises her face to the sun's rays.

"They're here." Her chin tilts down, allowing her eyes to find mine. "Do you feel them?"

She reaches down to slip off her sandals as I stand awestruck by how this trip has buoyed her. I watch silently as she digs her hands into the unusual sand before glancing back up at me with her head tilted to the side in an unspoken question that I'm too happy to answer.

"This place is a white shell magnet."

Her brows gather as her eyes glisten with unshed tears. "Oh my God."

Her breath catches on a sob.

"All of my life, I've wondered why she called me her pretty little seashell—*mi conchita linda*—and now I *finally* understand."

She looks back at the white seashells beneath our feet, dashing away her tears before smoothing her palms across the sand. Then she laughs aloud, grabbing a handful and grinding it in her fist before she looks up at me once more with a bright, wondrous smile. "It's out of this world. She never spoke of this before."

Wistfulness flits across her perfect face, and I quickly reach down to intertwine our fingers, gently tugging her against my side.

"Come on. It's *way* past lunch."

We journey closer to the white gazebo, and when she spots two smiling attendants waiting, she stops dead in her tracks to turn to me.

"Alex, today…today—no, this *entire trip* has been amazing. It's too much! It's—"

I cut her off, pressing my index finger over her lips firmly. "It's nothing less than you deserve, Reyna Mar…" I trail off for a beat, but quickly readjust my words to reflect my thoughts.

"It's nothing less than you deserve, *Reyna DeMarco*."

She inhales sharply, tears filling her eyes again as she roughly shoves my hand away from her mouth. "Alex, you don't need to say—"

And in that moment, something inside of me snaps.

I step closer, softly placing one palm over her mouth while the other grips the back of her head, keeping her in place even as she shoots shocked eyes to mine. "I've told you before, baby. I say what I *mean*, and I mean what I *say*. Those vows were *not* taken lightly; let me assure you of that."

She sucks a harsh breath through her nose, her eyes holding mine before she nods as much as this position will allow.

I step back, removing my hands instantly, even as the urge to kiss her almost overwhelms me.

Instead of following my baser urges, I force my lips upward. "Now, let's give Mari a send-off here in paradise."

Once we've eaten lunch, I give Rey some privacy to change into her bikini, resolutely ignoring the steady twitch in my pants when she remerges in a simple black two-piece.

When I'd shown her the racks of clothes that had been delivered last night, she'd stuck to the more staple items rather than the elaborate ones, though I have no doubt in my mind that she could wear a garbage bag and still be the most beautiful woman on the face of the planet.

My eyes drink their fill, and I can't help smiling at how her curves have begun to fill back out in the space of a few short days.

"What's so funny, pretty boy?"

I saunter closer, my smile broadening as I reach for her hand. "Remember when we went shopping at Bergdorf's?"

She slides her small palm alongside mine as she nods easily. "Mm-hmm. Why?"

I chuckle as I openly allow my eyes to drift the length and breadth of her body again. "I thought lingerie shopping might kill me...but it appears I was mistaken, because swimwear is giving me a fucking coronary over here."

She nudges me with her shoulder as a smile blooms on her perfect face.

I squeeze her hand in mine as my laughter dies in my throat. "Fuck, baby. I'm so damn happy to see you smiling again."

Her cheeks pinken up delightfully as her mouth tugs upward.

"It's all because of you, you know."

Doe eyes meet mine. "You've been my shelter in the storm, Alex. I could never have weathered it without you. *Any* of it."

I stop suddenly as we reach the water's edge to plant my hands on her upper arms so that I can twist her about to face me. "That's not true, Rey."

My hands rise to cup her cheeks, and I dip my knees so that I can make her see the truth of my words reflected in my eyes. "You are stronger than you know. Don't *ever* forget that!"

Our eyes hold for several long moments as the water gently laps at our feet. A small breeze skates across our skin, blowing strands of Rey's long hair across her face, and my free hand automatically reaches up to brush them behind her ear.

Her pupils dilate, and I *know* I'm being unfair when she clearly still harbors a crush on me, but the lines that once seemed so solid in my mind have been well and truly blurred now. So much so that I can't seem to find a single reason in my mind to deny ourselves any longer.

Maybe I *am* a serial screw-up, but for Rey…I want to do better. I want to *be* better.

And with her guiding light, perhaps I *can* be better than the people who made me.

For her.

Perhaps I can fix the broken parts of me. The ones I've long thought unfixable, but I now realize that she makes me feel whole in a way I've never imagined.

Is it selfish to want to keep that? To want to give her my all while taking all she has to give.

I cup her face in my hands, and her gaze darts to my lips. I'm slowly magnetized to close the distance between us until I'm inhaling her sweet exhalations. Her chest is rising and falling at pace, and my head is slightly fuzzy as I feel myself give in, as I give myself over to whatever higher power led me to her that day in Molly Malones.

Our lips dust across one another's just as the peaceful serenity of Playa Conchal is broken by the inimitable sound of an incoming helicopter.

I pull back instantly, and her closed lids flicker open as hurt dances across her confused features.

Clearing my throat, I plaster a smile onto my face and angle my head to the sky, simultaneously relieved and disgusted at the interruption.

Good timing, Ford!

Even so, I have to admit, part of me missed the dour fucker.

The chopper comes closer, and Rey twists about to watch as it descends slowly to the ground farther down the beach.

"Your wings are here, Sunshine."

REYNA

I settle back in against the seat of the small chopper, my hands trembling slightly while a stoic-as-ever Ford, who's left his trademark hat at home, lifts us into the air.

The rise is smoother than I'd have imagined, though the sound of the blades is overwhelming, even with the headset I've been equipped with.

"I've got you, Sunshine."

Alex's calm voice sounds in my ears, and I shoot him a grateful glance before I fixate my stare on my clenched fists resting on my lap.

I'm thankful for everything today—beyond thankful, really—

but our almost kiss on the shoreline has sent me spiraling into deep confusion.

Alex has never been anything less than honest with me following the omission of the truth the day he proposed, and recently I'd begun to think he'd started to see me in a similar light as I see him.

A look here, a touch there. His honesty about finding me attractive.

And maybe that's *all* it is. Maybe he just needs to blow off some steam.

Maybe our rule to not fuck other people isn't working for him anymore.

The thought makes my stomach lurch so harshly that I feel like I might throw up.

His gentle hand lands on my twisting fingers, quelling my anxiety about riding in this helicopter while sending goosebumps scattering across every inch of my skin from his simple touch.

"We're high enough, Ford."

Alex's firm voice echoes in my ears, and I shakily raise my eyes from our joined hands as Ford expertly handles the chopper, hovering precisely where instructed.

Alex shifts in his seat, and I meet his eyes, ignoring everything around us, focusing entirely on the comfort of his amber gaze.

"Rey." He blows out a heavy breath as his brows draw together. "I have thought about this for a while now, and *personally*, it feels like full circle. *However*, the choice is yours."

His eyes leave mine when he bends low to retrieve something from beneath our seat with his free hand, resurfacing a moment later with a wooden box covered with intricate carvings.

"Like you, when I read Mari's book, I understood the importance of this place. It wasn't until her personal effects were delivered from Sunrise Harbor that I realized what we could do for her. For *both* of them."

He passes the box onto my lap, and I can immediately see now that the carvings are all seashells. "Did you know that Mari never scattered Thiago's ashes?"

My breath catches in my throat on a gasp as I haltingly shake my head, running the tip of my index finger across the largest seashell on the lid of the box. My hand falters when I reach the opening, my intuition telling me precisely how special the contents of this box are.

Seeing my hesitation, Alex raises his hand and opens the clasp on the box. He lifts the lid to reveal two matching pewter urns with simple inscriptions.

MARIANA MARQUEZ
FOREVER IN OUR HEARTS

My eyes shift to the other.

THIAGO MARQUEZ
TOGETHER IN ETERNITY

I reverently brush my thumb across each urn, smiling through my tears as my mind finally realizes why we're here. I raise my emotion-stained face to Alex, a watery smile on my lips.

"Are we here to lay them to rest?"

Alex shakes his head, shifting closer as he lifts his hands to clasp mine, his forehead deeply creased with the intensity of his gaze. "No, baby. We're here to bring them *home*."

I blow out a shaky breath, glancing past Alex's concerned face to the window behind him. To the blue sky beyond, eventually scanning the horizon before shifting my gaze downward.

The sun hits off the water of the calm bay beneath us, almost winking at me, and a slow smile overtakes my face when my eyes settle on Alex.

"It's *perfect*." A matching smile lights up his features at my enthusiasm. "It's exactly what she would have wanted. What *they* would have chosen for themselves, given the choice."

My gaze drops down to Abuelo's urn, and I dust my thumb across the inscription once again.

Alex's hand grips mine, gently moving it across to Lita's urn so that my palm touches both of them at the same time.

The muffled sound of the chopper blades slicing through the air fills my ears until Alex softly murmurs, barely audibly. "Together in eternity, Rey. At their favorite place. Wouldn't any of us choose that for ourselves?"

I look up to find his eyes fixed intently on my face. My nod tugs a smile from his lips as I softly reply, "I'm ready."

"Sit back in your seat, Reyna."

Ford's voice fills my ears as I feel the chopper drop lower, and I quickly do what he says, settling the seashell box atop my lap with both my and Alex's hands gently gripping it.

The door on my side slides open, and a breeze ripples through the small space. Alex drops to the floor on his knees, edging closer to the open door. Fear threatens to overwhelm me until I glimpse the view outside.

We've dropped much lower, the serenity of the crystalline water below us interrupted by air swirling courtesy of the rotor blades' proximity.

Alex reaches the side of the chopper, dropping both legs out the side to sit as he calmly looks back to me, his palm outstretched in invitation.

Your intuition is your gift.

I know I'm safe with him, and so, despite my fears, I grasp his hand immediately, sliding closer across the seat until we're side by side, albeit at differing heights.

He looks into my eyes, nodding once before slipping the seashell lid from my lap. I reach for my abuelo and then my abuelita before depositing the box on the seat behind me.

My eyes close as I hug both of them against my chest for a long moment, and a feeling of complete tranquility overtakes me. When I open my eyes again, a peaceful smile parts my lips.

Acceptance.

I pass Lita's urn to a plainly shocked Alex.

His eyes are like saucers as he glances from me to her and back again. "Rey..."

My smile grows. "It's only fitting. As her *mijo*."

He swallows roughly against the emotions that are clearly etched on his handsome face. "It...it would be my greatest *honor*."

Side by side, we open the urns, and leaning out over the side of the hovering chopper, we simultaneously send my family back to their roots.

And even as sadness flows through every vein in my body, there's an overriding sense of rightness. Of closure.

And of destiny.

We watch the ashes swirl and twist as they make their descent, landing all along the water as Ford begins to shift higher.

Alex climbs back onto the seat with a sad smile as the door slips closed. He gently enfolds me in his embrace, and I willingly nuzzle in against his firm body, seeking the comfort of his touch.

The chopper circles once, then twice in muffled silence, before making a sharp turn away from Playa Conchal.

And instead of looking back, I fix my sights firmly on the

horizon, spreading my wings just like Lita said I would in her letter.

I press my cheek against the steady thump of Alex's heart. "What's your favorite place?"

He doesn't miss a beat. Instead, his arms lock more tightly around me as he softly replies, "Anywhere you are, Sunshine. *You* are my favorite place."

Twenty-Four

ALEX

"So the casa is—"

"Yes." Ford cuts me off with a single affirmative through gritted teeth. Unperturbed, I continue.

"And everything is set for tomorrow, right?"

Rey has slipped into the waiting SUV on the tarmac at Tamarindo, where we've returned with the chartered chopper, so questioning Ford now is hopefully not going to ruin any surprises.

He rolls his eyes. "This ain't my first rodeo, fucker."

I quirk a brow, my eyes encompassing his huge frame in one fluid movement. "You can take the boy out of Texas…"

He sighs heavily. "Christ almighty, DeMarco. I do *not* get what that ray of sunshine sees in you. You're a complete—"

Rey cuts him off when she pops her head back out of the open door. "Incorrigible asshole is the term I prefer to use."

Ford snorts as a smile blooms on his face, and in that moment, I notice smile lines I'd not seen before now, only adding to the mystery of why this young man has become such a hardened soul.

A broken man.

Takes one to know one.

Clearly, Vaughn Burton is a fan of taking in strays.

"It's all set. I'll pick you up in the a.m."

He tips his hat with a nod to Rey before stalking back toward the waiting chopper.

I usher her back inside the car, and our driver smoothly leaves the airstrip as Ford once again takes to the sky.

"What was he talking about?"

I press my lips together, absolutely failing to hide my grin. "You *know* I'm a top-tier secret keeper, baby. You'll just have to wait until tomorrow."

Her eyes narrow, but she doesn't push, knowing by now that I'm a motherfucking vault when I want to be.

It takes no time at all until we're back at the casa, and my mouth lifts in a huge ass smirk when the sound of music hits Rey's ears as the SUV comes to a slow halt.

She turns to me with wide eyes.

"Is that…'Despacito'?"

My smirk grows, transforming into a wide, bright smile. "The Bieber remix, I'll have you know."

Her eyes soften. "She loved that one."

I slip from the back seat, round the back of the vehicle, and open her door with my hand flourished.

"Come on. I have a surprise for you."

She takes my offered hand with a wry grin. "You and these surprises."

I tug her to my side, winking mischievously. "Me and these damn surprises, Sunshine."

We enter the casa through the front door, finding the property has been utterly transformed, with vibrant red, white, and blue exploding to life within, spilling out onto the pool area beyond. It looks like our own private street party, with platters of mouth-watering local Costa Rican cuisine interspersed throughout.

Music is pumping through speakers out by the pool, filling the entire house with a desire to move. To let the rhythm take control, and glancing sideways at Rey, I can't help but smile when I note the slight sway of her hips in time with the beat.

"What…what is this?"

Rey spins to face me, her eyes shining with delight, and my smile grows even broader.

I step closer, looping my arms around her waist to pull her closer to me. She places her palms on my chest, looking up at me with dancing doe eyes, and I can feel my chest puff out ridiculously under her obvious adoration.

"Dance for me, Sunshine."

Disbelief colors her face, and her brows pinch together. "*To this*?"

I chuckle deep in my chest, but nod as I hold her eyes with mine. "I've done my homework, Rey. To enter Pearson, you would have needed to be *well* above average, at the *very* least, in several other styles of dance. Correct?"

She nods warily, and I continue with a shit-eating grin. "So, I've decided…while we're here, I think it's only fitting that you showcase your favorite Latin American dances."

Her eyes narrow minutely, but she doesn't debate it. Instead, she throws her hands up in exaggerated exasperation, unable to hide her twitching lips. "Well, since you've gone to the trouble of doing your *homework*, pretty boy, what kind of wife would I be if I denied you?"

She rests her hands on my upper arms, quirking a playful

brow as my eyes fixate on her stunning face. My chest fills with light at her easy use of her new title, despite the initial rationale behind tying ourselves together.

It's becoming more and more apparent that my reasons for asking Rey to be my pretend girlfriend were thrown out the window a long damn time ago.

Because this doesn't feel pretend. And deep down, I know it never was.

From the moment we exchanged vows, I *knew* I would never let her go.

This is real.

We are real.

And the acknowledgment is fucking liberating.

"Well, Sunshine. To deny your husband one small request such as this…I'll go out on a limb here, but I do believe that would make you a little bit of an *asshole*."

She throws her head back, her slender neck on display to my rapt gaze as she laughs long and loud. Her face returns to mine as she extricates herself from my embrace to lift the hem of her beach kimono. She easily lifts it over her head and tosses it aside, her intensely pupil-dominated eyes never leaving mine.

"I can categorically state that I wouldn't want to join the incorrigible asshole club, pretty boy."

She gives me her back with a smirk, sauntering toward the wide-open space of the living area with a sultry sway of her delectable ass that I don't even bother attempting to hide.

When she turns back to face me, Cheat Code's remix of "South of the Border" comes over the speakers, and her eyes blow wide in clear delight as she begins to dance.

"Ooh, this is perfect for a bachata!"

My eyes drink their fill as she extends her hands gracefully.

"I had a feeling this one could be a firm favorite."

She pads closer, twisting her hips almost hypnotically. "You know Ed's my man."

She pops a brow before pivoting back across the room, her wider steps making her hips sway even more. And almost of my own volition, my feet cross the space, and the flat of my palm lands on one undulating hip as I bring my chest flush against her back.

"You mean *I'm* your man, right?"

Her gasp of shock sounds over the music, and her movements falter. I allow a small grin to play across my face as I bend my neck to ghost my lips along her ear.

"And I don't share what's mine, Sunshine."

REYNA

Alex's hot mouth by my ear sends a flash of absolute *want* straight through the center of my vibrating body. I'm putty in his capable hands as his feet quickly synchronize with mine.

He can dance?

"Don't stop, baby."

He threads our fingers together expertly, quickly twisting me around to press his hips close to mine. His eyes have darkened to almost black in their intensity, and I feel the air surrounding us electrify as he presses us even closer together. My chest is rising and falling at speed as I desperately try and fail to get a handle on my racing thoughts.

On my palpitating foolish heart.

"Box step."

I instantly comply, quickly following his brusque instruction while his eyes spear me. It's *easily* the most sensual box step of my fucking life, his muscular thigh damn near buried hard against my suddenly throbbing pussy.

"Pretzel. *Now*."

His voice takes on a dominance I've never witnessed before as I rush to do as he says, except he captures me in a half-pretzel turn, tugging me back to hold me firmly against his front while he continues to move in tandem with my feet.

With my hips.

I finally find my voice, even though it comes out in a whisper that's barely audible above the pulsing music. "What are you doing?"

"Being honest." He huffs a laugh, muttering almost to himself. "At long fucking last."

He buries his nose in my hair, and I can feel him breathing deeply. His exhalation ghosts across the curve of my shoulder, sending goosebumps scattering along my skin, turning my nipples to bullets beneath the thin material of my bikini.

"I want you, Rey."

My knees threaten to buckle, and my feet hesitate as I try to turn to face him, but he holds me firm. "I said *don't stop*."

I swallow harshly, focusing on staying upright and moving my feet, swaying my hips alongside his. His mouth hovers by my ear, and he murmurs softly, "I can't fight this any longer. And, more importantly, I don't *want* to."

My breath catches in my throat when his husky voice sends a flood of warmth straight to my core. I almost falter as I try my utmost to focus on the beat of the music, and the rhythm of our bodies.

He leads me into a rolling body wave, leading with his left foot before pivoting me around.

When I meet his heated gaze, I close my eyes as a shiver of anticipation runs the length of my spine, settling in my core.

He brings our hips together, his thigh firm between my legs as I slide into a booty roll under his strong, silent lead. A grin quirks his lips as I tug my lower one between my teeth, watching his reaction from beneath my lashes.

"I see your lady boner stage is still in full swing."

I feel my cheeks pinken as I bite my lips almost hard enough to draw blood.

And suddenly, Alex stills, bringing his hands to rest on either side of my flushed face.

"I have a confession to make, Sunshine."

He brings our foreheads close together as the music trails off, filling the air with a silence that's only broken by the sound of my heart racing in my ears.

"Our arrangement is off. It should never have happened in the first place."

My stomach dips at his words, so at odds with his soft tone.

I swallow roughly, slamming my eyes closed to keep the prickling tears at bay.

"This has *never* been fake for me, Sunshine. None of it, not for a moment."

My eyes fly open, finding his spearing me with golden flames. His words are spoken with such passion, such fervor, such *honesty* that it damn near takes my breath away.

"I'm a smart man, but when it comes to *feelings,* I don't know a whole lot. But what I *do know* is that I want to be with you. That I *need* to be with you. To care for you. To protect you. To spoil you. To worship you. To be your shelter from the storm. To be your *person*. I need—"

I cut him off when I crush my lips to his, stealing his words with a kiss filled with all my pent-up longing, with every ounce of love that dwells within my body.

His mouth opens under mine, a growl ripping through his throat when he pulls me tightly against his hard body. His thigh, still between my legs, moves back and forth against my core, adding another layer to this kiss that utterly consumes my senses, and devours my soul.

Heat surges through my body as Alex takes control of the kiss, deepening it and taking it to a new level. Rolling my hips, I seek the friction of his hard thigh against me.

I cry out against his mouth at the exquisite sensations, and he uses it as his chance to palm my almost bare ass-cheeks, lifting me into his arms. I wrap my legs around him, locking my ankles behind his back as I look down into his handsome face.

He doesn't take his eyes from mine as his long strides eat up the distance to our room, lit only by the light of a small lamp and the moon outside above the forest trees.

He sits on the bed, settling my legs on either side of him, and I can't hold back any longer. I cup his face gently, my eyes focusing solely on his dark whiskey pools.

"I love you, Alex." He blinks slowly; his brow furrowed as though he can't comprehend my words. "I'm *in love* with you."

The long-buried admission comes out on a whisper, and his face freezes for a beat before he appears to be lit up from within. His crooked smile is the last thing I see before he slams his mouth to mine, crushing me to him with a passion that almost overwhelms me.

His right-hand snakes around my neck, gently tugging the string tie of my bikini before making short work of the tie at my back. His left reaches between us to pull the material from my chest, flinging it across the room to bear me to his ardent gaze.

He drinks his fill, his eyes roving across every exposed part of me in reverence before he lays his palm on my breastbone, urging me to arch my back.

My head drops back as a moan spills from my lips when his hot mouth engulfs a nipple, sucking and nipping me into a frenzy before he moves to the opposite one.

"Oh *Jesus*. Fuck. Don't stop!"

He raises his head with a devilish grin as his fingers pinch my nipples into stiff buds. "Baby…"

He trails off pointedly before raising a sardonic brow. "I've been deprived of this deliciousness—"

His hand roughly squeezes my breast before dropping down to palm my aching pussy, making me jolt on his lap. "And this sweetness, for *far* too long."

He twists his free hand in my messy hair at the nape of my neck, pulling me closer until our lips brush. His words send a shock of electricity through me as wetness pools between my legs.

"Trust me, Sunshine. I won't be stopping any time soon. Maybe not ever."

Sucking a nipple between his lips, he swirls his tongue as his thumb expertly finds my clit. His eyes hold me in rapture, even as my eyelids threaten to fall closed from the sensations he's bringing to life within me.

He lets my nipple pop free, then flicks his pointed tongue over and back across the tip while his thumb mimics the movement farther south.

I cry out as my hips push themselves closer. "*Yes*!"

He sits back, watching my reaction as his thumb continues to stroke my wet heat. My chest is rising and falling rapidly, my hips thrusting against his attention.

"Nothing in this wide earthly world could stop me from doing what I'm about to do right fucking now, Reyna DeMarco."

"What's that?" My question comes out as a gasp.

And suddenly, I'm hoisted into the air as Alex grips me under the ass to spin around and drop me onto the soft mattress with a breathless yelp.

He stares down on me with an almost predatory gaze, slowly coming closer with each word he speaks. "I'm about to fucking *ruin* you for anyone else, Sunshine. I'm about to make sure you're so in love with me and how only *I* can play this body to per-fucking-fection that you'll never leave me."

He fits himself between my legs, caging me in with his forearms resting on either side of my head. Then he leans closer, his soft lips brushing over my cheek until they rest right by the shell of my ear.

"First, I'm going to take it nice and slow. Going to work you into a frenzy like you can't get enough of how I make you feel."

He rises up, finding my wide eyes fixated on him. Whatever he sees in my face makes his lips twitch. "Then, I'll lick your pussy until you come so hard you see stars. Until you can't stand the pleasure. Until you're pushing me away, your body humming in the aftermath of mind-blowing orgasms, your skin tingling with the promise of *more*."

Pressing a kiss to my parted lips, he rests his forehead against mine to feed me his words as he grinds our pelvises together.

"And then, Sunshine…*then* I'm going to fuck you hard, my irresistible *wife*. I'm going to make you scream my name until your throat is as raw as your pussy will be."

Twenty-Five

ALEX

Rey locks her ankles around my ass, pulling me closer. "I think I like this surprise."

I chuckle deep in my chest, closing the gap to slowly slide my tongue past her lips into her sweet mouth. Her low moan of pleasure makes my cock damn near combust.

I deepen the kiss, slowly entangling my tongue with hers. Her sweet floral scent—the one I've spent weeks pretending doesn't exist—fills my nostrils as I increase the tempo of our dancing mouths, and our simple kiss becomes something else entirely.

It feels infinitely more intimate than anything I've ever experienced before throughout my entire twenty-nine years. My heart is palpitating, my mind whirring, and my senses are wholly consumed by this tiny dancer, who *somehow* has fallen *in love* with me.

And the knowledge sends me spiraling to new heights.

She loves *me!*

Rey arches her hips, pressing her pussy against my raging

hard-on, and my body stills. My brain suddenly realizes that unless I slow things down, I'll nut in my damn pants.

I break our kiss and push her legs apart, forcing her to un-lock those ankles that have been holding her heels firmly to my ass.

She cries out, hands reaching blindly. I grasp both slim wrists easily in one hand, securing them above her head to pin her with my eyes.

"Kiss me, Alex. *Please—*"

I cut her off with what I know is a devilish grin. "Oh, Reyna, baby. I'm *all* about kissing you. Trust me. I'm going to kiss you *everywhere*."

I draw my thumb across her waiting mouth before pressing a kiss to her soft lips. "I'm going to kiss you *here*."

Then I slide the digit farther down, my eyes riveted to her luscious fucking tits. "And *here*, too."

I paint languid circles with the fingertips of my free hand across her bare chest; her darkened buds crying out for the attention of my mouth.

Instead, I place a chaste kiss on the crest of each globe before flattening my tongue and swirling it over first one nipple and then the other. My fingers skate lower south as I worship her perfect tits with my mouth. I swiftly find the seam of her bikini and tug it to one side to slide a single finger achingly slowly through her slick folds.

Rey throws her head back, crying out on a gasp. *"Oh shit!"*

I straighten, kneeling between her spread thighs so that I can loosen the strings on either side of her bikini. She watches in complete rapture, her eyes following my intentionally slow motions.

She gasps when I add another finger to her tight pussy as I peel her pants away, exposing her bare flesh to my hungry gaze.

"*Fuck*, your pussy is as beautiful as the rest of you, Sunshine." I pump my fingers harder, deeper, and her hips jerk against my hand. Her eyes squeeze closed with her forehead furrowed in concentration. "*So* fucking perfect, baby. Can you take another finger for me?"

The sound of her pussy taking my fingers deep inside fills the night around us. Her little breathless moans and circling, searching hips ensnare my senses, and when her eyes blow wide, she holds me hostage in their black pools as she unravels in sheer splendor.

"I—I'm—" She gasps as I add that third finger, the flush on her chest traveling up her neck and onto her face before she pants, "*Alex, I'm coming, Alex!*"

Her body loses its rhythm as she comes apart on my hand, and once the last vestiges of her orgasm travel through her trembling body, I waste no time shimmying down onto my elbows until my face is right in front of her dripping slit.

"And I'm especially going to take great pleasure in kissing you *here*."

I run my fingers through her glistening folds, parting them to reveal her arousal-slick clit. I look up along her body, finding her eyes on me as she nibbles her index fingernail almost frantically.

I smirk in complete roguishness. "See those stars yet, Sunshine?"

She nods as I part her pussy lips farther, my eyes fixating on her shimmering nub. "Yes, I—*oh!*"

I cut her off when I pull her clit into my mouth, sucking harshly. She arches against me, and I can't help but smirk against her wet core. "Oh, you ain't seen nothing yet."

I press her thighs flat against the bed, flicking her clit with the tip of my nose, making her gasp loudly. "Now lie back, baby. I need to eat this sweet cunt until you come all over my face. I *need* to tongue fuck you so hard you won't just *see* stars; you'll explode all over my tongue like a goddamn supernova."

A shiver ripples through her at my words, and my eyes hold hers as I flatten my tongue, sliding it from her slit right up to her clit. I swirl across that throbbing nub before sucking it into my mouth and sliding two thick fingers into her wet center.

She cries out as I begin to eat her in earnest, unable to stop my own moans of pleasure from filling the room alongside hers.

A pool of arousal sweeps across my tongue, and I swallow it down, eating her harder still, desperately in search of *more* of her sweetness.

"Oh fuck, fuck, *fuck*." Rey's voice is breathy with a frantic edge as her fingers tangle in my hair, holding me firmly against her pussy. I growl against her, my mouth almost feral in my attention, and my hips move of their own accord against the bed beneath me in search of friction.

Of relief.

In search of burying my rock-hard cock *deep* inside the gloriously wet cunt that I'm fucking devouring.

I feel a steady stream of precum leaking from my shaft as I grind against the bed, ramming a third finger into Rey's tight heat alongside the first two, and suddenly, she's crying out.

"*Don't stop, Alex*! Yes, yes, *yes*!"

Her hold on my head tightens as she uses my mouth to get off, and I watch in sheer euphoria as she peaks, her eyes fixed on mine, never once wavering.

As she descends from her pinnacle, her grip on my hair slackens, and her hands drop uselessly to her sides.

"I can't…I didn't know…oh shit…fuck."

Rey's breathy ramblings as she returns to earth, make me

chuckle while I clean my orgasm-covered face with the back of my hand. I waste no time sliding up along her naked body, quickly cutting her off when I take her mouth with mine.

She opens easily underneath my persistent tongue, slipping hers against mine, humming loudly when she tastes herself on me. The kiss turns almost primal as we devour one another until I can't hold back any longer.

I rip our mouths apart and yank off my swimming trunks in one fluid movement.

My cock springs free, and Rey's expression freezes.

"Monster cock."

Her whisper makes me belly laugh, and her wide eyes move up from my dick to find my mirth-filled eyes. I shrug with a lopsided grin. "I mean, it might look monster size to you when you've only fucked pickles before—*oof*!"

She cuts me off with narrowed eyes and a sharp jab to the gut. "Incorrigible asshole."

I lean over her, fitting my cock between her slick pussy lips and making her visibly melt with that single touch. "But I'm *your* incorrigible asshole, Sunshine."

Her smile makes me smile wider before I pump my hips forward once, hitting her clit with my hardness. "Shit, that's so good."

I circle my hips, grinding my cock against her in alternating hard and soft strokes. Her gasps of pleasure feed my need to be deep inside of her. She lifts her head from the mattress, brushing her lips across mine before nipping my bottom one between her teeth.

I take her mouth with a growl that rumbles from my chest, grinding my cock against her slick, wet pussy lips, desperate to slide into the paradise I *know* is waiting between her legs until she breaks the kiss with a whimper.

"I *need* to feel you inside me, Alex."

As though reading my mind, her words almost kill me. I swallow harshly, making to rise up on my knees to grab my wallet so I can suit up, but Rey stops me with her heels on my ass, holding me in place.

As I look at her with confused eyes, she just gently palms my cheeks. "You know I'm on the pill, right?"

I gulp, blinking rapidly as I nod, having seen her take it on previous mornings. "Yes, but, Rey—"

"Tell me you've always been safe…in the past…" She trails off, nibbling her bottom lip as her eyes plead with me to give her this.

So I give her my honesty. As always.

"Yes, Sunshine. I've *always* used protection. And I can show you proof that I'm clean if—"

She presses her index finger over my lips. "My intuition doesn't lie, Alex. I already *knew* what your answer would be."

Then she rises up on her elbows, quirking a brow as though in challenge, and fuck, if it doesn't make my cock throb against her clit. "So *ruin me*, pretty boy!"

Our mouths meet in an almost violent plundering as our hips undulate in the same hungry rhythm as our tongues. Her whimpers of agony and ecstasy are music to my ears, feeding my need to please her, my need to *ruin* her enough so that I can keep her for always.

The thought makes my chest swell with feelings I'm entirely unfamiliar with, but I funnel them into this most intimate of acts, stroking her soaked cunt with my equally wet cock.

She tears her mouth from mine, her hands finding my cheeks and holding me firmly. "Take me, Alex. I'm yours."

Mine. She's mine*!*

The knowledge nearly makes me blow, so I draw my hips back enough to stop teasing both of us. But she surprises the fuck out of me when she reaches between our sweat-slick bodies, grasping the head of my slick cock with her small fist.

"*Shit*, Rey." My hips jerk, loving the tightness of her hold. The softness of her palm gripping the hardness of my dick.

She looks down, smirking mischievously when she sees precum pearling at the top of my dick. Drawing her thumb across the slit, she gathers my arousal before bringing the digit to her mouth.

My balls tighten, and my jaw clenches almost painfully when she slowly licks her thumb clean before sucking it inside her mouth. She swirls it around, her hooded eyes fixed on mine, before releasing it with a *pop*.

"Holy fucking *shit*, you'll be the death of me, wife."

Her eyes blow wide at that, but I don't give her time to question my use of her title before I settle between her thighs, notching my cock right at the entrance to her pussy. I rub the tip along her folds, lubricating my dick with a mixture of our joint arousal, and the simple act makes my balls tighten, threatening to finish way quicker than I want.

"But before you kill me altogether, I need you to do something for me. Can you do that, baby?"

Her eyes are wide, and her jaw is slightly slack as she nods slowly.

"Take all of me, Sunshine."

I surge forward, seating my bare cock inside her clenching pussy in one swift thrust as she cries out at the invasion.

The feeling of her wet, warm pussy is like nothing I've felt in my life, and in this moment, I can see why wars are fought over women such as the one in my arms.

I would happily go to war to keep her, to keep this.

I edge slightly deeper, needing to get as far inside her heat as I possibly can. Needing to be wholly consumed by this woman.

My wife.

She arches her back as she cries out when I hit a spot even deeper, and I bury my face against the slender line of her neck, laving open-mouthed kisses all along her collarbone.

I hold myself steady for a moment, allowing her tightness to become accustomed to my size before the need to fuck—to fuck *hard*—overwhelms me.

I move my hips experimentally, circling them almost agonizingly slowly as I try my utmost to be gentle. Wanting to make it last, *needing* to make it exceptional for her, but the tortured pace sees me gritting my teeth as I try my hardest to keep from blowing my load too early.

As though she can read my mind, Rey brings her thighs up alongside my hips, squeezing tightly as she whispers against the shell of my ear, "Give. Me. *More*, Alex. Give me *everything*."

A shudder runs the length and breadth of my body before I crush my mouth to hers, groaning lowly as I angle my cock even deeper inside her wet core. Her eyes fall closed while she takes what she's asked for, and I'm only too willing to give it.

I kneel between her thighs, surging forward, feeding her sweet pussy my cock as she throws her head back, whimpering in pained pleasure.

"Oh fuck, Sunshine. You feel like paradise."

Grabbing her thighs, I rest her feet on my shoulders as I pick up the pace. Sweat beads on my brow, dripping down onto the flat of her stomach as she pushes her hips against my cock, taking everything I have and silently begging for more.

I reach between us, flicking my thumb across her clit, swirling her juices around the little bud and making her cry out.

"Oh fuck, yes. Keep doing that." Her hand snakes down to help mine, her fingers slipping across her slick nub alongside mine, and *fuck* if it doesn't turn me on far too much.

"Shit, Sunshine. You're going to make me come."

Her eyes are watching me when I lift my gaze from our joint actions. Her mouth is slack as she pants, a flush coloring her chest. "Fill me, Alex. Come inside me, *please*. I want to *feel* it."

Those words are the catalyst that sends me flying over the edge of a cliff so high I feel as though I'm falling endlessly.

Her tight cunt grips my dick like a vise as my balls tighten, and I groan heavily as I fill her convulsing cunt with streams of hot cum. Her cries of ecstasy echo in my ears as I fill her body with everything I have to give.

Together we ride the wave of pleasure until I fall forward onto her sweat-slick body, unable to bear my own weight on legs suddenly made of jelly.

She takes me into her warm embrace, holding me against her rising and falling chest as she gently brushes the hair back from my perspiration-soaked brow.

Her arms hold me impossibly closer as she twists about to fit our bodies together, legs tangled as I shift high enough on the bed to fit her in against the crook of my arm.

A sigh of contentment rumbles in my chest, and I tug her even closer until her cheek rests right over my thundering heart.

"I was wrong, Sunshine."

She angles her head up to find my heavy-lidded eyes with a questioning look. "Huh?"

I huff a laugh as sleep threatens to overtake me. "You're the one who's ruined me."

My eyes succumb to the weight of sleep before I can see her

reaction, but I feel her nuzzle against my chest, throwing a leg over mine to burrow ever deeper beneath my skin.

Silence reigns supreme as we both drift off until sleep has almost overtaken me when she softly whispers, "I love you, Alex."

Twenty-Six

REYNA

The rays from the morning sun hit my face through the sheer white billowing curtains lining the double doors that lead onto the patio, pulling me from the most relaxed sleep I can ever recall experiencing.

I roll onto my back, instantly noting that I'm alone in our bed, covered in part by our light bedsheet. Glancing down along my naked body, I stifle a smile when I note several small marks dotting my breasts and abdomen.

A memento from my clearly insatiable husband.

Alex had woken me twice through the night, first with his head between my legs, making me come three times on his talented tongue before I'd all but passed out from sheer pleasure.

And the second time, he'd woken me when he'd slipped into me from behind, whispering sweet nothings across the shell of my ear as he'd skimmed his fingers along every inch of my body, playing me like that sheet music he'd referred to back at the gala.

My stomach lurches, remembering the distance he'd put

between us after the gala…after he'd touched me. After we'd crossed the line. I can't have him checking out on me again.

I won't.

I'm about to throw back the covers and go in search of him, when he breezes through the slightly ajar patio door clad in only his Calvins with a huge breakfast tray in hand.

When his eyes meet mine, his face lights up with that lopsided grin that makes my heart flip-flop inside my chest. My own face is the mirror image of his, undoubtedly, and I fidget with my bangs nervously, tucking them behind my ears as he approaches the bed, gently setting the tray down at my side.

"I come bearing sustenance for my Sunshine."

My smile widens when I take in the spread of gallo pinto, fried eggs, platanos maduros—fried and caramelized plantains—and fresh fruit on the tray top.

"Thank you." My voice comes out in a mere whisper, and my eyes dart to the side, fearful that he can see my misgivings despite his sunny disposition of this morning.

Eventually, I look back at him, a frown marring my face, that sees Alex narrow his eyes before picking the tray back up to set it on the nightstand. He climbs onto the bed, straddling my waist and grasping my wrists to gently but firmly pin me to the bed beneath him.

"Last night was the single most spectacular night of my life, Sunshine. You have brought feelings to life inside of me that I didn't think I was capable of experiencing…"

He trails off with a small huff, glancing to the side as though unsure of how to continue.

"Alex, I—"

He cuts me off, his eyes swinging back to spear me into silence. "*Please* don't doubt that I want this between us. I want you. I want *us*. I want this to be a real marriage in *every* sense of the word."

I gasp as my long-buried feelings of hope dare to bloom to life.

He tilts his head to the side in utterly adorable confusion. "Do you not know what you mean to me by now, Reyna DeMarco?"

He slowly moves his face closer to mine with each word he speaks. "I want to see where this goes. I need to know that what you said last night...that you *love* me..." He gulps, exhaling heavily as my heart threatens to jump right out of my chest at these words I'd barely hoped to *dream* of.

His eyes are filled with sincerity that sends a wave of goosebumps traveling the length and breadth of my body. "I need to know that you can love the man behind the mask, Rey. Flaws and all. *Everything*. I need to know that you won't leave me. And in order to know that, I want to throw our arrangement away and see what we could have."

He pauses before dusting his knuckles off the back of my left cheek as our gazes hold. Tears threaten my eyes as a lump in my throat make speech an impossibility.

"Do you think we could try this, Sunshine?"

My eyes flick back and forth between his as my heart palpitates beneath my breast. My love for this man utterly knows no bounds, and I find myself nodding frantically before raising my head to press my lips against his softly.

When I pull back, he smiles.

Lopsidedly, of course, before it turns devilish.

"Just wait until you see the surprise I have planned for today!"

"Are we there *yet*?"

Alex chuckles as he grips my hand tighter. "Almost."

"You've been saying that for the last twenty-five minutes, ever since we passed that sign that was covered, and you made me wear *this*!"

I huff a sigh, fixing the accursed blindfold over my eyes with my free hand, when I feel Alex stop suddenly, and I instantly do the same.

"Hold on, Sunshine. We're here, but I just need to..."

He trails off as he drops my hand, and I reach out, searching blindly for him with both hands. "This isn't funny, asshole. I'm taking this off right—*argh*!"

Suddenly, I'm plucked from the earth by a set of strong arms and held against a broad chest in a bridal carry. I don't need Alex's unmistakable woodsy scent to fill my nostrils to know that it's him, and I immediately snuggle deeper into the safety of his embrace.

"You could have done this five minutes ago and saved me from almost stumbling to my death."

His chest rumbles, and I can't help a wide grin from splitting my face.

"Ah, but if I'd carried you, I'd have missed out on some truly excellent, free entertainment!"

I half-gasp, half-snort a laugh, and I can even hear the up-to-now silent Ford, who's trailing behind us, having piloted us here in that blasted chopper once again, exhale mirthfully.

"That's right. Laugh it up, pretty boy! Lita always said karma's a killer!"

He presses a smiling mouth to my forehead as he grinds to a halt. "I'll remember that the next time I screw up."

His arms tighten around me for a split second before he gently places my feet back on the ground. The hiking boots he'd insisted I wear have actually been a godsend, though the heat of the day is making me itch to take them off and immerse myself in a cold shower.

"Okay, we're here."

He rests his chin on my shoulder, wraps his arms around my waist as his chest draws up flush with my back, and I can't help but deadpan, "Whatever gave that away."

He snorts. "You're in top form today, I'll give you that. Maybe we should skip the surprise so that I can take you back to the casa to fuck the sass right out of you. Hmm?"

I bite my lip, my nostrils flaring at the imagery that flashes before my darkened vision. He barks a laugh. "*Clearly*, that's precisely what you want, my dirty fucking girl.

His teeth nip playfully at my ear, sending goosebumps dancing across the surface of my skin despite the heat of the day.

"Instead, you'll get *this*."

And at that, he tugs away the blindfold with a flourish.

I blink heavily, ramming my eyes closed forcibly to block out the sudden invasion of bright light. It takes several long moments before my vision begins to clear, and when it does, my breath catches in my throat at the beauty before me.

"May I present to you…the *Rio Celeste* waterfall."

We're standing at the top of a beautiful stairway, looking down on a stunning waterfall that's surrounded by the greenery of the forest. It's cascading down into a beautiful turquoise pool of water, and it takes a hot minute before I can tear my eyes away.

I find Alex watching me in silence. The edges of his mouth quirk upwards when my eyes meet his, and his gaze travels across the planes of my face in an almost reverential silence until he whispers, "Simply breathtaking."

My stomach dances as we continue to watch one another until Ford clears his throat behind me, drawing our joint attention.

"They're here, Alex."

Suddenly, the sound of voices reaches my ears, and I pivot on my heel to look back into the forest, my eyes following the path we must have taken to get here.

Several men and women descend, each bearing large black cases while amicably chatting among themselves.

I twist my head back to Alex. "Who are they?"

His face takes on an almost sheepish look, but he doesn't shy away, choosing to answer me outright. "Remember I mentioned the photo shoot we were booked to do with those media outlets on our wedding day?"

My brow furrows, taking what feels like forever to remember back that far, but eventually, the lightbulb comes on. "Yes...what has that got to do with—"

"Everly Events and Keller Media are two of DeMarco Holding's largest media competitors. They have sent representatives to shoot us *here* instead, and in exchange, when we return home, they will see to it that we are left in relative peace, for the most part, owing to the simple fact that they own most of the smaller outlets who peddle in meaningless gossip. The ones that buy the photos from the freelancers who pester us."

He smiles hesitantly, and I can see that he's concerned that this surprise is falling a little flat. While it's not ideal, I can see the merit behind it, and so I close the gap between us to wrap my arms around his waist.

My chin rests on his chest, and I smile softly when I look up into those whiskey eyes that *see* all the way down to the very deepest parts of my true self. "It's wonderful, Alex. And *kinda* genius, too!"

His face brightens, that crooked smile dominating his entire face, making my heart literally skip a damn beat before he plants a kiss on the tip of my nose. "I'm glad you agree, wife. Now, let's get changed!"

He extricates himself from my hold, leaving me with a furrowed brow as I call after his departing back. "Changed? Why?"

ALEX

Everly Events had opted for their shoot to take place in the forest surrounding the Rio Celeste, while Keller Media wanted a montage of us immersed in the beautiful turquoise waters of the waterfall to contrast.

We dress as quickly as possible inside a makeshift tent they've set up for us, though it isn't as fast as we *could* because I'm too distracted watching Reyna to focus on my own clothes.

They've provided simple matching white linen pants and a button-up shirt for me, alongside a casual knee-length white linen dress for Rey.

"You look fucking delectable, Sunshine."

She tucks her hair behind her ears, a hint of a smile tugging on her kiss-swollen lips as she fixes the thin straps on her shoulders, and I'm helpless to stop from tugging her to me so that I can kiss her again.

She grips my shirt, pulling me even closer to run the tip of her tongue across the seam of my lips, seeking an entry I'm too willing to give.

Her deep groan of pleasure fills the tent when I slide my palms around to cup her ass, holding her flush against my body. She breaks our mouths apart, panting as heavily as I am.

"Shit, Rey. Just when I think I've satiated my need for you, I look at you, and that's it. I'm lost all over again."

She smiles up into my eyes until Ford's voice beyond the pseudo-tent calls out, "Christ almighty, Burton owes me big time for making me babysit you two."

Everly's shoot is up first. It's a casual one peppered with a handful of innocuous, pre-approved questions.

Tara, the rep from Everly, questions from her place beside three photographers – because, clearly, one wouldn't cut it.

"How did you two meet?"

Rey takes this one, having previously determined that we needed to stay as close to the truth as possible. "It was *literally* a 'guy walked into a bar' type of situation."

She looks up at me from beneath her lashes, a secret smile dancing on her lips, and I can't help but intertwine our fingers to pull her close to my side.

"And you had absolutely *no* idea that the guy you met was the notorious Alex DeMarco?"

Rey chews her bottom lip for a beat before shaking her head. "I mean, I knew he was special, but I had no idea he was famous, or whatever."

Tara moves on, thankfully. She glances sideways at the clicking photographers before openly shrugging. "I know it's not on the pre-approved questions, but I'm absolutely *dying* to know—"

I cut her off with a sharp denial, terrified she would mention the circumstances of the huge ass wedding being canceled, forcing Rey to tell her about Mari's passing. "No. Unless it's preapproved—"

"It's okay, Alex." Rey cuts me off, twisting her head back to Tara. "Please, by all means. We are an open book."

Tara shoots her a thankful look before continuing – and absolutely *not* in the direction I'd anticipated. "How did he pop the question, Mrs. DeMarco?"

Rey's face lights up, and I don't even bother to fight the belly laugh that erupts from my mouth, unsettling several birds from nearby trees.

"Oh, now that's a story."

By the time Tara and Rey have quit giggling over my Maverick-style proposal, Tara is swearing blindly that she won't tell another soul when I spot a sloth high up in a nearby tree.

"Look, guys!"

Rey's reaction is something I will remember for the rest of my life. Her *face* lit up with all the splendor of a thousand suns when she saw the sloth, who was actually awake and moving, much to the delight of the entire crew.

All I could do was stand back alongside the snapping photographers with a cheesy-as-fuck grin on my stupid face, watching my wife stare in complete rapture.

We bid goodbye to Tara and the crew from Everly, with both ladies promising to stay in touch. When we got back to the falls, Keller Media had everything set up, and I'd quickly donned the simple black trunks they provided before wading into the pristine waters.

"Come on in, Sunshine. The water is blissful."

I look back to find Rey standing by the water's edge, her toes barely dipped. She's wrapped in an oversized white towel, her tan complexion absolutely glowing in contrast.

I pop a mischievous brow as I flick water in her direction, and she giggles lightly before I move off close to the falls with a swift, strong backstroke, leaving her to debate entering.

Her voice calls from the shore. "I'm coming in now."

When I stop and face her, I'm floored once more at her beauty, her effortless grace, and the effervescence that pours from every part of her, making everything surrounding her appear dull.

She truly is a veritable ray of light.

And she's mine.

The thought is damn near intoxicating as I wade through the water to take her proffered hand.

"You look…" I trail off, allowing my gaze to skim across every inch of her face, settling on her smiling lips before pressing a kiss to them. "Like a dream come true."

Her cheeks color adorably, and I waste no time hauling her into my arms to carry her farther into the pool. Her eyes hold mine until the water gets deeper, swirling around our bodies, and I ease her away from my chest.

She swims away from me with ease, her smooth strokes barely rippling the water, and I glance at the Keller rep, Tomas, for further instruction, only to find him with his eyes fixed on my wife.

A quick glance around the entire group makes me realize that every single pair of eyes present is utterly fixated on Reyna. I watch for long moments as some deep down, caveman urge to smash their faces in almost overwhelms me.

"Where do you want us?"

Instead of succumbing to my screaming baser instinct, I grit my question at the waiting Tomas, who literally shoos me with his hands, eyes still keenly watching Rey.

"Do whatever comes naturally."

Don't tempt me, motherfucker.

Jaw clenched so tightly, I'm *sure* to break some molars, I swim to join Reyna, who's flipped over onto her back to tread the water. Her hair is spread out around her like a dark halo, her tits are bobbing on the surface, and I *swear* I can make out pebbled nipples beneath the thankfully thick black fabric of her suit.

I'm suddenly all too sure that this was a huge mistake, and I want to grab that towel to cover the body that is only meant for *my* eyes.

I wasn't lying when I told her that I don't share what's mine.

And it's with that at the forefront of my newly acquired Neanderthal brain that I tug her to me, forcing her to loop her legs around my waist.

Her cry of surprise turns to laughter as she drops her arms around my shoulders, squashing her chest to mine when she holds me close.

"It's out of this world, Alex." She smiles softly. "Thank you. For *everything*."

I feel some of the tension ebb from my shoulders as she hugs me close, and I focus on her alone rather than the surrounding vultures whose eyes I can feel burning a hole in my back.

"You know I'd give you the world, Sunshine. In a fucking heartbeat, if you asked me to. Because the only thing that matters is *you*."

She pulls back enough to find my eyes, and I press my forehead to hers, needing her to know what she means to me.

"The world outside of this, now, *us*? It doesn't matter. Because *you* are my world now."

She swallows roughly before slowly brushing her lips across mine. "I love you, Alex."

I want to say it back to her. I *need* to say it, but the words stick in my throat, choking me. Suffocating me so that all I can do is slam my mouth to hers, inhaling her like oxygen, like she is the air I need to breathe.

She doesn't hold back, taking my passion and feeding me with a matching one of her own for long moments.

Her hips thrust forward against mine, and despite the coolness of the water, my dick springs to life.

Groaning into her mouth, I palm her ass cheeks and slide my pinkie finger along the seam of her bikini, making her whimper.

I rip my mouth from hers, dragging my lips along the side of her neck to lave open-mouthed kisses all the way to her collarbone as she throws her head back in abandon.

Suddenly, an ear-piercing whistle breaks the silence, and we pull apart, twisting our heads in the direction of the noise.

My hazy, lust-filled eyes scan the sides of the pool to find around a dozen or so Keller Media employees currently watching on in rapt silence.

Eventually, I spot Ford standing on the same bridge we'd arrived on earlier, the thumb and index finger of his right hand jammed between his lips, clearly making him the perpetrator.

He shrugs as he drops his hands, his eyes flicking back and forth between both of us while he shakes his head. "Just saving you from *another* potential scandal, DeMarco." Ford rolls his eyes as he moves away, calling over his shoulder. "Thank me later."

Twenty-Seven

ALEX

We exit the falls to find a barrage of texts on my cell, and Rey sits quietly by my side as I sift through them in silence.

VAUGHN

I hate to break up the party, but Grayson is NOT okay.

My stomach sinks before moving on to the next, which is a group chat between my siblings and me.

HENRY

Al, I think you need to check on Grayson, man.

MILA

I literally just spoke to him. He's going to Vermont the day after tomorrow.

Shit!

BAILEY

911.

Well, fuck. If Bailey is contacting me when he'd been *specifically* warned not to…

"Rey, we need to—"

She palms my cheek, leaning closer to brush her lips across mine. When she pulls back, her words whisper across my mouth. "It's time to go home."

Five hours later, we're on the jet, ready to depart Tamarindo, and even Ford seems sad to leave it behind.

"I'm glad you got…closure, Reyna. We all deserve that." He drops a hand to my wife's shoulder before sliding past us on the airstairs to take his place as co-pilot on the flight.

Rey takes one last lingering look back at the darkened landscape beyond the airport before slipping inside the jet after him.

Once we have taken off, I unbuckle my seatbelt and hold my hand out to Rey as I stand. "Come on, baby. Let's get some sleep."

She furrows her brow, then glances around, her eyes landing on two doors at the rear of the cabin.

Her eyes flick back and forth between both of them, and I answer her unspoken question as she takes my hand to rise beside me.

"The one on the left is a bedroom."

Her eyes widen even as her face lights with comprehension. "*Ah*! I thought they were *both* restrooms."

She palms her forehead with a self-deprecatory smile as I open the door, allowing it to swing wide to reveal a large double bed.

When her eyes land on it, she scurries past me, launching herself onto the mattress with a happy squeal. "Ooh, this is *awesome*!" Then she pats the bed beside her. "Come on then."

I close the door and settle onto the bed to draw her into the circle of my embrace. I can feel the tension ebb from her body and mine as we lie together in serene silence.

"I'm sorry the trip was cut short, Rey."

She presses a kiss to my T-shirt-clad chest right over my heart. "It couldn't have been more perfect." She turns her worried eyes to mine. "What's wrong with your friend? Grayson, was it?"

I exhale heavily as I nod. "Yeah, it's Grayson."

Pulling her in closer against my side, she tucks her head underneath my chin, ready to hear a story I'd prefer I didn't have to tell.

"About a week after Mari passed, I got a call from Gray. He was distraught, speaking in fucking riddles, but I eventually understood why he was so upset. His wife, Talia, and their twins, Gracie and Parker, had been in a car accident on their way to their vacation home in Vermont. Talia…"

I trail off, tears filling my eyes when I remember the day she and Grayson married only five years previously. The love between them was as clear as day.

"She didn't make it." I clench my jaw before blowing out a heavy breath as Rey gasps. "Gracie was airlifted to the hospital. Her injuries were…excessive. But with time in intensive care, she's on the long road to recovery."

Rey's arms tighten around my waist, questioning in a trembling tone. "And, Parker?"

"*Miraculously*, he walked away without a scratch."

Rey inhales on a sob. "Oh, your poor friend. I can't imagine the pain he's in."

Tears track down the sides of my face, pooling in my ears as I hold my Sunshine as close as possible. "Me either."

I press a kiss to the top of her head. "Now sleep, baby. I've got you."

REYNA

The smell of bacon hits my nose, physically hauling me from the deep sleep I'd fallen into on the jet last night. I'd only roused long enough to stumble to the waiting town car, and upon reaching our building, Alex had carried me from there to our bed.

I have a bleary-eyed recollection of spotting an openly seething, red-faced Krista with a toad-like old man—clearly Ralph with the saggy balls—as I'd been transported across the marble foyer.

The memory makes me smile as I stretch, taking up the entirety of our empty bed, a feeling of sheer, bone-deep contentment filling me from head to toe.

Being back in Manhattan following the events of the past couple of days made everything feel completely different while remaining absolutely the same as before we'd left. The only adjustment being the fact that I can touch my not-so-fake, fake husband anytime I damn well choose.

And at that thought, I'm filled with the desire to embrace these new changes.

I make short work of relieving myself before quickly washing my face in an attempt to wake myself up properly. Then I slip into a satiny robe to cover the simple white cotton T-shirt of his that Alex had thrown over my head upon our return home last night.

My descent down the stairs is on silent, bare feet, and I walk into the kitchen to find Alex sitting at the kitchen island with two steaming mugs of coffee in front of him as he scrolls through his cell.

"Morning, pretty boy."

He looks up with a start. "Shit, Rey. Are you training for the silent ninja Olympics or something!"

My smile is from ear to ear as I take a seat across from him, taking the offered coffee from his left hand. "Nope. Just wanted to surprise you."

I take a sip as he stands with a smirk. "You do that effortlessly, baby." Then he closes the gap between us to cup my cheeks with his large palms. "Don't ever stop."

My smile is utterly shit-eating as he kisses the corner of my mouth before moving off to grab a plated stack of pancakes and bacon that I hadn't noticed before now.

The sight makes my stomach complain loudly, and Alex eyes me with a quirked brow. "I was going to serve you breakfast in bed, I'll have you know."

The plate barely hits the countertop before I pluck a piece of crisp bacon from it, popping it into my mouth with a moan of bliss.

"I'm famished."

Another piece follows the first while Alex settles beside me. "You don't say."

I narrow my eyes playfully as I dump a mountain of syrup on top of my pancakes.

"I have a surprise for you."

I press my lips together to suppress a grin as I swallow my mouthful of bacon, feeding him his words. "*You don't say*!"

"I can guarantee you'll like it."

I moan in bliss when I take my first bite of fluffy, syrupy pancakes, but just then, the elevator dings, and Alex rises with a grin. "Ah, right on time. He's nothing if not punctual."

My forehead puckers. "Who?"

A tall man with a shock of ginger hair, who looks strangely

familiar, rounds the corner of the kitchen, smiling hesitantly as he extends his hand. "Bailey Malone."

I take the offered hand with a small smile. "Reyna Marq—"

Alex cuts me off when he clears his throat pointedly, and I chuckle softly as I rephrase my answer. "Pleased to meet you, Bailey. I'm Reyna *DeMarco*."

Bailey smiles warmly, and the familiarity deepens, though I can't understand why.

"Bailey is Darcy's son, Rey."

My face brightens with a wide smile, finally catching on. "I *absolutely* see the resemblance."

He blushes bright red all the way from the starched collar of his white shirt to the tips of his ears before clearing his throat and finding his stride.

"*Ahem*, so today, I will be your companion for the tour, and then we—"

"Tour? What tour?" I spin questioning eyes toward my grinning husband.

"Surprise, Sunshine!" He rounds the island to cluck me under the chin, his eyes dancing in contagious delight. "Today, you're checking out properties for that dance studio I owe you."

"That last place was *perfect*."

One thing I've learned about Alex's assistant today is that he's very quick to smile, and he shoots me a bright one now as he nods excessively.

"Agreed. It was absolutely ideal. That floor space. *That* view!" He shakes his head in wonderment. "Your face was priceless! Would you like me to put in a bid?"

"Hell no!" My brows almost hit my hairline. "I mean, I should talk to Alex first. It's a lot of money—"

Bailey cuts me off softly. "Mr. DeMarco was *very* specific that there's to be no budget when it comes to what you want."

I shake my head as the town car rolls to a gentle stop. "There's really no rush. It can wait until after I've spoken to him."

Bailey regards me with knowing eyes, despite the tender age of our tentative friendship.

"If you're *sure*. The owner did mention several other interested parties…"

My mind is so utterly conflicted, and although I don't doubt that what Bailey said about a limitless budget is true—and very in character for Alex—I simply *can't* commit to something as monumental before going over everything.

I shake my head, firm in my decision. "No, thank you. I'd prefer to wait."

Ford—who Alex had insisted I bring with me today, ever mindful of my safety, despite the agreement with Everly and Keller—opens the rear passenger side door, and when Bailey slides out, I realize with a start that we are outside Molly Malones.

Bailey looks at me, red-faced and slightly sheepish. "I told Mom I was shadowing you today, and she made me swear to bring you by. I should have mentioned—"

"Not at all."

I slide across the back seat and step out onto the pavement beside him and Ford.

"I think it's a great idea. Ford, I'll contact you when I need to go home."

My stoic protector nods once, tipping his hat. "I'll check in on Alex. I won't be far."

I nod as he gets back into the town car before slipping out into the busy evening traffic.

Then Bailey gently steers me toward the pub.

"I'm sorry I didn't get back to see your mother in recent weeks. She's a really wonderful woman, and I've been meaning to visit, but life…it's just been…"

"Full on?"

I nod at his suggestion as we enter the large wooden doors of the homely Irish bar, finding it half-filled with a handful of servers milling about like worker bees. "That's accurate."

"I'm sorry you had to cut your trip short."

"It was wonderful, regardless of how long we had."

As I smile at the memories we created, and in particular the intimacy we shared, Darcy spots us from her place behind the long bar, where she's unloading a dishwasher of glasses.

"You *can* take instruction when the mood strikes! There's hope for you yet, Bailey Malone." She shifts her gaze to me, her eyes lighting up. "Well, well, well. Aren't you a sight for sore eyes!"

With a speed I'd not have expected, she rounds the bar to pull me into her arms. "I heard the news from Bailey, lovely. I'm so sorry for your loss."

I cling more tightly to her frame, choking on a newly formed lump in my throat.

"You know you always have a place here, Reyna."

She pulls back, leveling me with a look that surely means business. "I mean it now. If you ever need us, we're here."

She glances at her watch before rolling her eyes. "Leonard is late, but we'll start without him."

Bailey grins as he leads the way beyond the bar, into the staff quarters beyond, and takes the stairs on our right.

"Start what without him?"

Darcy shoos me on with the gusto of a mother hen. "Dinner,

of course. You look like you need some good old-fashioned home cooking."

I follow Bailey with a smile. "I'd go for more of that stew. It was *so* good."

When I reach the top of the stairs, he ushers me inside a pristine white kitchen, and my nose is instantly hit with the smell of what promises to be a delicious dinner.

Darcy bustles in past me, bee-lining for the stovetop as I take a seat at the large dining table that dominates the space.

"When I told Bailey to bring you, I knew for *sure* you liked stew. So, of course, I've made it again."

She grabs a ladle from the pot and a dish from the counter before filling it. Then she passes the steaming bowl to her son, who sets it before me at the table.

I look into it, spotting cubed potatoes and carrots in a thick gravy-like sauce alongside large chunks of beef, and the smell is altogether mouth-watering.

I notice that this time, it's served over a dollop of creamy mash, and my stomach suddenly riots with a sharp pang of hunger, having not stopped to eat since leaving home this morning.

Darcy sets a round wooden plate with a round loaf of bread on it in the center of the table before sitting beside me with her own bowl.

She nods at the plate. "Use the soda bread there for mopping up the sauce."

"Thank you. This is so—"

The door of the kitchen swings wide, admitting a red-faced Leonard.

"I could've sworn you said we were eating downstairs."

Darcy slowly spins on her seat, shaking her head, even as a smirk tugs at her lips. "And when, pray tell, do we *ever* eat in the pub, brother dear?"

She spears him with a no-nonsense look as poor Leonard blushes red right up to his receding hairline.

"Hi, Leonard."

His face breaks into a smile when my welcome lands on his ears. "Good to see you're doing well, Reyna." His eyes twinkle as he takes a seat beside Bailey. "And I hear congratulations are in order."

It's my turn to blush. I nod as I slowly eat my stew, even as my stomach screams for me to throw out my manners and shovel faster.

"Thank you."

"And please tell him that the car is ready when—"

Darcy breaks him off with a stern tone. "Oh, sweet baby Jesus, for the love of all that's holy. Ever heard tell of a *surprise*, you great big eejit?"

Leonard's eyes are wide, his hand clamped over his mouth in terror, but before I can question him further, Darcy swings around to me with an eye roll.

"Some people just sound better with their mouths closed, am I right, or am I right?"

Twenty-Eight

REYNA

Having whiled away two hours in the apartment over Molly Malones, I bid a smiling farewell to the wonderful Irish family who's clearly taken me under their wing.

Bailey, ever the personal assistant, makes short work of calling Ford, who said that he was on his way back from a personal errand to pick Alex up in Tribeca but would pick me up first.

By the time I bid Darcy and Leonard farewell and made it onto the pavement outside the pub, the familiar black town car is waiting right where he'd dropped us only a few hours earlier.

"I'll be waiting to hear about the bid for the studio over on Staten Island. Just give me the nod, Reyna."

I smirk. "It might not be that one."

He narrows his eyes playfully. "The heart wants what the heart wants, Little Miss Sunshine."

My mouth tugs up in a smile at that as Bailey lightly squeezes my upper arm before I slip into the back seat of the waiting car.

Ford slides out into traffic, navigating the lanes with ease until we enter Tribeca, when he flicks a quick glance over his shoulder. "Stay in the car. I've got to run inside really quick."

"Inside where?"

He shifts slightly in his seat, his shoulders tensing, and if I didn't know better, I'd say I've made him uncomfortable with that simple question.

He clears his throat. "Ah, it's Vaughn's club. He's meeting Grayson there."

My brow furrows deeply. "He's meeting his *grieving* friend at a *club*?" I can't keep the incredulity out of my tone. "That makes *zero* sense."

Ford expertly parks the car along the side of a brightly lit street opposite a teeming club, with an entry line no less than half a mile long.

"I'll be right back." Ford exits the car, sticking his head back inside for a split second to emphasize his next words. "*Stay. Here.*"

The door shuts with a light click, and he jogs across the road. But instead of going to the door that's being manned by a burly security guard, he moves into the shadows and opens a door that I'd have mistaken for a wall had I not seen him surreptitiously slip inside.

His instruction knocks around inside my brain for all of a hot minute before curiosity gets the better of me.

My feet follow in Ford's footsteps while I scan the street for any hiding paparazzi, thoroughly expecting them to jump out at a moment's notice.

When I reach the secret door, I easily find a latch that allows me to slip through and into a dark alley beyond.

Despite reservations, I move farther into the alley, which becomes darker the farther I go. I'm legitimately about to shit my pants, thoroughly regretting my decision to leave my cell in the car to follow my erstwhile bodyguard, when a spotlight illuminates the blackness, almost blinding me.

"Who're you?"

A deep voice makes me jump, and I blink rapidly, trying to dispel the dots that dance in my vision.

"Are you the last lot for the auction?"

A tall, tanned, and very clearly ripped man comes into view with a thatch of jet-black hair and a full beard that hides most of his features. His eyes are shockingly blue and staring right at me, clearly expecting an answer.

Shit!

"Um, *yeah*?"

My affirmative comes out as a question, but he doesn't take any notice, instead propelling me through the door and into a bustling room filled with half-naked men and women of all shapes, sizes, and ethnicities.

The room is huge, but I don't get more than a fleeting glance as my companion—who bears a startling resemblance to the actor who plays Rip in Yellowstone—steers me through the crowd and into a dimly lit corridor beyond.

"We'll have to go in the back way. The guests have already started to arrive."

My stomach lurches as I stumble after him, trying to keep up, terrified of being left in this strange place that I'd *assumed* was the nightclub Ford had mentioned.

Up ahead, I spot a pink neon sign that reads *Ravish,* but before we reach it, the Rip-wannabe hangs a right, bringing me into a changing room of sorts.

Lingerie, heels, and wigs of all colors adorn the wall running opposite the door, and he gestures sharply. "Get changed. I'll tell

Vaughn you're here..."

Oh my God! This is *Vaughn's club.*

He trails off pointedly, clearly waiting for my name.

"Umm, it's Reyna."

"Lucia will come to get you when it's your turn." He narrows his eyes suddenly, as though something has just occurred to him. "This your first time at Rogue?"

I swallow roughly, managing a singular sharp nod before choking out a question. "C-can I speak to Vaughn?"

He chuckles softly. "Lucia runs this side of things, though Vaughn does visit upon occasion. You may see him when you walk onto the stage – perhaps he'll break his rule and bid for you himself!"

"Bid for me?" I glance around the room, and realization dawns with a bang. "Oh my God. *Oh my God!*"

"You'll be fine; you've signed the paperwork. It's all consensual. Remember that." He grasps my upper arm gently, his blue eyes softening. "You can say no at any time. Lucia's a hard-ass, but Mr. Burton would never make you do something you're not wholly comfortable with."

With that, he exits the room, leaving me in a mess entirely of my own making.

ALEX

Having set Rey up for a day of studio shopping, I'd quickly gotten the ball in motion for the Grayson intervention that was sorely needed.

Having convinced him to meet me there later, I drove myself across town, took care of some business with Ford, and strode into Vaughn's office in Rogue after a quick dinner, ready to pull together to help my hurting friend.

I'm confused when I find Vaughn in deep conversation on his cell behind his desk.

"Can't you put him in WITSEC or something?"

I stop short upon hearing the most random of phrases.

What the fuck?

Vaughn sighs heavily, scrubbing his palm up and down his face as the person on the other end continues speaking. After a long while, he straightens, resignation heavily painting his features as he stands to pace his office, something he does when he's stressed but won't admit it.

"I'll be at work, Joseph. You'll need to come here."

More muted chatter before Vaughn hangs up his cell without another word.

"Everything okay?"

My hesitant question is answered with an utterly un-Vaughn-like shout.

"*Fuck*!"

He flops down into his desk chair, leaning back to expel a heavy breath. I take a seat opposite him, checking my watch surreptitiously and finding we have another couple of minutes before Gray is due to arrive.

"I've known you long enough now, Burton, to know you don't lose your cool. *Ever*. So whatever that call was about, spit it out quickly so we can clear the air before Grayson gets here."

Vaughn regards me with an unreadable look, weighing something up internally before softly asking, "Did I ever tell you how I could afford to buy Verity out of this place?"

I shake my head, keeping silent, knowing inherently that there are very few people to whom he *has* told this story, and he continues.

"My mum died when I was twelve. We'd just moved to the States, and she was working diner shifts most nights while I was sleeping."

He stops with a defensive tilt of his chin. "We were *broke*. She couldn't afford a sitter. It made sense, you understand?"

I open my mouth to answer, but he moves on without waiting for a response. "Anyway, one morning, on her way home from the graveyard shift, she was mugged by some junkie who pushed her out onto the road into heavy traffic. A cab hit her..."

He stops as his almost black eyes glaze over with memories of a time long past.

"There was no one to take me, and I'd have gone into the system had it not been for Julia, our neighbor—and the mother of the older boy who would become my best friend, Lorenzo."

His face changes, brightening up in a way I've never before seen. "We had some good times when I moved into the Caputo's apartment. I shared a room with Renzo even though he was three years my senior, and we did *everything* together."

He looks at me pointedly. "And when I say everything, I mean *everything*. We lost our virginity to the same girl at the same time, for fuck's sake." He huffs a dark laugh. "I was only fourteen, but we were inseparable."

His brow creases as his gaze shifts away, a look I can only describe as haunted taking over his features.

"We developed an idea together – I was in his advanced physics class if you'd believe. I could have been *anything*. Mum always said I could."

His smile is sad, almost like he can't believe it himself.

"Renzo's brains and my drive saw it come to fruition. All of a sudden, companies were beating down Julia's door, trying to buy the patent for our…no, for *his* work. And well, when the US government came knocking—"

"No way!"

He stops at my exclamation, nodding in resignation. "Yeah. We sold it. Made a small fortune, and Renzo continued to work with them developing new projects while I finished high school, much to my disgust. Motherfucker *loved* it, though."

A broad smile lights his face. "But he loved nothing as much as he worshipped the girl next door, Sara Ricci. Christ, if she told him to jump off a skyscraper, he'd have asked which one."

He snorts with a shake of his head. "And when she told him she was pregnant—despite the fact he hadn't long turned twenty—he was over the moon. And it was because of that… because his dreams were coming true that he wanted to help me achieve mine."

Silence fills the office, snaking its way around both of us like a serpent until I'm compelled to ask the inevitable question. "And what was your dream, Vaughn?"

He looks me square in the eye with no hint of an expression. "To dismantle everything my piece of shit father valued. Namely, this place. And so, Renzo gave me enough money so that I could approach Verity with more money than she could say no to, and the rest is history."

My stomach sinks, having a decent idea of where this is headed, but asking regardless. "So, where is he now?"

"Dead."

His single-worded answer rebounds through the space like the sound of a gunshot echoing, and I can't help the shudder that runs the length of my spine as he continues, his gaze fixated on his steepled fingers resting on the desk between us.

"The dispute with the scum who needed *Ravish* to remain

open…well, it escalated to the point where I wasn't able to leave the safety of the club without a threat on my life. And Renzo was caught in the crosshairs when they couldn't get to me."

"*Fuck*! I'm so sorry, Burton."

"Don't be sorry for me." He snaps his eyes to mine. "Be sorry for Sara. A single mom before their son even arrived into the world. Be sorry for Lorenzo's kid, growing up without his father. She named him Ren, you know."

He smiles sadly. "He'd have fucking loved that shit."

With a heavy sigh, he rises from his seat and silently fixes drinks for us both at the small liquor cabinet by the wall.

As he hands me my tumbler, his serious eyes find mine. "I've ensured that they have both been taken care of financially. Nice house, all the best schools for Ren, more money than they could spend in a million lifetimes…"

He drops back into his seat. "The only way Sara agreed to take the money was if I was removed entirely from their lives. And I've *always* kept to the terms."

He exhales a deep sigh. "Until now."

I can't keep my question from spilling out. "Why now?"

"Because Sara vanished last week, and foul play is suspected in her disappearance."

Shit!

"There's a very real possibility that Ren is in danger, too."

He nods at his cell sitting on the desk. "That was Joseph Fratelli, the lead detective on the case and a personal friend of mine. He thinks the only place Ren will be safe is *here*. With me. But to do that means breaking my promise to his mother, and—"

The door of the office slams open, cutting Vaughn off to admit a disheveled Grayson Hunter.

His hair is longer than usual and falling into his eyes. His clothes are crinkled, and the pink polo shirt he's wearing has a dried-in blob of what looks like ketchup smack in the middle of it.

He looks nothing like his typical, well-presented self, but it's the wild look in his eyes that makes me scared for him. And for the twins.

"I'm here. What's so important that I needed to delay my trip?"

Twenty-Nine

ALEX

Vaughn stands to fix Grayson a drink as he sits on the chair beside mine, his eyes fixed firmly on his clenched fists.

My forehead creases as I can *feel* the pain rolling off my friend in waves. It's soul deep, and my stomach churns at the thought of what he must be going through.

"I hear Gracie has been discharged. That's great." The forced chirpiness in my tone hurts even my own ears. "How are you doing, Gray? How's Parker holding up?"

He exhales heavily before accepting Vaughn's offered tumbler containing a more than generous measure of Macallan.

"We're alive. Is that to be considered a triumph or something?"

I exchange a worried look with Vaughn, who takes it upon himself to steer the conversation where we need it to go.

"I know it's only been a month, but have you given thought to Talia's parents' request?"

Hector and Eleanor Rivera were desperately wanting to take

the twins to live with them, if only until Gray managed to pull himself together from what Vaughn had been able to discern.

He whips his flashing green gaze toward Vaughn. "Not fucking happening. Our kids won't be another trophy for their collection."

He takes a sip of his drink. "It's all about image to them. To my parents, too. Tali and I hated that shit. Even as kids, we agreed that we'd never put *our* future kids through what we went through. No way. Parker stays with me. *Always*. End of discussion."

And suddenly, I cut the shit and just skip right to it. "Why are you going to Vermont, Gray? You're cutting yourself off from everyone who cares for you. Surely, that's not—"

I slam to a halt when he rises suddenly, and in a move wholly out of character, launches his tumbler across the room. It shatters to pieces when it hits the liquor cabinet, and he rounds on me with fire in his eyes.

"Have you ever lived with loss, DeMarco?"

His question is spat through gritted teeth, and before I can answer, he rushes on.

"Not just the loss of the woman I love and miss beyond all imagining. But the loss of what *should* have been. The loss of what will *never* be. And if traveling along the last path that she took brings Parker and Gracie a semblance of peace, then I'll continue to do it until I can't anymore."

He slowly walks toward the door, shooting over his shoulder. "I'll be staying in Vermont for the foreseeable. I can't give you a date for my return to the office – and being frank, I couldn't care less if I ever—"

"I've lived with loss, Grayson."

Vaughn's softly spoken words see Gray twisting back around to face us, even as his hand rests on the door handle, ready to escape at a moment's notice.

"Do whatever you need to do to get by, but please remember… grief is like the ocean."

He swallows heavily, and his forehead creases as he stares at an unmoving Grayson.

"It's vast…and it's deep. Some days, the water is still and serene. While on other days, the waves almost drag you under with their ferocity. It's up to you to learn how to swim."

The two men share a look until Gray nods sharply before leaving us in a heavy silence.

Vaughn breaks it first. "There's an auction starting shortly, DeMarco. You might want to…"

My stomach sinks as he trails off pointedly, and I grab my cell from my pants pocket to text Ford.

ME

I'm ready when you are.

He'd mentioned needing some time this evening to secure a contract for his security business. He reckoned that it would put him on the map in the private bodyguard sector, so I'm surprised when my cell chimes less than thirty seconds later.

FORD

On the way.

"Do you need to head over to *Ravish* yet?"

Vaughn checks his watch and then shakes his head. "Nah. I'm good to wait with you."

I drain the end of my Macallan, softly placing it back on the desk between us before I move to clean up Gray's smashed tumbler.

As I gather the larger pieces of glass, Vaughn's voice draws my attention. "All we can do is be there for him, Alex. That's what being a good friend is."

I nod as I finish cleaning up in silence until there's a knock at the door.

"Come in."

Jules, the mountainous security guard who mans the staff entrance, is standing outside.

"Hey, boss! I've delivered the last arrival to *Ravish*. Pretty little thing called Reyna."

There's no way!

"That's a very unusual name, Jules. What'd she look like?"

He presses his fingers to his lips. "She was chef's kiss perfection, Alex. Big brown eyes and lips just made to be wrapped around my cock—"

I push past him, Vaughn hot on my heels as Jules calls after us. "What'd I say?"

Neither of us replies as we march across the staff floor, Vaughn pulling out his cell to quickly dial Lucia, who readies the clients for auction.

"She's not fucking answering!"

I break out into a run, my gut telling me that it's her.

My Reyna.

I round the corner into *Risqué* and run smack into a shocked Ford.

"I was just on my way to find you."

I don't preamble. "Is Rey with you?"

His forehead puckers. "She's…outside."

My stomach dips. "She's in *Ravish*. She's been mistaken as a lot in tonight's auction!"

Horror fills Ford's face, and the three of us rush toward *Ravish* in single-minded determination.

Rather than entering through the usual door, Vaughn ducks to the side, leading us into an empty room packed with minuscule undergarments and wigs in every shade known to man.

"She's already gone with Lucia. Otherwise, she'd be here."

He leads us through the room and out into a backstage area that's interspersed with scantily clad girls, some giggling softly between themselves, others sitting silently in wait.

All of them willingly selling themselves for their own reasons.

My eyes scan the area, almost instantly finding the woman I'm looking for wearing a hot pink wig and matching negligee while she argues with a clearly irate Lucia.

"Take me to Vaughn *now*!" I can hear the frantic tone in her voice escalate with each word she speaks while Lucia looks on in blatant disbelief.

"Nice try, but no one gets to Mr. Burton unless he bids for them." She folds her arms with a self-satisfied smirk. "And he *never* bids, sweetie."

"*Lucia*!"

Vaughn barks the single word, and his second-in-command snaps her head up. "Vaughn! What are you doing here?"

Rey spots me and dashes headlong into my waiting arms. "Oh, thank God, you're here."

I bury my nose in the top of her head, inhaling her sweet fragrance, filling my lungs in the hope of quieting my palpitating heart.

If she'd been sent out onto that stage, there'd have been no takebacks. She would have been fair game, and only attendees with a bidder's paddle would have been able to win the lot.

Those are the rules.

Bidding wars aren't uncommon, from what Vaughn has told me. And there's no doubt in my mind that a woman as stunning as my wife would have instigated one in a heartbeat.

Vaughn turns apologetic eyes to me, and I hold up a quelling palm. "No harm, no foul, Burton. Is there somewhere we can—"

He cuts me off. "Come with me."

Then turns to Lucia with a dangerous scowl. "I'll deal with this shit in a minute. Don't you worry about that."

He brings us out through another door and down a long corridor that I've visited before in my early days at Rogue.

The Voyeur Chamber.

It's lined with doors on either side. Most of them have a red light lit up over the architrave, and when he finds an unlit one, he leads us inside.

"I'm sure you already know that the mirrors are single-way. You have utter privacy here. Take as long as you need." He moves to leave, shutting the door behind him with a soft click.

"I'm sorry, Alex."

Rey's words are muffled from where her face is flush with my shirt-clad chest. I hold her even more tightly against me. "What's there to be sorry for, Sunshine? You did nothing wrong."

She exhales shakily, clearly not herself as she angles her head upward to find my eyes. "Ford told me to stay in the car. I—I should have listened. I shouldn't have come—"

"It's *okay*. Nothing truly bad happened, hmm?"

Her forehead creases at my words, and that fire I so adore blazes to life in the depths of her dark eyes. "But those women out there are being auctioned like cattle, Alex. How can you say nothing bad happened? It's *happening* as we speak."

I blow out a breath and palm her cheeks. "Rey, some of those women out there have a need for the money this place provides. Some just enjoy the rush of being sold. Of carrying out whatever fantasies they're not living in their everyday lives. And if it wasn't happening here, it'd be happening elsewhere – and perhaps in a less secure environment than here."

She pulls herself out of my hold, disgust painting her beautiful face.

Disgust that's aimed at me. "And you're *okay* with what's happening here?"

She begins to pace, and it's then I notice her lack of clothing. "Here." I quickly unbutton and shuck out of my shirt. "Take this."

But she slaps it away, rage flowing through her body, swelling fast like a rising tide.

"You're a member of this club."

Her words are a stinging accusation, and I can only nod as my chest tightens painfully. "Yes, but—"

She chokes on a sob. "My gut is telling me that it couldn't be true, but I need you to say it, Alex." She swallows roughly. "Have you used this club since we've been married?"

REYNA

As soon as the question has left my mouth, Alex drops to his knees, a pained expression in his whiskey eyes. His hair is unkempt, as though he's been raking his fingers through it in the way he does when he's stressed or frustrated, and the urge to smooth it back from his brow is almost my undoing.

Your intuition is your gift.

Lita's words whisper across the shell of my ear, and though I *know* the answer, I fix my gaze on my husband, *needing* his words more than anything.

"Reyna DeMarco."

Butterflies burst to life in my stomach the same way they always do at the sound of my married name, and I soften ever-so slightly at the pleading honesty that I can clearly see on his face.

"I'm no saint. I have never claimed to be. And I've fucked up more times than I can count, but when it comes to *this*..." He gestures between us. "When it comes to *you*, I will do everything in my power to be the man you deserve. I don't *want* any other woman because all I *need*...is *you*."

He edges closer on his knees until we're almost touching. "Reyna, I haven't so much as glanced at another woman—here or elsewhere—since the moment I first laid eyes on you. All damp hair and sad eyes, desperately in need of a time-turner."

I reach out, cupping his cheek, and he turns his head to press a kiss to my palm, his eyes never once leaving mine. "You're everything I never dared to hope for and everything I didn't know I needed. I'm *finally* at peace with the path my life has taken because every step I took was leading me to *you*."

Silence surrounds us as our eyes hold, tears filling mine at those words that mean the world to me.

"It's like you've taken my broken pieces and poured yourself inside of them. Inside of *me*." He exhales heavily, his eyes intent on mine. "Being with you makes me feel *whole*, Sunshine."

In a fluid movement, he stands, pulling me against him to crush his mouth to mine with a groan.

I wrap my arms around his neck, pulling him as close as possible as our tongues dance together. My nipples poke through the practically sheer babydoll negligee that witch, Lucia, had forced me to wear, and I can feel them scrape off his bare chest, the motion sending a jolt of want straight to my pussy.

I yank my lips from him, breathing heavily against his panting mouth. "I want you beyond all reason, Alex. It's like you've buried yourself beneath my skin, anchored yourself in my damn bloodstream. I can't think, can't see clearly – I can't *breathe* without you."

Pressing a chaste kiss to his lips, I hold his gaze as he peers into my soul with an intensity that robs my lungs of all oxygen.

I exhale my next words on a tremulous breath. "I *love* you, flaws and all. The man behind the mask, the one you give to me and *only* me, Alexander DeMarco. I love you, probably more than is wise, and still, I continue to fall deeper every single day."

I shift my hips closer, needing him more than air. "Catch me when I fall?"

"Sempre, mio raggio di sole."

I smile softly. "What does that mean?"

He dusts the tip of his nose across mine, a heart-stopping lopsided smile dancing on his lips. "It means 'always, my ray of sunshine.'"

And then he wraps his hand around the nape of my neck, yanking me closer to him to press our mouths together.

Pulling back for a moment, he rests his forehead against mine. "I am *yours*, Rey. Just as much as you are *mine*."

His eyes spear me with an intensity that makes my belly flip-flop. "And the thought of anyone else getting their hands on what's *mine* makes me fucking crazy."

I press my mouth to his, halting his words, needing to feel exactly how much he *wants* me. Reveling in the clear fact that he *needs* me.

His tongue massages mine slowly before I close my mouth around it, sucking hard and making him jerk beneath my demands.

"Oh shit, Rey. I need to feel you. I need inside you. Right fucking *now*!"

My legs go around his waist when he slams me up against the wall, and he draws his tongue along the line of my neck right up to my ear before swirling the lobe into his hot mouth.

"Tell me you'll take me, baby. *Please.*"

I cry out helplessly as I push my hips against his, seeking the relief of his cock buried deep inside me.

"Yes, oh please, *yes*. I need you, Alex."

He reaches between us, sliding my panties to one side before pushing his thick middle finger into my wet center.

I throw my head back, thrashing from side to side as I try to push against his hand, needing more. Needing it *now*. He stops laving my neck with wet kisses to pull back and look at me with a wide grin. "Such a greedy little pussy you have, Sunshine. The more I give her, the more she wants."

He adds a second blissful finger, even as I pump against his hand, eager for more.

"*Shit*! Your sweet cunt is just *begging* to be fucked, isn't she?"

His filthy words do things to my insides, and my head is suddenly hazy as he stretches me roughly with a third finger.

I cry out as he angles his fingers perfectly, making me crazy as he drives me closer to the orgasm that hovers *just* beyond my reach.

Until he withdraws his fingers from my wet pussy, and I whimper as though in pain. "Please don't stop!"

But leaning closer with a dark expression on his handsome face, Alex wraps his hand around my throat, tugging me closer so that I am inhaling his next words.

"Before I give your greedy cunt the fucking she clearly needs…" He trails off, bringing his thumb up to graze my bottom lip, tugging it down exactly like that night at the gala.

Except for this time, I suck it inside my mouth, swirling my tongue as his lashes flicker, threatening to fall shut, and giving me the ultimate sense of power at this moment.

"I'm going to need to see you on your knees, Sunshine, with my cock between these perfect lips as you choke for me…" He spears me with his whiskey eyes. "Can you do that for me, baby? Can you suck my dick like the dirty fucking girl I know you are?"

Thirty

ALEX

My wife's doe eyes darken before she drops to her knees, her hands working at the button and zipper of my dark pants to free my throbbing cock.

Her eyes shift down to take in my size as she grips my dick at the base to bring the tip between her lips, swirling her tongue across the top slowly. She looks up at me then, her eyes fixing firmly on mine.

The sight of her plump lips taking me into her mouth inch by inch turns me on so much that I can *feel* my precum leaking onto her teasing tongue.

"Shit, Sunshine. Your mouth is perfection."

Then she moves down along my shaft, sliding almost to the base when she sucks *hard*.

My hips jerk, and she starts moving her mouth up and down, working my cock deeper inside, hitting the back of her throat as she picks up speed.

Another hard suck almost makes me see stars, so I work my

hands into her long dark hair, balling it up on the top of her head and holding it tight to control the tempo.

"If you keep that up, I'll blow in your mouth, and then that hungry little pussy of yours will go without."

She allows me to hold her steady so that I can slowly pump my hips, feeding my cock in and out of her hot mouth. I hit the back of her throat, making her eyes water, and suddenly, she hollows her cheeks and sucks harder than before.

I pull my cock out of her mouth, a mixture of saliva and precum linking us as I roughly lift her to stand. Palming her ass cheeks, I pick her up into my arms, her eyes holding mine as their willing prisoner. Her legs wrap tightly around my waist as I press her against the wall, grinding my dripping cock against her wet heat.

Her low moan of pleasure is swallowed when I take her mouth with mine, sliding my tongue against hers, tasting my precum in the depths of her sweet mouth.

She cries out against my lips when I push my hips forward, circling them against her clit. "Oh, shit, that's *so* good!"

She gasps for air when I continue to grind against her, dropping my mouth down along her neck, nipping and sucking as I go until I reach her barely covered nipples.

I draw one into my mouth through the material of the negligee, swirling my tongue in a figure-eight motion that makes her whimper loudly, thrashing her head from side to side and raking her nails across my back. Then I move to the other, repeating the process, driving her wild with need.

She grips my shoulders, using them to leverage herself against me so that she can grind back against my cock, and suddenly, I can't take any more.

Using one hand, I rip the flimsy panties from her body, making her cry out in needy anticipation.

Then I reach between us to grab my cock, and bring it to her slick core, sliding it through her wetness before tapping the head roughly against her engorged clit.

She gasps. "Oh, fuck. Do that again!"

I smirk as I continue to torture her, gliding through her soaked folds to tap, tap, tap, tantalizingly against that swollen bud until she's squirming against me.

Notching the tip at her entrance, I reach out with my free hand to palm her throat and hold her in place. "Now I'm going to fuck this insatiable cunt the way she needs me to, baby."

I feed another inch into her, and her mouth falls open as her lashes grow heavy beneath the force of the sensations I'm bringing to life within her.

The feeling of her tight, wet pussy wrapped around my bare cock is almost enough to make me come, and I'm filled with the need to take her hard and rough. To fill her with my cum until it's dripping down the inside of her thighs. To push it back inside of her greedy little cunt so that she'll know *exactly* who she belongs to.

"I don't think I can be gentle this time, Rey."

Her eyes focus on mine, and she sinks lower onto my dick, taking me all the way inside her body as my hand tightens on her throat. "I don't need you to be gentle, pretty boy."

She pops a devilish brow as though she's just read my thoughts. "I need you to show me who I belong to."

REYNA

Alex surges forward at my words, seating himself fully inside of me, and we both moan together as our mouths clash.

His tongue rages against mine in a heated battle while his hips slam forward, and mine rise to meet him as I cling to his broad shoulders.

He drops his hand from my throat, slipping down between us to land unerringly on my clit, brushing firmly back and forth across the swollen nub, and I break our kiss when I throw my head back, crying out in sheer pleasure.

He peppers my face with kisses before latching onto the sensitive skin on the curve of my neck, sinking his teeth into the flesh in a painful pleasure that makes me want *more*.

Suddenly, he changes the angle, hitting impossibly deeper inside of me, and without warning, I'm thrown off the sheer cliff of ecstasy.

"I'm coming, I'm coming, *shit*!"

His growl hits my ears as I drown his cock with my pleasure, soaking both of us as I come so hard I feel slightly faint.

But I don't have time to recover before Alex pulls out of me and kneels with his head between my legs. "That's mine."

He hooks a shaky knee over one shoulder, then parts my pussy lips with his thumbs. "*Shit*, that's so fucking beautiful, Sunshine. The sight of your orgasm dripping down your bare pussy and pooling between your ass cheeks gets me *so* damn hard."

Then he latches his mouth onto my clit, sucking it inside his hot mouth and making me whimper as I steady myself by holding his sweat-slick locks.

He dips his tongue farther back, lapping at my wetness, his eyes fixed on mine as he cleans my orgasm from my sex, even as he drives me closer to another.

Two fingers dip inside my core as he presses his flattened tongue against my clit, devouring me with long, deep licks. He increases the pace of his fingers, matching the rhythm with his tongue, and his eyes fall shut as a low hum of satisfaction thrums through his chest.

My breathing comes in short gasps, edging closer and closer to another spectacular orgasm when he sucks sharply on my clit.

I hit the peak of pleasure and sob loudly as my whole body is engulfed in the fiery flames of exquisite euphoria.

As I'm descending from my pinnacle, I dimly note being lifted and carried across the space toward a previously unnoted low couch.

Alex gently drops me onto my knees, then kneels behind me to palm the middle of my back, urging me to bend forward. I press my cheek against the soft material of the sofa, as he grips my ass in both hands.

"Shit, Rey. This *ass* is fucking delectable."

In my peripheral vision, I see him bend lower and then disappear from sight. Then I feel his teeth nip the fleshy skin of my ass before he draws his tongue the length of my body, all the way up along my back, until his mouth hovers by my ear.

"And one day, I'm going to own this hole too."

His filthy words send a shiver down my spine, settling delightfully in my core, turning me on more than I'd ever have thought.

He lines his cock up between the cheeks of my ass, pumping against me with a low groan against the nape of my neck. "Has anyone else ever fucked you here, baby?"

My breath comes in short gasps as his hand snakes around my hip, his thumb dusting lightly over my cum-slick clit. My body ripples beneath him, and he thrusts his hips harder as I press my forehead against the couch, shaking my head in reply to his question.

"Mmm." His low growl of approval sends a flood of wetness

straight to my pussy.

"*My* dirty fucking girl."

And as though in reward for giving the right answer, he presses his thumb harder, flicking and pinching my clit in a way that sees me arching my back, pleading for more.

And he delivers.

He straightens to line himself up at my drenched core, thrusting forward to seat himself deep inside me, and we both simultaneously groan in sheer fulfillment.

My pussy clamps down on his cock as he slowly runs his palms almost reverently along my ass before grasping my hips with both hands.

And then he drives his cock as deep as he can, making me scream against the cushions while he continues to fuck me at piston pace.

He pulls me back onto his cock, shifting me upright so that his chest is against my back. Then he holds me in place with a firm palm wrapped around my throat.

His mouth is by my ear, whispering filthy words that set me on fire as his free hand grabs mine to bring it down between my legs.

"Play with your sweet cunt for me, Sunshine. I want her to drown my cock when I paint your insides with my cum."

He presses my fingers against my throbbing clit, harshly rubbing back and forth, and the pressure of his hand around my throat increases as my head falls back against his shoulder.

His rhythm begins to falter as he approaches his peak, and my own hips move frantically, chasing our joint rapture.

His cock pulses right when his thumb and index finger pinch my clit, and I go off like a firecracker as I feel him coming deep inside me. He continues to send aftershocks of cum into my pussy, each one making me gasp as small waves of pleasure continue to ripple between us.

Without a word exchanged, he slowly withdraws from my body before picking me up and laying me down on the low couch.

"Open your legs for me, Rey."

I do as instructed, allowing my legs to fall open to show him the evidence of our coming together.

I can feel his cum trickling out of me, down along my asshole, and pooling on the couch beneath me. All the while, his eyes are glued to the sight. I watch in thrall as his nostrils flare and his breathing becomes labored.

After a long beat, he slides his hand along my leg, all the way to the apex of my thighs, running his fingers along my pussy before dipping two inside of me. The sound of our combined orgasm being pushed back inside me hits my ears, making me gasp sharply.

My pussy clenches around his fingers, and his mouth twitches with an unsuppressed grin. "Such a greedy fucking pussy."

He lowers his head, pressing a kiss to my quivering clit as he pushes his cum farther inside of me. Then he looks up at me, that lovable lop-sided smile front and center on his handsome face.

"*My* greedy pussy, Sunshine."

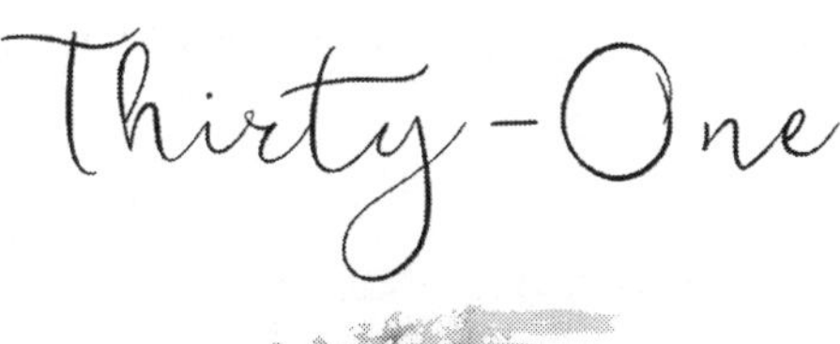

ALEX

Having mustered the wherewithal to clean up Rey and myself, I poke my head out into the corridor and find fresh clothes for both of us.

Thank you, Mr. Burton!

I silently vow to send him a cask of Macallan as I help Reyna get dressed, and moments later, we slip out into the corridor, returning the way we'd come.

We pass by the ongoing auction, with no sight of Vaughn, but Ford is waiting, stoic and still, by the side of the stage.

"Are you ready to go?"

He jumps at my question, clearly fixated on the sight before him, but he nods, turning to lead the way out through a different corridor until we come upon a door.

When he presses his palm to a biometric scanner, the door swings open. I immediately note that we're back in *Risqué* as Rey's eyes take in the level of debauchery this tier thrives on.

In the alcove to our left, two naked women—one masked,

one unmasked—are kissing passionately on the floor at the feet of a tall, slender, masked man wearing a very expensive-looking black suit.

He says something to them that we can't hear, and instantly both women stop what they're doing to crawl toward him as he unbuckles his belt.

Rey's eyes go wide when she glances around the alcove, taking in the other members all watching the ongoing show in silent delight.

We move on, the sounds of pleasure filling the dimly lit area until the sound of the low pulsing beat of the music from *Rapture* hits our ears.

Ford pushes open a hidden door, admitting us to the first tier of Rogue with a smile. "Take your time leaving. I need to go ahead of you to check that the area is clear, then I'll meet you at the car."

He ducks back into *Risqué,* clearly far more familiar with the nooks and crannies of this sprawling place than I am.

With time to kill, I pull Rey onto the dance floor, and hold her body close to mine. "Dance with me, wife."

She smirks up at me, then narrows her eyes. "Hey! You never told me how you learned to dance."

I'm helpless to stop my mouth from lifting in a huge grin. "I learned in my teens."

Her mouth drops open, and she shoves me half-heartedly. "You knew *all along*?! You asshole! Why did you tell me you had two left feet that day?"

I drop my forehead to hers as I cup her cheeks. "I knew within a moment of meeting you that I'd do *anything* just to see you smile."

Her eyes fill with tears as our gazes hold while we sway to the music until the song comes to an end.

I tug Rey in against my side as we leave the dance floor, and we make our way out of the brightly lit, jam-packed club to find none other than Chad Freemont exiting his town car.

Freemont's face is purple, mangled, with a split lip, swollen black eye, and Steri-Strip across his left eyebrow. His right arm is bandaged right against his body, and he's *clearly* limping.

He looks frantically from me to Rey and back again, his gait wavering as he internally debates what to do next.

I take a threatening step closer, and to my twisted delight, Freemont slinks back toward his town car, his immediate reaction to cower from me.

"What the *fuck* do you think you're doing here?" My words are a snarl even to my own ears, and the piece of shit flinches as though I've hit him – and not for the first time today.

"I *know* I told you to stay the fuck away from my wife, Freemont." Rey stiffens beside me, her quick mind connecting the dots almost instantly.

I take another step closer to him, and he holds his hands up. "P-p-please, I—I won't cause any more t-t-trouble."

"What do you need to say to Reyna?"

His eyes flit between both of us before he dips his head. "I'm the scum of the earth and don't deserve to be allowed to breathe after how I treated you."

He raises questioning eyes to mine, and I deadpan. "And the rest, Freemont. Don't forget the best part."

He swallows almost painfully, and I press my lips together at the sadistic joy that flows through my veins at his next words. "I'm sorry."

Rey just stands numbly, taking in the scene before her, so I bark at the prick, "Now you can fuck off. And I don't want to see your face here or at Malones *ever* again."

We move past him, stepping out onto the street to the parked black town car, Ford waiting at the rear passenger door with a grin.

Once we're safely inside, she rounds on me.

"*What* did you do to him?"

"Gave him what was coming, Sunshine."

"Are you sure this is the place?"

Ford just rolls his eyes at my question before pushing open the door to the pawn shop he claims is a front for a brothel upstairs.

"Can I help you, gentlemen?"

A short, squat man with a receding hairline and sleazy smile greets us from behind a desk.

"Watermelon, lollipop, daisy."

His eyes light up at Ford's crazy words, and he quickly reaches beneath his desk to press a button that allows the bookcase behind us to swing open softly.

"Have a good day."

He goes back to his business as Ford leads the way past the bookcase and up steep stairs leading into a dark hallway.

"I have it on good authority that he's in room 315, so keep your eyes peeled."

We move quickly down the hall, checking door after door until, eventually, *we find 315.*

Low sobs are coming from within, and we both exchange a look before a cry renders the almost silence.

"I told you to scream, *bitch!"*

Nostrils flaring, Ford draws back and kicks the door open, much to the disgust of a naked Chad Freemont.

"What the fuck is this? I'll sue you, you bastard. Get the fuck—"

He stops, spotting me behind Ford, and his indignation turns to amusement. "Oh, yes. I've been waiting on you to figure it out."

I step closer, rage dripping from every word. "If she'd told me sooner, I'd have kicked your ass long before now."

His forehead crumples in confusion as he tugs on a pair of shorts, finally covering his piss-poor excuse for a limp dick. "How did she figure it out before you?"

It's my turn to frown. "How did who figure what out? What the hell are you talking about, Freemont?"

He rolls his eyes and tuts loudly. "It's surprising that your wife would figure out my hand in the media leaks before you would…" He trails off and smirks.

"Though she did claim *to have been valedictorian, so…" He lets his words hang between us for a long beat.*

And suddenly, the massively intrusive media all makes sense. They've always been invasive, but since I met Rey, things have been unbearable.

And despite seething internally, I push it to one side, and firmly fixate on getting justice for this cunt's treatment of my wife.

"Doesn't matter anymore. It's all been taken care of." I cross my arms over my chest and pin him with a look. "Just means I'll go that little bit harder on you for being a bigger twat than I'd initially thought."

I turn to a stony-faced Ford. "Take the lady downstairs and call the cops. Shut this place down."

Chad's loud shout of protest reverberates through the room. "The fuck you will!"

"Just watch me, asshole!"

I step closer, menacingly. "But first, you're going to pay for laying your hands on my wife*!*

Reyna's face is lit up with a bright smile when I finish telling her about the errand I'd run with Ford earlier as she'd studio shopped with Bailey. My face mirrors hers before her lips hungrily seize mine with a ferocity that leaves me breathless and wanting a helluva lot more.

She breaks the kiss to pant against my mouth, "I told that prick once before that karma is a bitch – and hearing that he got what was coming to him makes my karma-loving heart so damn happy, I could burst!"

As we pull up outside our building, Ford catches my eye in the rearview mirror, the hint of a smile playing across his lips, and I press a kiss to the top of my Sunshine's head, feeling a sense of contentment I'd never dreamt of until now.

I wake to text messages chiming in on my cell, one after the other.

Ding. Ding. Ding. Ding. Ding.

"Jesus fucking Christ!"

I grab my cell from its place on the nightstand and mute it as Rey burrows deeper into the covers, not quite ready to face the day after our late night last night.

I swipe up the screen, unlocking the cell and tapping on the steady stream of texts that keep coming.

Most of the messages are from my brother, so that's the obvious place to start.

HENRY

The board are climbing up my ass here, Al. Is it fucking true?

I rub the sleep from my bleary eyes, dimly wondering what

the fuck rumor is circulating now as I scroll to the next message.

VAUGHN

Call me immediately when you get this.

I scroll on despite my friend's explicit instruction, my heart rate kicking up a notch.

FORD

I can have extra security in place if you require it today.

Why the fuck would I need extra *security now?*

LIV

I know it's not true, Alex. I'll deal with Henry. You focus on Reyna.

My stomach dips at the words from my best friend, and I gently push back the covers, padding softly to the bathroom so as not to wake my lightly snoring wife.

I close the door with a barely audible *snick*, but before I can key in Vaughn's cell number, an email pops up in my notifications that sends a shiver down my spine.

Sender: Caleb Jones (calebjones@demarcoholdings.com)

Recipient: Alexander DeMarco (alexanderdemarco@demarcoholdings.com)

Dear Mr. DeMarco,

The Board has received some alarming news and requests the pleasure of your company at your first available opportunity.

Contact my secretary to make the relevant

arrangements.

Caleb Jones

Chair of the Board of Directors for DeMarco Holdings

I swipe the email away and dial Vaughn as I try to get a handle on my panic. He answers on the first ring.

"Have you spoken to anyone else yet?"

I huff impatiently. "Look, fucker. I've just woken up after a busy-ass evening. I don't have time—"

"I have it on good authority that there's another shitstorm coming for you, DeMarco. Another woman out for a payday…" He gives me a second to digest what he's said, as though it's not a knife to the gut.

But it's his next words that twist that knife, bringing me to my knees in the middle of my ensuite.

"This one is seven months pregnant. And a paternity test says that you're the father."

ALEX

There's ringing in my ears, and the white tiles of my bathroom seem to go in and out of focus. My breathing comes in short bursts, and I manage to verbalize my wild thoughts.

"I can't…" I inhale a shaky breath. "I can't…"

I desperately inhale through my nostrils, but still, my lungs feel oxygen deprived. "I can't lose her."

My breath catches in my throat.

"She's *everything*, Vaughn."

My breathing speeds up, only to stall entirely when the feeling of betraying Rey, of being *this fucking close* to having something real, only to see it taken away by something I have no control over, robs the breath from my lungs, and I lean forward, pressing my forehead against the cool tiles.

"Christ, DeMarco! Breathe. You sound like you're having a motherfucking coronary over there. We can fix this!"

My breathing escalates, and tears fill my eyes, dropping right down onto the tile before my face, as the loss of Rey—the loss of what we could build together despite my unworthiness—fills me from head to toe.

"I'm sending in Ford. He's downstairs waiting to hear from me."

I try to force myself to speak, to say no, but the single word won't fucking come, and I silently curse myself for being such a damn screw-up.

No one loves you, Alexander. No one cares.

I can hear Vaughn on another call, clearly speaking with Ford as my mother's words break through the haze in my mind.

"SHE CARES!"

My words are a roar, bellowing at the top of my lungs before I let my body sag onto the tiled floor, repeating the words over and over again, even as my brain tells my mouth to stop.

"She cares. *She cares*. She *loves* me."

Rey appears in the doorway, a terrified look overtaking her beautiful face, and she runs toward me to fall to her knees.

"Oh my God, Alex!"

She gathers my head onto her lap, stroking back my hair with one hand, soothing me softly as she picks up my discarded cell from the bathroom floor.

"Vaughn?"

Whatever he says, she hangs up and runs both hands through my hair, the motion calming my racing thoughts and palpitating heart.

"Vaughn is on his way. And Ford, too."

She dusts her knuckles across my cheekbone, gently wiping away the evidence of my emotions.

"Whatever it is, I'm here." My stomach flips nauseatingly, and I twist my head to look up at her gentle smile as she feeds me my own words. "Rule three, remember? *I've got you,* pretty boy."

I swallow past the ball of emotion that's lodged in my throat and blow out a breath.

"*Please,* don't leave me, Rey."

She smiles softly, her thumb tracing the contours of my face as she shakes her head. "I'm not going anywhere, I prom—"

"Don't make promises you might not want to keep."

Her forehead crumples as concern paints her face. I clear my throat as my eyes fall closed. "There's a woman saying that she's pregnant with my child."

REYNA

"He'll be down in a minute."

Vaughn and Ford nod before they each take a seat at the kitchen island.

"Tea? Coffee?"

Vaughn shakes his head as he stands. "There's whisky in the home office."

When he steps out of the kitchen, Ford looks at me with intense eyes. "Did he speak with you?"

I grit my teeth as I nod.

"He said there's someone who claims to be having his baby."

I almost choke on those last words. Even saying it out loud doesn't seem real.

I've always used protection.

I flick on the coffee machine as Alex's words from Costa Rica swim around inside my brain, trying to make sense of everything.

"I know it sounds bad, but has a paternity test been—"

Ford cuts me off with a terse nod, and I turn away as tears

prick the backs of my eyes.

"Henry and the Board were the first to be approached, and they organized one immediately. From the looks of things, Rey, this has been in the works since before you went to Costa Rica, but the results only came through this morning."

My responding nod is slow, resigned, as Ford continues to speak.

"She's come forward to request a settlement, citing that she doesn't want to unnecessarily upset Alex's wife; otherwise, she's going to sell her story to Keller Media."

I make myself a cup of hot tea, and as I finish, I spot Vaughn hovering outside the door of the kitchen, his face frozen in thought.

"I'm going to call my guy. We'll dig deeper."

He walks closer, sets his whisky down on the kitchen counter, and pulls his cell from his vest pocket.

He keys in the number, his eyes locked on me as he barks instructions down the line.

"Research everyone she's ever come into contact with, starting with most recent interactions. Work colleagues, neighbors, her OB-GYN, and all records you can find. I need it yesterday."

He hangs up. "Now we wait."

By the time Alex has showered and changed, I have a whole new narrative ready to present.

"You want to *what*?"

Alex sits forward from his place on the opposite sofa, sloshing his tumbler of Macallan all over the leg of his pants.

I clear my throat and repeat myself. "I want to meet her. I need to speak with her in person. Woman to woman."

He scrubs his free hand down along his face with a weary sigh. "Can't we just pay her the damn money and put it to rest?"

"*NO*!" My voice rings out alongside Vaughn's and Ford's.

"We do our due diligence first, DeMarco." Vaughn leans across the coffee table, spearing Alex with an obsidian stare. "Something's not adding up."

"I don't buy it." My words have all eyes shooting to me. "It's too convenient. The timing. The circumstances. Going to Henry and the board to 'save my feelings.' It feels much too contrived. She's *assuming* that you'll do whatever it takes to stop this news from reaching my ears. That you'll pay out without a second thought."

Alex looks at his hands, clearly needing a minute to absorb what I'm saying before I softly murmur, "I'm not believing it, not for a second. No matter what that test said. It's *wrong*."

His eyes shoot up to meet mine, apparently hearing the conviction in my tone.

I slip from my seat beside Vaughn to round the low coffee table between us and slide onto my husband's lap. Cupping his face in my palms, I hold his whiskey eyes with fierce intent.

"Lita always told me that my intuition is my gift. She was right. *It is*! And it's telling me—no, it's *screaming* that this is bogus. *Something* is off."

He shakes his head, a frown firm on his usually carefree face, and the sight just about kills me. "Sunshine, I—"

Vaughn's cell begins to ring, cutting him off as all eyes in the room swing toward the sound.

"What did you find?"

Vaughn's guy obviously found something of note because as they speak on the other end of the line, Vaughn's eyes light up slowly.

"Keep digging."

And following that instruction, he ends the call, a smile tugging at his mouth. "So, get this. The girl—Iris—has a link to GenoCell, the lab that analyzed the paternity samples. Aidan Marsh, the father of her other child, works there!"

My mouth drops open as hope swirls in the depths of my stomach.

I shift about to take in my husband's disbelieving face, his mouth opening and closing like a goldfish before he manages to mutter, "At this point, I'm not sure if I need a time-turner or a nap because, *Jesus,* it's not even 10 a.m., and this day has made me age a good decade."

Once Alex touches base with Henry, the process goes a lot more smoothly.

Henry was able to act as the go-between for Alex and a very irate chairman of the Board, who really wasn't buying anything Henry was saying, much to his intense annoyance.

He immediately organized a meeting between himself and the illusive Iris for later in the afternoon, where he told her that he would give her the cash that she had asked for. She wanted to keep it discreet and in a neutral location, so asked to meet him on the main deck of the Empire State Building.

But, in what I have come to learn is true DeMarco fashion, Henry booked out the observation deck for the entirety of the afternoon, ensuring absolute privacy.

The ride in the elevator takes less time than I recall ever taking on my previous visits, and before I know it, I'm stepping out into the lobby that's weirdly empty.

I straighten my spine, fully confident in what I'm about to do, and march single-mindedly out onto the observation deck.

A pale, thin girl with lackluster brown hair falling almost to her waist meets me. She almost appears vaguely familiar somehow, and I can't help frowning at how she's not at *all* what I expected.

Her baby bump should be much bigger for being seven months along, and it again reinforces my instinct that everything is not what it seems.

"Iris?"

She turns her wide brown eyes to mine, blinking rapidly as she glances left and right, clearly taken by surprise at my appearance.

"Where's the other guy? The brother? He's the one I'm supposed to meet."

She turns to leave, realizing that we're eighty-six floors above the ground, her shoulders sagging as she turns to face me with uncertain eyes.

"I'm Reyna. I'm—"

She cuts me off. "I know exactly who you are."

I nod softly, something inside of me telling me that I need to take things gently with her.

"I only want to talk." I hold up my hands, palms facing her. "Is that okay? Can we talk?"

She shakes her head rapidly, her long hair swishing around her face. "I can't talk to *you*. He'll—"

She stops suddenly, as though she's said too much, and I tilt my head to the side in question.

"Who? Your boyfriend? Ex-boyfriend?"

"I don't have a boyf—"

I step closer, cutting her off softly. "We know about Aidan, Iris."

She flinches, and my chest tightens, feeling her conflict on a visceral level. "Oh, Iris, is *he* making you do this?"

This woman is an innocent party. She doesn't want to be here.

I can feel it in my gut.

"*No*! God no. Aidan loves me." She cradles her small bump protectively. "He loves *us*."

"Then who, Iris? I *know* Alex isn't your baby's father."

Her eyes blow wide as she begins to shake her head. "We know Aidan works at GenoCell. It's just a matter of time before the authorities are involved and you both wind up behind bars."

She presses her lips together, shaking her head as tears well up in her eyes. Her nostrils flare when those tears crest over her lashes, streaking down along her face, and a feeling of overwhelming sorrow flows through my veins.

I approach her slowly, speaking soothingly, as though to a small child. "And who will take care of your baby then, Iris? Use your head. *Think*! We can help. No one will hurt you—"

"*No*!" She cuts me off, holding her hand out for the bag holding the cash that Henry gave to me. "I'm not falling for it. He's right. Tough times don't last, but tough people do. I'm stronger than I look."

Tough times don't last, but tough people do.

A shiver races up along my spine, hearing those words as though spoken from the mouth of the man I hate more than anything.

The man who tried to ruin my life.

And I'd stake my life on the clear fact that he's the one who's trying to do it again.

I narrow my eyes as I look at Iris now, my gut telling me *exactly* what's happening here.

"It's Victor Marquez, isn't it!"

I bark the words, letting them echo around the observatory, and she flinches openly. "No, don't—"

I approach her slowly, afraid to spook her. "How did he get to you? Debts? Gambling? They're his usual wheelhouse."

She shakes her head, swallowing a sob as she tries to back away.

"I can *help* you, Iris. *Please*! Is he behind this?"

She closes her eyes, inhaling a breath through her nose before opening them again. Her face is filled with a resolution that wasn't there before.

"He's my father."

I freeze at her words, shock traveling through every inch of my body as she looks at me with pleading eyes.

My mind races to catch up with what she's just said as she takes a step closer, sincerity painting her eerily familiar features, and suddenly, it all makes sense.

She takes another step, her words low but firm, and I feel the truth of them in my bones. "Reyna…I'm your half-sister."

Thirty-Three

ALEX

"Absolutely fucking not. There's no way that's happening, Rey."

I fold my arms across my chest, spearing her with a look that brooks no argument, only for her to cock her head to one side with her eyes narrowed to slits.

"I'm doing it, and you *won't* stop me, Alexander DeMarco."

Rey had come back from the meeting with Iris holding some hugely valuable information.

Firstly, and thankfully, the baby in question is *not* mine.

Secondly, her father is behind the extortion and has been forcing her younger half-sister to do his bidding by threatening to harm Iris and Aidan's three-year-old son. He'd put Aidan in the hospital last night with a concussion and a ruptured spleen when he'd tried to stand up to him.

Finally, third and most unsettling for me, she wanted to go with Iris to confront their father. We now know that Victor is waiting for the money at Iris's house, and my tiny wife is dead set on getting concrete evidence that he'd committed theft and fraud when he left her and Mari penniless.

Her determination to make him pay would be a complete turn-on if the thought of putting her in danger in order to achieve her goal wasn't giving me a damn stomach ulcer.

"I could have *been* her, Alex! Don't you *see*? I had Lita in my corner. Iris had no one. Her mom didn't protect her from him, but *I can*. I can guarantee that he can't hurt anyone else ever again."

Tears fill her big brown eyes. "I *can't* let him get away with everything he's done."

A tear crests her bottom lashes, tracking down her flushed cheek. "He can't ruin her life too. He needs to be stopped, Alex. He needs to *pay* for his sins!"

And it's my undoing.

"Oh, sweet Jesus." I gather her into my embrace, holding her far too tight as I press a kiss to the top of her dark head. "I have conditions before I allow you to enter the lion's den, Sunshine."

Her gasp of surprise sees her pulling back to look up into my face, delight pouring from every pore of her unblemished skin. "I'll do everything you tell me. I promise."

"You can bet your sweet ass you will."

Her lips twitch with the hint of a smile, and I heave a sigh of resignation.

"Okay, here's what we're going to do."

"I don't like this, Rey."

"Of course you don't. I'm hardly jumping for joy over here." She shoots me a quelling look, arching her brow pointedly as Ford finishes taping the wire to her chest. "But a deal's a deal."

She shifts her gaze to Ford. "Are we done?"

He nods, glancing sideways at me before addressing Reyna. "Everything is in place. The surveillance team is a stone's throw down the street, and we'll be in the vacant house beside Iris's, listening to every word. I've done a sweep with an infrared drone and have no reason to believe he's packing."

Gripping her upper arms, he gives her a bolstering smile. "Let's get that motherfucking son of a bitch."

Rey snorts, shaking her head with a low chuckle. "If you're calling my abuela a bitch, you'd best watch your back. She was a big believer in karma, Ford."

"I—I didn't mean, oh shit, I wouldn't ever…" He trails off uselessly, only for his mouth to drop open when both Rey and I burst out laughing.

He recovers enough to roll his eyes before striding toward the elevator. "I'll be in the car, *assholes*."

His off-the-cuff insult makes us laugh even harder, thankfully lightening the seriousness of the moment until we're doubled over.

I sober first and gather a still giggling Rey against my chest. "The first sign of trouble, and I'm putting a stop to this. Okay?"

She nods with a tremulous smile before raising her face to mine. "Now kiss me good luck."

I dust my mouth across hers, a bare brush before I run the tip of my tongue along the seam of her lips. She opens, ready to take me inside, and I indulge freely.

My tongue massages hers gently, teasingly, with the promise of so much more.

I pull back, breaking the kiss, and she whimpers at the loss, even as I grin, pecking the tip of her nose playfully. "There's plenty more where that came from, wife. Just hurry back into my arms, and I promise I'll never let you go again."

Her eyes soften at my words. "You mean that?"

I palm her flushed cheeks, a frown claiming my face as I hold her gaze with an intensity that borders on violence.

"Tu sei il mio sole, la mia unica luce. I can't be without you, Reyna DeMarco. I *won't*."

"Am I going to need to learn Italian, pretty boy?"

I bark a laugh at her ability to center me when the world is spinning on its head. "You are my sun, my only light. That's what I said, Sunshine."

My brows furrow as I fill my words with every long-buried emotion my tiny dancer has swirled to life within me. "That's what you *are*. The light that has chased away the demons ingrained within me by the misdeeds and downright neglect of my parents."

She swallows heavily as I continue. "Today is a day I will never forget, but not for the reasons you're thinking, baby."

I draw the pads of my thumbs across her cheekbones, committing to memory the way she looks right now, at this exact moment, as I share my truth.

"The thought of losing you—of losing the possibility of what we can have—shook me to my very foundations. It was in that instant that I knew beyond any doubt that I don't ever want to know what my life is like without you in it. I can't go back to my gray world when you've shown me what it's like to live in technicolor."

A frown mars her forehead as her eyes glisten with unshed tears.

"So let's get today over with. I'm ready to find out what life has in store for us, Sunshine."

REYNA

The surveillance team let us out at the usual bus stop that Iris would use when traveling to Manhattan from her rental house in New Jersey.

Having checked my wire one last time, Ford gets back inside the van with a small nod before they drive farther up along the street to park closer to the house.

Iris and I fall into step beside one another as she slings the bag supposedly containing the payment over her shoulder. The tension between us is palpable, and I search my mind, quickly finding a subject to alleviate the strain.

"What's your little boy's name?"

Iris's bottom lip trembles as she whispers, "Dean."

She looks down at the sidewalk beneath our feet, clenching and unclenching her fists, and it hits me again that I truly can't imagine how hard she's had it.

"When did he tell you about me?"

She looks up at my question, her eyes lightening at the change of topic. "I found a magazine at my last OB appointment that had a true Cinderella story inside."

She smiles softly as she remembers. "I brought it home to show Aidan…I wanted to show him that fairytales *do* exist."

Her eyes darken then, and she shifts her gaze away. "Victor saw your picture, and that was the start of it. He's in the hole to some loan shark—"

I cut her off with an eye roll. "What else is new!"

Her head bobs with a nod. "Yeah, well, he saw you as his ticket out, so…" She shrugs. "Here we are."

She stops, pointing to our left at a small, well-kept house, not unlike the one I rented in Staten.

Except this one is colored with love.

There's a huge mural of a rainbow on one of the windows that I'm assuming is Dean's room, and the flower beds that line the porch are teeming with an array of brightly colored flowers.

I shift my gaze to my sister with admiration in my eyes. "Do you tend the garden?"

She blushes furiously as she nods. "It's kept me sane since *he* moved in."

My stomach lurches at that, even as I straighten my spine and follow her up along the path to the deep green front door.

She cracks it open and sticks her head inside, calling out quietly, "Victor? I'm back."

My breathing picks up when I follow her over the threshold and into the dark open-plan living space. All the curtains have been pulled despite the beautiful sunshine outside, and I'm instantly transported back to my childhood when his mood would blanket the entire house.

I can *feel* it now, just like I did then.

"You better have it, Iris, or you'll get the same treatment as your boyfriend. Knocked up or not."

Goosebumps scatter across every inch of my skin at the unforgettable sound of my father's voice, and nausea stirs to life in the depths of my stomach.

Then he appears at the door that leads from the living area to, what I'm assuming, is the bedrooms.

"I brought you something even better." Iris's words, though previously discussed, make me shiver openly.

His eyes shift from Iris to me and then back again before his lips part in a grin that makes my skin crawl.

"You brought me something even better?" He nods at her. "You absolutely did."

He stares at me for a long moment, as though he can't believe his eyes, before turning to Iris. "I locked your brat in his room when he shit his pants."

He grimaces. "Fucking animal."

I swallow down my rage at his inhumane treatment of his grandchild as Iris moves toward him, clearly desperate to get to her son, but his bark stops her in her tracks.

"Leave the bag on the floor." She drops it instantly. "And don't fucking move until I say you can move."

His dark eyes are even blacker than my memory allowed me to recall. He looks unkempt, unshaven, and utterly dangerous, but even so, I know I need to play the part to get what I want.

"I can't believe you'd trick me like this, Iris. I wanted to help you!"

Iris buries her face in her hands, emotion overtaking her thin frame. "I had to do it."

"You're just like him!" I spit my words as I move past her, focusing on the smirking face of the man before me.

"So, what's your move, Victor? You want to ruin my life for a second time, is that it?"

He narrows his eyes, never once taking them from my face for a beat before he tilts his head to one side, a calculated look in his dark gaze.

"You're like a damn cat, *niñita*."

I barely suppress a shudder when he uses the only name that he's ever called me.

Never Reyna. Always *niñita*. Always little girl.

"It's ingrained in you. Remember, tough times don't last, but tough people do." He spreads his arms with a shrug. "You sure did when you spread your whore legs for a real-life billionaire! He might even pay more money to get you back."

"If you do this, you'll end up back behind bars where you damn well belong. You mark my words; I'll see to it that you do."

He pouts exaggeratedly. "Aw, boo hoo. *Niñita* gonna make me pay for my sins, is that it?"

I don't reply. Instead, I remain perfectly still under his slow perusal, forcing him to speak again.

"You won't find *anything* on me. I bury my skeletons *real* fucking deep."

His lips lift with what can only be described as a sinister smirk. "Your mother would know *all* about them."

My forehead creases at the turn the conversation has taken, even though I try my best to remain impassive, and he barks a rough laugh. "Have your attention now, don't I!"

I give what I'm praying is a nonchalant shrug as my bottom lip curls. "I could care less about your fucking games, Victor. Do what you want—"

Then he cuts me off with a snarl as he closes the distance between us.

"*Don't* you disrespect your father, *niñita.* Disrespect is one thing I *won't* stand for." He holds his hand up to his mouth and stage whispers, "Just ask those skeletons, hmm?"

I stand my ground, tilt my chin, and stare right into those unfathomable dark depths as though I'm looking into the bowels of Hell, asking the question that I need answered.

"What happened to you, Victor? What made you become *this* despicable? Truly, I want to know—"

He leans down into my face, spittle from his mouth flying out and landing on my cheek as he roars, "You want to know, do you?"

Then he grabs me by the shoulders, making me yelp in fright before he steers me toward a mirror by the hallway. He grips my chin between his thumb and forefinger, making me look at my reflection.

"You're looking at the damn reason, *niñita*."

My face crumples as I shake my head in confusion, shifting my gaze to his in the mirror. "I don't understand."

He forcibly shakes my head, pinching my chin more tightly. "It's *you*. You're the reason." His brown eyes sear into mine as he hisses, "You never should have been born."

"It's *my* fault? I never did a damn thing to you, Victor."

He leans down by my ear, holding my eyes in the reflection as his words make my whole world shift on its axis.

"Your mother changed when you came along. She used to be fun, always liked to party and have a good time with me – until *you*. She forgot about me. Her new priority was you. Gia wanted to give you a different kind of life than the one we had been living. A life that didn't include me…"

I shake my head. "My mother didn't want me. She left me at the church—"

"To hide you from me!" His bellow rips through the house, and he increases his grip on my chin, making me cry out in pain.

He repeats himself in a lower tone. "To hide you from me, *niñita*. So that you wouldn't meet the same fate she knew I intended for her."

My eyes go round as saucers while my stomach swoops uncomfortably. Victor's sadistic smirk grows impossibly broader, and a bolt of pure fear runs through my entire body.

"Wh-what do you m-mean? My mother l-left me…"

Suddenly, he spins me around and slams me to the wall, getting right down in my face. His breath is as sour as I remember, and I fight the urge to vomit as he watches me in silence.

"Your mother never left you, *niñita.*" He brushes my bangs back from my forehead, his eyes fixated on the action.

A shudder runs the length and breadth of my body, knowing what the answer is before I even ask the question. "Wh-where is she then?"

His laugh is totally unhinged, his sour breath turning my stomach and making me wretch.

His hand moves to grip my neck, holding me firmly in place to hiss from between his clenched teeth. "She's in an unmarked grave in the woods behind our house. Just a pile of bones and dirt by now, and nothing less than she deserved for trying to leave me. *For you*!"

Sweat beads my brow, and I pray Alex is on his way, because the look in Victor's eyes turns demonic as he smiles sadistically. "And now, without your abuela here to protect you, I think it's about time you joined her, *niñita.*"

Thirty-Four

ALEX

"What happened to you, Victor? What made you become this despicable? Truly, I want to know—"

"You want to know, do you?"

There are sounds of movement over the feed from Rey's mic before she cries out, and I'm on my feet, moving to leave the living area instantly.

Ford's hand lands on my shoulder, forcing my feet to stop. "Don't. Move."

I tilt my head back to face him, and he just nods sternly with a finger to his lips as Victor speaks again.

"You're looking at the damn reason, niñita."

There's silence for a beat, and I meet Vaughn's eyes across the room before Rey speaks. Her voice is wavering. Unsure. And I crave nothing so much as to go to her and protect her like every cell in my body is crying out for.

"I don't understand."

"It's you. *You're the reason."*

Victor's response is nothing short of venomous, and I'm floored at the level of hatred he's spewing for a daughter he is in no way deserving of.

Then he hisses. *"You never should have been born."*

Reyna begins to speak, and I've had enough. I grab Ford's hand and shove him away.

"I'm going in there. And you won't fucking stop me."

He pushes me hard against the wall, his face turning thunderous. "Give her more time."

I push him back. "We have enough evidence to get him for extortion. Get out of my way, damn you."

"What would Reyna want?"

But I don't even get to answer as Victor's bellow booms through the speaker.

"To hide you from me!"

Then Rey cries out, and I'm done being patient. I'm done thinking about what anyone else might need or want.

I only know that I need to get to her and shield her by any means necessary.

And with that at the forefront of my mind, I slam my fist into Ford's unsuspecting face, watching as he stumbles backward with a grunt.

Vaughn roars at me to stop, but I grab the door handle and run as fast as I can, leaping over the low wall that separates the houses before flying up the front steps of Iris's house.

The front door slams open, the sound echoing through the space as Iris yelps softly from her place by the front door.

Victor and Rey are at the far side of the room. His hand is on her throat as he swivels about to meet my enraged glare. "Take your damn hands off my wife, *now*!"

He chuckles deep in his barrel chest as I feel Vaughn appear at my back, and Victor stares me down. "You're welcome to watch as I choke the life out of—"

At that moment, Rey brings her knee up sharply between his legs, driving it full force into Victor's groin, and he lets her go with a howl. She takes the opportunity to fly across the living room and straight into my waiting arms.

I gather her to me, pressing desperate kisses to the top of her head as I run my hands up and down her body, checking for any sign of injury.

"I'm okay, Alex. I'm okay." She repeats herself over and over before I tilt her chin upward. Her eyes are filled with tears, her face is red and blotchy, and I've never been more grateful for anything else in my entire life than to have her back, safe in my hold.

"Get back here, *niñita*, or I won't hesitate to kill Dean."

Iris cries out desperately, and Vaughn gently catches her arm, buoying her as Rey turns to face a sneering Victor. Her face is resolute, her gaze filled with sheer hatred as she calmly responds, "Make *one* move, and I will kill you with my bare hands."

Victor's mouth twitches with a grin, but before he can say whatever is on the tip of his tongue, the surveillance team and the associated authorities slam through the front door, guns pointing directly at him.

Iris cries out, "*Please,* I need to see my son."

And at that moment, Ford strides past everyone, his black Stetson firmly in place, to march right past Victor and down the hallway toward the bedrooms.

As the authorities crowd around a thrashing Victor, who's roaring his innocence for the world to hear, Iris dashes past them to meet Ford as he returns with a very upset little boy who looks so like Rey that it makes my heart hurt.

The boy reaches for his mother with a cry, and she takes him with an answering one. Then Ford tips his hat to them with a small smile before he goes to stand at Vaughn's side, a silent, stoic sentinel.

Rey turns back into the safety of my embrace, her arms locking tightly around my waist as we shut everyone and everything out.

People are in and out of the small house, milling around, gathering evidence, and taking statements, but it's just the two of us in our small bubble.

Exactly as it should be.

I deeply inhale her sweet floral fragrance until my senses are swimming in everything Reyna DeMarco, and I press a soft kiss to her forehead as I whisper with a grateful heart, "I've got you, Sunshine."

REYNA

Seeing the authorities cuff Victor is one of the most empowering moments of my entire life, and I gently place my arm around Iris's shoulder as together we watch him be taken away.

Forever!

The evidence from the mic is irrefutable, and it's safe to say, Victor Marquez will die behind bars.

"It's nothing less than he deserves."

I don't realize I've spoken the words aloud until Iris catches my hand and gently squeezes it in her own small one.

"I can hardly believe it." Her eyes widen with incredulity. "We're free, Reyna."

She turns to little Dean, who's propped on the top of her bump. "We're safe now, sweetheart."

His smile is heart-stoppingly similar to Lita's, and my chest constricts as Dean burrows his face against his mother's neck.

Iris slides her arm around my waist, pulling me in closer to them, and we share a small smile of solidarity.

Alex finishes his conversation with one of the detectives as his cell rings, and he steps away to answer it. His face lights up, and he lifts his gaze to me and Iris as he closes the distance.

"Iris, I have someone special who needs to talk to you."

He passes over his cell, and Iris accepts it, placing it to her ear. Her face transforms as she cries out, "Aidan! Oh my God, baby. It's over, he's *gone*!"

Alex laces his fingers through mine, tugging me away to give Iris and her little family some privacy. I press my shoulder to his, looking up at him with a grateful smile.

"Thank you for that."

He smiles lopsidedly with a shrug. "I reckoned if I were in her shoes, I'd give just about anything to talk to my person. To get to you."

It's his turn to press his shoulder to mine, his smile widening, sending butterflies soaring in my stomach as I'm filled from head to toe with pure, unadulterated love for this beautiful man.

"I'd walk through Hell to get to you, Sunshine."

He bops me on the nose with his index finger, and I melt at his next words.

"With a smile on my damn face, knowing that what's awaiting me is my very favorite place to be."

ALEX

It's later than I'd like by the time we return home. The interviews and paperwork had taken far longer than I'd hoped, and Rey had insisted upon ensuring that Iris and her son were housed at a hotel in the city to await Aidan's hospital discharge, rather than the home that had been tainted by a madman.

Ford drops us off, opening the door for Rey with a gentle smile that sees her stop to draw him into her embrace.

"Thank you for everything, Ford. You've been…" She draws back to look right at him. "You're always welcome in our home."

Ford's brows pull together, and his throat works harder to swallow as he palms my wife's face with a soft smile. "I appreciate that more than y'all know."

I can't help but grin at the slip of the accent he hides daily before it's my turn.

"Thank you. For everything…and…what she said."

I break off with a shrug. "Emotions are her thing, not mine."

Ford chuckles as he closes the rear door of the town car before he slips back into the driver's seat. "Sure thing, asshole."

When we reach our penthouse, both of us are still smiling, but as Rey moves off toward the stairs, I reach out to tug her back to me.

"I need to tell you something. And it *can't* wait another second, Sunshine."

She swallows heavily before nodding with the slightest hesitation and allowing me to draw her into my arms.

I press a soft kiss to her brow before whispering, "Hearing Vaughn say that another woman was having my child...well, shit, Rey, all I could think was how much I wanted that to be *you* carrying *our* child."

She jerks back, confusion coloring her features. "But you said you didn't want—"

I press my index finger over her lip. "That was before *us*, Sunshine. Because any child that comes from you will be perfect, *just like you*. You said you wanted a house full of kids, right?"

She nods slowly with wide eyes, and I can't help but grin. "I told you before that I'd give you the world if you asked for it. Growing a family together sounds like an adventure, and there's no one else I'd ever dream of doing it with."

Tears fill her eyes as she whispers, "Oh my God, we're really in this."

My mouth parts with a lopsided grin, and I shake my head as I cup her cheeks. "I don't know about you, but I've been *in* since Malones, Rey. Since I asked if you needed a time-turner. Since we shared a waltz, an Irish stew, and part of our souls."

I drop my forehead to hers as tears fill my eyes. "I've been in love with you since the moment I set eyes on you, Reyna DeMarco. I'm just sorry that it's taken me this long to say the damn words."

She exhales on a sob, tears flowing freely down her pinkened cheeks as I press my mouth to hers in a kiss that shows her just how precious she is to me.

I break the kiss and hold her gaze as I whisper across her parted lips, "I love you, Sunshine. And I'm going to keep on loving you the way you deserve for the rest of our lives – *that* is my solemn vow."

I angle her head down to press a slow kiss to her brow, and when I pull back to find her eyes, her smile is as radiant as her nickname.

"So, what do you say we get started?"

Her forehead crumples in adorable confusion, and I can't stop the chuckle that tumbles from my mouth as she questions, "Get what started?"

I quirk a brow. "Growing that family, Sunshine. I hear it's a tough job, but my monster cock is *absolutely* up to the task."

A wide smile spreads across her face as she shakes her head before leaning up on her tiptoes to wrap her arms around my neck. "You really are a truly incorrigible *asshole*."

She kisses my mouth softly, then smiles into my eyes.

"As propositions go, I must say, it's decent, pretty boy. I'll take it under consideration—"

She breaks off with a shriek when I throw her over my shoulder and lightly swat her skirt-covered ass. "What are you doing?"

I take the stairs two at a time, intent on my destination as I ignore her question with a smirk. Instead, I just massage the luscious ass cheek by my right ear, laughing outright when she pounds at my back indignantly.

"Put me down right the hell now, or so help me—*ouch*!"

I cut her off when I turn my face to gently nip the side of her ass with my teeth before I toss her onto our bed. She yelps as I look down on her with a smile.

She scrambles farther up the bed, her eyes narrowed and directed right at me. The sight just makes my smile grow even bigger as I kneel on the bed and follow her oh-so slowly.

"You'll take it under consideration…is that right, Sunshine?"

She nods, raising her eyebrows in exaggerated innocence, and I narrow my eyes devilishly. "Allow me to persuade you that I'm the right man for the job."

I reach her ankles, and roughly push her legs apart, making her dress rise in the process. My mouth drops open when I see the paradise that awaits me, and I raise questioning eyes to her laughing ones.

She lifts the hem of her dress higher until the bunched fabric is pooled around her belly button. "I took them off before you got in the car when we left Iris at the hotel."

I drop to my elbows, throwing her calves over my shoulders so that my face is buried right against her bare pussy. Then my gaze travels the length of her body to find her eyes locked on me, pupils blown as she tugs her plump bottom lip between her teeth.

"Good girls get *rewarded*, but dirty fucking girls…well, they get *worshipped*."

Then without further warning, I clamp my mouth down on her sweet sex, making her throw her head back as she arches her body closer to me.

"Oh *fuck*!"

Her cry is ripped from her throat as my tongue sweeps across her silky, slick pussy, swirling in circles that see her hands shoot out to find purchase in my hair.

She holds tight as her hips move against my mouth, keeping me in place while she uses my face to chase her pleasure.

And *fuck*, if it's not the hottest thing I've ever seen in my life.

I moan against her, and my eyes fall closed as I worship my wife's sweet cunt. Her low cries of rapture are music to my ears, and I'm altogether consumed by my need to bring her to blissful completion when her legs clamp around my head.

"Yes, *right there*. Lick me harder. *Fuck*!"

Her demand makes my cock throb against the mattress, pleading for attention.

But, internally, I tell the fucker to get lost because I'm solely one hundred percent focused on eating my wife's delicious cunt until she shatters on my tongue.

The thought makes me double down on my efforts, making her hips falter, and her grip on my hair tighten painfully.

Her hooded, pupil-dominated eyes are fixed intently on me when I open mine again. I pop a brow when I see that she has unbuttoned her dress and pulled down the fabric of her bra to roll a dusky nipple back and forth between her thumb and her index finger.

And I can't help the deep growl of possessive desire that rumbles through me straight to my wife's drenched cunt.

"I'm coming, *shit*, I'm coming!"

Her orgasm floods my mouth as her body soars to untold heights under my relentless attention, and I don't stop until her thighs slacken, her hands falling away from my head to flop uselessly to the bed beneath us.

"Fuck, you taste divine, baby." I run a finger through her shimmering pussy lips, dipping inside. The move makes her shiver as I gather even more of her musky sweetness.

I slide up along her body, extending my dripping finger in offering. "See for yourself."

She immediately opens her mouth, and I slip the cum-soaked digit along her tongue before she closes her lips around it, humming loudly when she sucks hard.

My eyes almost roll back in my head, and I drop my face to her perky tits, taking a pointed nipple inside my mouth. I bite gently, making her cry out and arch against me before I sweep my tongue across the hard bud.

I alternate between nipples, driving her higher and higher, making her lift her hips desperately in search of friction to satisfy her renewed need.

"Shit, Sunshine. I'm so fucking *hard* for you."

I stand suddenly, without warning, and she cries out as I pull her to the edge of the bed.

She watches, propped on her elbows, as I unbuckle my pants and shove them along with my Calvins down my legs, allowing my swollen cock to spring free between us.

She reaches for it with wide, eager eyes that, on any other day, would see me fucking her face into oblivion. But today, I gently grip her wrist, stopping her from reaching her desired destination, and she lifts her chocolaty eyes to mine.

"Not a chance, baby. You touch me now, and it's game over."

I rub my cock over and back across her wet cunt as she moans beneath me. Her fingers are playing with both nipples now, eyes glassy with need as she watches me.

"Are you still taking this family-growing offer under consideration, or have I convinced you sufficiently that I'm up for the task?"

Her face lights up with a mischievous smirk. "I'm still not convinced..."

She trails off, and I palm her ass cheeks, lifting her hips so that her dripping hole is lined up with my dick.

"I got a couple more surprises up my sleeve." I wink as I pump my hips, lubing my cock with her wetness. "I *guarantee*...you'll like this one."

REYNA

All oxygen is driven from my body when Alex surges forward, filling me in one delicious thrust. His jaw slackens as his eyes glaze over, and *Christ,* if I wasn't desperately in love with him before, I'd be all in now.

He's sheer perfection. And he's *all mine.*

"Holy *fuck*, you feel so good, Sunshine."

I moan when he hits deep, letting my eyes fall closed to heighten the delicious sensations.

"So fucking wet."

His husky baritone fills my ears, sending shivers down my spine.

"So damn tight, baby. You take me so good."

He starts to move, and each pump fills me more than the last as he hits places so deep I didn't know they existed.

He sets a brutal pace that sees me climbing again despite already coming so hard that my entire body turned to mush in the immediate aftermath.

"I love how your greedy little cunt sucks me in so deep, baby." Alex reaches between us, strumming his thumb back and forth across my clit, making me moan as I writhe beneath the sensations. "I love how your pussy was made to take my cock *so* perfectly. Like we were made to fit."

I can feel his dick pulsating inside me as his own orgasm begins to build, and the feeling sends me higher, within touching distance of another mind-blowing orgasm.

His grip on my ass tightens, and my eyes fly open, needing

to see him. I rake my nails across his tight abs, and he grunts as indentations mark his olive skin.

He fucks me even harder, and I cry out as I push back desperately against him, wanting nothing more than to take him inside me as deep as possible.

His thrusts increase in pace, almost knocking the breath from my body, and I rock against him, circling my hips. Without warning, his palms leave my ass as he drops me down onto the bed to bury his face in the nape of my neck.

I wrap my thighs around his frenzied hips as I lift myself to meet him. His pelvis hits my clit so fucking exquisitely, I know I'm on the cusp, about to explode all over his beautiful dick.

Lifting his head enough to rest his mouth by my ear, he continues to drive into me while I dig my nails into the muscles of his upper back.

His heavy pants of exertion reach my ears, the sound pushing me higher. But it's when he whispers against the shell of my ear that I come undone.

"I love you."

The power behind his words and the steady rhythm of his thrusting hips and pulsing cock send me flying off the precipice.

I cling tightly to his sweat-slick skin, and we fall together. His groan of completion mingles with my own cries of pleasure as I feel his dick fill me with his hot cum.

He collapses onto my heaving chest with a moan, and I gather him close against my breasts, pressing a kiss atop his dark head as we both come back to earth.

We hold one another for a long while, until he eventually removes his delicious weight from my body, moving in the direction of the bathroom. He returns with a warm, damp towel, and then, pushing my still-quivering thighs apart, he cleans my well-loved pussy, eyes glued to the process.

Once he's finished, I palm his cheek as I sit up and scoot off the bed to take his hand in mine. "Come with me."

He looks at me with a furrowed brow, but does as I bid, interlocking our fingers so that I can lead him out of our room and down the hallway to what's *technically* my room.

I bring us directly to the ensuite, open the bathroom cabinet, and remove my pill packet. Then I drop them into the trash before turning to him with a smile.

"I was convinced before, but I expect this level of dedication in all future family-growing endeavors."

He smiles—lopsidedly, of course—then picks me up, spinning me around as I laugh like a lunatic. His eyes never leave mine as he slowly sobers, lowering me back to the tiled floor with shining eyes.

"I don't think I've ever been as grateful that time-turners don't exist, because Reyna DeMarco…"

He trails off to press a chaste kiss to my swollen lips. "I don't want to miss one damn second of our time together. Not a single one."

Thirty-Six

REYNA

I wake to an empty bed, the bright sunshine beaming through a slit in the bedroom blinds as I stretch my limbs, embracing the delicious ache in every single part of my thoroughly loved, absolutely satiated body.

As I stare at the ceiling, I can't help a smile from overtaking my face when I remember my husband's words from the night before.

"I love you, Sunshine."

My heart flip-flops beneath my breastbone at the memory, and my stomach fills with butterflies when I suddenly realize that I need to see him.

I need to know that it wasn't a dream.

And so, I throw back the covers, leaping from the bed to stride through the bedroom door, grabbing Alex's shirt from yesterday from the jumbled mess of discarded clothes on the floor before I walk into the hallway.

I take the stairs at top speed, the smell of flowers hitting my nose and making me stop to look around.

The entire open-plan area is filled to capacity with vase after vase of stunning ballerina bouquets – ornate rose lilies and soft butterfly ranunculus in varying hues of pink – covering every surface.

My eyes well with tears at the sight as I make my way past them toward the kitchen, only to find it empty.

I glance around, suddenly bereft, only for my eyes to light on a single white envelope, and my greedy hands reach for it immediately, knowing that it's from Alex.

Needing to know where he is.

His familiar neat writing is front and center, and I make short work of ripping it open to pull the contained papers out, along with a single white seashell identical to the ones from Playa Conchal.

My throat tightens as my nostrils flare, and I hold the shell tight inside my fist while I open the documents inside.

Firstly, I read the handwritten letter.

> To my beautiful, blissfully sleeping wife,
>
> I have just spent the last three hours watching you as you slept. Devouring every single curve, every contour. Soaking up every little morsel of unfiltered Sunshine that I can physically handle.
>
> And the sight has sent my thoughts into overdrive.
>
> First, every single bouquet here is for all those shows you missed. For all those nights when you would have shone brighter than the

sun as you danced to your heart's content.

It's not even half of what you deserve, but it's all the florist could do at 5 a.m. I'll do better in future, I promise.

Second, my beautiful wife, I know I am utterly undeserving of you, but I want to try to be better as we move forward.

Our beginning needs a second chance, and it's with that in mind that I ask you to please go back to the start with me.

You'll find me where we began.

Love always and forever,

Your husband

I read and re-read the letter three more times before I move on to the printed document, and my eyes blow wide at the content.

It's the deed for the studio I wanted. The one on Staten Island, despite the fact I'd not even mentioned it to him.

Bailey!

I laugh to myself and glance around at the bouquets dotting the entire penthouse, totally overwhelmed by the outpouring of love.

It's so utterly unexpected that I sink to my knees, gripping the letter and deed to my chest as tears overwhelm my entire body.

Once I've allowed my emotions to dominate me, I rise to stand with renewed purpose.

Ready to go back to our beginning.

ALEX

"You sure she's coming, pretty boy?"

I turn to Darcy with a wry smile. "I know my wife, Darce. She'll be here."

I grip the ballerina bouquet in my hand tightly as I take a quick glance at the bar clock. "She'll be here."

I repeat the words more for myself than for her before she moves off down the bar toward a silently waiting Bailey.

Bless him; when I'd rung in the early hours, he'd been ready and willing to help. He'd had no issue harassing a local florist at 5 a.m. and chasing the ballet studio owner along with my lawyer to ensure Rey's sole ownership of her studio, all before she woke.

I take a quick glance around at him, and he shoots me an encouraging smile. "She's coming."

My nod is sharp, and I turn back to the door, heart on my damn sleeve as I send up a silent prayer of thanks for this beautiful family who've had our back since day one.

The door moves just then, and I stand to attention with a bright smile on my face, only to wilt as an unsuspecting Leonard saunters inside.

"Oh, for Christ's sake, Leo. You're woeful."

My eyes follow Darcy as she moves swiftly across the pub to usher her brother behind the bar while he protests softly, "I had to get the car ready—"

"Shut it, eejit." Darcy cuts him off with an eye roll. "She'll be here any second."

"Who'll be here?"

I spin toward the door, my eyes landing on my Sunshine,

who is lighting up the bar with all the radiance contained in her megawatt smile.

My breathing becomes labored as I take in her unparalleled beauty, her hands clasped uncertainly at her midriff.

"You came."

My words are whispered on an exhalation, and her eyes spear mine. "Of course I came. Where else would I be?"

Without another word, I close the distance between us, unmindful of the family surrounding us, and I reach into the back pocket of my jeans to flourish a very important piece of paper.

"Sunshine." Her eyes are wide and utterly beautiful as she holds my gaze.

"We began on a lie. Right here. In this place. I told you I couldn't dance. I told you I was near perfect when I'm absolutely fucked up…and yet you claim to love me. *Flaws and all.*"

My eyes hold hers as I pour every ounce of emotion into my next words. "We started off *wrong*. And now, I can make it *right*. No arrangements. No deals. Just two people falling in love and wanting to be the other one's person."

I blink heavily, nodding at the paper in her hands. "This is how we start fresh. And with our truth at the center."

Her brows crease as she rips the proffered paper from my hands. Her eyes scan the document once and then twice before she raises them to mine as frustration overtakes her stunning features.

"Divorce papers? *Really*?"

I nod with wide eyes. "Yeah, I thought—"

"Not a fucking hope, pretty boy." She folds the paper in half, and then rips it right down the middle.

I blink several times as I watch her shred the document into tiny pieces. She scatters them across the floor before moving closer to palm my cheeks, holding my gaze with hers.

"Alexander DeMarco, don't you realize? *This* was never fake. For *either* of us. Every single emotion, every single word…" She trails off as she leans up to brush her lips over mine. "Every damn touch has been real. I don't need a redo to know that *this*—"

She lays her hand over my palpitating heart and my jaw tics with barely constrained emotion.

"*This* is where I belong, pretty boy. Here, and *only* here. In your heart. In your arms."

I swoop down to pluck her from the floor and spin her around as I laugh out loud, the sound joining her whoop of delight.

When I set her back down, I hold her gaze even as Darcy, Leo, and Bailey begin to chat excitedly behind us.

I press a kiss to the top of her head as I hold Rey even closer, my emotions taking charge. "You came into my life—so unexpected, and so perfect—I'm still in goddamn awe that you could care for me, let alone love me like you do." I angle her jaw upward, holding her deep brown eyes. "Was it any wonder that I fell head over damn heels for you, Sunshine? Hmm?"

My eyes devour her perfect face as her nostrils flare. Her eyes hold mine, and I feel sheer joy fill me from top to toe.

"I *adore* you, Reyna DeMarco. More than I could ever put into words."

Her smile consumes me as the Malones approach from behind.

"Well, Christ almighty, it was touch and go for a hot minute there, but it all came right in the end, eh?"

Darcy slides up beside us, smiling broadly. "Glad to have helped play matchmaker of sorts." Her exaggerated wink makes me laugh while Rey slips into Darcy's waiting embrace.

Bailey taps me on the shoulder, a knowing grin overtaking his face as he glances at my wife with a cheeky wink. "Told you she wouldn't go for the redo."

Rey returns to my side, giggling happily as I shake my head. "So you damn well did."

Then I glance at Leonard, giving him a nod that sees him throw keys in my direction with a shit-eating grin.

"Now, Sunshine. How's about I bring you around the corner to show you the epic refurb Leonard has so kindly done on your piece of shit Corolla, hmm?"

Her gaze shoots to mine as her jaw unhinges. "What?"

And I chuckle loudly. "Surprise, Sunshine!"

Epilogue

ALEX

SIX MONTHS LATER

"That's wonderful, sweet girl. I'm so glad you are all settling well."

My best friend sighs softly on the other end of the line as I slip from my car, disconnecting the cell from the Bluetooth.

"It's so nice to be home, Alex. But I do miss having you guys around the corner."

Liv and Henry flew back to London three days ago once their newborn twins had gotten the all-clear from the pediatrician.

Jonah and Kate, the newest additions to my brother's rapidly expanding family, are six weeks old now and utter perfection.

"We'll visit as soon as we can."

The sound of a crying newborn hits my ears, followed by my brother's booming voice in the background. "Jonah needs a boob, Peach!"

Liv snorts a laugh. "Never a dull moment."

I chuckle as I pull open the door of my wife's ballet studio.

"We'll chat soon. Kiss the kids for me, and tell Ri that I've signed those contracts he requested."

"Will do." Liv disconnects the call, and I pocket my cell with a smile on my face.

Silence hits my ears as I walk through the entryway of the studio – the one that Rey adores so much that she would quite happily live here on Staten Island, just a stone's throw from Sunrise Harbor.

The bay outside the floor-to-ceiling windows is beautiful, the sun glinting across the water and lighting up the space.

It isn't until I step inside the main room that I hear the unmistakable bars of the *"Dance of the Sugar Plum Fairy"* over the surround sound speakers, and my skin comes alive as goosebumps scatter across my entire body.

"Now, Dean, arabesque…and *good*! That was beautiful, *mi amor*."

My wife's demure tone resonates through the entire space, and I open the double doors wide to find her with our soon-to-be four-year-old nephew, Dean, who's watching his godmother with an adoring smile.

My own mouth mirrors his when I take in her pastel pink leotard and tights, gently rounded with the swell of her four-month-pregnant stomach.

"Where's Mama?"

Dean's voice rings out through the space, and I smile before I answer.

"How would you like to spend the next couple of days with your Auntie Rey and Uncle Al, hmm?"

"Uncle Al!"

Dean's big brown eyes light up when he spots me, and he takes off across the floor, dead set on finding his way into my arms.

I catch him with a grin, swinging him around as Rey watches in smiling silence. "Where *is* my sister, anyway?"

I hold Dean snugly against one hip as I close the distance between us and my watching wife. I pull her in against my other side, ensuring to smooth the palm around her waist over our precious cargo while smiling into her chocolaty eyes.

"She's on her way to Costa Rica with Aidan and baby Adam, Sunshine. We join them in three days."

Rey's face blooms to life with a smile. "*Seriously*?"

I nod with a wide grin. "You *know* I love to surprise you, Sunshine."

She shakes her head with a chuckle. "I know you do, pretty boy."

My smile becomes entirely lopsided when I tilt my head. "The Malones are joining us too, baby. Bailey's due a vacation since his latest promotion."

My ex-personal assistant has found his niche in the HR department of DeMarco Holdings, much to the delight of Darcy, who's become like a surrogate mother to my beautiful wife.

Rey squeals with delight, pressing her cheek against my chest in a side hug before she looks up into my eyes.

"This is perfect. I've been teaching both Darcy and Leonard to speak Spanish!"

I chuckle. "I know you have." Then I shake my head exaggeratedly. "My poor bleeding ears!"

She shoves my chest even as she laughs.

"Why are your ears bleeding, Uncle Al?"

Dean's small voice is too damn cute, and I can't help but preen under his attention.

"Oh, don't you worry, little dude. My ears are just fine."

I bop his nose with my index finger. "How about you show

me what your Auntie Rey taught you today before we bring you home for some tamales?"

Dean's big brown eyes blow wide. "Lita's tamales?"

Rey nods with a bittersweet frown. "Mm-hmm. I made extra yesterday, and they've got your name on them, *mi amor*."

Dean flashes us a blinding smile before scooting off to the barre, excited and motivated to show me what he's learned.

I slip my arm around my wife's shoulder, watching our nephew plie and jete to his heart's content before she snuggles close into my chest.

"Christ, I love our life, baby." My whole body fills with a familiar sensation. One that will never grow old for me. One I've chased after and felt unworthy of my entire life.

Love.

She nods. "Me too." Her smile is clear in her soft voice.

We stand in silence as my hand drops to her gently rounded stomach and a feeling of absolute contentment comes over me. I press a kiss to my stunning wife's temple before she tilts her head up to meet my gaze.

"I had an OB appointment earlier."

I nod with a smile. "I remembered, baby. I'm sorry I had to work."

I drop a kiss on her upturned nose. "I'll be at the next one."

"I have a surprise for you."

Mischief mingled with happiness dances in her chocolate gaze as my skin erupts in a wave of goosebumps. My tiny dancer is silent for a long beat as her eyes bore into mine before she whispers, "It's a girl, pretty boy. We're having a girl."

It takes a long moment for Rey's words to sink in, but when they do, I turn and carefully, as though she's made of the finest porcelain wrap my arms around her while red-hot tears fill my eyes.

I press our foreheads together as we breathe each other's exhalations.

"I can't wait to hold her in my arms, Sunshine." The words escape my throat in a deep, emotion-filled tone. My nostrils flare as I attempt to find the right words.

"We're having a mini-Rey!"

She shakes her head as tears fill her beautiful eyes. The movement makes the tears spill over her long dark lashes, streaking down her smiling face.

"No, Alex." Her words drop to a whisper as her eyes pierce mine with nothing short of sheer adoration. "A mini *us*."

I wrap my arms around her, holding her in my embrace, and a smile lights up my face as the realization hits me.

"She's it, baby."

My wife turns wet, questioning eyes to mine, and I smile even wider, my heart filling to almost bursting as I feel everything come full circle.

"We've danced in the rain, and now she's our sunshine after the storm. Our baby girl is our rainbow's end."

Epilogue Two

VAUGHN

UNEDITED AND SUBJECT TO CHANGE

"This shit is going to stop, Lucia, or I swear…"

I trail off, fists clenched almost as hard as my jaw while I stare at the uncompromising face of my second in command.

She arches a brow. "You swear *what,* Bossman?"

My nostrils flare as my stomach lurches at the nickname I *know* she used for Valentine Burton – the previous owner of Rogue and her long-deceased fuck buddy.

Her eyes are unwavering as she crosses her arms in defiance.

Truthfully, I have little issue with Lucia Romano other than the fact that she's a remnant from a time I wasn't part of this place. From when *he* ran the show, but the fact of the matter is, she's gotten a little too fond of managing *Ravish,* the cesspit at my club, Rogue, that I'd rather didn't exist.

And I can't have that. She needs to know who's in charge.

Before she can blink, I've crossed the space between us to grip her upper arms hard enough that she flinches openly.

Her startled eyes meet mine, and I almost smirk.

"Just because I'd prefer to wash my hands of this shit show doesn't mean I'll allow you free reign, Lucia." I increase my grip, and she grits her jaw as she furrows her brow, clearly determined to stand firm.

And so, I bridge the gap between our faces until our noses are almost touching. Her chest is rising and falling rapidly despite her otherwise cool composure.

"*Don't* forget who runs this show now, Miss Romano, because if you do…" I narrow my eyes into slits. "I can guarantee you won't like the outcome if we need to have this conversation again."

My cell chimes in my pocket, saving my power-hungry employee from the full force of my wrath, and I pluck it out to check the message.

JOSEPH

I'll be at Rogue in the next five minutes.

I shoot him a quick thumbs up, then with a final dark stare for Lucia, I pivot on my heel and stride from the changing rooms adjoining *Ravish*.

As I make my way back toward my office, I breathe a sigh of relief that Jules—following his fuck up with Alex DeMarco's wife several weeks earlier—had alerted me to Lucia taking a bigger cut from our lots at the auctions than even the lots themselves got.

I mean, I don't want *Ravish* to be part of my club. My *legacy*. But the reality is that when I bought this place and attempted to tear it asunder, I'd not realized the extent of my sperm donor's reach. He had dirt on a great many powerful people, but they, in turn, had no qualms in strong-arming me into keeping Valentine's crown jewel.

Much to my disgust.

I'd learned to play the role following the untimely death of my best friend, Lorenzo, and the guilt I carried as a result of leaving the love of his life, Sara, a single mother to their son, Ren.

The same boy I'm due to meet tonight.

The same boy – or almost man considering he's recently turned twenty that I'm claiming some sort of guardianship over – for no other reason than to tame the guilt that continues to haunt me daily.

I reach the stairs leading to my office and take them two at a time, raking my right hand through my messier than usual black hair as my left grips the door handle.

I step inside, expecting to find the room empty, only to stop short when my dark eyes land on a woman with a warm brown high ponytail leading down to a slender neck atop narrow shoulders covered by a simple white T-shirt.

She twists about on the seat, her mesmerizing grey eyes locking on mine with an intensity that makes my feet stall and my heart freeze in my usually empty chest cavity.

"Are you Mr. Burton?"

Her husky tone sends a jolt of desire straight to my cock, and I step closer, silently thanking whoever sent this motherfucking vision my way.

"One and the same." My lips tug upward. "And who are you?"

Her lips tug up on one side as her eyes darken. She stands and closes the distance between us until our toes are almost touching.

Her entire self is petite, slender, and utterly reminiscent of a small brown bird that used to land on my mother's front porch all those years ago.

The need to care for her flows through me like never before, but I shove it roughly to the very back of my mind, instead focusing on the physical and what her body can do for mine as I've done my whole adult life.

My fucking palms are itching with the need to touch her, but I refrain, needing my lovers to voice their assent more than anything. But *shit,* I've never experienced such a visceral reaction before.

It's like I'm magnetized to her. The desire to plow into her hard against my desk rushes through me like a fucking tornado.

And so, I'm helpless to bring my hand up between us and brush my knuckles across her smooth cheek.

"Who are you, my little bird? *Tell me*. I need your words."

She holds my eyes unflinchingly as she darts a pointed pink tongue out to wet her pouty lips.

Lips that are utterly perfect for sucking my dick. God help me.

"I'm—"

The door opens behind me, and I twist about, thunder in my black orbs. "Who the *fuck*—"

Joseph Fratelli steps inside, a chagrined look on his slim face. "Sorry I'm late—"

His eyes narrow as they take in the girl before me, even as my hand falls away from her smooth cheek.

"Christ, Jo. Heard of knocking?"

I round the desk, my face hardening with each step. As I take my seat, I look at the girl who's taken the same seat I found her in, her hands folded and resting across her slender stomach.

"And you may *leave* now, little bird."

My words sour in my mouth even as I speak them, and I open a drawer at my desk, pretending to mess about with paperwork that I could care less for.

"Leave? *Now*?" She barks a laugh. "I fucking wish."

I swallow harshly when her words hit my ears, and I lift my head, ready to retort, only for Joseph to cut me off.

"Vaughn, meet Wren Caputo. She will be staying with you while we search for her mother."

Vaughn Burton and Wren Caputo's forbidden age gap, Rogue Villain, *is coming later this year.*

Acknowledgments

This entire story has been a learning curve for me.

Don't take people at face value. Don't think that behind the façade, each person you encounter is okay.

In a world where you can be anything, please always choose to be kind.

We all mask our demons in different ways. Alex is the epitome of that.

Now, I'd like to take this opportunity to thank some truly exceptional people who have been a part of this wild ride.

As I have been blessed with such amazing alpha/beta readers, I need to make sure to thank you, wonderful ladies. Adi, Selena, Jen, Aimee, Joan, and Amy – I am so grateful for you and the precious time you give to help shape my stories. Thank you, from the bottom of my heart, for everything you do. I value you more than you could ever know.

Adi – would any story of mine be complete without letting you in on the very obvious fact: you are awesome? I don't think so!

You cool my jets when I need them stalled. You let me spiral when I believe there's nowhere else to go. But, you bring me back to earth with your wisdom (that's truly beyond your years), your banter (that's fucking excellent), and your general amazing self, and I cannot wait to squish you for real someday (please, God, soon!)

To Karina and Becky, my girls who made my Spanish and

Italian translations for this book so seamless. THANK YOU both, I am so so so grateful!!!

To my Street Team. Girls – you're all legends! When I tell you that your presence in my life means more to me than you know…

You are THE BEST! And I'm beyond blessed to have you in my corner.

To Sara, my kickass, utterly inspiring PA. You are *amazing*. Thank you for being so damn awesome, my love. Your input on these two has been so helpful, and your cheerleader self has just buoyed me so much. I adore you!

In 2020, I discovered T.L. Swan and her beautiful prose. I discovered how she'd begun writing—having been entirely unfamiliar with the indie world prior to that—and upon further investigation, I found she had, in her infinite wisdom, decided to pay it forward, setting up a Cygnet group for aspiring authors. Thank you, Tee, for paving the way for so many others. I'm forever in your debt.

To my beautiful friend, Lilian Harris. When I grow up, I want to be you. You are one of the most beautiful people I have met in this industry. You give your all and expect nothing in return. I swear, you have me for life!! Roll on Denver 2024!!

To my writing sisters – KJ Michaels, K. Woods and ER Sloane. There's no one else I'd rather be figuring this out with! I love you guys so much xxx

To my sister, Michelle. I have been a terrible bridesmaid while writing this book—*again*. I'll be better. I promise! Bring on the 'I Do's'.

Thank you to my parents, William and Bernadette, for your support and encouragement. I know you have no idea what this is all about, but your acceptance is everything! (PS: Dad, I know you're proud but please stop recommending my books to your friends!)

To my five miracles. If there's one thing I teach you in this life, it's to march to your own beat. I'm so proud of the people you are becoming. Each of you can be whatever you want to be so long as you keep chasing those dreams.

James O'Rourke. I love you. You are my favorite person. My rock. You pick me up when I'm feeling shit. You make me laugh every single day. And you put up with all my flaws because when you've found your person, the world feels right. Thank you for being my biggest cheerleader, my unpaid PA, and my number one fan.

And *finally*, to each and every person who has read my words. Who has read my stories and *enjoyed* them. To each reader who has been transported from their life into the world that I have created.

To every reader who has contributed to making my dream a *reality*.

THANK YOU SO MUCH!

I see you.

I appreciate you.

I am so honored that you took a chance on my newest book baby.

Vaughn Burton's story is up next in *Rogue Villain*, which is releasing this fall.

Also by Pamela O'Rourke

THE BROTHERHOOD SERIES

1. *Painted Truths*
2. *Unwritten Rules*
3. *Broken Strings*

ROGUES OF MANHATTAN SERIES

1. *Rogue Romeo*
2. *Rogue Villain* (COMING FALL 2023)
3. *Rogue Knight* (RELEASE TBA)
4. *Rogue Angel* (RELEASE TBA)

Pamela O'Rourke lives in Ireland with her husband, James and their five young children. Life is hectic, but she wouldn't change a single second of it. She loves sunny days, strong coffee, and daydreaming about writing your next book boyfriend.

Rogue Romeo is the first in the Rogues of Manhattan series.

Rogue Villain will follow Vaughn Burton.

Rogue Knight will follow Ford Holloway.

Rogue Angel will follow Grayson Hunter.

The Brotherhood series, including Alex's brother Henry's story in *Painted Truths,* is complete and *free* to read on Kindle Unlimited.

In the meanwhile, come and join my Facebook reader group for a first look at sneak peeks and teasers. Please note that this is a private group, so only other members can see posts and comments.

Follow on social media!

Newsletter: https://bit.ly/PORourkeNews
Facebook: www.facebook.com/authorpamelaorourke
Instagram/TikTok: @pamelaorourkeauthor
Amazon: https://tinyurl.com/PORourkeAmazon
Goodreads: www.goodreads.com/pamelaorourke
BookBub: www.bookbub.com/profile/pamela-o-rourke

Made in the USA
Middletown, DE
14 March 2024

51515384R00222